5 2 W...
TO MAGIC
AMERICA

James Flint was born in 1968
and is a contributing editor at *mute* magazine.
His first novel, *Habitus*,
was published by Fourth Estate in 1998.
He currently lives in London.

For more information on James Flint visit
www.4thestate.com/jamesflint

52 WAYS TO MAGIC AMERICA

James Flint

FOURTH ESTATE · *London* and *New York*

This paperback edition published in 2003
First published in Great Britain in 2002 by
Fourth Estate
A Division of HarperCollins*Publishers*
77–85 Fulham Palace Road
London W6 8JB
www.4thestate.com

Copyright © James Flint 2002

10 9 8 7 6 5 4 3 2 1

The right of James Flint to be identified as the author of this
work has been asserted by him in accordance with the Copyright,
Designs and Patents Act 1988

A catalogue record for this book is available from
the British Library

ISBN 1-84115-524-1

All rights reserved. No part of this publication may be
reproduced, transmitted, or stored in a retrieval system, in any
form or by any means, without permission in writing from
Fourth Estate.

Typeset by Rowland Phototypesetting Ltd,
Bury St Edmunds, Suffolk
Printed in Great Britain by
Clays Ltd, St Ives plc

For Marianne

52 WAYS
TO MAGIC
AMERICA

Once, long ago,
in the time before Internet,
there lived a magician.

His name was Martin.

Look at Marty. Look at his hands. Long hands, slender fingers, unobtrusive knuckles with joints so efficient they might be components of some elegant machine. Look at his hands; don't look at his face, a tapering face with a nose sharp, triangular, a little equine. Don't look at his hair, a gelled mullet, a barnet that'll pass as high cool in five or six years when the eighties come back into style but which right now looks parochial, sad, overtly soft-rock. Like I told you, don't look at his face or his hair or his purple velveteen suit or that black satin shirt, which he likes to wear buttoned up to the neck, or those eyes of Microsoft blue, a colour he's not familiar with yet. Don't look at any of that. Try to concentrate on his hands.

His hands. Just what is it that they're doing?

Well, nothing, you say. They're hanging down by the seams of the trousers, apparently inert.

But look closely.

Not at the eyes. Jesus Christ. Not at the eyes. Look at the hands. They're holding something. Can you see? They're each gripping something, each holding something palms down so that you can't quite see what it is though that doesn't matter because now you suddenly realise you already know. Or at least you think you know – much more important because in Marty's line of work it's what the punters *think* they know that's the key. And knowing what the punters think they know, and *knowing how they come to know it* – well, that's the crux of it. That's how it's done.

Which is why you must never look at the eyes, see, because the eyes will tell you they love you when all they want is to stop you from wandering – and wondering – elsewhere. To keep you close. Once you take a peek at those eyes you won't care any more, you'll never have seen eyes quite like this before, you'll just want to look at them, you'll want to believe. They're glossy, plastic, all surface. They're without mystery. They fascinate.

So don't look at the eyes. They're there to distract you. Look at the hands, those hands fine enough to be photographed wearing Rolex or Tag, sporting De Beers, offering Gold Diners' Club, Platinum Visa, Plutonium American Express. Can you see what they're holding, what they're concealing, can you see what is caught in the arch between those soft supple heels and those eight fingertips capped with eight manicured nails, the ulnas perfect as eclipsed suns cast between leaves down on to the sand? That's right. Not credit cards, no, they're not credit cards. Calm down. They're playing cards, and there are three of them: two in one hand and one in the other, though whichever way round you think they're arranged I'll guarantee you are wrong – Marty's good, too good for that. Too good for you, anyway. (Don't look at the eyes.)

So. Three cards, two hands. 'Find the Lady', that's the trick, that's the game we're playing. You know that one? It's an old one. Everyone knows it. 'Three Card Monte', as the Americans say. Everyone's been hustled by it at least once at the fair or out in the street. Find the Lady. Find her – it's easy. Three cards: two jokers, say, and a queen. You've got to pick out her Royal Highness from among them and as long as you don't look at the eyes you've got a one in three chance of getting it right. Find the Lady, that's all there is to it. Pick a card. Find her. Find her and make off with her heart.

Look at Martin. Look at his mother. His mother is ill and she's been ill for some time. She has cancer, lung cancer, and little Martin has not yet turned ten. He has to be quiet around the house when he comes in from school because Mum's home all day now, sitting on the sofa, star-pattern-diamond plush comforter draped across her knees even though it's summer.

'Quiet, Martin!' his big sister Rebecca tells him whenever he bounces in from school, wants to watch TV, lets the fridge door slam closed. 'Mum's resting.' Which drives Martin nuts because he *knows* Mum's resting, how could he forget? What with her always in the living room locked into the sofa or lying uneasily on her daybed, coughing all day long and all through the night, spitting all that he loved about her up and out and into carefully folded tissues which fill wastebin after wastebin, wastebins that it's somehow turned out to be Martin's job to have to take out and empty. How could he forget?

How could he forget when Mum is turning herself inside out, how could he forget when already she's not there to protect him any more, neither him nor any of them. Not Rebecca, sister no. 1 (two years Martin's senior), whose response has been to take on her mother's role and treat Martin like a child, which he is, of course, but then so is she and just because Mum's ill he doesn't see why it should mean that she gets to boss him around so much. (Though he's alone in this: every time he tries to raise the issue Rebecca tells him don't be stupid; or his dad clips him round the ear; or Mum tells him, 'Please, Martin, darling, please don't argue, I just don't feel up to it. Why don't you go upstairs and play?') Neither sister no. 1 nor Karen, sister no. 2 (three years Martin's junior), to whom at least he can feel superior, she being officially 'too young to understand' and not party to the secret that the grown-ups know (the grown-ups, by this definition, including Martin, much to Martin's delight and pride).

The secret being, of course, that Mum is going to die.

And then she won't be there to protect any of them any more: not Martin, not Karen, not Rebecca, not even Martin's dad, who is maybe in need of the most protection out of all of them. Which is not something Martin knows but something he senses, owing to the way in which Dad has changed over the last few months. Dad-before, you see, was short and dark and gruff and hard and terse, and either an architect or builder, Martin can never work out which, though he tends towards the latter on account of having seen Tony Quick operating cranes and working concrete mixers and humping great bags of cement, which with all his might Martin can't even budge an inch; on account, in other words, of seeing his dad generally involved in building things, things like the big workshop and games room he put up last year at the bottom of the garden, Martin helping to dig foundation trenches and lay the bricks and cinder blocks, and saw important bits of wood that might (or might not) be crucial to the final assembly of beams and joists and rafters. And while Dad-after is quite similar to this in many respects, being also short and dark and gruff and grumpy, he's not quite so hard and terse, being someone whom Martin now sometimes surprises crying quietly to himself outside in the new workshop or upstairs in the master bedroom. Most significant of all, though, is that Dad-after is someone who these days doesn't heft and hump and mix quite so much, having somehow hurt his back, a fact which – Dad-after has explained to Martin and Karen and Rebecca – has a lot to do with why Dad-after's not going to be an architect or even a builder any more but a builder's merchant, which is sort of the same but different, more like being a kind of big shopkeeper. Or was that big-shop keeper? Martin didn't really understand, though he knew that it made his mother very happy. Which little did, not now.

★

Shortly after Tony Quick made the big-shop decision, into this small collection of frightened people a stranger walked. Harry was Martin's step-uncle, Martin's grandmother having married twice and her first husband having left her for America. When he'd finished school Harry had gone to visit him and not come back, not permanently anyway – and not at all for the last seven years, which was further back than Martin could remember. He was tall and fair, and had a dash of grey in the left-hand fringe of his short and slightly wiry hair that looked as if someone had just flicked him with a whitewash brush. He got this from his mother, where the trait was manifest as a long single silver fore-lock, just like JoBeth Williams's character gets after rescuing her daughter at the end of *Poltergeist*, and Martin had it too, though his was sparser, fainter, more accidental. He hadn't liked it at all till Harry came; before then he'd always felt it was a defect, tried to trim it out with scissors, had even attempted to dye it once using a wash-in henna dye he'd found in his mother's bathroom cabinet (although he'd managed instead to turn the left side of his head bright red, much to the amusement of his sisters). But once Martin met Harry and realised that the strange white flick was part of what made him so great, he changed his mind about the flash of colour and a few years later, as a vain and peacock teen, he even went through a stage of using Tippex to make it bigger.

Thing was, with Harry the flick was part of the magic. Martin had always found it hard to look into people's eyes, felt somehow if he did they could see right down inside him, see some secret he was keeping. But with Harry it was easy because the white flick was always there to look at so you could look at his eyes until you got scared, then at the flick, then – when you were ready – back at the eyes again, and you could keep on doing this until you'd built up the courage to see his whole face which, in fact, nearly always turned out to be friendly and smiling, and which spoke in American, and which had a look of wanting to extract the maximum enjoyment from everything in life. Which as far as Martin was concerned was all good.

He couldn't understand why his dad was so reserved around Harry, why he didn't leap to agree with Harry's seemingly endless stream of fun suggestions quite as readily as he and his mother and his sisters did. Suggestions like all going bowling or skating, or taking Martin to the video arcade, or forgetting about cooking dinner and ordering in pizza or a big Chinese, or taking everyone for an evening at the dogs (though Tony Quick was somewhat keener on that last one). Or the Saturday morning he'd announced he'd hired one of those new eight-seater people carriers so they could all drive Mum down to Brighton for the day, an idea that Mum had to be talked into, not feeling up to it (this at a time when she rarely felt up to being wheeled out into the garden). But in the end Harry persuaded her and they'd all piled into the space-age-looking vehicle and spent the best day anyone could remember on the road and on the pier and on the beach, doing fairground rides and video games and trampolining. Even Martin's dad had looked really happy, and that night was the first for ages that Martin hadn't had to lie awake till really late listening to his mother's coughing.

All this was good, but none of it was what was best about Martin's recently rediscovered relative. What was best about Harry wasn't the white flick of hair or the fun trips out or the fact that he was more or less American. What was best was that Uncle Harry was a magician.

A magician. Really. He had a magic show in Las Vegas, that was his job. And though on one occasion Martin heard his dad complaining to his mum that he'd give any money Harry only performed in strip joints and the like (whatever they should happen to be, a confused Martin being sure that stripping was the kind of prosaic thing that builders did, not glamorous magicians) – and though Martin's mum said in reply that the only thing she wanted Tony to give it was a rest – that was good enough for him. A magic show. *In Las Vegas*. Wow. Just like on TV, like Paul Daniels or something. Meaning, of course, that Harry could do magic. Within a fortnight of his arrival he'd decided that Martin should be taught how to do it too.

Not without prompting, it should be remarked. Since Harry's first night in the house, when he'd entertained them all after dinner with an hour of extraordinary tricks – not just card routines (which Karen found hard to follow and Martin too, though he would never have admitted it) but tricks with notes and coins and cigarettes and cups and balls and scarves and magic knots and flames – Martin had nagged Harry almost incessantly to tell him how everything was done. With what Tony Quick thought was a self-important attitude Harry resisted, parrying Martin's requests for knowledge with patient explanations that the secrets of magic were not something to be taken lightly. To a quiet chorus of derisive huffs and sniffs from Marty's father, Harry told Marty that there were two sides to magic, dark and light, just as there was to the mysterious Force in *Star Wars*. Marty wouldn't understand this yet, Harry explained. Reaching understanding was something that took the course of your entire life. Even he, Harry, though he might look like a master magician to someone as young as Marty, was himself a mere acolyte.

Martin was confused by lots of this. The word 'acolyte', for example, though becoming unconfused about that was simple enough – he asked his mum and she told him it meant 'trainee'. But all the stuff about there being two sides, dark and light – that all sounded to him like real, proper magic, like more than just card tricks. Though Martin was old enough not to believe in real magic, he was still young enough to want to. And what Harry had told him sounded like genuine mystery. He burned with the desire to find out more.

Harry told him. The trouble with magic, he explained, is that it *is* just all about doing tricks – or illusions, as he preferred to call them. There's no magic, not really, not in the sense young boys think. There is magic in the world, but that's something else, that's something to do with the understanding he was talking about before, and that kind of magic would come naturally to Marty when he was older. Or he hoped it would, Harry said. Either way, it required a different kind of training (he winked at Martin's mother here). But the kind of magic Marty wanted to learn about; well, that was tricky – and in a very precise meaning of the word. Tricks, illusions – they were about acting, performing, about telling stories. Most important, however, they were about telling people something that isn't true – and not, never, never except to a fellow magician (and sometimes not even then), admitting it. To be a great magician, Harry said, you have to be very good at lying – and at the same time you have to keep a firm grip on the truth. To be a great magician, you have to be completely pure in heart.

'Why?' Martin wanted to know.

'Because being good at lying is a very dangerous thing. The trouble with making a living by lying to others', Harry said, 'is that one day you might start lying to yourself. And people who lie to themselves are rarely good or happy.'

Tony Quick lost his patience at this point. 'You're confusing the poor kid, Harry, can't you see? He can't get all this stuff you're going on about. Why don't you just teach him some bloody tricks?'

So Harry did.

★

Harry stayed with the Quicks much longer than he'd planned – three whole months by the end of it, including all the summer holidays, during which time he spent most of his time in the company of young Martin – or Marty, as Harry called him, something of which his dad also disapproved but which (partly because of that) Martin himself really liked.

'Marty' wasn't the only new word imported into Martin's lexicon over these days and weeks. There were the magic terms, of course: 'pass' and 'flourish' and 'routine' and 'vanish' and 'misdirection' and the marvellous 'prestidigitation', a word it took

Martin two days to learn how to say and which was almost magical in itself. Then there were terms for items Harry showed him and, eventually, gave him – 'feke'* and 'thumb-tip' and 'egg-bag' and 'sponge-ball' and 'shell' – and the Americanisms: 'kind of' and 'sort of' and 'period' for when you wanted to let someone know you'd finished your sentence, and 'sidewalk', and 'comforter' (e.g. the one that lay across his mother's legs, brought for her by Harry from the US of A). Then there were words like 'truck' and 'deck' and 'deuce', which instantly displaced the far more mundane-seeming 'lorry' and 'pack' and 'two'. And last but not least were the names of great magicians: Houdini and Malini and Maskelyne and Devant and Chung Ling Soo and Robert-Houdin, names which wrapped up everything Marty was learning in an ancient mystique and made of it an entire new world.

Some of the things Harry was teaching him Martin found very hard to learn, but Harry was very emphatic that he should practise through all those hours when for whatever reason he had to stay put in his room, hours which stretched almost to infinity when Mum was moved off the daybed and into the hospital (pre-pubescent sibling politics making it impossible for him to join in with the games his two sisters played – or the 'deuce of broads', as he'd privately begun to label them). But though practising had a special kind of boredom all its own, at least it gave Martin something to do. He'd long ago tired of most of his toys, and practising double lifts and Emsley counts and one-handed fans and Hindu shuffles and finger palms and all the rest of it did more than just occupy his body and his mind. It became his secret life.

It wasn't the repetition. Though Martin didn't know it, his mind wasn't quite mature enough to dissolve itself in the rhythm of pure practice just yet. So it wasn't that. No – he'd discovered another way, a young boy's way, a way that involved an old black

---

* Pronounced 'fake' and meaning any of the many kinds of trick or imitation coins, cards, cigarettes and so on which a conjurer will substitute for the genuine article in the course of performing an illusion.

pillbox hat he'd found wrapped in tissue in a forgotten leather box at the back of the airing cupboard and which must've belonged to his grandmother before she'd passed away, a black skirt of his mother's that he'd 'borrowed' out of her wardrobe (and which he didn't feel too guilty about borrowing, seeing as how Mum didn't wear most of her clothes any more), and his mother's tall faux-mahogany dressing mirror, a rickety free-standing thing she'd been given as a wedding present, and which had since suffered a snapped leg; damage that Tony Quick had repaired with a wooden splint and strong wood glue, an interim solution that was less than satisfactory, being not only ugly but also on at least two occasions having given way on Mum, both times when she was tizzing around, getting herself ready for going out. In the days when she had still gone out, that was. Since she'd been ill, the mirror had been fine.

Martin's spell was simple:

1 Wait till all the grown-ups were out and the deuce of broads were playing downstairs or outside.
2 Go into his parents' bedroom.
3 Take the skirt, which was a wraparound and lined with scarlet satin, and throw it round his shoulders, transforming it into a cape.
4 Place the pillbox hat upon his head, ensuring his white flick was still allowed to show.
5 Practise flourishes and fans and coin productions for several hours.

And . . . *hey presto* . . . Martin Quick would somehow vanish into the mirror and in his place there'd be the Great Martini: magician, adventurer, seducer of beautiful women and all-round international man of mystery extraordinaire.

Just like Harry.

Easy.

Just like that.

★

Harry told him he had good hands for magic. They were pale with long and slender fingers and though they were a bit on the small side now, given time that would change. One day, Harry told him, he would be a great magician and whenever he got upset about his mother he should try to concentrate on that. They were his mother's hands, he said, and his grandmother's too, and everyone in their family who had the white flick in their hair also had these hands, which was part of what made them all so special. Look at my hands, Harry said, and Martin did. They were like his own, it was true, but that much bigger and with scars across the knuckles which, when Martin asked him how he'd got them, Harry had done something he almost never did and looked away, said something about tripping down some steps and falling through a plate-glass window.

'So your hands are even better than mine,' Harry said, 'because they don't have scars – and you must make sure you keep them that way if you want to be a great magician. Whenever you miss your mother, all you need to do is look down at your hands and remember that she's there in them, so she's always with you, even though she's gone. Okay? Will you remember that?'

Martin nodded. He was crying now. Mum had gone a week ago; then there'd been the funeral and now Harry was going too. Everyone was leaving him, it seemed. He was scared, he didn't like it any more, he didn't want to be left alone. He didn't understand why Harry had to go. But Harry did.

By the time the taxi carrying Harry to the airport turned the corner at the end of Lincoln Avenue, Martin could hardly see it through his tears. He was too upset even to throw a tantrum, which was what he normally did when things didn't go his way. First his mother and now this; it seemed like he'd never done anything but cry. He wished the world would stop; he was prepared to stand there in the street for ever and ever, until that taxi somehow came back: first the taxi, then Harry, then his mother, like the climax of the most amazing magic trick.

But the climax didn't happen. This was no illusion. The bleak sun, the dirty–laundry clouds, the blank tarmac of the road, the

15

row of frowning houses were all completely everyday and real. And when his dad put his arm round his shoulder and led him back inside Martin didn't protest.

'Harry left you something,' Tony Quick told him once they were in the living room, which without the presence of Mum's daybed seemed emptied out a thousand times. Not really caring, hardly even hearing, Martin shook his head. But his father went over to the sideboard and, opening one of the drawers, took out a small parcel wrapped in purple paper studded with silver stars.

Wiping his nose with the back of his hand, his tears slowing, Martin took the gift. 'What is it?'

'I don't know. Harry just said it was a special present for you, something very valuable, something you must look after. A reward for being his best ever student.'

Martin stood and studied the parcel, as if he wasn't sure what he should do next.

'Why don't you unwrap it?'

'Okay.' He knelt down on the shaggy old soft-cord rug that lay between the sofa and the fire, and eased the Sellotape away from the star-studded paper, opening the parcel much more carefully than he'd ever opened any kind of present before. Turning back the folds of paper one by one he slowly revealed whatever it was Harry had left for him.

Two things lay within. A postcard of Mickey Mouse dressed as the Sorcerer's Apprentice, casting his famous mop and bucket spell, and a tatty old book with a stained blue cover and curling, uneven pages, a book that looked decidedly unusual. 'Marty,' said the card, 'there aren't many real magic books left in the world, but this is one of them. Guard it with your life, study it well and never show it to anyone. And one day you'll be a great magician too. Be strong. Love, Harry.'

'*Jarrett Magic and Stagecraft, Technical*, by Guy Jarrett' was printed on the cover of the book. Martin picked it up and flicked through the poorly typeset pages, pausing whenever he came to one of the unusual-looking diagrams or pictures.

Tony Quick peered at the volume over the boy's shoulder.

'Well. A real magic book. That's nice of Harry, isn't it, Martin?'

Martin nodded. Then he closed the book, wrapped it back up in the paper and looked his father directly in the eye. 'Dad?'

'Yes?'

'Can I please be called Marty from now on?'

Tears came into Dad-after's eyes; to stem them he patted his middle child on the head. 'Okay, son,' he said.

Jarrett Magic and Stagecraft, Technical, by Guy Jarrett – referred to by magicians simply as '*Jarrett*' – was written, printed, bound and published by the author himself in 1936. Carny pitchman, acrobat, actor, illusionist, inventor, philosopher, health freak and all-round eccentric, Jarrett had for years designed illusions for many of the great magicians of his era, before deciding to commit the greatest of his ideas to paper. When he did, however, the effects he described were so extreme and revolutionary – and the textual descriptions of the illusions intercut with so many acerbic and plain off-the-wall comments aimed at the state of magic and other magicians – that he couldn't find a single publisher willing to take on the task of mass-producing the great work.

Jarrett, being Jarrett, remained undaunted. It was only to be expected, he told himself, that his genius would not immediately be recognised by lesser men. To give the world a leg-up on its path to enlightenment he went out and bought himself a second-hand 'foundry' printing press – old-fashioned even in the 1930s – and proceeded to set and print the book himself, letter by letter, page by page. He had the illustrations done at an offset house and inserted them at the appropriate points, before stitching the pages together by hand and binding them with blue binding fabric.

The manufacture of four hundred copies took him a year, four hundred copies which he proceeded to try to sell at the then hefty price of $5 apiece. Yet, with the exception of a few fellow obsessives, the magic world greeted the arrival of Jarrett's masterwork with scorn. Reviews, the few that it received, were largely scathing. Several purchasers tried to return the book and get their money back, claiming it to be the unreadable ramblings of a maniac. One place the book did sell well was Nazi Germany, where Jarrett's occasional (if unfocused) anti-Semitic outbursts no doubt endeared it to its audience. But his Central European readership alone was not enough to save him and, unable to shift fully half of his already modest stock, Jarrett advertised a sales drive in which he announced his intention to drop the price of each book to $1 and increase it by a dollar a month until the price reached $10 a copy, at which point he would burn any stock that remained in a public ceremony dedicated to the condemnation of a nation of short-sighted and ignorant 'drugstore magicians' (a favourite phrase).

The book-burning never happened. Nor did the price increase scam. Jarrett ended up giving away as many copies as he sold and what stock he couldn't clear sat around mouldering on the shelves in sundry shops, his own included, until it was sold on in job lots or just thrown out to free up more valuable space. But in the way of these things, those copies of *Jarrett Magic and Stagecraft, Technical* that still exist today are collectors' items, their value more or less beyond price, their contents considered ground-breaking, extraordinary, touched by both madness and genius.

★

Of Guy Jarrett Terri Liddell knew precisely nothing. She certainly had absolutely no idea of the existence of Marty's copy of one of his books and not even the tiniest inkling that it presently lay, nine years after Harry had made him a gift of it, wrapped in velvet and revered and preserved inside a small gunmetal-grey child's strongbox inside the locked bottom drawer of a cabinet in Marty's room, though the day when she would know of it was not far off. She didn't even know of Marty – though that day, too, was coming.

What Terri did know quite a lot about was Darren Watt, whom

she was seeing and whom she liked despite his gingery hair and freckles, because he was both quite sporty and, she reckoned, quite intelligent (plus he had a red Triumph Spitfire that he'd done up by himself). He was quite well off, was Darren, and his parents were still together. His dad was a stockbroker or something – she'd forgotten now, but something like that in any case – and they lived in a house with two receptions and a double garage one side of which was what Darren called his den. Here was where the Triumph had been reconditioned and it had jacks and toolboxes and spray-cans of body paint, and that oily smell of engines that Terri had always liked because it reminded her of car trips with her own dad when she was little, especially of how he always used to bring her a mini-present – a bar of Toblerone, a key ring, a Smurf, something like that – every time they stopped for petrol, a habit that went on for long enough to make sure she spent most of every journey wishing the petrol gauge towards the 'empty' zone. In fact, she still did: even today whenever she climbed inside a car Terri automatically imagined herself into the situation of the engine, a greedy engine, hungrily devouring Daddy's fuel. Memories and mechanisms which were all mixed up with and somehow contained within that hot-engines-on-a-forecourt smell, the same smell she'd discovered lingering in Darren's den, though the Triumph was no longer kept in there, and the jacks and toolboxes and so on had all been pushed aside to make way for all sorts of other stuff: bundles of dowel and stacks of two-by-four and sheets of ply and a Black and Decker workbench and coils of wire and pricey sets of wall-mounted tools and pots of paint and a shelving unit crammed with tatty boxes filled with screws, electrical components, and any number of other random bits and bobs. And, most important of all, the cabinet that he was building.

This cabinet was about the size of a small wardrobe and fitted with castors; these, Darren had explained, had been salvaged from an old drinks trolley his gran was throwing out. On first viewing, Terri remembered, the cabinet had seemed both slightly tacky but also a bit mysterious, coloured as it was with misty air-brushed blues and golds overlaid by runes and stars and silver moons. She didn't need to guess at its purpose because Darren had already told her: it was a sword cabinet, and it had to do with the new hobby he'd taken up ever since, the Spitfire finished, he'd got bored of cars.

In a way Terri had met the hobby before she'd met the boy. The first time she'd encountered Darren – in the pub nearest college, where she was in the habit of drinking on Fridays with a regular group of friends – he'd come over and tried to chat her up by showing her a card trick.

The trick was actually quite cute. Terri even thought it a little bit romantic, though admittedly this was before she'd met lots of other magicians and had come to realise that this is what all (male heterosexual) magicians do, use tricks to chat up girls – that was why they learned tricks in the first place, most of them, for this very purpose. Darren's trick had gone like this: after cornering Terri while she was standing at the bar and delivering an awkward line or two, he'd asked her if she fancied seeing some magic. One of his lines had (almost) managed to make her laugh so she'd said yes. Darren had promptly produced a pack of cards from his back pocket, fanned them out and asked her to pick one of them. 'Look at it,' he said, 'and then put it back and don't tell me what it is.' (It was the two of hearts.)

When the card was safely back inside the pack, Darren told Terri he was going to try to read her mind, but that he could only do this if she let him hold her hand. Terri agreed, though it felt a bit funny, letting this total stranger take her hand the way he did, between both of his, and squeeze it hard like that. It made her wonder if perhaps this wasn't a trick at all, or not a magic trick at any rate but rather some weird boy trick that would turn out to be just an excuse to get into physical contact with her and which would be revealed as such any second now to the amusement of his friends, two of whom, she had noticed, were already beginning to giggle at them from where they were sitting a short way off, in their group.

'Well?' she asked, now that her paranoia had reached this

dangerous pitch. 'So what's the card then, Mr Mindreader man?'

Darren said he didn't know, that he couldn't tell just yet. She was difficult to read, apparently. Removing his hand, he took out a pack of cigarettes, offered one to Terri (she declined) and lit one for himself. He smoked it quickly, without inhaling, until there was a caterpillar of ash curling off the end. This he knocked into his palm, smoothing it into a soft circle with his thumb before asking her if he could take her hand again. 'Well, I don't know,' she said. 'I don't know if I want to get all covered in ash.'

'No problem,' he told her. 'Then all you need to do is just hold it out, palm down. Like this.' He demonstrated. 'It's your hand. If it wants to express itself it will.'

This sounded fair enough so Terri held out her hand as Darren asked while he brought his ashy palm flat up to hers and just touched her very delicately, moving his hand in small circles in a manner that was much more intimate and sexy than the heavy way he'd held her earlier. And that must have been the magic because when he'd told her her card had been the two of hearts and she'd asked him how he knew he'd answered, 'Your skin told me, just look.' So of course she turned it over and right there, sitting in her palm, just like on a playing card but made out of ash, were two grey hearts, powdery and insubstantial but two grey hearts nonetheless.

Which had completely blown her away.

*

All through the first sixteen years of her life, Terri had always been completely adamant that she didn't believe in sex before marriage – or sex before you met the person you were going to marry, at any rate. But two years of turbulence in late adolescence were to change her point of view. This period began quite abruptly and out of the blue when, only two weeks after her fifteenth birthday, her parents announced they were to divorce. Shockingly, Daddy was leaving the family nest to go and live with his 'other woman' who, as it transpired, had for quite a number of years now been at the other end of lots of those long car journeys on which Terri had accompanied him, the other woman happening to work in a sales office on an industrial estate outside Luton. Now Terri could make sense of those long meetings he'd had while she'd had to stay put in the car, meetings from which he emerged smelling sweaty and more strongly of his Lynx body spray than he had when he'd gone in. Appalled by her new knowledge, she was for a long time put off the prospect of sex altogether. What good was it if it led to such awful heartbreak?

While her mother played the martyr, Terri was distraught. It was such an incredibly *selfish* thing for Daddy to do. Especially since her GCSEs were coming up. And she wouldn't be able to get that pony that she'd been promised since she was ten nor – even though Graham was paying child benefit and had left Avril with half their savings, her pension and the house – would she be able to stay on at her fee-paying school once her exams were over and done. Not unless Avril were prepared to go back to full-time work, which at her age (forty) was apparently unthinkable.

It was a bad year for Terri. Not only did she feel obliged to terminate her membership of the Pony Club (sending a copy of her official resignation to her father's new address in a calculatedly pointed and symbolic act), three months later during the qualifying rounds for the county gymnastic championships (gymnastics being the one thing at which she was actually really good) she lost her grip while performing an inbar kip to V-press handstand on the parallel bars. She slipped, fell and badly hurt her wrist. After which she gave up gymnastics too.

Worst of all was changing schools. The other kids attending the sixth-form college weren't what she was used to, not at all. To begin with there were boys, when her previous school had been single-sex, and secondly hardly anyone at the new school would speak to her, except to take the piss. While her new female peers listened to Rebel MC and the Ragga Twins, Terri thought this was music to frighten horses with. While they wore Reeboks, hugely baggy Madchester jeans and Space Baby tops from Red or Dead, she favoured clothes purchased from the same catalogues and stores as her mother's. Her idea of dressing down was wearing tight stonewashed jeans, strappy little heels, and hot pink angora sweaters that showed off her navel. Even her school uniform – which Avril Liddell had insisted on buying even though it was optional and which she was one of only five girls in the entire school actually to wear – looked like it had been ordered from Freemans or Littlewoods.

Still, she was resilient enough and she learned to cope, adopting strategies that included the surreptitious swopping of school uniform for more casual attire (casual by Terri's standards) in the public toilets en route from home to school and the deepening of her interest in palm reading and astrology, which certain other girls soon began to realise she was comparatively expert in and quickly gravitated towards. She needed something to draw them to her; being tall and slim and austerely pretty it was easy to make enemies, even among the boys, most of whom found her too posh and pretty to approach.

What the girls were concerned about were signals, she realised. Before, at her all-girls school, she and her friends had competed among themselves to be the most beautiful, the most ethereal, the most dainty, the most affected. Less attractive classmates had hated them for this, but that had been part of the fun. Here, though, there was no tight group of friends, and behaving preciously would quickly get her hated by everyone.

Gradually, then, Terri toned down her more solipsistic excesses. Yet she remained resolute about the vow she'd made one evening to her mother soon after her father had left home: that whatever happened to them in the future she'd stay true to who she was, a vow which turned out to mean always sitting down at the table to eat, not starting smoking or experimenting with drugs and keeping the furry animals piled up on her bed until she was nearly twenty-one.

But everyone needs at least one way to rebel, and Terri was no exception. Which is why she lost her virginity to Darren within a month of his showing her the trick with the two ash hearts, a release of good-girl tension which – along with the astrology – helped to keep her sane.

★

Now that Terri was Darren's lover it seemed only natural, given her gymnast's training and his increasing interest in his hobby, that she should also become his assistant. She was a little unsure about this at first. If she'd learned one thing in the last six months it was that it was as a rule unwise, in her new situation, to draw too much attention to herself. But Terri was nothing if not an attention-seeker, and like all the parts of her personality that aspect required its outlet too. At least once she was up on a stage she was *supposed* to be showing off.

They rehearsed a little show and tried it out on their friends – Darren being able, Terri noted, to garner a surprising amount of respect for his magic from among his sporty set of mates – and over the next year or so they moved on from doing performances at parties and school events to adding cabinets and routines for a series of occasional appearances at the local arts centre. At which point, buzzing with their own slightly unexpected success, they began to talk about entering for the televised competition *Young Magician of the Year*. Which in the end is what they did.

The preparation period for the competition should have been a happy one, but oddly, perhaps because the two of them suddenly found themselves bound together as a couple more tightly than they'd bargained for by the high visibility of the project, tensions began to appear in their relationship. Darren's response, consciously or not, was to disappear into his workshop. Having decided that they needed an important new prop, he set out to build it himself, a project that involved angle iron and hacksaws and hired welding gear and great chunks of his time during which he wasn't free to entertain Terri quite as much as she would have liked him to. Worrying that his interest in her was perhaps on the wane, she'd turned up at his den one day wearing a new outfit she'd put together specially (a sleeveless, ruched black-mesh top that unzipped at the front over an impossibly short PU/PVC snakeskin-print miniskirt in hot-red multi) to find him struggling with something, she wasn't sure quite what, but some kind of very large and awkward metal frame.

Darren's neck, Terri had noticed, was swollen and thick, and his face had turned the colour of aubergine. He was also swearing a lot – swearing being something of which Terri did not approve – on account of his throbbing right thumb, which he'd managed to trap in whatever it was he was grappling with and which was rapidly turning the same colour as his blood-forced cheeks. His overall condition was one which – if Terri had been in his place – would have meant stopping right there and paying out/pulling in whatever funds or favours she had available in order to get someone else to come in and make for her whatever it was she was trying to build. Certainly it wouldn't have involved her continuing to struggle like this while her recently post-virginal girlfriend whom she hadn't seen for days stood timidly by, all made up and delicious, all desirous of a hot bout of fresh, clean and still-technically-teenage sex, an option that most men would kill for if Terri knew men (which she thought she did). Most especially it wouldn't have involved her continuing to struggle if she'd had the remotest idea of how much attention that recently post-virginal girlfriend had been getting from other boys 'n' that, on account of all the leaping in and out of cabinets and trunks she'd been doing in that skin-tight little costume of hers, the white Lycra one with all the sequins sewn on it.

Yes, Terri had been getting attention all right. She'd known she'd been getting it because of how, when she emerged from whatever it was she'd been hidden in wearing that tight little outfit she liked so much, she could *feel* the eyes watching her. And she now discovered that she *liked* the eyes watching her, for the first time, really, since she'd smashed her wrist. Out on stage each little sequin seemed to capture one of those eyes and transform its stare into a perceptible electrical buzz, and when all these buzzes were experienced together, when they were all added up – like at the climax of a trick when she held up her arms in a double swan's neck like a dancer, stretching the Lycra so taut between her shoulders and hips that the material fluttered against the sensitive zones in the arch of her back and tugged at the folds of her groin – it felt as if hundreds of careful fingertips were tenderly brushing over every inch of her pearly white Home Counties skin.

It was certainly something to experience. There was only one problem with it that Terri could see. Two of the eyes always happened to be Darren's, and since that day when she'd arrived in his workshop all dolled up and pretty and he'd hardly glanced up from whatever it was he was grappling with, Terri had been forced to acknowledge that his eyes didn't work like that on her any longer. Which was a tricky one. Because it meant, when it came down to it, that Darren was at heart a tinkerer, rather than the dedicated lover Terri felt she required. And that really wouldn't do.

Much to their surprise (not to mention everyone else's), Darren and Terri made it through to the finals of *Young Magician*, which were to be broadcast to the nation from the Crucible Theatre in Sheffield, the last event in the calendar before the annual snooker championships got under way. The finals were no small affair: four categories of acts, six acts in each category, ten minutes allotted to each act plus changeovers and intervals and prize ceremonies, and time put aside for the inevitable technical hitches . . . it was a veritable monster, though only highlights were to be televised, of course. 'The Demonic Darren Watt and Terri Electric' had been allocated a slot about two and a half hours into the proceedings, the fourth in their category, sandwiched between a comedy magic duo who'd later get a Highly Commended and a bloke who called himself Martin Mystery. They came on to the opening strains of Van Halen's 'Jump', which Darren had decided would be their theme tune. Terri didn't like the song much; she thought it 'very boy'. If she'd have had her way they'd have had something by Whitney or Madonna or even Sister Sledge ('Lost in Music' would've been her ideal – she still had a tendency to think of magic like it was figure-skating). But Darren had choreographed the whole act around 'my man Van', as he referred to him, so that was that; she didn't want to tell him to go back and do it all over again.

Though they'd rehearsed it backwards and forwards until the moves and routines ran as smoothly as the engine under the bonnet of Darren's red Triumph, by the time their slot came round they were both wound up tight as springs. When the first power chords of their soundtrack reverberated around the theatre, Terri was shaking so much that she could barely keep her fingers locked into the clingholes on the back of her cabinet, the same cabinet Darren was now wheeling out on to the stage. It seemed an impossibility that she'd be able to get through her moves at all, let alone get the timings perfectly right – especially with the memory of her disaster on the parallel bars from three years before so present in her mind. But it was too late for thinking, or for fear even: they were out before the audience now and she could sense the crowd and both feel and see the lights, and they had begun.

The glare softened for a moment as Darren flipped the lid back over her head and dropped open the front, and banged his hand round the insides to demonstrate to the assembled company that the container was empty. Then the front was clipped back up and the top flipped forward, and Terri pressed the button that released the secret panel in the back, transforming it into a double set of doors which opened inwards. Feet first she slipped inside, a move which involved a quite extreme contortion, and having managed that she shoved the doors closed behind her with her elbows and heels. Then, with her back hard against the false panel, she pulled the two mirrors fitted flush into the sides of the container inwards until they met in the centre and formed a V, a V just big enough for her to hide behind.

To make things harder, by this point Darren was spinning the box round on its axis so that the audience could see there was nobody hanging off the back. Once, twice, three times he spun it, the idea being not to disorientate Terri but to give her plenty of time to get into her new position so that when the magician did what he did next – i.e. unlatch the front for the second time and show the inside of the cabinet to the audience – it would still appear that there was nobody inside.*

* This works because the mirrors reflect the black side walls of the cabinet, creating the illusion that you're not looking at a V of mirrors at all but at the same black back wall that the magician showed you earlier.

With this important stage of the illusion achieved, Darren closed the cabinet and spun it round again, before leaving it for a moment in the centre of the stage. Inside, Terri released the mirrors and waited while her boyfriend walked over to stage left and retrieved a giant yellow sack, which he held open at the mouth and pulled quickly through the air in order that the audience could see that it was solid at the bottom – a proper bag, in other words, rather than a mere tube of cloth. This thus demonstrated, he arranged the bag – mouth still open and uppermost – upon the lid of the cabinet, taking care to un-Velcro the false seam that they'd both pass through before walking over to the wings again to retrieve a second item, this time a small set of aluminium steps, which he used to climb up on to the box.

Terri heard his feet above her right on cue, the cue being the beginning of Van Halen's guitar solo. Climbing into the sack, Darren pulled it up over his head, tapping the lid three times with his toe as he did so. This was Terri's signal to release the secret panel in the lid and squeeze up through it and into the sack behind her boyfriend, stripping the black panels of his suit away from their press-stud attachments as she went and stuffing them into a pocket sewn into the back of the sack just to her rear, revealing the spangly red costume he wore beneath. Then she reached up and took the sack from where he was holding it above his head, allowing him to drop to his knees and slip into the box through the secret panel. At this point Terri's nerves came back. It seemed to be taking Darren an age to get down inside the box. What if he'd put on weight since their last rehearsal and suddenly couldn't fit? But now his legs were in: and now his stomach (the primary danger point); and finally his head, and she set her posture, looked wide-eyed and pretty, heard the panel click shut and let the bag drop to her feet.

It was the eyes. All the eyes were on her. The eyes and the lights. A real stage, a giant audience. Her two thousand sequins blazing with two thousand watts or volts or amps or whatever they were called. Terri Electric, on fire, that was the main thing. Terri Electric.

Alive.

★

They came off stage and leapt into each other's arms, jumping up and down with relief and excitement. It'd gone okay, they'd pulled it off – and what's more it had been a pretty much perfect performance. Running backstage to the Green Room, they collected congratulatory hugs and handshakes from the loose bunch of people they'd befriended in the course of the competition. This being *Young Magician*, the consumption of alcohol was subject to heavy restriction, but like most of the participants Darren and Terri had a private stash of booze – in their case a bottle of cheap champagne – which they now cracked open. It didn't matter too much if they won or not, they'd done it and that was what counted. Or so Darren announced, clutching his plastic cup in a trembling hand and holding it aloft.

Terri nodded but couldn't help thinking otherwise. While Darren seemed more nervous now than before they'd gone on, for her it was just the opposite – the fear and tension she'd experienced earlier had vanished and all she could remember was the wonderful buzz of the eyes upon her skin. Sure, it didn't really matter if they won. But it would be *nice* . . .

Then she spotted Marty.

He was on the television in the corner of the room, the CCTV screen on which pretty much everyone in the Green Room was watching the unfolding show, either sitting silently, blinking like birds, trying to keep a handle on their fear and nerves, or chatting noisily and making facetious comments about the rival acts as they came on, which was another way of achieving the same goal. But even the critics found themselves with little to say, now that Martin Mystery had started his act, the sudden drop in noise being the reason Terri had looked over from her and Darren's small celebration to find out what was going on.

With his slim build, fine features and highly styled mullet of raven-black hair that looked as if it might well be dyed, Marty would have looked distinctive enough without the strong fleck of white hair sprouting from the corner of his forehead (which, unbeknown to Terri, had been enhanced especially for the occasion). Dressed in a black polo-neck sweater and saffron satin

31

lounge jacket, with salt-and-pepper trousers piping down his legs to the crêpe soles on his feet, he looked relaxed and laid back, moving about the stage slowly and evenly, his groin pushed forward a little.

His soundtrack was 'Who's that Lady?' by the Commodores and the illusion he was doing was the three card trick Find the Lady, the one where you have to guess which of the three cards is the queen. Nothing remarkable there, except that the playing cards easily measured eight feet by five and the lady was real. Hanging from a rail with three-foot gaps like washing from a line, their bases clearing the ground by about two feet, the cards were large enough to fill most of the stage. Behind each card stood a stool, which you could see, and on one of these stools stood a girl, whom you couldn't. But behind which of the cards was she standing? It was never the one you thought it was going to be. Marty would show her and then she'd be gone; he'd show her again and she'd vanish again, and though he did this over and over it was impossible to see how she could move from behind one card to another. As a finale he removed all the cards, carrying them off stage one by one, and when the last was removed the girl had disappeared altogether. When she came back on from the wings to take a bow alongside the magician she got such a huge round of applause that it was worrying.

It was a great illusion, really original – or so Terri assumed (whereas, in fact, Marty had taken the trick from his copy of *Jarrett*, who'd credited it to a 1920s vaudeville magician who went by the name of Amac ('A Most Amazing Conjurer') and who had a successful travelling show in which it was the only attraction).

'Was the rest of the act any good?' she asked a girl sitting nearby, a Goth from Stoke called Julie whom Terri had earlier seen lying in a velvet padded coffin while her boyfriend, dressed as a vampire, sawed her in two.

Julie nodded back, bangles rattling. 'It were *brill*-yant. He's going to win.'

Terri looked back at Martin Mystery and his assistant, bowing to rapturous applause on the screen, her eyes flicking from one face to the other. His face was beautiful, she thought, hers an oval dish of light.

Terri wanted her face to be like that.

Soon it would be.

Everyone was back in the main auditorium, the performers and their guests sitting at tables, the public arrayed in the raked seating behind. Princess Di was presenting the prizes, which probably had something to do with the venue being both so large and so full. Darren and Terri, as it turned out, were to receive a Highly Commended for their efforts, which pleased them immensely and meant they were among the first to get called up on to the stage. It seemed to Terri she was even more nervous going up and meeting the Royal than she had been performing the act, but on this occasion there was much less pay-off; this time she could sense that the eyes weren't focused on her. Other than her mum's, of course – while she was standing there giving Diana the obligatory peck on the cheek it was as if she could hear her mother back there in the audience whispering to her Aunt Fran, who'd accompanied her in lieu of Terri's absentee dad, that didn't Terri look like Di, now they were standing side by side you couldn't mistake the resemblance, it was just as she'd always said.

Which was true, she had always said it. And she was right: Terri did look a little like Princess Diana – and also a bit like Jill Dando and Anthea Turner, though less like Anthea than the other two, what with her tallness and thinness and her (as she thought of it) slightly beaky nose, and her hair worn in that George Michael style that she favoured: short and bouffant, and highlighted as if to mimic the plumage of the tawny owl. And very eighties which, as Terri was in the habit of pointing out, were ready to start coming back (and on which point she'd turn out to be right, if a little premature).

All this meant two things. First, that Terri was beautiful in that thoroughbred way that's favoured by the aristocracies of this world, with their lizard tastes for racehorses and ballerinas and competition dogs and fashion models, and other living machines bred into the narrow conduits of human specificity, their value apparently set in inverse proportion to their evolutionary usefulness. And second, that in the weeks following the *Young Magician* competition Terri's mother would persuade her to look for work as a Diana lookalike, going so far as to get some photos of her daughter taken by a portrait photographer with a small studio above a dentist's in Guildford town centre (and, unknown to either of them, a thriving sideline in bondage pictures, which back then he sold through small ads in the pages of *Tied 'N' Teased* magazine but which these days are punted out mainly via his website) and have them sent to a West (very West) London agent who'd been recommended by a friend, efforts which did, in fact, lead to Terri getting a bit of paid work opening the occasional car park or school fête (not to mention several other rather more distasteful offers which she quickly and embarrassedly declined).

So Darren Watt and Terri Electric kissed the princess and collected their runners-up plaques and retook their seats, and felt all round pleased with themselves and waited to hear the roll call of results that led upwards, in incremental steps, to the overall winner. Who turned out to be Martin Mystery, just as predicted by Julie the Goth.

If Marty was surprised to discover that the mannerisms, expressions and attitudes proper to a rampant young talent that he'd so long been rehearsing in concert with his magic exercises were now going to have to be put to use, he didn't let it show. Exuding the practised Olympian charisma that had looked so good in that mirror of his mother's ever since the age of ten, he bounced up out of his seat and, with his sister Karen in tow, bowled through the crowd and up on to the stage, brushing past

Terri as he went. At this moment of contact, Terri inhaled sharply and grabbed at the patch of skin on her shoulder where the winner's jacket had touched. She absolutely had to, she decided as she listened to Martin Mystery's gracious acceptance speech, she absolutely had to make sure she spoke to him at the after-show party.

★

Talking to Marty at the after-show party was not, as it turned out, a particularly difficult ambition to realise. The new god of magic had already logged Terri with his female-o-scope; as the next act in the schedule he'd watched her slip in and out of her sphinx box while he waited in the wings, and he'd been paying extremely close attention when she'd walked up on stage to kiss the princess on the cheek and be handed her plaque. And that brush on the shoulder? It wouldn't, I think, be remiss to point out that it wasn't entirely an accident.

Unlike Aunt Fran, Marty didn't need to have Terri's similarity to the Royal pointed out to him. Indeed, it was the thing that most drew her to his attention. For Marty had a bit of a thing about Princess Di and for Jill Dando too (and, later on, even for Anthea Turner). In fact, Marty had a bit of a thing for any slender, white, blonde, short-haired woman who looked like she might have modelled underwear for Kays catalogue between 1983 and 1985.

Reasons are hazy at the best of times, but Marty's preferences might well be traced to his discovery, aged thirteen, of his mother's old cache of mail order catalogues which Tony Quick, being understandingly sentimental about his dead wife's things, hadn't yet been able to bring himself to throw out.

Ever since his thirteenth birthday, puberty had begun to displace magic in Marty's young mind. Practising card and coin manipulations in his mother's old dressing mirror – which he'd asked his dad if he could have after her death and which Tony Quick had given him, much to his older sister's fury, as she also laid claim to it – no longer seemed as interesting as standing naked before it (naked except for a pair of towelling socks) watching his erection rise and fall, or carefully counting his slowly sprouting crop of pale pubic hairs.

Rebecca's girl logic dictated that as both the eldest daughter and eldest child (as well as the sibling with the finest bone structure) *she* should have the mirror, which though cheap and broken had somehow been imbued by Maureen Quick's death with the status of priceless heirloom. As had Mum's make-up bag and her jewellery box, and her matching hairbrush-and-clothesbrush set, and her hairdryer, and certain of her clothes, all of which would be surreptitiously fought over by the two girls for some years to come until, like a series of small French villages trapped between trenches, they had been so pulverised by argument that they had no inherent value left at all and were barely even capable of functioning as bridgeheads to their mother's memory. But the mirror wasn't like that. You might have thought Rebecca wanted it because it had so often held her mother's image or something meaningful like that, but that was not the case. The objects that the two sisters wanted had somehow to have been in contact with their mother in some way, and she rarely touched the mirror except on those occasions when, trying to get it to stay in the right position, she'd caused its leg to collapse. No. Despite her rationalisations to the contrary, Rebecca had wanted the mirror purely out of vanity.

This was understandable. Thirteen when her mother died, she was in the same place then that Marty was now, more or less (a bit further ahead, in fact, in that way girls have), and the need to keep careful tabs on her swelling hips and breasts, and how they changed her body's relationship with the clothes she wore and – by extension – the wider world around her was at that time her primary driving force. Marty, on the other hand, just needed the mirror for practising his magic tricks, and since there was no point in giving him the hairbrush or the jewellery case or any of those other things, Tony Quick decided it should be his. By the time he wanted it for the same reasons as Rebecca, his sister had turned fifteen and acquired a full-length mirror of her own, as well as an extensive wardrobe and a well-developed interest in the opposite sex that was already underpinned with a healthy amount of empirical data.

Some of this knowledge trickled down to Marty, of course. Until he discovered the catalogue cache Rebecca was the best example of woman he had to hand, though boys at school rumoured that there was more to the breed than his big sister's girlish posturings suggested. Then came the catalogues, discovered accidentally in a box stacked up with others out in, of all places, his father's workshop.

Some of them were still in mint condition. Some were even still sealed inside their prophylactic polythene wrap and when Marty ripped it open he couldn't believe his eyes. Here was woman after woman carefully displaying herself for him in a provocative but unthreatening way – in sharp and refreshing contrast to the one or two porn mags he'd seen, which compared with this were like a heroin injection, forbidden fruit that was too blatantly linked with violence and death to be anything but completely terrifying.

Inevitably, it was the lingerie sections that most interested him, even though viewing them produced in him a quite extraordinary level of shame and guilt. By looking at these pictures – by becoming aroused by them – was he somehow wronging the memory of his mother? Marty hadn't yet sorted out all that life and death stuff to his complete satisfaction, and he couldn't be a hundred per cent sure that Mum wasn't up in heaven right now, looking down on him. Yet despite all this he couldn't help himself, those hormones were raging, so in the end he reached a compromise. He wouldn't look at the pictures of women who looked like his mother, by which he meant women who had any kind of haircut approximating that which his mother had had immediately before she'd lost all her hair to the chemo.

This haircut was the only thing about Mum that Marty could really remember with absolute clarity, apart from her smell and even that was fading. For most of his life his mother's hair had been ash-blond and worn shoulder length – neither she nor

Rebecca nor Karen, who were darker, like their father, had any echo of Granny's white strand as Marty did. But around the time that she'd become seriously ill, to make it easier to manage she'd had it cut into a feathered bowl just like Lady Diana Spencer's, the young English beauty whose engagement to Prince Charles was at the time the subject of so much speculation.

Charles and Diana were married the summer that Harry was staying; the family watched the wedding together on the telly. But by this time the bowl of fair hair that Marty's mum sported was no longer her own. Her son saw her without it only once, when he and Dad dropped in to see her in hospital as a surprise, and Marty was so shocked to find out that his mum had no hair – and that he hadn't detected the change between real and artificial – that her barnet stuck fast in his memory.

So there it was: mother, Princess Diana, the Royal Wedding, his dead mum. The two women, the two events, would for Marty be linked for ever, if only because by making a conscious attempt to avoid having sexual thoughts about any of the women in the catalogues bearing the remotest resemblance to one or the other, he ensured that he ended up desiring precisely that type of woman all the more.

★

For the next year or two, magic's place in Marty's mirror was displaced by his increasingly image-conscious self, the tricks and routines and prestidigitations rejected as a childish thing that girls would look down upon. Until, that is, one fateful night; a night spent at an early teenage party when he was around fifteen and a half, where he discovered that the exact contrary was true: that magic could help him become the centre of attention, imbue him, indeed, with a glamour and attractiveness with which all but the most charismatic of his male peers found it difficult to compete. Someone had heard he used to do magic tricks – people teased him for it occasionally, which was one of the reasons he'd stopped doing them. They asked him to perform one for them – they'd found a pack of cards in one of the kitchen drawers of the house they'd all descended on like locusts (the owners being foolish enough to have gone away on holiday and leave their son in charge) – but sure that they were looking for an easy way to take the piss, Marty'd said no, he didn't do that any more. They'd asked again, he'd declined again. But on the third request he'd acquiesced and one short routine later he'd found himself holding court to an audience of astonished boys and girls. Pretty girls. And that was that: once back home, out came the forgotten Paul Daniels magic set, the silver half-dollars, the thumb-tip Harry had given him, the streamers and the scarves; out came the dusty old copy of *Jarrett Magic*; over the next few months Marty found himself practising and practising and practising routines and sleight of hand to the detriment of his GCSEs. Before he knew it elements of his old magical persona had taken up residence inside the mirror, fusing with his narcissistic teenage self to form a perfect new identity.

Martin Mystery was born.

★

So it was magic that helped Marty to survive puberty and school. With it he could get almost anyone to like him, it appeared – or at least to admire him, which seemed to Marty to be pretty much the same thing. He loved the looks that crossed people's faces when he'd fooled them; he got a huge buzz when he coaxed wonder into the expression of a girl he found attractive; nothing beat forcing respect from a boy who previously had picked on him. The next stage – getting the girl to agree to come out on a date, getting the boy to become his friend – he didn't find so easy. But right now that didn't seem to matter; it seemed enough just to be able to show people something they couldn't understand, laugh at their laughable explanations for how he'd done what he just did, watch envy puffing out their eyes and necks and shoulders. That was addictive, that was a joy in itself. And if it filled up the void left by his mother's death by making him the centre of attention – then that was also to the good.

Around the time he turned seventeen, Marty decided to move

up from doing purely close-up magic and so, with one eye on the great magicians of the past and the other on the contemporary American greats he idolised, he built himself an Indian-style sword casket out of fibreglass in CDT using a design he'd taken from a Paul Osborne book he'd bought from International Magic on the Clerkenwell Road in London's Farringdon district, the place where Jerry Sadowitz sometimes works. Squat and round, it stood about fourteen inches high and, according to the instructions, was just big enough to take one curled-up girl. But while the instructions were detailed and comprehensive on the subject of the sword basket's construction, they didn't have a great deal to say – or really anything at all – on the subject of how to find (and curl up) a girl, a task Marty quickly discovered was to prove about as difficult as it was proving to find a girl willing to have sex with him. It didn't help that his first choice for both these roles was Miranda Swales, acknowledged by one and all as the best-looking girl in the school and therefore already very much in demand (though it was fair to say she'd never been asked to clamber in and out of a fibreglass laundry basket before). Unfortunately Miranda also belonged to the small set of people who remained distinctly unimpressed by Marty's magic tricks, judging them creepy and manipulative, and too clever by half.

'Miranda, how would you feel about –' Marty ventured one day while the two of them were queuing for lunch.

'Absolutely no way.'

'Oh. Okay. Then what about . . .'

'Not that either.'

'What then if I promise to sto –'

'Forget it, Marty. The answer is no.'

As Miranda was popular with girls as well as boys, her refusal meant that no other female would now take the job. No one, that was, but Sarah; Sarah who had long harboured a secret and intense crush on Marty, but who was asthmatic and what you might describe as glandular, but more than willing to try to squeeze into the basket if that would please the object of her desire. The object of her desire being desperate, he agreed to a trial run, which unfortunately did not go well. The problem was that Sarah didn't fit, a situation which made her embarrassed and upset, and Marty annoyed and angry. When Sarah foolishly presumed to ask if perhaps the casket might be rebuilt to accommodate her better, Marty couldn't keep himself from remarking that perhaps it would be easier for Sarah to rebuild herself to accommodate the cabinet, a comment that made poor Sarah burst into tears. Marty's attempts to pour oil on these troubled waters more closely approximated a tanker spill and the row which followed was sufficiently heated to flatten Sarah's crush for ever and ensure that the two of them would never exchange a single civil word again.

All of which left Marty with a single, final, dismal option, an embarrassing last resort: to get down on his knees and beg his younger sister, Karen (the older and more glamorous Rebecca having left home to study drama at the University of Glamorgan), to help him out, knowing that not only would this make him look stupid in front of his friends but that it would provide her with a golden, extended and not to be passed-up extortion opportunity that would last from the second he asked her until the moment the magic show was over and done.

In exchange for a percentage of Marty's allowance Karen agreed – just this once – to help him out. But the show – included in their school's end of year revue – went so much better than either she or Marty had expected that she ended up doing the next show and the one after that and, indeed, the one that followed, until she and her brother had completed several dozen proper performances together, graduating in the process from the school revue to a Winter Season slot at Beckenham's little independent theatre. It was after Marty snagged a summer run at Bognor Butlin's during the summer holidays off the back of this that they decided to have a shot at *Young Magician of the Year*.

Young Magician, though, was to be the last show Karen did – three years younger than Marty, her GCSEs were coming up and with Rebecca going off to study drama and his son neglecting his studies for all this magic, Tony Quick was determined that one of his kids at least would get a proper education. So Marty was notified that once the competition was over he would have to find himself a new assistant, not that he was particularly bothered by this piece of information. Despite their success, working with his sister had always had a slightly uncool taint to it and over the past year or so persuading girls to do things had become much less of a problem for him. Ever since he'd proved to his peers that he could handle himself up on stage, more than a few members of the opposite sex had begun to see him as something more than an entertaining sideshow to gawp at at parties, and Marty had quickly turned this to his advantage, usually by torch-light in the back of the second-hand white van his dad had bought him for his seventeenth birthday to help him him cart his magic props around, usually while parked in a car park or layby somewhere on the outskirts of Beckenham or Bromley.

Besides this, what else do we need to know about Martin Quick, aged seventeen/eighteen?

- He stands a little under six feet tall.
- He is strong but hates physical exercise.
- Because of what happened to his mother he doesn't smoke, nor does he take drugs, and though he drinks it is rarely to excess – he has quite strict rules about that, which stem from his deep belief that he's saving himself for bigger things. He's read enough magic books by now, you see, to realise that discipline and purity are key to becoming a success, and since he's got his sights set on being the next David Copperfield success is always uppermost in his mind.
- He hasn't seen or heard from his Uncle Harry since he was ten, a fact which has imbued his ambitions with a portentous air of personal quest and ensured that his heroes and role models are all American: not just Copperfield but other Las Vegas supremos like Lance Burton, the double act Siegfried and Roy (famous for staging the most expensive magic shows

ever and breeding the white tigers used in their performances),
Doug Henning – the man responsible for reinventing magic
for the age of television – and, of course, the master himself,
Harry Houdini.

- He loves Elton John, has all his albums; he also likes Mike
Oldfield and Sting, and has a complete collection of early Gen-
esis. At the harder end of the spectrum he enjoys T'Pau and
Simple Minds. He's not too up on really contemporary music
like rap or acid house, though he does like Peter Gabriel world
music stuff (sort of), and Terence Trent D'Arby, and Simply
Red.

- He is picky over food, preferring ready meals to self-prepared,
frozen veg to fresh; ever since the wig incident the boundary
between natural and artificial has been a touchy one and if in
doubt Marty will always tend aggressively towards the latter.

- He is meticulous in his personal habits to the point of obsess-
iveness, insisting on showering at least once every day and
preferably twice. He maintains a huge array of deodorants and
anti-perspirants in his bedroom as artillery in the ongoing war
he wages against his pores, having recently discovered that he
doesn't like his own body smell or sweat; and is forever fiddling
with his hair which is currently dyed jet black (flick enhanced
with Tippex) and styled into a mullet that owes far more to
Nik Kershaw than to the Beastie Boys.

- He still lives in Beckenham, in the same house as when he was
ten, behind the same high hedge of combat-green leylandii
trees, trees which his father – in his Dad-after role of builder's
merchant and minor property developer with a sideline in landscape gardening – has been responsible for planting in vast
numbers in and around the town of Guildford throughout
Marty's teenage years.

- He has sweaty palms, these being among the few areas of his
skin from where his barricaded perspiration can escape. These
palms have their uses – things tend to stick to them, things
like cards, coins, lighters, knives; things that pass with little
friction through most people's hands seem to have an affinity

for Marty's dainty claws. The same was said of Max Malini, by the way, a Polish émigré who was taken to live in America by his parents while still a child in the late 1870s and who went on to make a living as an entertainer on a private circuit that included the salons of several presidents, the King of Siam, and almost every monarch throughout the continents of Europe and Asia. Despite his tiny stature and childlike hands, he is widely acknowledged to be one of the greatest close-up magicians in history, one of his favourite stunts being the production of a large block of ice from underneath his hat halfway through a lengthy formal dinner, no easy feat at the best of times, let alone in the days prior to electric refrigeration. 'The last of the mountebanks,' is how the magician and historian Ricky Jay refers to him.

- He is into riverdance, has two of Michael Flatley's videos.
- He likes, whenever he can, to dress up in a suit, an external indicator, perhaps, of the personal sense of natural aristocracy that he is privately developing, in odd contrast with his actual background, which is really quite mundane.
- He's decided not to go to university but instead to leave school following his A levels in order to try to pursue magic as a career.

And that's it, pretty much.

'So how d'you get into this scene, then?' Marty'd asked Terri when she appeared at his side at the *Young Magician* after-show party, pleased beyond measure that his sudden elevation in status allowed him to pull girls merely by brushing them with an item of his clothing.

'Oh, you know. Through Darren, really. My, erm, partner.'

'Your partner, huh? The rugby player type? Yeah, think I saw him earlier – you two were in the slot in front of mine, right? So how'd *he* get into all this?' Darren might not have been the world's most talented magician, but it wasn't something you got into casually. You had to put in too much practice for that. You had to really want it. Or so it seemed to Marty, anyway.

'I'm not sure. I think it's cos he likes building things.'

'Building things?'

'Don't get me wrong, he's really talented, is Da',' Terri assured him. 'He is, he's got so much talent. I mean, that's what I thought right away when I first met him – I thought he's just got so much talent has that boy. But he's not committed like . . . like you are. I mean, like you seem to be . . .' Terri blushed. 'Darren . . . you know. Darren wants to be an engineer.'

'An engineer?'

'Yeah, I mean, we just entered this for fun really. He's waiting to hear if he's got a place at Southampton Uni.'

Marty raised his eyebrows a little – he couldn't imagine anybody wanting to be an engineer, not when they had a chance of

being a magician, of going to Vegas, of being on TV. Not that
he was really sure what an engineer's life consisted of, but he
couldn't imagine that anything remotely industrial could in any
way be preferable to living out his own glamorous dreams. 'So
what about you, then? Do you want to be an engineer too?'

'Oh – oh no. I'm a gymnast. Well. Was.'

'Was?' Marty queried, keen to find out more.

So Terri told him a story that quite possibly wasn't true at all,
a story of how, on her fifteenth birthday, while performing on
the parallel bars at the county championships, she lost her grip
and fell and shattered her wrist. 'It never properly healed,' she
explained sadly, when Marty asked her why that'd stopped her.
'At least, not like it was before. It's the tensions and pressures,
see; at competition level, the slightest little thing can make all
the difference.'

He took the damaged wrist between his fingers, hoping that
Terri would think it sexy, his presuming to touch her like this.
She did.

'Looks all right to me,' he said.

'Oh, it's fine for most things,' Terri replied with a little toss
of her head, leaving her hand to linger in his for a moment,
enjoying the way he twisted her joint back and forth with his
prestidigitator's certainty. 'You know, day-to-day stuff. But for
the paras you need maximum flexibility. Ninety-nine per cent
isn't good enough.'

'You're sure it wasn't just fear? That put you off?'

'What? Don't be silly. Scared? Don't be dumb.' And she pulled
back her hand and started doing demi-pliés, using the function
room's dado as a barre. 'Though Daddy had just run off with
his mistress, which didn't help my concentration much.'

Before Marty could express an appropriate measure of sympathy, Darren appeared.

'Oh – Darren. This is Marty. Darren Marty, Marty Darren.'

'Hi.'

'All right.'

'Liked your act,' Marty lied – he'd hardly seen it, waiting as

47

he had been in the wings, and what he had seen he'd thought tired and unoriginal.

'Cheers,' Darren replied. 'Liked yours too.' Which was also a lie – watching Marty on the CCTV he'd thought the new *Young Magician of the Year* was a bit of a poseur, that the thing with the cards was too simple to be any good, and he couldn't understand at all why Marty had walked off with first prize like that, it being obvious to anyone who knew anything about it that he'd used the cards themselves to obscure the movement of the girl between each one.

'Ta.'

'Congratulations and all that.'

'And to you.'

Interlude of nods, shrugs and shuffles.

'I was just telling Marty about how we ended up working together,' Terri said. 'About how my gymnastic training makes me perfect for getting in and out of the cabinets. Even now my body's very flexible.' She turned to Marty, not quite managing to look him in the eye. 'I could have been a contortionist, almost. Couldn't I, Da'?'

Darren was too narked by the fact that someone as weedy and effeminate as Marty should have beaten him to be aware of any strange undercurrents. 'Oh yeah. You should see some of the stuff she does. It's incredible.' It was odd – earlier on he'd been pleased to have got that Highly Commended. But now he felt angry and jealous. 'Er . . . either of you two want a drink?' he asked, hoping to escape.

'You should lay off the bitter,' Terri told him, patting his belly. 'You can hardly get into your trousers as it is.'

'Oh ha, ha, very funny, Terri.' Darren glowered, trying to smile but unable to stop his neck flushing purple.

Marty tried changing the subject. 'Terri says you might be off to study engineering?'

'Yeah, at Southampton. Well, you know. Waiting to hear.'

'Not going into magic, then?'

'I think not. I mean, it's hardly a career, is it?' Darren replied, pleased by the subtle quality of his put-down. 'Just a bit of fun. I'm no way good enough. It's just a hobby really. But I wanted to ask you something about that first vanish you did . . .'

'How about getting those drinks in first, honeybun?'

'Oh, yeah. Sorry. Back in a sec.' And Darren dutifully trotted over to the white-tableclothed table on which was laid out, in ready-poured wineglasses and uncapped beer bottles, the limited amount of alcohol deemed sufficient by the competition organisers for oiling the wheels of the *Young Magician* after-show party.

Terri watched her boyfriend deliver his order to the uniformed waiter, feet snugly slotted into his favourite old brogues, each heel firmly planted, toes pointing out. 'Oh, la,' she tweeted, before turning back to Marty with a shrug and a smile. 'He's such a sweetie. Hey, you know, while I think about it, have you got a number or anything? I mean it would be nice to keep in touch and that.' She started poking about in her bag. 'In fact, do you want to take mine?'

Instantly Marty had reached into his pocket and brought out a pen. If Terri had been scared off gymnastics after breaking her wrist, he'd decided, she wasn't ever going to let on.

Ten days after the *Young Magician* final Terri and Marty established telephone contact. Nine days after that they made a date for meeting up. Wednesday week they had their first clandestine encounter, which climaxed in a kiss. Seven days later Darren received a letter telling him he'd got a place to study engineering at Southampton Uni. Six days elapsed before it occurred to him that the thought of his going away must be upsetting Terri and that this was the reason she was behaving somewhat strangely around him. It took him five days to pluck up the courage to broach the subject with her; he managed this just four days prior to her and Marty's second secret assignation. Three days later Terri and Darren tearily ended their relationship, it being the most sensible thing, they both agreed. Two whole days now passed before Terri and Marty spoke again on the phone. The following afternoon they had sex.

It came as something of a surprise to Darren when Terri told him during one of the (for him) slightly heart-wrenching phone calls that he still made to her from his hall at Southampton that she'd decided to go and work as Martin Mystery's assistant. Following his success at *Young Magician*, Marty was definitely going to turn professional, she said, and he needed a new partner because his sister couldn't work with him any more owing to how she had her exams coming up.

'Okay. I see. So how did he get in touch with you, then?'

'Oh – er, I gave him our number that night we all met.'

'*Our* number?'

'Well – mine. I couldn't remember yours; I was so drunk.'

Darren wasn't sure he believed her, but there didn't seem much point in pursuing the issue. Drawing upon traditional male resources of comfort and strength, he went out that night and drank himself blind with his new bunch of friends, who ended up wheeling him home in a shopping trolley while he yelled repeatedly to anyone who wanted to listen (and a great number who didn't) that Terri Liddell was a whore and a slag. Meaning it was easier for him to claim not to care when on the next (and last) occasion the two of them spoke, Terri informed him in a roundabout kind of way that Marty and she were no longer two individuals with separate agendas but had entered into that mystical union the English refer to as 'love'.

In the beginning it was fun. Marty was into her as Darren never had been. He looked at her as though she were some kind of valuable vase, ran his fingers over her features with gentle reverence, brought her to her first proper orgasm. And Tony Quick made her welcome in a way that Mr and Mrs Watt had never done; they'd been very nice but they'd never've allowed her to stay over and sleep with Darren in his bed, as she could with Marty at his house (the back-of-the-van years having officially ended when Marty'd turned eighteen).

Actually, although she'd never had to have sex in it, the van was still a bit of an issue for Terri. That this was Marty's sole mode of transport was a slight disappointment to her after the deep engine throb and leather upholstery of Darren's Spitfire, but as Marty explained, it wasn't his ideal choice of a vehicle; he needed it for transporting his props, some of which were pretty substantial in size. Like Darren, he built these at home, having commandeered the old games room as a workshop long before. For rehearsal he had for a long time used the dining room, which only got used now for eating at Christmas when his older sister was home and not always even then.

Marty started off by teaching Terri the routines he'd used at the *Young Magician* awards, exactly the same blocking he'd choreographed with Karen. The first question she'd asked had been what are the hooks for, those heavy-duty hooks cemented opposite one another in the dining-room walls? For Find the

Lady, Marty'd explained, and had shown her how the trick worked, an explanation that had astonished her because of how nimble Karen must have been to carry it off (she hadn't believed Darren when he'd tried to explain to her, coming home from the award ceremony, how the trick was done).

But it was a challenge she would just have to rise to. Find the Lady, an adapted Creo* and a trunk escape/costume swap not unlike the one Darren had done but closer in style to that performed by the Pendragons (i.e. using a trunk); these illusions formed the core of Marty's set, a core which he now planned to alter and expand with the help of the prize money he'd won.

But the money was only half the story, Marty told Terri. You could have all the money, all the talent in the world, but without the right assistant – an assistant with talent, commitment, grace and natural glamour – your act would be useless. The whole 'magician and assistant' thing in itself was very misleading, apparently; it made the relationship sound like it was some kind of master-servant thing when in reality it was a partnership, like in figure-skating, like Torvill and Dean, and though it might look like the man was calling the shots that was just the way the form had evolved.

But what tipped Terri into loving her new partner rather than merely being impressed by him was his emphasis on purity. 'Success, real success, only comes to the pure in heart,' he liked to say, his blue, blue eyes not blinking. 'This is something I learned while still very young, something my mentor taught me. To be a great magician requires total dedication, physical and mental. That's why I keep myself fit, don't smoke or do drugs, hardly even drink. I've given up these passing pleasures in order to pursue a higher aim. Most people can't do that, Terri. But one of the reasons I think we get along so well is that you're the same as me. You're willing to make sacrifices in order to succeed.'

Terri nodded, her little heart fluttering like a netted bird. She

* Another *Jarrett* illusion, one in which the magician dresses up a showroom dummy which, once dressed, comes to life.

was willing, yes she was. She *hated* smoking, and she was scared of drugs. She didn't even like drinking much – it hardly seemed a sacrifice to her that Marty didn't rely on the usual local pubs for dates, as Darren had, but drove her into the West End to see the shows. To her mind that was far more glitzy and romantic, even if they did have to travel there and back by van. Marty seemed to be offering her a bond of love and trust and purpose stronger than the one that had bound her parents, and this is what Terri wanted more than anything. So what if his vehicle was a little lacking and the shows were so expensive that most of the time they ended up staying in? He'd lost his mother, she'd lost her father – their love was meant to be.

As for work, he was as good as his word: he asked her opinion on blocking and thematics and design instead of just telling her what she had to do, and he taught her stuff about misdirection and magical stagecraft that Darren either hadn't known about or hadn't bothered to mention. When, on one early date, he complimented her on her outfit and she told him she'd made it herself he asked her if she wouldn't like to be in charge of making their costumes. Flattered and delighted, she'd said yes. Marty and her. They were a real team.

For his part, Marty simply couldn't believe his good fortune. Terri was delectable, she was timid, she looked like Princess Diana and she was going to take care of the tricky and expensive issue of costumes for him (which, though she didn't know it yet, would include doing all his laundry). Nor had she made a murmur about wanting to be paid. She stared up at him all the time with those big, blank, trusting impala eyes and if he asked nicely did pretty much whatever he said. She was sweet and she seemed positively delighted to be able to sit with him in cheap seats at bad shows that he often went to in order to see just one single effect. She worshipped the ground he walked on, it seemed, although – as Marty was careful to remind himself around this time with some frequency – that was only to be expected, what with his being a young god and that.

There was, as far as he could make out, only one fly in the

ointment, only one fault in the mirror. Try as he might to persuade her, Terri wouldn't go down on him. Somehow, somewhere, she'd got it into her head that oral sex was dirty and wrong, and this was the one subject on which Marty could not get her to budge. He did manage, finally, on his birthday, to persuade her to suck him off just the once. But then she was furious with him for days afterwards because he'd come in her mouth when he'd promised he wouldn't and it had nearly made her throw up. He'd had to tell her maybe forty times that (a) he'd been very drunk and (b) she'd looked so beautiful down there that he just couldn't help it, before the subject had been smoothed over sufficiently for it to be dropped.

In the wake of *Young Magician* Marty had got himself an agent
and a spate of cabaret bookings, and a couple of months into his
and Terri's collaboration the new double act packed their stuff
into the van and started off on their first magical mystery tour:
a series of hotel engagements at Brighton and Eastbourne and
Worthing, followed by a six-week residency at a holiday camp on
the Welsh coast. The hotel gigs were fun in contrasting ways: in
Brighton they were treated like royalty, looked after personally
by Roy, the ex-Stones roadie who handled car parking and stage
management; in Eastbourne nothing had been organised, nobody
seemed to know that they were coming, everything was seat-of-
the-pants. But it was Prestatyn Pontin's that gave them the biggest
shock.

They'd arrived to discover they'd been booked for over-sixties
fortnight. Theirs was the after-dinner slot, during which they
found themselves performing for the benefit of only about half
the audience since the other half weren't up to shuffling their
seats round in order to take in the show. Terri came off stage
the second night and announced to no one in particular that it
was like playing to a bunch of zombies, a remark that the compère, an ex-butcher from Wakefield named Ted Preece (a man
whose showbiz career had been kick-started when he'd won a
Homer Simpson lookalike contest at his local working men's club
in the late eighties, since when he'd never looked back), unfortunately overheard. From that point on he took the mickey out of

them incessantly for being young, green, English and southern.

For two weeks they alternated between the geriatrics in the evening and children's shows in the afternoon, getting pelted with fairy cakes and Ribena as often as not (and that was just the geriatrics). When Terri started throwing nightly strops, Marty started finding it increasingly difficult to cope. Depression and despair were imminent when, four days into their third week, sitting eating a silent breakfast in the staff canteen, they were approached by a bearded fourth-member-of-the-Bee-Gees type called Glen. They'd seen Glen around – his preferred attire of white slacks, heavy gold neck chain and Hawaiian shirt made him difficult to miss – but they'd never actually spoken to him. Now, however, Glen spoke to them; Glen being, as it turned out, a booker for Far Side Cruise Lines, or so he said. The company needed a new act at short notice, the sword swallower they'd booked having punctured a lung. It was a three-month contract on board a ship which would be touring, on a rotating itinerary, the Western Caribbean, the Eastern Caribbean and the Deep Caribbean. ('The Deep Caribbean not meaning the underwater bit,' Glen had laughed in a prepared-joke kind of way, his bleached and ringletted curls jogging up and down like a clutch of office party paper streamers, 'but Martinique, Barbados and Mayreau.') The catch was that they'd have to be in Florida by the end of the following week, which would mean dishonouring the Pontin's contract.

'We'll have to think about it,' Marty said.

Think about it he and Terri did, for precisely three-quarters of a minute, at which point Terri got so excited that she spilt her coffee across her breakfast tray. Endeavouring to keep up at least an appearance of professionalism, they waited till the following day to notify Glen of their decision. When they did, however, he seemed curiously slow to move to action. He'd call the company tomorrow he said, today he was busy organising a party for that evening. In fact, would Marty and Terri like to come? His wife Marie-Claire would be there and so would one or two other couples.

Worried that if they did not attend their golden booking might slip from their grasp, the young duo accepted the invitation and arrived at the party to find that Glen and his wife and one other couple were indeed present. And that was all, except for what Glen explained were complimentary tablets of Ecstasy and what Terri could see for herself was a bowl of condoms and a two-litre tub of Bodyshop *crème de massage*. Breaking into fits of giggles she insisted that they leave, which they did, Marty perhaps a tad more reluctantly than he might have done but no matter. Running from the chalet, they hid out in the pool bar, appalled and amazed and crippled with laughter, their hilarity tainted by the loss of the Caribbean cruise.

But their luck would hold: Glen appeared bowl-eyed at their chalet door late the next morning and apologised, said he hoped they weren't offended, swinging wasn't everyone's thing, he'd misread the signs, but he was worried that they might have thought the cruise was a ruse designed to get them into . . . well, whatever. Which it wasn't, it was for real, he'd already called the company and everything was organised; the contracts were being faxed through that very afternoon. If they were still interested, that was.

Still interested? They couldn't sign fast enough. Frightened that the staff at Pontin's might find some way of stopping them if they found out, the duo left without warning the next day at 5 a.m., though they didn't escape without promising that on their return to England they'd give Glen and Marie-Claire a call. By the end of the following week the young magician and his assistant were in Florida.

★

To the two young hopefuls the cruise seemed the height of glamour. While it was true that the passengers tended to be a little on the venerable side, they were nowhere near as ancient as the Pontin's geriatrics and it didn't matter anyway because most of the staff were under thirty and knew how to party. Marty and Terri had fun, got tans, made new friends. By night they danced and drank, and dazzled audiences with their magic, by day they lazed on deck and made elaborate plans. Lying side by side on their loungers, gazing out at the peppermint sea, Marty infected his girl with his dreams and talked endlessly about the fabulous riches that lay at the end of his own particular rainbow, a rainbow that Terri began to picture in her mind as a wondrous pathway once she'd heard how it circled round Britain a couple of times, touched upon London for a clutch of impressive bookings, then arched over the Channel (or under now, what with the Tunnel), all the way to Paris. From Paris it would most likely circle round Europe a bit – perhaps dropping by Rome, possibly swinging through Berlin – before gathering the energy requisite for bursting into the rarefied bubble of television or even actually leaving the ground altogether, skyrocketing up into the stratosphere and bridging the curve of the earth in order to carry the two of them to the Magic Castle in Hollywood, the home of American illusion. From this fabled location their path of glory and fame would be a yellow brick road leading out of LA and into the desert; along it they would travel in a giant white American convertible, the wind in their hair, the sands stretching away to vistas filled with Monument Valley-style rock formations on either side, until, tanned and self-assured as a couple in an advertisement, they arrived at their utopia, the Mecca of Magic . . . the one and only Las Vegas.

It was an American dream and it all seemed so simple, and Marty was a genius and Terri was in love, and the sea air must have done something for her because nearly once a fortnight she found herself going down on her boyfriend in their tiny cell of a cabin and even managing to swallow a couple of times.

What a summer it was.

★

And what a winter it wasn't. They returned to England in the autumn, their Caribbean memories fixed in flat chemicals and the Caribbean sun inked deep into their soft English skins, the future as boundless and plastic as the scudding shoals of cloud over the

Lesser Antilles, to find that there was no work waiting for them, no work at all.

Marty thought at first his agent was punishing him for cutting out on the Pontin's gig. Which Michael confessed he wanted to, before going on to explain that wasn't the reason for the sudden lack of employment. The cabaret circuit just wasn't what it had been. High season was one thing, you could usually expect to link together some kind of string of bookings, but through the winter months? The only real options were support slots for Davidson or Monkhouse or Davro or Starr, or (perish the thought) local panto and Marty just wasn't in the frame for that yet. He wasn't old enough, experienced enough, quality enough for the first option; he wasn't humble enough for the second. He needed exposure, Michael said.

'But how does he expect you to get experience and exposure if he can't get you a gig?' fumed Terri when Marty reported back to her, so frustrated that she actually stamped her foot. The last few months had given her confidence, it seemed; it was her opinion that they dump Michael, find themselves new representation. She could talk to the guy who handled her lookalike stuff. He'd be bound to have contacts.

Perhaps strangely, Marty was not altogether keen on this idea. 'I don't know, Tel,' he admitted.

'I've told you not to call me that!' Terri snapped back.

'Sorry, sorry, Terri; sorry, sugar. But Michael is one of the best in the business. He's truly respected and he's been really good about the whole Pontin's thing. And, you know, I trust him.'

'But Marty, he's so obviously not good for you. I mean, he can't get you work and if he can't get you work what use is he? You've got to remember that your agent works for you. Not the other way round.'

'Yes, but . . .'

Terri shook her head. 'I think you're crazy. Crazy! And it's not just your future here. It's mine too, you know. It's mine too.' And she started to sob. Panicking slightly, Marty tried to take her in his arms. He still wasn't much good at dealing with tears.

How did this ever happen? He'd sold Terri his dreams and she'd bought them, it seemed. So how had it turned out that he was the one who was paying?

Marty couldn't understand it. Why call an Indian restaurant '*Le Madras*'? And why, more to the point, hang a blue neon saxophone outside the window and play Delta blues over the house PA? It wasn't exactly authentic. Anyone would have thought the place was owned by a white man. It wasn't, though. Mr Hiranandani was definitely Indian. And if he wanted to add magic to his cultural mix, who was Marty to argue? (Though argue Marty did, as Mr Hiranandani wouldn't pay him a fee, insisting that he was already being more than generous by letting the magician busk his tables for tips.)

It wasn't surprising that Le Madras had such a low class of clientele, Marty thought meanly. As he went from table to table making some woman's wedding ring disappear, predicting yet another bloke's playing card, or tearing his five hundredth five-pound note into pieces, crumpling it into a ball and then unravelling it into magically reconstituted perfection he told himself that this was all just a setback, that Henning and Daniels and Copperfield had all had to go through this, that in the long run it'd be good for him. Character-building, or something.

Marty had dumped Michael, not that it had done him much good. The friend of a friend whom Terri's mother's friend came up with couldn't find any work for him either – nor for Terri, as a matter of fact, lookalikes having apparently gone out of fashion – and as winter set in the two of them had found themselves spending far too much time stuck in behind the leylandii in

Beckenham watching daytime TV or – more entertainingly – staring out of the living-room windows at the trickling rain. At least this gig he'd found at the Le Madras got him out of the house.

'Oi. I saw that.'

Marty snapped out of his reverie. 'What?'

'I saw what you did with that card.' The man's head was thicker than his neck; his arms were smeared with bleary tattoos. Marty disliked him already, though he wasn't afraid – he came across at least two or three of these types every night. It wasn't how they looked that made them the same – they could be in their fifties and wearing sports jackets and polka-dot cravats as easily as Levis and a Hilfiger shirt. What they all shared was the inability to bear the fact that their girlfriend's, or wife's, or partner's, or lover's attention was no longer wholly on them; that their female should be impressed by this kid who was confident and good-looking, and who knew how to do something that they couldn't.

'What did I do with it?'

'You put it up your sleeve.'

'Oh, stop it, Malcolm – you're spoiling the trick.'

'But I saw him put the bloody card up his sleeve.'

'It doesn't matter, does it?'

'Of course it matters! He's supposed to be a professional magician. Not much good doing magic, is there, if everyone can see how it's bloody well done.' Malcolm beamed, as if he'd just ejaculated a sensational bon mot.

With a sigh, Marty held out his arm. 'Go on then.'

'What's that?'

'You think it's up my sleeve? Why don't you find out?'

From the look on Malcolm's face, Marty might have been asking him to lick round his balls.

'Go on, Malcolm,' said the girl, giving Marty a wink. 'Undo his sleeve. See what he's got up there.'

Malcolm grumbled and started fumbling with Marty's button. When he rolled back the sleeve it was empty.

'So where is it then?'

Reaching across with his other arm, the magician touched the girlfriend lightly on the neck. 'Behind your lovely lady's ear.' He smiled, as the card appeared in his hand.

It was a sweet little victory, made sweeter still when the woman – clearly buzzed by having had the opportunity to watch her boyfriend getting brought down a notch – slipped Marty a twenty at the end of their meal. But triumphs like that came too seldom for the big picture to be much affected. The bottom line was that Marty hated these evenings. He'd liked doing close-up at school to impress all his friends, he liked doing it in bars to impress pretty girls. But doing it for men, dour men, thuggish men, self-satisfied men, superior men, men and their dowdy, unappealing wives . . . he just couldn't stomach it. He didn't feel it was to his benefit to be associating with these people, felt that contact with them would bind him harder and tighter to Beckenham, prevent him from ever being able to escape.

Instead of being pleased when a man he did the coin inside the glass routine for one night turned out to be in charge of corporate events at the Moathouse Hotel on the Bromley Road, next door to the Harvester – and took his number and called him up and booked him for a whole series of dinners, money up front – Marty hated himself even more. Though it was regular work and good pay, and the corporate crowd was as a rule more subdued than the cross-section of the public that ate out in Beckenham High Street, he couldn't help feeling like a sell-out. Knowing this was irrational didn't help matters; all it meant was that he hated himself for being irrational too and so compounded the hate.

Marty was very particular (some would say precious). He knew what he wanted to do and how he wanted to do it, and doing it any other way seemed to him like a compromise. And compromise was degrading, particularly to someone whose dreams were so close to his heart. Working tables made him feel like a prostitute, that's what it was. Close-up magic, with all its patter and smiling obsequiousness, made him feel like a whore. He wanted to be a king, not a whore. He wanted to be in control.

Terri was just as particular as Marty, it seemed. More so, in fact: she was refusing point-blank to go out and look for a job. 'I'm a performer as well,' she insisted when Marty suggested she maybe get some bar work, something to help see them through this bad patch. 'Why should I pull pints while you get to practise your art?'

They were standing in Next on Beckenham High Street, Marty sitting on a canvas director's chair outside the changing rooms while Terri flitted before him in a succession of outfits, all of which she liked, none of which she could afford.

The magician looked as glum as an unhappy gonk. 'You know perfectly well how much I hate doing table magic. I thought one of the things you liked about me was that I didn't "get off on doing crappy little tricks like most magicians" was how I think you put it. And you don't have to pull pints if you don't want to. It was just a suggestion. You must be able to think of something that you might be able to do. Can't you see if you can run an aerobics class at the gym or something like that?'

Terri frowned and ignored him. 'Does this make my thighs look fat?'

'No – no, not at all,' Marty said, having long been conditioned to produce the correct and Pavlovian response.

It wasn't until a day or two later that he discovered his words had had some effect. Coming downstairs from the bathroom, he found Terri in the hallway, donning her hat and coat and preparing to go out in the rain.

'Where you off to, then?'

'Nowhere,' she answered him lightly.

'Come on. Where? Tell me!' He started fooling around, grabbing her by the waist, tickling her.

'Ow! Get off! Okay, okay – I'm going to the gym.'

'What? What for?'

She stuck out her tongue and vibrated her eyelids to keep the shame she was feeling at having backed down from bursting out on her face. 'To see if they need someone to run some aerobics classes, stupid. Get off! Ow! Get off! No, come on, get off, you can play with me later.' Twisting from his embrace, she ran through the door and out into the street, skittering slightly on the front pathway like a veal calf on ice.

But there was no room at the gym. Terri managed to get past the offensively unhelpful receptionist to talk direct with the shift manager, but there were no openings of any kind, especially for someone without the relevant qualifications or experience. Which really got her goat. Having used up two whole days to think herself into taking the drastic step of looking for work, she was shocked and distressed to discover that the world didn't jump at the chance of having her pretty little shoulder help in the task of turning the great human wheel.

'I can't believe you need like a degree to be a flipping fitness trainer,' she moaned to Marty later, while he lay beside her on his bed, fiddling with the fastener on her Triumph International 'Amourette' bra, with Busty-Girl® padding and lace pansy filigree. 'Like, a degree in what? Stretching and bending? I mean, it's so pathetic. It's not like it's exactly complicated. Jesus. And you should have seen this woman, she was such a flipping *freak*. I mean like *hello*, like do *you* have a degree? I don't think so.' Marty's love of all things American was starting to rub off on her, it seemed.

'Poor you,' Marty mumbled, through a nipple.

'Marty! Are you even listening to me?'

Marty pulled back, looked up, hair slightly matted. 'Yeah. Yeah, course I am.'

'I thought you were the one who wanted me to go out and find work in the first place?'

'Well, yeah. But you can't expect to walk into the first thing you go for.'

Terri shrugged away from him and pulled down her bra. 'You are just such a wanker, you know that?'

'What! Why?'

'I don't even want to talk to you. Just get out of my way.' She pushed herself up off the bed and stormed out of the room, pulling on a cardigan as she went.

'What?' said Marty, shocked and surprised. 'What? What the hell are you on about?'

He got up to follow her but she hadn't gone far: she was sitting on the stairs, crying, clutching a small slip of paper in her fist.

'You are so fucking ignorant!' she said, through a cute curtain of phlegm.

Gently, Marty plied free whatever it was she was holding in her hand. It turned out to be a flyer and it looked like this:

WANT TO BE YOUR OWN BOSS? START YOUR OWN BUSINESS?
WANT TO MAKE MONEY WORKING WITH FAMILY AND FRIENDS?

WELL WITH **FILTRO-AQUA**™ YOU CAN!

If you have what it takes to join our ever-growing
fleet of independent sales managers, *if you have what it
takes to make money fast*, call this number.

0181-777-AQUA
NOW!

Don't dealy. Only limited career opportunities are available.

'What the fuck's "dealy" supposed to mean?' Marty started to say, before thinking better of it. Instead, he encircled Terri with his arms and carefully kissed away her tears. 'Were you going to have a go at this?' he asked her in his gentlest voice.

Terri nodded. 'You see,' she bubbled snottily. 'I hadn't given up. You just think I'm no good at anything.'

He kissed her forehead. 'I think you're amazing,' he said. He was getting better at this. 'You're the most amazing person I've ever met.' Good, Marty, good. 'You know that, don't you? And I think this is a brilliant idea. You should go for it. Yeah. You've got what it takes, I know that. I believe in you. Of course I do.' Fantastic, Marty; well done indeed. It looks like you're finally learning.

'Have you called them yet?' he asked her when eventually she'd stopped sobbing.

'No, not yet.'

'Well, we'll do it tomorrow. There's no hurry.'

'No, no I'll do it now. But . . .'

'What, honeybun?'

'Oh God, you're going to think I'm so stupid.'

'No. What? Why?

'I can't say.'

'Come on. I won't laugh. You can tell me.'

Terri sucked her lip, composed herself, looked down at the paper (now damp). 'Well, it's this number. 777-AQUA.'

'Yeah? What about it?'

'I don't understand is. How is it dialled?'

Marty swallowed a smirk. 'Oh, that!'

'I knew you'd think I was an idiot,' Terri burst out, voice bending into a wail.

'I don't think you're an idiot at all! How should you know! It's an American thing. You just need a phone with letters on the dial. There's one in the spare room. I'll show you how. Come on.'

★

'We'd like to make clear that this is not in any way similar to pyramid selling,' the voice of Filtro-Aqua assured Terri when she'd finally plucked up the courage to call.

'Oh, no, no, I didn't think it was,' she said, wondering what pyramid selling was, exactly, wondering if there was any way to find out without sounding ignorant.

'We don't condone that practice here.'

'Oh, nor do I. Not at all.'

'And we have to insist that none of our representatives would follow that sales model.'

'Absolutely. And no, I mean, I wouldn't, I wouldn't dream of doing that.'

'Just so that we're clear on that.'

'Of course, of course.'

'So would you like us to send you some literature?'

'Oh, yes please.'

'And what is your address?'

★

When, three days later, the envelope arrived it was with some excitement that Terri spread its contents across the living-room floor.

'What's the story?' asked Marty, breaking off from an intense hour practising coin palms in his bedroom to come downstairs and see how she was getting on. The array of diagrams and spreadsheets reminded him of the almanacs and calendars she laid out whenever she was preparing to draw up an astrological chart.

'It looks pretty cool,' she said, holding out a shiny catalogue for his perusal. 'It's water purifiers, see? They look like this and you just install them either on the end of your tap or underneath the sink depending on the type you need.'

'And what do you do? Work out of a shop or something?'

'Oh no, no it's better than *that*. That's the whole point, I don't have to work in a shop or anything horrible. What I do is, I build a team of five distributors, which is what they call my subdivision, which makes me a subdivision manager. And we all pledge to sell twenty purifiers each, which means we have to sign this thing here, which is the Purifier Pledge. Right? And when we've sold those twenty, which shouldn't be so hard, then the members of my subdivision can choose either to carry on as salespeople under me or become subdivision managers of their own.'

'How do you make your money?'

'Okay, well, what happens is, we all sell the purifiers on to the end-consumer at £20 each, okay, but I buy them at £8, and my distributors have to buy them from me at £12. So on each one I sell myself I make £12 and on each one I sell to them I make £4, so that means that' – she ran her finger down the column of carefully labelled figures on page five of the Filtro-Aqua sales manual – 'if I perform according to the company average I'll make £700 profit on every £1000 I invest. Which I think is pretty good. Oh – wait a sec.' She turned the page and stared at it for a few seconds. 'Oh. That's not counting delivery costs. So that's, oh, I see: £640 on every £1000 I invest. Which is still quite a good rate of return.' *Rate of return* – she was getting into this.

Marty flipped his coin into the air. 'Where's the cash coming from?'

'Well, from sales of course.'

'Yeah, but the investment. The grand you need up front?'

'Not from you, obviously.' She sounded a little annoyed at the question. 'Mum's going to lend it to me.'

'Avril is?'

'Yeah. She's got some money put aside for me, which she says I can have some of. Originally it was meant for my wedding,' she added, a little more quietly.

Marty miscaught his coin and sent it spinning across the room, where it disappeared under the sofa. 'And who you gonna sell them to?' he asked, trying to steer the conversation back to its proper subject.

'*Friends*, stupid. Who d'you think?'

'All right, calm down. I was only asking. It wasn't a criticism.' He got down on his hands and knees and started to try to fish out the half-dollar, making an elaborate affair of the task in order to avoid Terri's gaze. He didn't want her guessing from the look in his eyes what he really thought of this whole Filtro-Aqua thing (or of the prospect of getting married).

'Mum's going to be one of the distributors, and Aunt Fran too. I'm going to get Liz to help cos she's got a car, and if I get Liz I reckon she'll bring in Pete –'

'Pete?'

'Her *brother*, Marty. You know Pete. God! What are you like? And all I need then is one other friend.'

'And you don't want me to help?'

'No, thank you. This is *my* business venture. You can concentrate on your own. See if you can get a gig that actually involves the two of us.' It was intended to sting a little, that remark, and it did. 'But I won't be intending to support you when I'm raking it in, we might as well get that straight right away.'

'Got it,' he said, meaning his coin.

'Aunt Fran says we should go door to door. Round the estates and stuff. We'd make a killing, she reckons, what with water the way it is these days, all recycled and everything. According to what they say in the catalogue most of the water in London has been through three other people's bodies before you get to drink it.'

'No way?' Marty said, flipping the retrieved coin into the air once again, thinking of the surface scum that varnished the surface of ninety per cent of all cups of tea. 'That's gross.'

He had to admit it all seemed pretty straightforward. In theory at least.

★

In theory, maybe. But almost exactly three months after that conversation took place – three months out of which life shaped a learning curve bitter in its steepness – Marty was to be found driving alone to the local waste tip, one hundred and eighty-three unsold boxes of Filtro-Aqua product jittering about in the back of his van like unwanted kittens on the way to the river, after which trip the subject of water purification would never be mentioned again.

The following week Marty called Michael in secret and begged to be taken back into the fold. After making him squirm for a while, the agent relented and it must have been the right decision all round because before a month had passed Martin Mystery and the fabulous Terri Electric had been booked for their second cruise.

Marty and Terri hadn't been on board ship more than fifteen minutes before they met an old friend. Ted Preece, he of the Homer Simpson lookalike competition, was occupying the cabin next to theirs. He was, it turned out, the ship's master of ceremonies.

'Well, if it isn't Charles and Di.' He chuckled, sticking his head through his door as Marty and Terri struggled down the narrow hallway with their bags. 'Pontin's are still looking for you, you know. They haven't forgotten. Hooo-no. They want your blood. Not that I'd tell them I'd seen you, of course. I wouldn't go and do a nasty thing like that.' The chuckle turned into a cackle as Preece ducked back inside his cabin, not to be seen again until later that evening when he arrived on the small stage in the Captain's Cabaret, shaking his hand in the air.

'What's frightening and stuck on the end of your arm?' he yelled out to the assembled.

'We don't know,' an enthusiastic passenger gamely shouted back.

'A terror wrist,' came the laconic reply.

On the second night Preece broke the ice by telling the audience that two idiots had been sitting on the floor when one fell off, which as Marty pointed out might have been funny if they hadn't been on board a ship. On the third night ... on the third night Marty and Terri weren't in attendance, as they were down in their cabin searching for their sea legs. Terri located hers soon enough, but Marty seemed to have left his at home, if he'd ever had any in the first place. While the ship rode gaily over the tumult of waves fleeing beneath it from an area of high pressure hovering just south of the Faroes he vomited freely, remarking in a moment of respite that it seemed incredible how a person could keep on being sick even when there was absolutely nothing left to throw up.

'Ugh, Martin, please try not to talk about it,' said Terri, who wasn't feeling that special herself and was less than overjoyed by the corrosive stench of puke that had by now insinuated itself into every item of clothing and bedding in their already cramped quarters.

Marty was upset by her attitude. 'It's not my fault,' he moaned. 'I wasn't sick last time. Maybe it was something we ate.'

'Last time we were on a cruise ship,' Terri pointed out, 'I don't seem to remember seeing too much in the way of wave action. I suppose Michael didn't bother to point out that "Iceland and the Fjords" in late September was hardly likely to provide the same glassy seas as the Caribbean in June, did he now?'

The hammer of Terri's scorn slammed against the concrete carapace lining the inside of Marty's skull and further jellified his brain. She was still simmering over his having signed on again with Michael without telling her and the magician couldn't help but entertain the possibility that she might never actually forgive him. He curled tighter into the small ball he'd made of his aching body in the base of the shower unit, a position from which he could raise his chin up and over the edge of the toilet bowl in less than a second, should it suddenly become necessary (which it quite often did). But Terri was right: 'Iceland and the Fjords' might have been on a different planet from the 'Deep Caribbean' for all the resemblance the two cruises bore to each other, as might 'Capitals of the Baltic', the itinerary with which their ship would alternate its present one, week in week out, for the next two and half months. These weren't voyages for idle sun worshippers who fancied a change; this was hardcore cruising for hardcore cruisers, the last option for people who'd seen it all, done it all and wanted to see Latvia before they died.

Oddly, the only comfort Marty was able to find was in the words of Ted Preece's terrible jokes, which floated back to him now across a memory sea of awful calmness and transparency. 'I'm half Irish, by a friend of my father's' was the gag Preece had liked to open with at Pontin's, his preferred set tending to revolve around the telling of tall tales about his family. 'And I was born in a place name of Wedlock. Well – just outside it, in fact.'

'It's better to be illegitimate than gay,' he'd continue. 'You don't have to tell your mother. My mother was a fine woman as it happens, or was until she married my father, who was a hopeless case. The man was doomed. Everything he turned his hand to went wrong. When she met him he was selling hearing aids over the telephone. He gave that up and bought a paper shop, but it blew away. When my mother was pregnant with my sister, the old man insisted they call the baby Eileen, if it were a girl. It was hard for me mam not to blame him when she was born with just the one leg.

'But you've gotta hand it to my father. He set about altering the family home so Eileen could get about as easily as the rest of us. I remember the day he rang up a local building firm. "I want a skip outside my house," he told them. "We're not stopping you," they said.

'Next thing that happened he saw a billboard out by the airport saying "Drink Canada Dry", and we haven't seen him since.'

At the memory of this particular line Marty heaved again. Bored with playing nursemaid, Terri departed from the cabin and went to sit on deck, where she drew rectilinear animals with her outstretched index finger across the giant silver Etch-a-Sketch that had replaced the sky.

'Well, that's three people clapping and I did pay for eight,' Preece complained.

And so the cruise went on.

Marty and Terri weren't interested in the splendours of the land of ice and fire. The fjords left them cold and the wonders of St Petersburg failed to move them. They could sort of see the point of the Winter Palace, but they couldn't get past the state the streets were in. After the first month they didn't bother taking shore leave any more, mainly because it upset the sea legs Marty had had such a hard time acquiring. They preferred to spend most of their free time on board, playing Hearts with Preece – with whom they'd formed a working détente – and the various members of the Ken Farlow Glenn Miller Tribute Big Band.

The thing of greatest consequence that happened to them throughout this period was Marty's deciding to grow his hair out. Lying on the floor of their tiny bathroom, throwing up, he'd had what he thought at the time was some kind of epiphany, a sort of moment of truth; at least, that's what it seemed like to him. Though Terri and the ship's doctor had repeatedly assured him that he wasn't, he'd been frightened he was going to die and this pang of mortality had let him see himself for what (he thought) he was: a vain and conceited twenty-one-year-old with an exaggerated sense of his own talent.

Preece's Charles and Di crack had hit a nerve, it seemed. Marty'd always thought the heir to the throne was basically a prick and now that the press was beginning to suggest the perfect Royal marriage might be a total sham the thought was getting a lot of confirmation. Similarities between himself and the prince reflected prismatically through his mind; he didn't want to be like that, he told himself. He wanted to be straight and loyal and true. And if he was going to puke himself to death, or if this ship he'd somehow ended up on was going to disappear beneath the heaving waves of the North Sea, then he wanted to go out feeling good about himself in some kind of fundamental way.

The upshot of this was that he made four crucial decisions, all of which would be carried out before they finished touring the high seas.

(a) He would henceforth cease to dye his hair jet-black.
(b) He would no longer enhance his white flick with Tipp-Ex.
(c) He would calm down on the mullet, get the hair that currently curled over his collar trimmed right back.
(d) He would inform Terri that he loved her.

Terri greeted all these announcements with enthusiasm, especially the last, which she'd been trying to bully Marty into admitting for quite some time. She was worried a bit about the colour change, though; she quite liked the black and wasn't sure she'd still fancy Marty if he went back to being blond.

It couldn't be worse, however, than the halfway house: after six weeks of putting up with looking at pale roots and black split ends Terri could stand it no more. Marching Marty into the cruise liner's beauty salon she sat him in a chair and gave the stylist strict instructions on what she wanted done. An hour later her man emerged looking about a million times better. And she *loved* that little grey wisp he had in front – so much better than the Tipp-Ex, which she'd always thought was a little bit dumb.

'You look great, Marty!' she cried, clapping her hands excitedly. She grabbed his shoulder, turned him to face a nearby mirror. 'Look! And – wow. Isn't that bizarre? Don't you think you look a little bit like me?'

It was true. Now that he'd ended up with almost the same haircut as Terri – short, blow-dried, moussed-up – it highlighted quite striking similarities between their skin tones and their fine, even features.

Marty glanced from his own reflection to his girlfriend's and back again. 'Nah,' he said, wrinkling his nose at his new haircut, which he wasn't altogether sure yet he was all that much in favour of. 'Don't be silly. Nothing like.'

★

The cruise had taken the fight out of them and they returned to Beckenham demoralised, their battered collection of costumes and cabinets in tow. Home was quiet and cold; the house gave off a vague scent of decay. Karen had gone off to college, to Durham, to study history, and Tony Quick had started seeing a woman he'd met through his ten–pin bowling club, at whose place he was now spending the greater proportion of his nights. There was nothing in the fridge. There wasn't even much mail to welcome them, though what there was included a short note from Michael.

'Call me when you get back,' it said. 'Good news.'

Marty called.

'You're going to be pleased,' the agent told him.

'Oh yeah?' Marty said.

'Totally, totally.'

'So what you got?'

'Are you ready?'

'Hit me.'

'*A low season round-Britain tour.* What d'you say to that, eh?'

'You are joking?'

'Nope – no joke. I've really swung it for you. This kind of thing just doesn't come up at this time of year.'

'"Round-Britain"? I take it that means no London. No Europe. No telly.'

'Hey, Marty, come on! These things take time to build. And it's tough times for everyone.'

'I know, I know. It's just that the cruise . . . the cruise was terrible, Michael.'

'Yeah. I'm sorry about that. I had no idea you'd be so unlucky with the weather. Those storms brought down half the trees in Central London, for goodness sake. But this will be better. I promise you.'

★

They took the tour and the one that followed and were on the road, on and off, for the next two years, during which time the gap between their dreams of a glittering path of glamour that would carry them to Vegas and the reality of working the exhausted domestic circuit grew ever wider. Pretty soon Marty could boast of having chopped Terri in half in the Camberley Lakeside; of having made her hover on columns of water at the Gaiety Theatre in Ayr; of running her through with half a dozen scimitars at the City Varieties, Leeds; of slicing out her stomach at the Sale of the Century Theatre in Norwich; of cremating her at Waverley's Inn on the Park; and of reconstituting her by pouring the ashes into a Terri-sized mould at the same. But the only Caesar's Palace he played was in Watford; the only Golden Nugget that welcomed him was Woking's; the only Strip he worked was a false shuffle that used cards cut to be thinner one end than the other; the only Sands he wowed was the Bognor Sands, not much of a place in the sun.

By the end of it these venues had all blurred into one; one long parade of battered Green Rooms, chipped gilt work, stale cigarette smoke and those terrible, horrible, unpalatable acres of ancient red velour. It felt old, it felt tired, it felt over. It felt British.

★

It was from the Inn on the Park that late one night, after a show, Marty called Michael on his home telephone. He didn't bother with preliminaries. 'Michael. It's Marty. You've got to get me out of this.'

'Marty? Are you drunk?'

'I need TV, Michael.' He made it sound as if it was some kind of life-saving medical treatment. 'I'm going nowhere. And fast.'

'What do you mean? You've played all over the country! You've supported Freddie Starr, Jim Davidson . . . I mean, need I say more?'

'Don't you understand I'm not even making a living! I still live at home with my dad for Christ's sake. What if Terri and me want to get married, have kids? I can't even afford to do that. I need to get up to the next level.'

'Fame and fortune take time, Marty boy. And this is magic we're talking about here. Most magicians have to work day jobs. You're one of the lucky ones.'

Marty hiccuped but beyond that made no reply.

'Marty?'

'Yeah?'

'You okay?'

'Yeah. F-fine.'

'How much have you had to drink? Is Terri there with you?'

'. . . No, really, I'm fine.'

'Look. You want to get bookings in London, break into TV, you've got to give me something to work with. You've got to give me something new. Finish this tour. See if you can't use it to come up with a new angle for the act. Something people haven't seen before. I've got it organised that you're playing the Mississippi Showboat in Blackpool in February, so you'll be there for the convention. Here's what I'm going to do: I'm going to book you for the Championships. Come up with something new, use what's left of the tour to really knock it into shape and see if you can't walk off with a prize in the competition. If you can do that, I reckon I'll have a good chance of getting you a guest slot on the *Paul Daniels Show*. What do you say?'

Silence.

'Marty? Hell-oo? Marty?'

'Yeah, I'm still here.'

'So what do you say?'

'Yeah, yeah. I'll do it.'

'Well don't sound too enthusiastic.'

'. . .'

'Marty?'

'Yeah.'

'It's going to be okay. Come on. You can do it. This is Martin Mystery we're talking about here.'

'Yeah. Whatever. I'll give it a shot. Thanks, Michael.'

Was that sarcasm, there? If it was, Michael ignored it. 'Don't mention it. And get some sleep, okay?'

★

Bognor, Eastbourne, Dover, Southend in December; Clacton, Skegness, Scarborough, Fishguard through Christmas and New Year; New Quay and Portmadog for January, then one half-decent city date in Manchester and two weeks' break before going up to Blackpool for the Mississippi Showboat and the annual Magicians' Convention. They had the best part of a month to prepare before it began, which should have been plenty of time to rejuvenate the act. But with regard to coming up with anything new, Marty just couldn't think. He felt desiccated and barren, like a forgotten seed pod. What two years previously might have looked like an original idea now seemed naïve, stupid, ridiculous. He thumbed his *Jarrett*, his Osborne's, his *Compendium of Great Illusions* searching for inspiration, but nothing jumped out. Everything was too ambitious, too dull, too eccentric, too old. Everything needed special equipment he couldn't afford or extra assistants he didn't have access to. His sword cabinet – the same one he'd built himself at school, his first real prop – was battered and beginning to seep a dangerous fibreglass dust. The bulbs on his shadow box had blown and the hinges had torn free from their screws. His doves were losing their plumage and one of his rabbits had what Terri claimed was myxomatosis. His saw cabinet had two broken wheels.

He had no ideas.

They went back on the road.

Every February in Blackpool there's a convention of magicians. In 1996 five or six hundred practitioners attend, travelling to the famous seaside resort from all over the world. Perhaps it was a glamorous destination once, Blackpool, but not any more. When they come – these Americans, these Japanese, these French – they do little but moan about the quality of the food. They make jokes about mad cow burgers, about the local speciality of fish and chips being safe to eat on account of being pre-irradiated by effluent from nearby Sellafield. And when it's not the food they're griping about it's the hotels, or the poor shopping facilities, or the climate. It's bitter here; the coastline bordering the Irish Sea's no English Riviera; the wind that rakes the promenade is arctic thanks to Ireland keeping the benign influence of the Gulf Stream well at bay.

But the locals don't seem bothered. Of a Friday night the girls are out in force regardless of the temperature, parading from pub to pub to club in arm-linked twos and threes, dressed in short shiny slips from Top Shop or Etam (or Miss Selfridge if they've made the trip to Manchester or Liverpool). In these groups they march, calling out to clots of boys in pastel shirts worn with the tails ironed and hanging out, shirts by Hilfiger or Ted Baker or Hugo Boss, the trousers underneath black polyester-mix with waxy perma-creases, shoes black loafers with pewter trim and cleated toes and heels.

The girls call to the boys, the boys call back. The girls are laughing, screaming, swaying, their bottle-bleached hair dragged back into topknots, buns and ponytails, hairstyles designed to help them slide faster through the night. The boys shout to the girls and the girls jeer back; above their heads brutal Blackpool Tower punches up into the tarry sky, the only stars its embroidery of yellow lights. 'Blackpool Girls are Magic' it says on some teenager's red baseball cap. 'Blackpool Girls are Magic' it says in neon all down Queen's Promenade. 'Blackpool Girls are Ace'.

This weekend more than usual magic moves among them. With five hundred magicians loosed upon the town, with five hundred freelance sorcerers swaggering like gunmen through the streets, Blackpool looks like a jamboree for visitors from a parallel reality. Barmen can't take a ten-pound note without it changing to a fiver in their hands; girls can't ask for a light without being shown a match that lights three times. Anyone sitting in any vaguely public place for more than fifteen minutes is likely to be accosted by an apprentice mage desperate to hone his patter and his sleight of hand.

We join our duo on the Saturday, just after lunch, as they take a turn through the Winter Gardens complex, its halls of Victorian ironwork and glass the venue for this year's convention. Terri wears a boysenberry trouser suit in luxury cupro fabric with climbing-ivy detail embroidered down the long-line jacket and right leg; a long-sleeved cream tunic blouse in sheer georgette; patent-leather charcoal-grey court shoes with stretch vamp. Marty wears a Nehru collar suit in black with flap pockets and single-pleat trousers over a black crew-necked T-shirt in ribbed marl fabric. His feet sit in a pair of Ben Sherman 'Brabham' loafers with metal trim; a spangle-faced Swatch adorns his wrist.

They have changed; they are professionals now, and adults, more or less (Marty's just turned twenty-five, Terri, twenty-four). They're not married yet, and they've entered that limbo period during which mention of the M-word is prohibited by tacit and mutual embargo. Neither wants to bring the subject up for fear of the answer they might get, and neither knows the answer they'd give were the other one to ask.

They should, you would have thought, be pleased about themselves. Over the last few years they've added experience to their good looks and youth; they should feel poised for bigger things. But they're not happy, not really. Deep down, despite appearances, they're both quite scared, worried that they're at the end of something rather than at its beginning, both beginning to wonder if perhaps they've made some kind of big mistake.

It's perspective, really, that they lack. While they've been changing, the world around them has been changing too, but not in ways they've begun to feel they comprehend. Take the Winter Gardens scene. The convention is no longer dominated, as in previous years, by ageing British maestros swanning around in tweeds or evening dress, their cloned protégés shadowing them closely; nowadays any older Magic Circle members wearing black tie or worsted country suits look a little disorientated and lost. Faces ruddy from years of starchy collars, expressions slightly forced (occasionally with drink), those who are there wander through the crowds like the charitable invitees at a cocktail party, raising half a hand at imaginary friends seen across the busy rooms, nodding to themselves, cruising on auto-smile. Often, if they happen to have been involved in some minor way in the convention's organisation, they dash about bent over at the waist, worrying like grandmothers, trying to look efficient, harrying the younger officials who humour them for a minute or two, then pay them no further heed.

Which is pretty nice of them, when you think about it, considering how they have their hands quite full enough already trying to deal with the tentacled horde of teenagers that has occupied the Winter Gardens as an amorphous and bottom-dwelling sea creature occupies a pleasing shell, regardless of the wishes of the existing tenant. These kids don't bother with respect, not in the way the old school understand it, anyway. They don't wear DJs or even suits but broken-backed trainers, shapeless anoraks, untidy jeans; they stand around in groups showing off their two-hand fans, their Elmsley counts, their Milk shuffles, their waterfalls, their coin rolls, their Ascanio spreads. The only magic they've really seen is on the telly; they don't understand the old club circuit. Theatre is more or less irrelevant to them – they are students of the screen. It's all so different from how it was in our day, their elders moan; it's not performance any more, it's not about the audience. It's all ego now, all spectacle.

One thing, though, remains the same: these are still the boys who've been excluded from girls and games, the boys who need to accrue reputation and respect in some way other than the purely physical. The envious looks they keep flashing Marty as he wanders through the dealers' mart with Terri on his arm unsettle him. On the one hand he sees the old Magic Circle aristocracy fading as he always knew it would (if young, ambitious men only know one thing it is that their elders will one day turn to dust; often their only real wish is that they'd do it sooner). On the other he sees this unruly mass of eager hopefuls gnashing at his heels. The wheel is turning but he feels he's missed his footing somehow and has lost his place upon it. His time is now and he should be doing the doing but he's not – and this frightens him because everywhere he looks he can see other people keen to gobble up the action and leave nothing for him.

And the people doing this? They're not the youngsters and they're not the oldsters either. For the most part they're American.

You can tell the Americans by their careful hair and large jaws and even skin, and by the way they sit back on their hips and square their shoulders instead of slumping. They look as though two or three smaller and more reticent English people might be sewn inside each of their skins. They also look like they're in charge, like hip-shooting Romans running rings around the Magic Circle Greeks.

Some are exuberant and loud, and riotously ugly – the magician Marty and Terri are about to go and see lecture being a typical example. Others are calm and suave; they drift weightlessly around the glass and wrought-iron halls, perusing the stalls and stands, their manicured assistants drifting gently with them, clipped to the maestro by an arm and projecting a calm Marty feels that he and Terri can scarcely hope to emulate.

A good example is gliding by right at this moment, though he's a little older than the others (meaning Marty shouldn't compare himself with him, although he does). He's a Merlin type: tall, with a granite-grey ponytail of long schist-like streaks, hairline honed into an elegant dagger by symmetrical recedes. His salt-and-pepper beard is neatly trimmed and he wears a black lambswool sweater with polo neck, chalk-flecked grey slacks, Cuban heels and – get this – an actual cape. His skin is the powdery terracotta tone of a sunbaked street in a Western frontier town, his eyes are scrunched around with wise-looking wrinkles, a platinum signet ring bands one of his fingers, he's carrying a silver-capped and highly polished cane. He has a strange, slightly other-worldly air about him that's hard to put your finger on; the nearest I can get to it is to say that he's somehow reminiscent of a Gerry Anderson puppet – from *Stingray* perhaps, or *Thunderbirds*.

In case you're grinning at this description of how this person looks, thinking that Marty's the only one who could be at all impressed by it (and then only on account of his being a journeyman and insecure), dripping off Merlin's arm is a woman who seems to have slid off the cover of *Elle* for the day in order to grace the flabby realm of us mere mortals with her presence. She's perhaps fifteen years the maestro's junior and with him because he clearly is no joke. The cape, for example – not least because it is only waist-length – would be laughable if the magician didn't have the good looks and gravitas to carry it. Which he does: he looks like the Hollywood actor/writer/director Sam Shepard and has without doubt worked extremely hard at removing all divisions between his art and his life in the way that these days seems common among all walks of life in the United States. When the celebrated nineteenth-century sage Robert-Houdin (a performer so admired by Harry Houdini that he took the man's name for his own, though in the way of these things he was later to denounce his prestigious forebear as an inferior and a fraud) commented that 'a conjurer is an actor who plays the part of a magician', he might have had this character in mind. He is no doubt able to laugh at himself and with studied irony. Apart from a handful of sour, hard-bitten characters, failures of one kind or another, *everyone* here wishes they were him.

Marty included. Though he cannot for the life of him see how that is likely to come to pass.

'I'm a magician,' said the American, 'and I'm going to magic for you.' Pause for effect. 'Aren't you glad I'm not a wizard?'

When the laughter came he leapt on it, surfed down its face. He'd come up on the stage, opened with a very slick little card production routine, stood stock-still for a moment in a comedy posture, then moved straight into the joke. He looked out at the waspy faces arranged in wide ranks before him. He already had them. He could tell.

'Wait, no, you – yes, you, my friend. Could I trouble you to help me out up here, just for one minute?' He was big, this American, big and tall, different from a lot of magicians who in Marty's experience tended to be shorter men. Tall and bulky, though his limbs tapered off with unusual rapidity and the hands and feet at the end of them seemed oddly small. The effect was startling, as if parts of him were disappearing into the distance. It made you a little embarrassed just to look at him, as though he were deformed. Marty didn't want to be caught ogling what could be some weird kind of birth defect, so where possible he kept his attention focused on the American's eyes. Eyes which, like his own, were an almost artificial shade of blue.

He was very good, this magician. He was, in fact, overwhelmingly good. He'd come out on to the stage wearing this ridiculous wig and when he took it off to reveal the hair underneath, that was more ridiculous still, all corkscrews and cartoon sprigs spraying out into an unkempt sort of mullet (the haircut of the gods, or so they say). With this hair thing, and the comedy posture and the jokes and everything, he got you laughing straight away – and he kept you laughing right on through till he'd finished his performance. It wasn't that he needed you to laugh because his magic wasn't up to standard, not at all. On the contrary. It was superb. He did this one thing, it was a whole routine, in fact, but it was built on this ability he had to palm four coins, four silver half-dollars with eagles on the back, palm four of them at once in those impossible tiny palms of his and then drop them out of his hand, one by one, at will. It was poetry. It was. Watching him transport the coins all around his body was poetry, even if you knew how it was done, which Marty did. It was poetry because the elegance and rhythm weren't contained in the secret of the trick but in the magician's perfect timing, in the way he made everything flow, in the way he used his jokes and moves and mania – and his icy glance and pregnant smile and very stupid hair – to make all the different pairs of eyes before him swivel round as one, travel round his body like the roller coaster cars half a mile away down at Blackpool Pleasure Beach. Though at the Pleasure Beach, of course, the roller coaster track was plain for all to see whereas here it was ineffable, invisible, laid with finger palms and false transfers just a beat or two ahead of the leading carriage of the trick.

It was extremely entertaining, but entertainment wasn't necessarily the point. This was a lecture, not a show; part of the programme of the forty-third Annual International Magicians' Convention, it was taking place not in a theatre but in the Spanish Hall, an extravaganza of a space on the first floor of Blackpool's famous Winter Gardens. The Spanish Hall was fairly magical itself: its interior had been designed with the aim of giving its occupants the illusion not of being in Blackpool; not, indeed, of being in Britain at all, but of cruising off the eighteenth-century Iberian coast on board some kind of square-rigged Napoleonic frigate. This was an effect not so much achieved as lunged at by the architect, who had built four miniature hillside towns complete with tiny stucco buildings and pocket-sized city walls into each of the four corners of the pillow-vaulted ceiling, which curved up to a rectangular roof light of iron and glass, and was supported by a kind of cloister or arcade of sandstone-coloured pillars.

The effect was, to say the least, unusual, especially after dark when all the miniature windows set into the miniature stucco buildings set inside their miniature city walls were lit up from within by dozens of miniature bulbs in all the candy colours of Christmas lights. But someone must have liked it and on liking it decided that it would be the perfect venue for these teach-ins on illusion, so they'd erected a plywood stage and two giant video screens in front of the sandstone-coloured pillars and set out several hundred chairs.

The Convention's lectures all took place in here and each lasted fifty minutes. The first ten to fifteen of these were taken up with the magician running through his (always his – all the lecturers were male, as were the vast majority of the audience, which lent the whole event the kind of atmosphere you might expect to experience at a congress on the subject of 'How to Pick up More and Better Girls') routine at double normal performance speed; the remainder with him showing step by step just how everything was done, how he'd fooled them, how if you did it just like him you could fool them too. The structure of the current presentation offered no variation on this general rule.

★

Suddenly the magician pointed at a man sitting in the middle of the front row. 'You, my friend, a moment there! You, yes, you! What *is* your name?'

'Les,' the man said somewhat apologetically.

'Less? Less? Did you say Less? Your name is Less? You're kidding me? What d'you get given at your baby shower, an inferiority complex?' More laughter, pained this time, as the audience saw spelled a truth about the difference between Americans and themselves.

'Lez,' the man said, effacing his soft Lancastrian lilt so the magician could hear him better.

'Oh. I see. Not Less, but Lez. Is that it? That's weird. Is that short for something?'

'Short for Leslie,' the man informed him.

'Oh! Leslie, huh?' The magician nodded. 'But you don't like Leslie, so you've gone and junked some of those dull extra letters. Okay. I see. Lez. Lezzzz. Not just lost some, but changed them, too. Dropped that boring old "s", put in a "z".' (He pronounced it 'zee'.) 'And how does your mother feel about that, huh, Lezzz? The name she gave you not good enough? I'm sorry, Mom, but that name you gave me, "Leslie", it's just too self-aggrandising, too upbeat, too dang positive for me. I want something that makes me feel real small and insignificant. I want something that makes me feel real *British*.' The magician adopted a sort of foppish accent when he said that last bit, which made the audience laugh extra hard. 'Maybe you should have gone for another letter, while you were at it,' he continued, feeding off the enthusiastic response. 'I mean, why "z"? You could have gone for "p". Lep. I kind of like that. Lep. As in lepton. As in even smaller than the already smallest possible thing. Better than Lez, don't you think? *Lep*. Kind of got a ring to it, hasn't it?'

Les said nothing. He couldn't think. The roller coaster was moving so quickly now; he hadn't known it was going to go this fast when he'd climbed on. All he'd done was say his name and now here he was, alone, a figure of national embarrassment, the audience – his countrymen – all laughing at him. All he'd done was say his name. It was like being back at school. It was like being back the first day at school when you find out that some piece of you that you'd always thought of as normal, admirable even, was in the eyes of other people a kind of horrible disadvantage or deformity.

His prey all dazzled and confused, the magician moved in for the kill. 'My guess is, Lep, that your mother's deeply offended by this name change thing you've got going on here. I think you're inflicting a deep hurt on her with your disrespect.'

They'd stopped laughing now, the crowd, perhaps suddenly aware of their own complicity, their own potential for destruction. Or perhaps they just wanted to hear where this was going. Poor Les, though, he was still laughing, still playing catch up. 'I'm willing to bet on it. You wanna know why, Lep? You wanna know how come I'm so sure?'

Les wasn't sure whether to nod 'yes' or shake 'no' so he tried to do both at once, ending up by moving his head round in a circle. He was no longer Leslie or Les or even Lez: now he was Lep, and as Lep he was, for the time being at least, completely in the hands of this other person, with whom he'd not done more than exchange one single word. He hadn't even got up yet from his chair.

Just as things were getting painful, the magician lightened the tone. 'Okay, Lep, well, come on up here, I'll show you how. Everyone give Lep a big round of applause.' Okay, okay, this was entertainment again and the audience could breathe a big sigh of relief as Lep stood up and, looking happy, climbed up on to the stage. He even took a little bow and started grinning with all the attention until the magician let him know that he was standing in the wrong place, on the wrong side, he wanted him here, no, not there, over here, back one step, yes, just about there, standing there on his right.

Lep, it turned out, was youngish, early thirties perhaps, with mousy hair, a ruddy Angle complexion, a rugby player's build, soft chipmunk cheeks. He wore a sports jacket over a rugby shirt with broad green and yellow stripes, ill-fitting jeans. He probably had a wife, one or two young kids.

'Come stand over here, Lep,' said the magician, repositioning the man yet again. 'You see, the reason I can tell your mother's not pleased with you is she's not looking after you properly. Look here.' Doing it so that the audience could see, the magician reached over and grabbed the left-hand panel of Lep's jacket, holding up the material. 'Your button is loose.' Everyone looked, Lep included; certainly, there was a button next to where the magician's thumb pinched up the material. And certainly it looked like it might be a little loose: the thread wasn't quite tight around it – the people in the first few rows could see that unassisted, while the people further back could watch it on the video screens.

'It's no good having you walk around with it like that,' the magician continued. 'At some point it's gonna fall off and you're gonna lose it. And you might not find another to match.' The magician shook his head. Lep shook his head as well. 'No,' the magician said, drawing the word out long and deep. 'But – don't worry. Because even though your mother's given up on you, I haven't. Yet.' Bending forward, he lowered his head to the level of the jacket, closed his mouth round the button and – with a waggle of his jaw – bit it clean away.

Straightening up, the magician showed the button held between his teeth, a thread dangling from it, his face radiating outwards from a spectacular grin, his eyes brilliant and blue and captivating and electric.

'Delicious,' he said, throttling the word like a comedy ventriloquist. Still keeping hold of that pinch of material with his right hand, he inspected the jacket again, picking some loose threads away from it with the fingers of his left. Then, reaching up, he took the button from his mouth and brought it back down to the level of the jacket, back to where it had started, moving the material now from his right hand into his left.

'Now, Lep,' he said, 'watch carefully, I'm going to do what your mother would have done if she weren't so offended by your foolish name antics.' Everyone watched: Lep watched his jacket and the front two rows watched Lep and everyone else looked at the magician's curiously small hands on the video screens, now that he'd given them permission to do so. Everyone watched while he slowly rubbed his chubby little thumb round in a circle; everyone watched as he slowly took it away. To reveal the button, sewn neatly back on to the jacket.

'You can clap now,' the magician told them. And they did.

★

After the lecture, directly after, even before the magician had actually managed to get off the stage, there was a small stampede. What began slowly, what started as a trickle when it became clear the talk was drawing to a close, with lone men dressed in blue cagoules or padded anoraks peeling off from the ends of the rows and hurrying towards the back of the hall with a stiff-legged gait, what began in this staid English manner was instantly transformed into a torrent of bodies the moment the final farewell round of applause had commenced.

Within seconds, the tables at the rear of the room were deluged and the items that had been laid out on the wood-effect tables by scarlet-sweatshirted convention staff during the magician's lecture had been engulfed. For fifteen minutes there was chaos as eager husbands and frustrated fathers and sallow teens and vicious pensioners battled for the limited-edition booklets and video cassettes and coin packs and fekes provided by the magician.

For here were secrets and, like all secrets, these were powerful. Those who had command of them possessed the power of giving names. Those who had command of them possessed the power of America.

★

While Terri had been watching Lep's ritual humiliation, America had shone in her eyes. Though she and Marty had been sitting towards the rear of the room, thanks to the video screens they'd been able to see the performance in all of its detail. In particular she'd enjoyed the routine with the button; simple though it was, it was the most enchanting thing she'd seen all weekend. When the button reappeared sewn back on to the jacket, she'd clapped like a battery-powered toy, her palms parallel and her fingers pointing straight out. She'd even bobbed up and down in her chair.

'Isn't he great, Marty, isn't he great? God, he's so fucking cool.' She bounced round to face her boyfriend. 'Wasn't that cool? I've not seen that before.' As always she wanted to ask how he'd done it but as always she didn't, because when you're among magicians you just don't.

97

Marty shrugged. He couldn't take Terri seriously when she expressed enthusiasm like this; there was something about her manner that always suggested acting, that gave him the impression she was only pretending to be enthused. Plus he was jealous. Did Terri ever think that way about him, did she ever think that he was 'so fucking cool'? Presumably yes, since she was, after all, going out with him, but that didn't occur to Marty right now. He was too busy picking over his own insecurities.

Four years before, when Marty had first come to Blackpool, American lecturers had been the exception, not the rule. Back then it had been him in the scrum at the tables. Young and keen, he'd managed to get himself a video cassette, he still had it somewhere, one of Wayne Dobson's, from back before he was struck down by MS. But now it was a little beneath his dignity, all of that. Dignity – that's what British magicians always had had. So why wasn't it them up on that stage? What was it about these Americans that made them so much better, so much more glamorous, so much more exciting to watch? It wasn't a matter of technique, clearly. Marty knew British magicians who could do all the tricks he'd seen in the lecture and more. But this guy, he had an air about him, an ease. He'd actually been *insulting* the audience – and they'd loved him for it. It almost seemed that, because he assumed people were going to love him, they did. He had none of the self-deprecating humour of his British counterparts and – curiously – none of their arrogance either. His manner said 'I am like you – and you, and you', even though he wasn't at all. It was very disconcerting. Marty wasn't sure it was something he quite understood.

'It's an old Max Malini routine from the 1920s,' he'd informed Terri. 'It's in one of Dai Vernon's books. It's just a little mime routine, 'sall it is. He's using a feke – it's probably still in his mouth. He'll probably make a move in a minute to retrieve it. Watch.' Indeed, as the magician had prepared to carry on with his main routine of making the coins appear in the tumbler – from which this had all been a diversion, no doubt a way of depositing the coins at new locations around his body – he passed his hand up and in front of his mouth.

Marty sniffed. 'Malini would have swallowed it.' A joke occurred to him and, without thinking, he let it spill out of his mouth. 'So now you know the difference between a good magician and a great one,' he said dourly. 'A great magician swallows, a good one only spits.'

He turned to Terri with a laugh, but she had a look of genuine shock and horror on her face. 'Jesus, Marty! How . . . how could you? That's so . . . so *fucking* offensive.'

Marty did a double take – he knew she was serious, as Terri hardly ever swore.

A second later he was pursuing her across the room, batting away some teenager who approached right at that moment blab-bering something about seeing Marty's show at the Inn on the Park and wanting his autograph.

'Terri, honey, Terri! I'm sorry, baby, I really am . . . I didn't mean it like that. I was just making a joke. It was thoughtless of me. But that was all. Honestly. *Terri*!'

It was a bad time for an argument: within the next few minutes Marty and Terri were supposed to be meeting up with a couple of friends from the magic circuit in the Galleon Bar, and straight after that the Cabaret Championships began – the same Championships in which all of them were entered. Experience told Marty that a comment like the one he'd just made could send Terri into a sulk lasting several days and he needed her on top form tonight: ever since the telephone conversation with Michael he'd felt the entire future of his career was resting on the next few hours. Which perhaps accounted for the insecurities that had been plaguing him all day.

He tried to explain this to his girlfriend as he chased her down the stairs and in the direction of the bar. 'Terri, darling, I wasn't *thinking*. It's because I'm nervous about tonight.'

'Don't be pathetic, Martin.'

He hated it when she called him that. Who did she think she was? His mother or something? 'I'm not, honestly not, I'm not . . .'

'You *are*.'

'Really I'm not, I didn't mean it like that, I promise, I would never . . .'

'But you just did.' She was enjoying this, as she did most of the opportunities she had to make Marty crawl.

'But I *didn't*. You just *thought* I did.'

'Look, Marty, you might be able to make an audience think

that black is white and vice versi' – Terri hadn't got that last word quite right, she thought, but no matter, she must carry on – 'but not me, okay? I know what I heard.'

Marty felt a change of tack was necessary. 'Okay, okay. Well if I did, I'm *sorry*. Really.'

'So you admit it?'

'*Terri*. That's not what I'm saying . . .'

'Then what are you saying, exactly?'

'I'm trying to tell you!'

'Don't raise your voice to me!'

'I'm not!'

Marty tried again. 'Terri, look, I'm sorry, okay? I didn't mean it, and if it came out that way I'm sorry.'

She still wouldn't look at him. 'I don't know what you're getting so worked up about. It's not that big a deal. I'm used to that kind of thing from you.' Terri sighed and rolled her eyes upwards to the ceiling. They were by now at the bottom of the stairs and the plastic beams of the Galleon Bar loomed before them like a giant ribcage. 'Are you going to calm down, or are you going to let Tanya and Harvey see us rowing?'

That kind of thing . . . How fucking dare she? He never made sexist comments like that! It was completely out of character. But he kept his mouth tight shut, knowing that for now at least she'd beaten him. He'd bide his time; sooner or later he'd have a chance to get her back.

*

While Tanya had gone for a walk along the seafront, Harvey had spent the afternoon dividing his time between watching the heats of the close-up championships in the Renaissance Room and browsing the stalls of the magic dealers' mart, set out beneath the hooped conservatory roof of the adjacent Pavilion Suite. As ever, he didn't have too much money to spend, but he had treated himself to a doctored fifty-pence piece with a spring-loaded 'bite' of the kind he'd seen David Blaine deploy in one of his street magic TV specials and a top notch latex thumb–tip,* which was of far superior quality to the standard-issue plastic ones that lay in bowlfuls on the vendors' tables, looking like props from a finger-fetish slasher film. Less successfully he'd blown twelve quid on a stupid horseshoe-and-chain trick, not an illusion at all but a mere puzzle: if you knew how, you were supposed to be able to pass the horseshoes past one another and tie a knot in the chain that linked them together.

Harvey had noticed the horseshoe hawker when he'd arrived with Tanya on the first morning of the event; their purveyor had sorted himself a place on the coveted square of tables in the entrance hall, an excellent spot on account of its being both right in front of the ticket desk and yet outside the security barriers for the event, allowing access to a captive audience of magicians queuing for their passes as well as to any curious members of the public who happened to be wandering by. The salesman's old-style (i.e. belligerent) sideshow hawker pitch ensured a crowd was gathered round him at all times. No matter if you'd watched him demonstrate the trick four or five times in a row, when you had a go – and everyone did, it was totally irresistible – for the life of you you just couldn't do it; it seemed totally impossible. Which, of course, was precisely the idea, the plan being that out of the pure frustration of not being able to suss out something so apparently simple and obvious you'd buy one of the puzzles in order to take it home and work on it. Which many did, Harvey included, only to find they still couldn't figure the damn thing out.

It would be at this point that most people would realise the truth, which was that what they'd really paid for was the instructions. These they'd now consult (in secret, when they were alone), only to find them so incoherent and poorly photocopied as to be next to useless, thus denying them even the baseline gratification of knowing the solution.

* A standard prop for any magician, a thumb–tip is a hollow, artificial thumb designed to be slid on and off a real thumb at will, creating a small cavity inside. In this space small items – a folded banknote, for example, or a crushed length of silk ribbon – can be easily concealed. When the hand is in motion even a crude thumb–tip is almost impossible to see.

In the case of older gulls the horseshoe-and-chain trick would now either be thrown out of the window or be repackaged and given away as a gift to some subsidiary male relative who was (a) young enough to have a chance of doing it and (b) old enough to know better than to complain at having such a dodgy and clearly second-hand item palmed off on him or her. The trainee teenage tricksters who'd bought the things, on the other hand, were not yet wise enough to negotiate this more adult course; they could be seen in corners wrestling with the horseshoes all weekend – and wrestling simultaneously, no doubt, with the terrible and mounting fear that the puzzle represented some kind of crucial journeyman-type challenge in the path of their route to a lustrous magical career. Would their failure to solve it be a sign that they should give up now, that they weren't possessed of that mysterious and elusive quality known as 'talent'? That it was over, that they were through? That they might as well go home? No one seemed to know the answer to this most vital of questions.

Unfortunately for Harvey, he seemed to have found himself firmly positioned in this second camp, and by the time he and Tanya turned up for their six-o'clock rendezvous with Marty and Terri he too was feeling a little insecure. Before Harvey had fallen under the spell of David Blaine, his current idol, the magician he'd been most influenced by was Marty. Harvey was from Liverpool; almost four years Marty's junior; as an impressionable fifteen-year-old he'd seen him win *Young Magician of the Year* on the television, since which he'd travelled as far afield as Leeds and Wakefield to watch him perform. As a star-struck young hopeful practising furiously in his bedroom, Martin Mystery was everything Harvey wanted to be.

When the two had first met in person at the previous year's convention they'd quickly become good friends, though Harvey had been so nervous around his role model that the relationship had only got past its initial stages because their girlfriends had hit it off. Over the last twelve months the two couples had made a point of travelling to see each other's shows, and this year they'd organised to stay in the same guest house during the convention. To further cement the relationship, Harv had invited everyone to come and have lunch with his parents in Liverpool on the Sunday which, this being Saturday, meant tomorrow.

By the time Marty and Terri arrived, arguing, in the Galleon Bar, Harvey and Tanya had got themselves drinks and a table. The Galleon Bar occupied the room directly beneath the Spanish Hall. Its interior was contrastingly dark and deeply rococo, a grand cocoon of giant plastic-oak planks and beams fitted with curlicue mouldings and glowing yellow barrel lanterns and false ship's windows, which taken together simulated the upper coach cabin of the vessel upon the deck of which Terri and Marty and the rest of the magic lecture audience had been sailing only a short while before.

Terri came over and sat with the two Liverpudlians while Marty went to get the drinks. To Harvey she seemed a little bit on edge – though with Terri that wasn't anything unusual. But when Marty returned, handed his girlfriend her drink without looking at her and demanded to know what was in his plastic bag even before he'd managed to sit down, he guessed that they'd probably had a tiff of some kind.

Dutifully, he fished out the horseshoe-and-chain puzzle.

'I can't believe you got one of those,' Marty said as soon as he set eyes on it. 'What on earth d'you get one of those for?'

'I think it's kind of cool.'

'You don't think it's cool. You were suckered, mate. What good's this to you?'

'I think it's kind of interesting, I –'

'How much d'you pay for it?'

'Not all that much. Twelve –'

'*Twelve quid*? Jesus, he saw you coming. What else d'you get?' Afraid that Marty would also demean his thumb-tip, Harvey produced instead his final purchase of the afternoon, a copy of Jim Steinmeyer's edited reissue of *Jarrett*. 'Nice one,' Marty said, taking the book greedily and examining it. It was a hardback, in pretty much mint condition, its black-and-white dust cover not marked or torn, though the fold on the back flap had been reinforced with Sellotape. First edition too, published by Magic Inc., 1981. It wasn't like having a real *Jarrett*, of course, but if there'd been one of those on sale here Harv would never have been able to afford it – or even get to it. Worth today what? Marty blinked and did some quick calculations. Six, maybe seven grand? It was fifty squids just for this repro – there was the price in pencil at the top right-hand corner of the frontispiece, two long digits and a dash written in a bookseller's semi-elegant scrawl.

'This is more like it,' he said, leafing through the pages. 'Not an original like mine, of course, but the next best thing.' By Marty's standards this was a compliment. He nodded to himself as he turned the pages, reverentially murmuring the names of some of the illusions: 'Creo'; 'The Easel and Pedestal'; 'The Water Barrel Escape'; 'The Bangkok Bungalow'.

'I've never read it all the way through,' Harvey confessed.

Marty was incredulous. 'You're kidding me.'

'Nope. Never have.'

'It'll change your life. It's genius.'

'Yes, well, we all know what you think,' Terri interjected, straightening her back and shifting in her seat.

Still smarting from his defeat, Marty ignored her. All he needed now was her embarrassing him in front of Harvey and Tanya. 'If I had the money,' he continued to Harvey, 'that'd be the basis of my show, that book. No one's doing those illusions, not like he did them. Not with the dedication, the attention to detail.'

'What about Copperfield?'

'Well, obviously Copperfield's brilliant, but he's not doing Jarrett's stuff.'

'But he's so fucking cheesy,' Tanya said, breaking off from whatever it was she'd been saying to Terri to interject. Marty had a tendency, in her opinion, to be a bit of a bully. He could do with taking down a peg.

'He is cheesy,' Harv agreed. 'But I still rate him.'

Tanya sighed. This was exactly Harvey's problem, that he

didn't have the guts to stand up for himself. Half hoping that Marty would leap down her throat with some ill-considered comment she remarked that David Copperfield wasn't as cute as David Blaine.

Marty took the bait. 'Face it, Tanya. Blaine is bollocks.'

'No, Marty – c'mon,' Harvey said, unwittingly winning himself a couple of Brownie points on his girlfriend's mental score sheet. 'Blaine's really good. He's reinvented magic.'

'Like fuck he has.'

'He *has*, Marty,' Tanya said, pressing home the advantage. 'Harv's got a definite point there.'

Marty shook his head. 'He's just put it on TV. And then he only does a bunch of card tricks and a levitation. A *levitation*. On *TV*? I mean what's that about?'

'I thought it was totally excellent, that. I couldn't work out how he did it.'

'*Exactly*. That's my point *exactly*. It's filmed so you can't see the apparatus.'

'I don't know. It looked like they filmed it all the way round. And there were people there. I mean, members of the public. They seemed pretty convinced. Some of them were completely freaking out.'

Marty shook his head, took a sip of his pint. 'You don't understand.'

'What don't I understand?' Marty had made a mistake, he realised too late, in getting Tanya all worked up over this. Once you got her started she could be impossible to stop. 'What? Come on, smart-arse. How does he do it? How would you do it?' The magician shrugged and reddened but gave no reply. 'You just don't like him because he doesn't wear a suit.'

'That's not true. Lance Burton doesn't always wear a suit. But he understands that sometimes you have to . . .' Marty knew before he said them that the words would come out wrong. '. . . that sometimes it's important to recognise that magic has *tradition*.'

'And that's why you always wear suits, is it, Marty? Because you respect tradition? Or because you think it makes you look good? Which it doesn't, I might add.'

Marty smiled thinly, determined not to rise to this. 'That's not the point,' he said.

'So what is the fucking point?' Flipping her hand at him Tanya turned away, picking up her conversation with Terri where they'd left off.

Harv was disappointed. He'd been enjoying the discussion – he liked discussions, they were in the spirit of democracy he felt; there should be more of them. He also knew that Marty had no idea how to pull off a straight standing levitation, especially in the middle of the street. The twat had backed himself into a corner. Still, mates were mates. *He* wasn't going to give him a hard time over it. At least not in front of the girls. 'So who else do you rate then?' he asked Marty, throwing him a lifeline. 'If not Blaine.'

Marty didn't hesitate. 'Siegfried and Roy – they're the only ones ever to have pulled off Jarrett's elephant vanish. Houdini and Devant, naturally, but we're talking alive, not dead. Doug Henning –'

'Doug Henning!' Tanya shrieked. 'Henning? What, the Freddie Mercury of magic?'

'What's wrong with Freddie Mercury?' Harv asked, earning in the process a Tanya black mark that nullified the two Brownie points he'd gained.

Terri was confused. 'Wasn't Henning the weird one, the hippie?' She always got mixed up between Henning, Jerry Sadowitz and Jeff McBride. She didn't pay as much attention to this stuff as the others did. She was a gymnast, not a magician. She was an acrobat.

'He was the one who completely lost it,' Harv informed her. He wouldn't have wanted to talk about it, not here anyway, not in the bar, but he'd spent a great deal of time pondering the strange case of Doug Henning. Henning was recognised the world over as a master magician and according to a lecture he'd heard some bloke give at a Magic Circle evening the previous year, the series of television specials the famous magician had made during the seventies were pretty much responsible for reinventing magic for the pop culture mainstream, drawing it out of the cabaret doldrums it had wandered into in post-war America. Harvey remembered some of these specials from when he was a kid, and when the lecturer had claimed that without Henning there'd have been no David Copperfield, no Paul Daniels, no David Blaine it had seemed fair enough.

A slim, effeminate man with wavy long hair, buck teeth and a self-conscious handlebar moustache, Henning favoured spangly, skin-tight costumes with outrageous ruffles and flares both on stage and off. His thing was whimsy. A vegetarian, a health freak and a Buddhist, his shows were full of elves, fairy tales and the 'childlike wonder of magic'. Which would have been fine, Harvey thought, except that by the time the eighties came round Henning seemed to have lost all perspective.

Abandoning magic for politics, he came to England to stand as a candidate for the Natural Law party in Blackpool South, the key plank of his policy the promise to promote the technique of yogic flying in order to 'improve brain coherence and bond society'. Having somehow failed to get elected, he went on to work for the Maharishi Mahesh Yogi, where he helped to draw up designs for a spiritual theme park that would feature buildings hovering in the air upon giant jets of water after the fashion of his own most famous illusion, which involved the levitation of a woman atop a four-foot fountain. Harvey didn't know what had become of this last project but he assumed it had been shelved – word was that Henning had cancer, and was dying.

Harvey viewed Henning's tale as a cautionary one. Every time he did a trick he was haunted by the thought that on a very basic level – on, indeed, a magical one – he was cheating someone; and he couldn't help wondering what the long-term consequences of spending your life doing this might be. It seemed more than possible that all those little bluffs and falsehoods would pile up ever higher on the backbone of his soul until, one day without warning, it would snap beneath their accumulated weight. He didn't know what that would mean, exactly, but it didn't seem a fate that was likely to be at all desirable.

'Forget about that. I'm talking about his magic, not the other stuff,' Marty snapped. 'The point about Henning is that he was pure, that he believed. And he was awesome on stage. Ever seen the film of his illusion "Things that Go Bump in the Night"?'

Harvey shook his head, and Marty proceeded to describe it to him as magicians generally describe illusions: in loving detail, but in a way that made them sound more than a little dull.

Of this dullness Marty wasn't completely oblivious. But he had to say something, he had to keep talking, he had to stretch whatever it was he wanted to say into the lengthiest possible spiel. He had to do that because if he didn't he'd have to sit there silently and listen, sit there silently and think about how he'd missed the mark with his joke, about how Terri was putting the screws on him, about how he felt powerless to do anything about it. Most of all he'd have to think about how terrified he was that they wouldn't win tonight and that Michael would drop him, so flushing his career and all his dreams down one of life's many busy sewers in one simple, single motion.

But even the talking couldn't stop him thinking altogether. *I don't want to be here*, an inner voice kept reminding him between breaths, between sips of his beer, between glances at Tanya to monitor the likelihood of her having another go. *I don't want to be here, I shouldn't be here. I should be under lights, under lights in Las Vegas, far away on the other side of the sea.*

★

Like the *Young Magician* event Marty had won a few years before, the Magical Cabaret Championships were no small affair. Indeed, the parallels between the two events were worrying; like some kind of Nietzschean rerun, the Blackpool championships also featured four categories of acts with six acts in each category, ten minutes of performance time being allotted to each and every one, a series of coincidences that further deepened the general feeling of gloom and portentousness that had taken hold of Marty ever since Terri had drawn up their charts a fortnight previously and concluded from what she'd found that some kind of major change was imminent.

'Jupiter is in the ascendent for us both this month,' she'd reported from her position on the bedroom carpet of whatever guest house they'd been staying in at the time, a carpet whose artificial weave and violently repetitious pattern were heavy competition for the sorry assemblage of aromatic candles and small pieces of crystal she'd laid out about her, objects whose purpose was to create a 'zone of socio-psychical interruption' (her phrase) conducive to horoscope construction. 'Over the next days and weeks, coincidence will play a significant part in both our lives, to the extent that things may begin to seem like a rehash of events long ago.' Her eyes saccaded between the pages of a well-thumbed paperback and the sheet of A3 paper that, in the course of the previous few hours, she had covered with a variety of words, diagrams and symbols. 'New solutions to old problems may be needed in order to stave off disaster. Relying on what you know may mean making the same mistake twice.'

Marty, suspicious of his girlfriend's astrological dabblings at the best of times, didn't register that second bit. Instead of listening properly he nodded, murmured something about it all sounding very interesting and went back to reading the latest Michael Crichton.

But now he found himself desperately trying to remember what, exactly, she had said. Strange omens were appearing with disarming regularity, and it was difficult not to give way to superstition. Not only was cabaret competition an uncanny echo of *Young Magician* (although this may have had something to do with the fact that – unknown to Marty – the same person was responsible for organising both), but they'd arrived at the venue to be told that Ken Dodd, Honorary Life President of the Blackpool Magicians' Club and compère for the evening, had been forced to cancel because of illness.

'Who've they got in to replace him?' Terri asked the stage tech who'd broken the news.

'Some bloke called Ted Preece, whoever the hell he is.'

Marty groaned, his feelings of foreboding suddenly magnified tenfold. 'It's like a fucking haunting.'

Terri didn't miss a beat – smiling primly, she told her boyfriend not to swear. Though the admonishment hadn't been directed at him, immediately the stage tech blushed (Terri's ability to induce such embarrassment was what she called the 'Diana Effect'). Marty, on the other hand – having long developed Diana Effect immunity – felt a sudden spurt of fury rise upwards in his gullet. This kind of behaviour was, he knew, part of the punishment for that spit or swallow comment he'd made. He wanted to say something, he *so* wanted to say something, but he couldn't think of anything to say and anyway, he couldn't run the risk of sparking another argument. He had to capitulate. 'Well, it is,' he mumbled disconsolately.

'There's still no need to swear.'

★

The flag went up at eight and by the time the audience was finally allowed to stagger disorientated from the venue – the Winter Gardens Opera House, a vast, multi-tiered hall dripping with decaying plasterwork and a look about it of having been salvaged from the *Titanic* – shortly after two, it had become known to our protagonist that, perhaps due to the movement of the stars, or to the operation of some cybernetically self-correcting karmic mechanism, or to any one of a host of possibilities that now came into his mind (all of which had in common the fact that none of them took his own performance as root cause) Martin Mystery's Mysteries had failed to get any kind of placing.

The first prize of five thousand pounds plus a month's residency at the Talk of London had gone to an act from Newcastle called the Power of Light. The Power of Light had a vanish cabinet made of fluorescent tubes and a light box with neon lights and a variant on the old sword through the torso routine that used lasers instead of cold (if bendy) steel. The Power of Light had a soundtrack by Orbital. The Power of Light changed a girl into an albino chow. The Power of Light . . . everyone except Marty seemed to love the Power of bloody Light.

Second prize, as was traditional, was awarded to a dire comedy magic troupe that was all orange wigs, big shoes, back-firing tricks and pratfalls. Third prize . . . Marty couldn't remember to whom third prize went, only that it didn't go to him. He was already drunk by the time the results were announced and the booze had made quick work of whipping up his disappointment into a clumsy and solipsistic fury – so much so that he'd failed to congratulate Harvey and Tanya when it was announced that they'd scored a Highly Commended, giving Terri the opportunity to get on her high horse with him yet again. At which point Marty, unable to bear it any longer, had run away.

His TV dreams in tatters, he'd walked straight past the door-way to the Gents and disappeared to sulk in the warehouse-like area backstage, where the twenty-four competing acts had rigged up makeshift dressing rooms. With everyone front of house for the announcements these enclosures, constructed of wheeled curtain rails and each accompanied by its own huddled pile of costumes and props, had a desperate, displaced and eerie air about them, like the wind-blown remnants of a Berber village ravaged by some awful magical apocalypse.

Creeping inside the most secluded clump, Marty sat down on the concrete floor and started picking at his soul. What was wrong with Terri? She seemed almost pleased they hadn't won. She knew what the competition meant to them. He needed her sympathy, not her damn guidelines to polite behaviour. When she'd started telling him to be a bit more gracious about losing to Harvey and Tanya he'd wanted to smack her in the face. How fucking dare she? It was so out of order, so beyond belief.

The bitch. *She* was to blame for them not winning anything. Not that she'd actively messed up their routine or anything; she was far too scheming and manipulative for that. It was just her attitude. That had been enough. She'd been robotic and lacklustre, that's what she'd been, and in a competition like this – where the judges were looking for enthusiasm as much as anything

– lack of drive and sparkle was always going to be completely fatal. Didn't she understand?

Well, it was her loss, Marty thought petulantly. If Michael dumped him now and his career nose-dived into the sand, that would be her future ruined too. Then what would she do? Why couldn't she have believed him when he told her he hadn't meant that remark the way she thought he had, that it had just been a random comment? Why was it that every time he said the slightest thing that might be construed as being somehow targeted against her she became Little Miss Stroppy Bitch from Hell?

Fuck her, Marty thought, fuck her fuck her fuck her. Even if he had meant the spit or swallow thing subconsciously, did she need to punish him by destroying everything that he – that they – had worked for? It made no sense.

'So that's where you are.' It was Harvey. Flushed with his own success he'd come to look for Marty, not absolutely sure whether he intended to comfort him or rub it in. 'What are you doing back there? We've been looking all over for you. Aren't you coming to the party?'

'Not in the mood.'

'Don't you want dinner?'

'Not if it's going to be that shite Lancashire hotpot they dole out every other year I don't. Fucking shite food.'

As Harvey clambered through the piles of magic kit in his direction, Marty experienced a nasty tremor of self-consciousness. It was one thing for him to sit around being maudlin and pathetic; quite another to have his friend see him that way. It would upset the balance of power if the acolyte were allowed to see his sensei being weak.

Standing up he smoothed back his hair and rubbed any traces of tears from his cheeks. 'All right, Harv,' he muttered as the visitor loomed into view.

Harvey's reply made it immediately apparent that the balance of power had already begun to shift. 'What you doing back here? Poor Marty upset cos poor Marty didn't win?' He felt sorry for Marty, he really did; he'd been unlucky not to take away a prize, though the compère's introducing him and Terri as the Charles and Di of the British Magic scene couldn't have done much to tip the judges in their favour. Still, he couldn't resist a little twisting of the knife.

'I see that one small sip of success has already gone to your head,' Marty replied bitterly.

'Fuck you.'

'Fuck you double.'

Harvey pouted, looking hurt.

'Oh, all right. Well done.'

The pout turned to a smile. 'Ta.'

'I just can't believe it,' Marty whined. 'I mean, I can understand losing out to Power of Shite, at least they were original, but that comedy troupe were total crap.'

'That go for us too?'

'Aw Harv, come on. You know that's not what I meant. You deserved to win a prize. You deserved to do even better than you did.'

'Come on, you twat. Have a drink.' Harvey swung over the vodka bottle he was carrying.

Marty grabbed it, took a swig. 'Got a fag?'

'Thought you didn't smoke?'

'I don't. Got one?'

Harvey fished one out of his pack and handed it over, then sparked up his lighter in such a way that the flame appeared to be emerging from his thumb. Lighting the cigarette, Marty took a drag, only to leap into the air a moment later as it exploded in a blaze of sparks. He hurled the burning mess away from him and it landed among the folds of a giant paper Chinese dragon that had been deployed to minor effect by one of the other unsuccessful acts, meaning that the two of them had to spend the next few minutes desperately trying to retrieve what was left of the smouldering cigarette before it set the prop alight, an episode made more burlesque by the contrast between Harvey's fits of giggles and the crackling stream of swear words that fell like firecrackers from Marty's lips.

'Arsehole,' Marty said when the embers had finally been snuffed out. 'I suppose you think that was funny.'

'You should thank me. I just stopped you from starting smoking.'

'Shut up and pass the vodka.'

The time: early-ish the next morning. The place: the Guest House Eldorado, one of three standing together in a terrace to the south-west of the Winter Gardens, opposite the multi-storey car park and in the shadow of Blackpool Tower. The people: Harvey wheezing bags down the stairs and out to where his van was double parked outside, lights flashing, Marty still in bed, doing battle with the memory of mixing vodka and red wine; Terri fixing her make-up at the MFI dressing table, an oversized doll's house number in white plastic veneer with excessive gold-paint scalloping that wobbles every time she puts weight on it; Tanya sitting at the end of the bed, smoking and dabbing clear nail varnish on a run she's discovered in her tights.

'So you're not coming, then?' Terri asked Marty, in reference to the trip to Liverpool to have lunch with Harvey's parents.

'I told you, I don't feel like it. I feel fucking terrible.'

'You just want to sulk some more.'

'I'll be sick if I get in the van, that's all.'

'Harvey's really angry with you for not coming, you know.'

'He'll get over it.'

'All right, sulky. I'll see you tonight.' Terri dropped her make-up into her handbag and snapped it shut. She had in the end given him some sympathy the previous evening, and though there hadn't been much of it – a ruffle of his hair and a quick hug – it had been better than nothing. Tanya had pointed out that it was totally ludicrous of Michael to expect her and Marty

116

to win a prize before he could get them better work; she reckoned he'd probably just been winding Marty up, perhaps with the aim of getting him to stop moaning so much and get on with life. Which, when he thought about it, Marty had to admit was probably right.

'We're on at eight, don't forget,' he reminded Terri. 'I want you back here by six thirty with the van, no later. We'll need an hour at least to shift all the props.' It was their slot at the Mississippi Showboat Marty was referring to; they'd done a week there already and though Michael had made it a condition of the contract that they'd had the previous evening off for the competition, tonight it was back to the grindstone.

'All right, Mr Hitler, keep your hair on. I'll be here.' The girls looked at each other and tittered.

'You know the way okay?' Marty asked, making an attempt to be more civil.

But it was too late for that. 'Oh, I think I can manage. Come on, Tan, let's leave Mr Grumpy to his own devices.' And the two of them waltzed out of the room, slamming the door closed as they went.

Marty swore and pulled the covers back over his head, glowing for a moment at the prospect of finally getting some peace. But it was not to be: the glow was dispelled just seconds later when the three of them yelled up at the window that he was a grumpy cunt (though Terri replaced the 'cunt' with a 'rat' and even then giggled over-excitedly at letting herself be so closely associated with such a public display of obscenity). It failed to return even after he'd heard them drive away.

He lay there for quite a while until the pounding of his head and the nagging of his bladder forced him to make a trip to the communal bathroom to seek relief and medication. Once back in bed, his headache gradually moved down a notch or two from completely debilitating to merely nauseating, which would have been great if annoyance and embarrassment and anger and regret hadn't quickly moved in to fill up the vacated space. He wanted to sleep but he couldn't, bouncing instead between the various areas of turmoil in his brain until he could stand it no longer. A shower, he thought, would help matters immeasurably. But when he got to the bathroom the shower didn't work. So then he thought: breakfast, and pulled on some clothes. But this was a guest house and even on Sundays – as the brisk landlady now reminded him, while smiling the kind of smile that nurses give when disposing of something distasteful and dubious – breakfast was over and finished by nine. She then took the opportunity to give Marty a stringent telling off about the amount of noise he and his 'crowd' had made when they'd returned to the B&B in the early hours of that morning, not to mention the awful language she'd heard not an hour before, right outside the window. The reprimand continued while Marty returned to his room, retrieved his duffle coat, and fled the building's dread pot-pourri embrace to brave the rain and seek refuge in a caff.

His first thought was to try inside the Winter Gardens. Crossing the car park, cortex throbbing, he slipped beneath the impressive fan window that hovered like a giant ice-cream wafer above the side entrance to the complex, passing quickly through the clutch of frantic video games that choked the hallway and continuing along an arcade of tiled pillars until he reached the Palm Court café, which he knew from bitter experience was the best chance he had of finding a passable cup of coffee this side of Manchester.

Straightening up in order to maintain his dignity in front of any other magicians who might happen to be inside, Marty pushed the door open and ambled in, only to slip on a discarded chip punnet, lose his balance and knock over one of the artfully arranged fake plastic trees. The two dumpy and sullen girls manning the checkouts had screwed their faces round towards him and fixed him with Egyptian eyes until he set the toppled plant right side up again and scooped all the white gravel he'd spilled back inside its pot.

Head hung low again he slid towards the buffeteria, hoping that none of the other customers had noticed him. But at the drinks machine he sprayed a cloud of scalding steam containing high-velocity bullets of superheated fluid across his hand.

'*Shit*!' The world was clearly conspiring against him.

'If you don't behave we'll have you thrown out,' one of the girls announced.

He tried again. The trouble was that the buttons weren't obvious. It was one of those machines with a smooth metallic plastic control panel (what exactly *was* that material?) that invited you to make your selection by pressing where the words were. But the words were quite close together and written on a diagonal slant, and it was all much more complicated than it should have been.

On his third attempt the machine spat ersatz cappuccino into his mug and Marty moved on to the haven of calm and efficiency that was the toaster. When he was done there he presented his forage to the kohl-eyed beauty who'd earlier admonished him. She sniffed and rang up his bill, and he gave her a wan little smile and went to sit down at one of the two or three unoccupied orange tables.

Across the corridor, visible through partitions of decorated glass, a second video arcade was jangling away. Stirring sugar into his drink, Marty stared wall-eyed at its spiralling displays. Something about the lights was simple and calming. Something about the simplicity of putting a coin in a slot, pressing a button, getting something back suddenly appealed to him. The kids hammering away at Ridge Racer and Time Crisis didn't interest him, they were too intent on the thrill. It was the stout old women at the fruit machines, they were the ones, pumping in coin after coin, the ash of their fags and the draught of their bellies dropping a little lower with every nudge. They'd got it sorted: the spin of the drums and the patterns of the lights gave them, as far as Marty was able to tell, all they needed from life. Winning only mattered to them in that it allowed them to stay in the game. It was a Tao thing, he reasoned thickly through the soup of his hangover, kind of a Zen, like in those Japanese Pachinko parlours he'd seen on TV, filled with people addicted to jangling thousands of little ball-bearings down through the mechanisms of what looked like coloured washing machines. There was no ego element, no feedback in terms of personal fulfilment. You just played for the sake of it and that was enough.

Marty wished he could play just for the sake of it. But his actions, whatever they happened to be, only seemed to matter if someone was watching. It occurred to him that he was like Terri in this. Perhaps this was what attracted them to one another.

Depressed by this insight, he finished his coffee – which had tasted of nothing – and shuffled through the main lobby towards the front exit. He would go and take a look at the sea. Maybe that would help him make sense of things. He'd read somewhere that watching the ocean was meant to be like looking at the human unconscious and right now that sounded like it might be a good thing to do. Something higher order, meditative, something in contrast to all the yearning and desiring he'd been wasting so much energy on recently.

Sticking his nose out through the main doors, he peered up at the sky. The clouds still hung low but the drizzle had stopped, for the time being at least. Deciding to risk it he followed the slope of the road down into the Sunday town centre and along a locked High Street – three portcullised sportswear outlets, four clamped charity shops, a barricaded bookmakers and two shuttered banks – arriving finally at the entrance to North Pier. He'd had it in mind to stroll out over the waves to get his sea view but for whatever reason the pier was closed too, so he made do with crossing the tram tracks on to the promenade and walking down past the red fortress that was the Hotel Metropole, the cold digging deep into the hollows round his eyes.

In front of him the sea wall banked and curved, and the promenade prepared to break into three lamp-posted and colonnaded tiers, which led with some majesty northwards to Fleetwood. The sea was up and waves thumped in short period against the stone bulwarks, breaking their backs on the small mole that ran out from the promontory. One in every eight gathered enough backwash and momentum to jet a thick, matted feather of spume up over the white safety railings, which though freshly painted were already suffering around their joints from blooming liver spots of rust. Two small boys were playing chicken with the spray, their trackpants soaked and slapping in the wind like sails that have missed stays. Above their heads a group of seagulls had joined their game and were busy gyring about in the updrafts and crosswinds, screeching maniacally. Another example, Marty noted, of doing something purely for the sake of it.

The sea wasn't blue or green or even grey but sandy and oily, the colour of tea, the foam scurfing its surface identical to that drooled on to his coffee by the Palm Court café drinks machine. It didn't seem natural, somehow, not that Marty was really sure he knew what natural meant any more. The whole of life felt artificial these days; there didn't seem to be anywhere unartificial left to go.

Consumed and morose, he watched the water twist and mutate for a while, until the effort of tracking even the one small square of it staked out between four of the great steel uprights that supported the pier's boardwalk brought his hangover back on. Shit. This sea-watching business clearly wasn't working. Giving up, he turned and lodged his back against the safety rail, looked inland to where he hoped things would feel more permanent.

Directly before him was the cenotaph, a tall beige needle scratching at the February sky, a huge wreath of red poppies propped against its base. The red disc captured the whole of Marty's ebbing attention – he thought it looked like a gunshot wound in the stone and he stared at it until distracted by the figure of a girl cutting across the emerald ellipse of grass that pooled around the monument. She was dressed in a black padded jacket like the one Terri owned – like the one everyone owned, these days – and she had one of those impish camel-coloured pixie hats (which someone had told him once were Afghani or Tibetan or Peruvian or something, he couldn't remember which) pulled down hard upon her head: something else you could buy pretty much anywhere these days, and the kind of thing that Tanya liked.

It was an odd combination, that hat with that jacket, which

Marty told himself was the reason the girl had first come to his attention. Nice pins though; jean-clad and shapely. It was probably worth trying to catch a glimpse of her face, he decided, just to see, you know, just to make sure that he didn't actually fancy her, just to be certain her existence didn't threaten the strength of his loyalty to Terri. Not that he was sure any more whether that loyalty counted for much.

The big triangular cheek flaps that hung down from the hat made the girl's face hard to see, and Marty had to shift his position in order to improve his view. The move brought him closer to the boys and the gulls and the danger of getting a soaking, but it was rewarded by a glimpse of the girl's nose and chin. Even at this distance they seemed oddly familiar. Walking forward a pace he narrowed his eyes just as the girl stepped from grass into road, glancing to her right to check for oncoming traffic and giving Marty his first unobstructed view of her face.

Of course she looked fucking familiar.

The girl *was* Terri.

But what was she doing here? And dressed in that hat? She hated those hats. And he could have sworn she wasn't wearing that coat when she'd left the guest house this morning. He hadn't thought she'd even brought it with her. Why wasn't she in Liverpool? Had she ever left Blackpool at all? And what was this, then? Some kind of disguise?

Instinctively Marty yelled out her name, but a moment before he parted his lips an eighth wave had arrived at the mole; now it smacked back into the wave immediately following it and with a giant impact a huge jet of spray erupted into the air and over the rail. The jet drenched the two boys and even caught out the seagulls, and though it didn't quite reach to where Marty was standing the noise it made drowned out his cry. Fifty yards distant Terri had clearly heard nothing and carried on walking just as before, away from the cenotaph now and south along the landward side of the seafront, completely oblivious to the fact that she'd been spotted.

Her not hearing his shout gave Marty time to reflect and now he hatched a new plan. He wouldn't confront Terri right away: first he would follow her. He wanted to know what she was still doing here, why she had lied. Because she must have done. Why else would she be hurrying through Blackpool this way, when she was supposed to be sitting down to Sunday roast with Harvey and family in Liverpool? To Marty, the hapless possessor of a mind already twisted into melancholic self-pity by the events of the previous twenty-four hours, the implications were obvious. Terri was having an affair.

It would explain so much, he told himself as he darted between two cars and a tram in order to get behind his quarry: the excessively brittle behaviour, the lack of sympathy, the apparent glee at losing . . . And how fitting it was that as his career got flushed down the pan he should discover that his relationship was going the same way.

Strangely, Marty felt almost gleeful at this prospect of impending apocalypse. It woke him up, banished his hangover, brought him back to reality.

There was nothing like someone stealing your girlfriend to do that.

When he was within twenty yards of her he dropped out of his jog and matched her pace, heart racing, mind churning with various interpretations of the available facts. Terri was walking purposefully but seemed relaxed, not too intent. It wasn't at all the attitude of someone carrying out a deception, although he supposed that, whatever it was she was up to, she was hardly going to be skulking along like some character in a cartoon. Then again, she was heading in the direction of the Eldorado, so maybe all that had happened was the van had broken down (quite likely, the state it was in) and she'd had to get a bus back or something, borrowing Tanya's hat and jacket to ward off the rain. If there was an innocent explanation, Marty was already telling himself, then his following Terri would be funny, one big joke (though what kind, exactly, wasn't yet clear). And if no innocent explanation was to be had, well, then . . . well, his behaviour would be justified. Wouldn't it?

Alternative explanations for the strange situation forked out before him like the branches of a tree and, leaping between them like a monkey on speed, Marty felt awed by the infinite possibility of the world. It was just as he sometimes felt when trying to work out all the things that could possibly go wrong with a trick: like possibility was suffocating him, like he might drown. He wanted to stop asking questions, wait for the facts to speak for themselves. But he couldn't help himself: the questions kept coming, and with questions came answers which led to more questions . . . soon he was hardly paying attention to following Terri, his thoughts were so busy.

He was jolted back to the task in hand when his target turned sharply left, mounted a couple of steps and vanished. Caught off guard, he dodged into the recessed doorway of the pub he happened to be passing, tentatively peering out round the edge of the battered stonework to check that his girlfriend wasn't about to reappear from whatever building it was she'd gone into. When she didn't show he eased himself out of his hidey-hole and, unaccountably, looked up.

The knuckles of Blackpool Tower gripped the sky above his head – he'd been so preoccupied he hadn't even noticed. So that was where she'd gone.

The plot thickened.

There was no queue to get into the Tower but Marty had to pay a fiver for the privilege. Once he was past the oak entrance doors, however, it wasn't clear which way he needed to go next. A corridor walled with chipped oxtail-coloured tiles led not to a bank of lifts, as he'd imagined, but to a wide staircase that according to a floor schematic double-backed its way up through seven storeys' worth of leisure-tainment. Only after you'd negotiated that, apparently, were you allowed to ascend the tower. Terri could be anywhere.

For want of a better idea Marty climbed the stairs and began to search the first floor, planning on gradually working his way skywards. Even if the viewing station at the Tower's summit was the most likely spot for a clandestine romantic rendezvous, it made sense to check out the rest of the building as well. But the place was a labyrinth and the hundreds of kids swarming throughout, crying and screaming and busy with their own games and concerns, made it more disorientating still. Soon Marty was lost.

One minute he'd been in a relatively straightforward amusement arcade, the next he was groping his way along a darkened corridor lit only by giant fluorescent arrows painted on to the floor, a corridor which eventually opened out on to what appeared to be a simulacrum of the cargo deck of some giant interstellar cruiser walled with video screens ablaze with hurtling forms, the silhouettes of proto-teens jerking and swaying in front of them. Dark portals led off this main arena into two more rooms. On investigation these turned out to contain not Terri and her lover but, in the first instance, a bunch of young kids dressed in FuzzyFelt jumpsuits sticking themselves at a wall of luminous Velcro and, in the second, a collection of slightly older children competing furiously at a long bank of networked racing games.

Ascending a flight of stairs, Marty emerged inside a huge jungle gym, two storeys high and brilliantly lit. It was filled with dozens of disturbingly maggot-like children yelling and screaming as they clambered up and down fibreglass trees, swung along cat's cradles of rope ladders, dived into vats filled with coloured plastic balls or crawled in and out of the eyes of the giant extruded foam skull that was fixed high up on one of the timber-clad walls. Attendants dressed in khaki safari outfits stood idly by, gossiping and eyeing Marty warily for any signs of ambiguous intention.

With their eyes upon him he moved on: another doorway, another staircase; this time he ended up trackside in an indoor racing arena where two boys hurled go-karts around a tiny, waisted course, practising reverse steering and filling the air with blue fumes and vibration. But with the exception of the two drivers, the attendant and three boys huddled around a Sega Rally booth the room was empty. Skirting round the track, Marty exited through the door opposite in the expectation that it would lead to somewhere new.

It didn't. As though trapped in a giant game of snakes and ladders, he found himself back on the interstellar cargo deck. Annoyed now, his hangover coming back, he chose a portal he didn't remember seeing before and climbing a staircase emerged in a well-lit corridor decorated all in red, with a dado rail and framed black-and-white photographs of Victorian Blackpool screwed to the wall. This led in turn to a small vestibule that was home to the entrance to the lifts that ascended the tower.

There was a big queue here. The line of people zigzagged up and down the hall, guided towards the snapping metal doors by a complex series of barriers and trailing off out of the vestibule, along a corridor, round another corner and along a second corridor before it reached its end. Terri wasn't in it.

The flat, bovine look on the faces of those waiting suggested to Marty that they'd been standing in line far longer than he'd been in the building, meaning that either Terri was by some fluke already at the top or that wasn't her destination. Either way there didn't seem much point in hanging around to find out. He'd search the lower floors for ten minutes more and if he hadn't found her by then he'd leave and return to the Eldorado – via a decent pub. The confrontation could wait for later on.

The queue came to an end right before a red set of double doors, and pushing through them Marty stepped into a kind of low-ceilinged archipelago of junk food outlets, the channels between them choked with plastic chairs and tables. In one corner of the room – the 'mainland', he supposed – was a green dais which, apparently, was the parents' zone. Here they all were, at any rate, the parents, smoking fags and chatting over half-gallon vats of soft drinks while their kids were wreaking havoc up and down the blue linoleum waterways.

Tiring of his hunt, Marty felt like joining them; instead he blundered his way through the shredded ribbons of cigarette smoke and chip fat fumes that festooned the room. He was moving quickly now; his headache pounding, the flickering strip lights, the shouts of the children, the reek of frying meat and the jangle of manufactured pop streaming from the hidden loudspeakers almost overpowering him. He no longer cared if Terri saw him or not; he just wanted to find her or get out, whichever was the easiest. The building had started to feel like one great haunted house: the ribbons of smoke cobwebs catching in his hair; the pale round faces looming up around him those of curious ghouls; the waitresses at American Chicken a witches' coven; Pizza to Go! a murder scene.

On the far side of this personal house of wax was a doorway and Marty made for it, bursting through and hurrying up the short flight of steps beyond. Immediately – as if by magic, even – the music, images and smells were gone and he found himself standing in an ethereal corridor of light. For a moment he had the impression that he was falling forwards into nothingness; it was as though he'd stepped out on to a ledge with no building beyond it at all. In fact, he was standing at the rear of a steeply raked balcony while to his left a bank of windows revealed a sky in which the clouds had parted and the sun blazed through, bouncing its rays off the polished parquet underfoot.

The balcony served a giant and sumptuous ballroom almost as large as the Winter Gardens Opera House and even more opulently decorated (and in better nick). Stepping in among the raked rows of velvet-covered seats, Marty could see down to where – on the distant stage, easily fifty metres to his right – a white-suited man sat at an electric organ and pressed out an over-harmonised version of 'Nights in White Satin' for the benefit of the seven or eight elderly couples who were spinning gently, like clockwork toys, across the polished dance floor. The scene was so bizarre and unexpected that he felt almost as if he'd slipped through some kind of tear in the fabric of the universe and had fallen backwards in time.

Bemused, he sat down on the spring-loaded seat nearest him and rubbed his eyes, letting the mesmeric music wash over him while gathering his wits and allowing his nausea to recede. Then, after a minute or two of glorious blankness, he spotted her. She was sitting at a table in the shadow of the balcony opposite, still wearing that ridiculous hat and talking to a man.

A man. All those branching possibilities he'd explored earlier suddenly compacted themselves into a single, solid trunk. So. His suspicions had been correct. It was shocking, but calming too, in that way that reality can be when it confirms your deepest fears. He didn't recognise the man. He had a long black ponytail and pale skin. Could he be one of the other magicians from the conference? One of the Americans? It was possible. From this distance it was difficult to tell.

Suddenly he was hurtling down the spiral staircase that connected with the lower floor, one hand clipped to its polished oak balustrade, the other clenched into a fist. Despite the apparent determination in his movements it wasn't until he was crossing the wooden parquet, bright and pale as a caramel glaze, that he resolved to confront Terri and her lover. Not until she looked up directly at him, saw him approaching, then carried on her conversation without the barest vestige of surprise apparent on her face did he become absolutely positive that he would kill her and whoever it was she was with.

He reached the table, blood pounding, heat radiating off his face and stood there for a full five seconds before she deigned to look up at him.

'Yeah?' she said.

'What happened to Liverpool?' he exploded.

'Lost to Wimbledon 2–1. Where 'ave you been?'

'What? What the fuck . . . ?' he began to say. But reality had just slapped him for the third time that day. The girl's accent, the girl's voice. A local accent, a Blackpool accent. Not Terri's. Not Terri's at all.

The girl wasn't Terri.

'What the fuck are *you* on?' the girl demanded.

Her friend stood up. 'You got a problem, pal?' he said, poking Marty's shoulder with a finger as broad as his vowels.

The prod jerked Marty from his daze. 'Oh, God. Oh, shit – I am . . . I am *so* completely sorry. I really am. I can explain . . . I am such a total idiot.' Somewhat desperately he looked away, only to have to look back again. 'I thought you were someone else. No, honestly. I really did. I'll, er, I think I'll just leave. Sorry to have bothered you. No offence. Honest.'

But he couldn't do it. He couldn't leave. He couldn't tear his eyes away from the girl, not even when ponytail prodded him again.

'Are you gonna fuck off or what?' the man asked. There was silence. 'Nights in White Satin' must have ended because the dancers had stopped moving.

Marty had the feeling that people were beginning to stare. 'I'm sorry,' he said again, blinking stupidly. 'I'm really sorry. It's just that you're . . . you . . . you really look the spit of my girlfriend. The total spit. I thought you were her. I'm sorry. But it's weird. It really is.'

'Look, you southern twat . . .'

'Easy, Paul,' the girl told her friend. 'He's just made a mistake.'

Marty nodded eagerly. 'Honestly,' he said. 'Wait.' Digging in his pocket for his wallet he pulled out a photobooth picture of Terri and passed it across. The girl looked at it, raised her eyebrows, handed it to Paul.

'This isn't your girlfriend,' Paul announced. 'This is Jill Dando.'

'Be serious,' said the girl. She turned to Marty. 'I'm called Jill, too,' she told him. 'Paul's taking the piss. Everyone says I look like her. It's really annoying.' She took back the photograph, considered it again. 'What d'you think, Paul? Does she look like me?'

Paul shrugged, sat down in his chair. 'I s'pose so.'

Jill returned the picture to Marty, who slipped it back into his wallet.

'Look – would you like to meet her?' he asked suddenly. 'Terri, that is.'

'Why?'

'Well, it . . . see . . . it's . . . I'm a magician.'

'Up for the convention, were you?'

'Yes. Yeah. But we're booked at the Mississippi Showboat as well. Terri's my assistant, see. You know the Showboat?' Jill shook her head. She was a little heavier set than Terri, a bit more darkly complexioned, her eyes green instead of brown. But the resemblance was still almost hypnotic.

'I do,' grumped Paul, who seemed to have accepted that communication was going to take place whether he liked it or not. 'It's that place with all the Americana shit, i'n't it? Used to be an all right place a few years ago.'

'We've got a show tonight, nine o'clock. I'll leave your names at reception. If you can't make it later, don't worry – we're on all week. Just show up any night, ask for me. I'm Marty, by the way.'

'Oh – by the way,' Paul mimicked.

Jill told Marty to ignore him. She seemed cool, he thought. He suddenly wondered why he'd always disliked those ethnic hats so much – this one, at least, looked great on her.

'If you do come, hang about after the show. I'll buy you a drink.'

'Yeah. Yeah, all right. Maybe. I'll see.'

'Okay, then,' he said, turning to leave. 'And you know, sorry about the mix-up and everything.'

'That's fine. Don't worry about it.'

Paul spoke up. 'I'll let you off if you show us a trick,' he said kind of quietly. Marty stopped where he was, thought for a moment, scratched his nose. Now Paul had calmed down a bit he didn't seem that threatening any more. In fact, he even looked like a bit of a nerd.

'Well,' Marty mused, a magician again. 'I haven't got my cards on me. But maybe . . .' He started searching through his pockets, hoping he had some kind of prop or feke with him – he usually did. In the inside pocket of his duffle coat he got lucky – his fingers touched a ten-pence piece he'd drilled through a year or two before, when he was doing table magic at that Moathouse outside Bromley. He retrieved it, slipped it into a finger palm, brought his hand out and held it as if it were empty. 'Hm. I'm all out of hats and rabbits. But if you can lend me a cigarette and a ten-pence piece I can show you something, I think . . .'

The real Terri returned to Blackpool on schedule and while they shifted their gear across from the Winter Gardens to the Showboat Marty told her of his encounter. 'It's unbelievable, the resemblance,' he said as they waited for the lights on Topping Street, the first diners of the evening disappearing into the row of Italian restaurants on their right. 'It's uncanny. If I hadn't've known you were in Liverpool I'd've thought she was you. Apart from the hat, of course.'

'The hat?'

'Yeah, she was wearing one of those impy woollen ethnic rave hats. You know the ones. Like Tanya's got. She was a bit of a raver all round, I reckon. None of your taste.' Marty grinned, leaned over, kissed his girlfriend on the cheek.

But Terri's thoughts remained focused elsewhere. 'And you just ran into the two of them in Blackpool Tower?'

'Yeah. She was sitting there in the ballroom drinking tea with this guy.' Strangely, perhaps, Marty had decided not to acquaint Terri with the details of his stalking activities and his suspicions of infidelity.

'And what were you doing in the Tower?'

'Oh. You know. I was bored. Fancied a spot of tourism. So. You looking forward to meeting her?'

Terri swivelled her head round to face him, as if it were mounted on an axle, not a spine. Her cheeks were red, her pupils contracting. 'I'm going to meet her? When? Why?'

131

'I thought you might be interested. I don't know when exactly. I – I said she should come and check out the show.'

'I don't know that I want to meet her, Marty. I mean, what's she to me?'

'Well, she looks like you.'

'Princess Di looks like me,' Terri said, her voice locked tight with sarcasm, 'but I don't want to meet her either.'

'You already have,' Marty pointed out, somewhat unhelpfully.

'You know what I mean,' the girl snapped back.

Marty back-pedalled fast. 'No, seriously, come on, Terri darling, I wouldn't've asked her to come if I thought it'd upset you. And she probably won't show up in any case. I think she thought I was barking, coming up to her like that, saying she looked like my girlfriend. She probably thought I was trying to chat her up.'

'Maybe you were.'

'Don't be an arse. She was with her boyfriend, in any case.'

'And if she hadn't been?'

'Jesus. What're you like? It wouldn't've made any difference. You know that's not what I mean.'

'Do I?'

'Christ, Tel, come on. She's just someone who looks like you. Chill the fuck out, will you? Like I said, I doubt she'll even show.'

★

But Jill did show and that same evening, too. She probably wouldn't have bothered, but from the Monday she was back on nights and she mightn't have another opportunity to check out Marty's offer. Actually, it was a relief to be off the day shift; to her surprise it had proved to be the busier of the two, though nights did have the two hours either side of midnight when a nation's worth of pissed single men were rolling home and the lines all jammed and the girls' throats got so sore with talking they might as well have been kneeling in the bushes, sucking the customers off.

For those two hours they tended to be monosyllabic, gruff, brief. When they spoke it was orders, descriptions, put-downs, abuse; you knew when they'd cum because the phone went dead. After one you got less of those. After one it was more often blokes who were just lonely, who started off by trying to do the sex but then gave up, preferring straightforward talk. She always asked them for their names and often they gave them, first names at least, though probably sometimes they made them up. Sometimes they'd tell her what they did for a living, where they were (she always asked them where they were, it was part of her training, like asking for their age, which she had to by law). But what they did, that was generally volunteered. Though if they told her she was supposed to ask them about all about it – anything to keep them racking up the minutes. Half the time they'd want to go on about how their girlfriend had left them or whatever and then it was more like being a Samaritan, which is easy, comparatively, because then they do most of the talking.

On days, though, there were hardly any Samaritans. It was mostly sex. Yesterday she had had a Welsh plumber called Reece phoning on his mobile – he'd had a hands–free unit apparently, the latest thing, and he was just leaving Cardiff on the motorway and wanted to crack one off while he was weaving through the traffic. He'd asked her to imagine herself kneeling on the transit's central passenger seat, facing backwards, naked (naturally), arse in the air, one hand on the headrest to steady herself and the other hand on his leek while she lowered herself down on to the gearstick, its vibrations particularly wild on account of his white van being a Ford and that, and nigh on ten years old, and the gearbox being pretty fucked. (Har har. He laughed at that one all right, God it was just so fucking funny.)

After him she'd had that Scouser who called mid–afternoon at least once a week because, as one of the other girls suggested, that's when the schools got out and maybe he had a vantage point or something from where he got to watch the kids leave from the gates. Not a great deductive leap to make, considering how it was schoolgirl fantasy he always wanted; on that occasion he'd wanted her to play at being kept back in detention and locked up in the books cupboard, let out only on the condition that she dropped her pants, leaned over his desk and took a caning with a ruler before allowing him to fuck her in submissive gratitude.

All the girls (they called themselves girls even though most of them were mothers and several were well into their forties) had done him at least once or twice, even the ones who thought he was too sick the first time and termed the call. They'd got him tagged now as a local TV newsman who did the lunchtime news on local BBC, or that's what they reckoned, at least. Jill wasn't so sure but she had to admit the voice was pretty close.

After him she'd taken her break and gone out back to smoke half a spliff, watch the sunset for a bit, and when she'd come back in she'd got this wanker who wouldn't give her his name – or any name – just his initials which were, he said, NB (he missed out an O, she thought immediately). He'd told her how she was his little fuckbag and how he wanted her to slide her cunt right up to his nutbag while he sat in front of his computer screen and watched looping MPEGs of two Serbian girls getting passport stamps in the form of jism face masks from four semi-clad guards inside a Portakabin border post on some remote Schengen frontier. Jill hadn't got a clue what he was on about but she'd played along and made the appropriate sounds. He was a Londoner, though this didn't come as much of a surprise: she could tell that from the way the wishbone of self-importance twanged like a Jew's harp in his voice, even before he'd told her how he lived on some street called Westbourne Grove (which was apparently just up from some place called 'the 'Bello, you know, right near All Saints, as in the band?'. Like she gave a shit. 'Is that Kula Shaker you've got playing there?' she'd enquired, pretending to be turned on by how cool he was for being into that bunch of sad-fuck trusters while silently imagining the pleasure she'd get from sinking her teeth into the battered glans of his hand-chafed little prick, spitting whatever she'd bitten off on the floor and grinding it to a state well beyond the reach of reconstructive surgery with the high-grip injection-moulded sole of her made-in-China-in-sweatshop-conditions-not-unlike-the-ones-she's-currently-being-subjected-to right cross-trainer).

She really hated this job.

She hadn't slept with anyone since she'd been working at the call centre. It was like she'd frozen up down there. Not even frozen up. Gone numb. Though maybe it was the other way round, maybe the numbness was a result of everything she'd been through with Gavin, what'd allowed her to take work like this, the only work that had been going, pretty much. Either way, sex seemed nothing right now, not even practical, not even degrading. At best it felt like a weird, sick joke, a stupid game she'd grown out of like skipping or drinking snakebite or caring about the pop charts, and for a while it'd seemed like a sort of confirmation to mash it up like this, to turn it into words and sell them down the phone to strangers who'd boxed up their desires and locked them away in the small attic rooms of their minds like idiot children, feeding them on a diet of the filth she provided, filth that could be conveniently shoved through the one small ragged hole they'd left behind when they'd sealed up the door.

Though it had to be said that any such novelty had pretty soon worn off.

★

And so.

Gavin.

A couple of years previously, Jill'd been involved with a bloke who had hit her. He'd been older, a divorcee, with kids. They'd been at each other's throats all the time, there'd been all sorts of screaming matches and fights in public, and much worse behind the scenes. It'd only lasted six months, and it was Paul who'd both convinced her to get out of it and had faced Gavin down on her behalf, told him to stay the hell away from her or else he would personally kill him. Which was pretty brave of him considering that no one else'd had the guts to do it; all these supposed hard men she knew were apparently too afraid. But Gavin turned out not to have the balls for that. It was only women he was capable of beating up.

But even when it was over there was something about Gavin

that Jill missed. Not the violence. She'd hated it when he hit her, no doubt about that. But there'd been an excitement about it too, something perverse, something she couldn't even admit to herself, a thrill she'd got out of seeing how far she could push him, before his anger or rage or whatever it was took him over and turned him into this kind of heaving, spasming, terrifying man-machine. And there'd been more than a few times when he'd threatened to slap her or actually had slapped her in the middle of sex and she'd not only come but come monstrously, like a mountain had cleaved open inside her.

Her mother – as always, what was it with her mam; it was like she knew everything, that woman – had seen it for what it was and had told her she was being a bloody idiot, that she was doing nobody any favours hanging around with a man like that. And she'd been right – though Jill hadn't given her any thanks for telling her, not until later, not until it was over and she'd crawled back to her parents' place, face black and blue, a total wreck. Which was when Paul had stepped in.

The sanctuary she'd received from her mam had been different from what she'd been given by Paul. With Paul there'd been plenty of chat, buckets of tears, hours of discussion and attempts to explain, but at the end of it she'd known that he still didn't truly understand what it was all about, what it was about Gavin that had hooked her into him. With her mam there'd been plenty of tears too, but though the two of them had hardly spoken a word on the subject her mother had *known*, there was no doubt about it. Which made Jill wonder if hers was a weakness that could be somehow inherited – an idea that for some reason scared her even more.

Either way, she'd not been able to bring herself to reveal herself to her mother, not through words, anyway. It would've been the same as admitting the perversity, right? And she couldn't do that. Like now, with the job. She'd lay good money that her mam had some idea of what she was doing, but Jill would never, ever tell her about it. It'd be way too much shame actually to say the words. When she'd got the position she'd told her it was a helpline job and left it at that.

Anyway, if Mam knew, she wouldn't've said anything. That wasn't how she worked. She was more subtle than that, was Jill's mam. She had the guts – and the patience – to let her kids make their own mistakes. And Jill was pretty sure she was just pleased, for the time being, that she'd stopped seeing Gavin and had come back to live at home.

But living at home had its pluses and minuses. It had been okay for a while but at twenty-three she was too old for it really, especially with the kids still not having left school. The truth was it was beginning to drive her nuts.

Take Friday, a fairly typical day. By the time she gets home from the centre the others have all had their tea, but Mam's kept back a portion for her to heat through in the microwave. She shows it to her in the kitchen and asks her how work went, and Jill says 'same as usual' because it's easier than making something up. Then, reaching in the fridge for her Diet Coke, she finds it's vanished, Mandy or Neil must have taken it and to prevent any further questions about her day, which she's not up to parrying, she says, 'Aw, Mam, they've taken my last can.'

'The little beggars,' says her mother, who's been folding laundry, 'as if I haven't bloody told them time enough.' Setting her face into one of her determined looks she finishes her folding, then puts the information down atop the short stack of sheets and starchy underwear and carries the whole lot out of the kitchen door and up the stairs. As Jill turns and sets the microwave she can hear her mother calling, voice slicing through the walls. 'Mandy!' she yells. 'Have you been at yer sister's colas again? And turn that ruddy music down!'

'No, Mam!' trills Mandy softly, like butter wouldn't melt, Jill knowing even from this distance that she's lying but her mother – duh – believing her and yelling 'Neil! Neil!' until her brother's grunt thumps through the house, washboard dull: 'Wha?'

The question is repeated. 'No, I ain't!' Neil shouts, totally indignant. 'It were Mandy.'

'No, it weren't,' Mandy screams back straight away. Lying little bitch, thinks Jill – as does her mum, but she knows how many days of sulking teenage grief she's in for if she pursues the matter with her younger daughter. 'Neil!' she says, finding a solution. 'Run down the corner and get some colas for your sister.'

'Aw, Ma!' His voice betrays a feeling of total injustice and incomprehension, as if he'd been asked to walk to Edinburgh and back.

'*It's all right, Ma!*' Jill shouts up, in a hopeless attempt to stop the process she's set in motion. 'He doesn't have to.' But those upstairs are into their own thing now and even though she's the victim her opinion's no longer relevant.

The voices bounce around the house for another minute or two until they begin to impinge upon the patriarch's enjoyment of *A Question of Sport*.

'Neil!' Boom. Plaster flakes fall from the ceilings. Door jambs vibrate. 'Do what yer mother tells ya!'

Silence. End of problem. Neil troops out, slamming the door behind him, swings into the kitchen twelve minutes later with Jill's can, though she's eaten her dinner by now and doesn't really want it, and it's full-sugar anyway and so no good. She makes a cup of tea instead and reads through the *Mirror*. Mam comes in and mutters around her for a while, exasperated, makes tea for herself and the old man, then goes off to join him in the front room, pot and mugs rattling on a tray. A B&H is trapped between her fingers, matching streamers of cigarette smoke and steam trail over both her shoulders. The house is quiet again.

Jill takes the phone from its holster on the wall and calls Mags, but it's engaged so she does the crossword, a doddle, knocks it off in fifteen minutes, then switches on the portable that sits, stained with cooking fumes, atop the microwave atop the fridge adjacent to the back door through which Marvin the cat – fur and one eye dirty white, the latter from an ancient fight, and one ear ragged from a more recent contretemps – now comes skulking in. Leaping straight up on to the table, he inspects Jill's empty plate. The TV fizzes on and it's the news; an Internet paedophile ring's been busted and later, on *Newsnight*, there's a special feature on the New Economy. Jill changes channels: a *Dad's Army* rerun; a straight-to-video movie on ITV; an episode of *Friends*; a documentary on teenage prostitution on the brand-new Channel 5. She watches ten minutes of Chandler agonising over whether to get a circumcision in order that some stuck-up bint he's infatuated with will sleep with him, before killing it and going upstairs to run herself a bath.

An hour later she comes back down, swathed in a worn towelling robe, to tell the olds she's going to bed. She sticks her head round the door: Dad's passed out in his armchair, can of McEwans balanced on his belly, grey jogging pants that have never been persuaded past an amble on his legs and small sounds grating out of his nose; Mam's on the sofa flipping through a Kays catalogue and demolishing a carton of Quality Street, building a petrol pool of wrappers beside her on the maroon velour. In the corner *Newsnight* flickers, Paxman whining on about the economic viability of e-commerce business models. Tomorrow, Jill decides, she's gonna go into Blackpool, see Sonya and Paul.

So that was Friday and then last night she'd been out on the razz with Mags and Sonya, and this afternoon in the Tower ballroom she'd had tea with Paul – the ballroom long being a favourite rendezvous because the doorman was Paul's uncle, meaning both that they didn't have to pay and the place was guaranteed Gavin-free. Then that freak Marty had turned up.

Paul disapproved, of course, but he would. That's what mates were for. But she couldn't go on like she was going on and maybe this was her chance, at last, to get the fuck out of Morecambe. She reckoned it had to be worth at least a look. And even Paul had to admit to liking the thing Marty did with the cigarette and coin.

So late that late-February afternoon Jill Kingcraig found herself killing time in Blackpool beneath a psychedelic sky, waiting for Marty's show to start. Being on days, she'd seen more of these sunsets lately, catching them during spliff breaks in the car park of the call centre. But this one was really spectacular; so much so that it was keeping her pinned down on the promenade, holding off from going to cadge a cup of tea over at Sonya's place in Stanley Park.

Really spectacular. Orange and vast. That was one of the things she'd always loved about living up here, the vastness of the skies. Like America, almost, or so she imagined, the sunset pulling her thoughts north-west past Iceland, past Greenland, up to Canada and Alaska and the frozen diadem of the globe, this sunset tinged tangerine in anticipation of summer, these purple clouds standing crude and prideful as cardboard cut-outs in a child's puppet theatre. These clouds parading west just like her thoughts, where they too formed a mass large enough to envelop the whole world.

★

Marty caught sight of Jill in the midst of sawing Tel in two. She was sitting at a table to the left of the stage, on her own, and he didn't recognise her at first: the hat was gone and chestnut-coloured hair of a much darker hue than Terri's fell down around her shoulders, masking the strange familiarity of her face. He forced himself to look away, to concentrate on the task in hand, but just knowing she was there was enough to strip away the security provided by the music and the footlights. He felt strangely naked, embarrassed even. And her sitting there – though he didn't know her, perhaps because he didn't know her – made him see his show for what it was: the glib and hackneyed arrangement of defunct elements, designed not to entertain but to self-promote.

He saw his show, he saw himself. The doubts that had been festering away inside him ever since that Baltic cruise now broke out and shrieked at him, sucking away his concentration. Suddenly, impossibly, there was this girl, and with her for the first time for a long time there was a glimmer . . . and the doubts, they didn't like it. They wanted to stay where it was warm.

'Pull the bloody blade out, dickhead,' Terri hissed through clenched teeth, her smiling head protruding neck-up from its box. Marty had faltered, forgotten where he was in the sequence of events, stared into empty space for long enough to realise there was something wrong. 'So where were you tonight?' she continued once they came off stage, kicking off her heels. 'I nearly got a flipping cramp you left me sitting in that box so long.'

'Sorry,' Marty said. He was apologising a lot today. 'I think all the voddie I drank last night's done for my brain.'

'Well, come on, then, help me get out of this costume.'

'Yeah, yeah, in a moment. I've just got to pee.'

'Oh, Ma-arty!' Terri whined, stamping her little stockinged foot.

Marty slipped out of the Green Room and tunnelled along the passageway, breeze blocks flicking past his eyes, feet oblivious to the stage set histories scrawled across the cold concrete floor in musky squirts of paint. He reached the toilets and carried straight on by, rounding the corner and coming up behind the door that let out on to reception. Leaning through it he signalled to the young woman behind the desk. 'Hey, Sarah, do me a favour, will you? Can you get Brian to send a glass of champagne over to that girl with the long brown hair? Tell her that it's compliments of me and I'll be out to see her in about fifteen minutes. Thanks. You're a star.' Then he retraced his steps to take a piss and work out how he was going to handle Terri.

★

The Mississippi Showboat was in fact a glorified hotel bar whose most recent owner had decided to transform it – with the help of a collection of hand-painted signs, wood-effect room partitions, louvred swing doors, brown mahogany-finish spindle-back bar chairs, some locally mass-produced American Civil War memorabilia and the set of Confederate flag waistcoats that the bar staff were now obliged to wear – into an approximation of what he imagined the interior of a nineteenth-century Mississippi paddle steamer might have looked like.

To make the verisimilitude complete – or rather to make absolutely sure it brought in the punters (which was after all the object of the exercise) – he'd added a resident dance troupe. The Mississippi Showgirls he'd named them, predictably enough, and just as predictably he'd had them dressed in co-ordinated outfits of silver Lycra micro-bikinis, silver-sprayed cotton canvas ten-gallon hats, white waistcoats with long leather fringes, silver snakeskin high-leg platform boots with turned-down upper cuffs and rhinestone studding, and open-buttock chaps in silverised PVC. In the wake of Martin Mystery's Mysteries the showgirls had occupied the stage, to somewhat warmer applause.

Despite his growing sense that it was the showgirls who were the main event of these evenings, the magic mere padding, Marty didn't have too much objection to sharing the hardly lavish backstage facilities with the dance troupe, two of whom were former lap dancers and not exactly shy about their bodies. But Terri had made no secret of the fact that she held the other women in low regard. She'd set up her mirror in the corner of the room and, after making it clear that this was her space and it was not to be invaded, had angled the glass so that she could simultaneously put on her make-up and monitor Marty's ogling. She sat there now, blotting her cheeks with cleanser and cottonwool, while she determined her reaction to the news Marty'd just given her: that this girl he'd run across, the one who looked just like her, had turned up after all and was sitting in the audience waiting to meet them both.

Terri wasn't stupid. She wasn't unaware that of late things hadn't been going exactly according to plan. She'd been sold on Marty's dreams as much as he had been himself and they were largely what had kept her with him. But bouncing out of disintegrating sword baskets in second-tier venues in out-of-season Blackpool was not her idea of glamour. The way she reckoned it there weren't too many twists and turns in store for the two of them before the end of the road loomed into view, especially not if Marty carried on behaving like he'd been behaving recently: sullen and sulky and silent, and increasingly remiss in his attentions towards her, both off stage and on. To her way of thinking he hadn't been polishing his girl machine – and the girl machine was not at all pleased.

And now this other woman. Terri had a pretty good idea what

her boy had in mind. No, not that – well, she bloody well hoped not that, though she wouldn't put it past him. So not that. The other. She'd give it a chance, she decided, she'd give it just one chance. But if it didn't work out she wasn't going to be in any mood for messing around. That's how it was with Terri: she'd suck it and see, but once she'd made up her mind, wild horses couldn't shift her. As Marty well knew.

By the time she'd got rid of her stage make-up and put on her regular face – this girl might look *like* her, but she didn't want to run any risk of her looking *better* – the showgirls had finished the first segment of their stint and were filing back into the tiny dressing room.

Much to everyone's relief Terri soon announced that she was ready, and taking Marty by the arm she led him down the concrete corridor, out into reception and back into the bar where Jill was sitting alone, drinking a pint, her complimentary glass of champagne standing untouched.

'Jill! You came!' Marty chimed, taking her hand. 'Jill, this is Terri, Terri, Jill.' The two women regarded one another cautiously.

'I don't really know why I'm here,' Jill began, trying to avoid looking at Terri's face. 'I feel pretty stupid.'

'Oh, don't,' Terri said, figuring attack was the best form of defence. 'It's all Marty's doing, as usual. He's the one with all the silly ideas. Go on, Marty, go get us a drink. I'll have a VAT, please. Jill – what are you having?' She looked at the table, confused by the two different glasses.

'Oh. Lager. Thanks. I don't really drink champagne.'

Pursing her lips, Terri glanced up at her boyfriend and sussed the little white lie. Deep within the psychic rope that held their relationship together, another fibre quietly snapped.

'Well, there you go. That's Marty for you. Always making assumptions instead of letting you decide for yourself what it is you might like.' She released a fluttery little laugh and waved the magician away. 'Go on, then. Drinks!'

Somewhat disconsolate at having already been outmanoeuvred

by his girlfriend and worried by what might be occurring in his absence, Marty sloped off to the bar. By the time he returned the girls were chatting to one other amiably enough, Terri explaining to Jill something about one of the illusions they'd performed.

Taking a seat, Marty smiled broadly at Jill. 'So,' he said. 'I'm surprised. I didn't think you'd come.'

She looked back at him, her gaze hard, slightly hostile. 'I nearly didn't. But I've got to be back in Morecambe by tomorrow. And I thought if I didn't now I never would. Anyway, I've never met any magicians before.'

'Back at work?' asked Terri sympathetically.

'Signing on.'

'Oh. Right. Of course. Not too many jobs around here, I suppose.'

'Not at this time of year. Not in Morecambe, anyway.'

'We've never been to Morecambe, have we, Tel?'

'Don't bother.'

'That bad?'

'Washed up and forgotten, that's all.' Jill reached into her bag, pulled out a pack of cigarettes and lit one. 'Want one?' Terri and Marty shook their heads. The whole situation seemed suddenly extremely odd. 'He showed me this thing,' Jill continued, sensing the tension, 'with a cigarette. And a coin. Show us again.'

This caught Marty out. 'What? Now? I don't have it on me.'

'I've got a cigarette. Here.'

'No – but it's the coin I need.'

'I've got a coin, too. I do have money, you know.'

Marty laughed uneasily. 'You don't understand. It's a special coin.' Was she stupid? Surely she'd realised that?

'Oh,' she said. 'So it's a trick?' She dragged on her fag. 'Thought so.' The couple exchanged a couple-type look.

'How old are you, Jill?' Terri asked.

'Twenty-three. Why?'

'No reason. It's just that you look older, that's all.' She blushed. 'Oh, I'm sorry – I didn't mean . . .'

But Jill didn't seem to care what Terri meant.

'So what was your last job, then?' Marty asked, trying to move things along.

'So what is this? An interview?'

Composing himself, the magician fixed her with his eye, just like Harry had taught him to do all those years ago. 'Maybe,' he said.

Jill returned the stare, but not quite as rigidly as she'd hoped. So, he *was* offering her a job. After she'd thought about this for a moment she looked away and answered him. 'Fatty's. Fatty Arbuckle's.'

'Oh, yeah? Here in Blackpool?'

'No – in Morecambe. In the zone.'

'The zone?'

'You know. Bowling alley, multiplex, Taco Bell, video arcade, car park big as the town. The zone.'

Marty had already noticed that he wasn't the only one playing games with his eyes. The girls were at it too. They'd both been looking at him a disproportionate amount and he realised now that this wasn't because of some natural authority of his but because they so wanted to find out whether they looked alike that they were embarrassed actually to do it. He wondered how they'd managed to get any conversation going at all while he'd been at the bar, sneaking glances at each other all the time like this.

He leaned back in his chair in order to get both girls inside his visual field at once. He hadn't been mistaken. It was as if someone were holding up a mirror to Terri – a tarnished and discoloured one, perhaps, but a mirror all the same. It was captivating. The only fundamental difference was in their complexions. Close up, Jill's grainy and visibly pored epidermis, slightly oaky in colour, contrasted strongly with Terri's soft porcelain sheen. But a little foundation would cure that. Jill's features were in fact a little finer, Marty thought, her skull a tad more elegant, like the bones in her animated hands. But that wouldn't show. He might see it, but an audience wouldn't notice.

'So what was your job?' As she spoke Terri looked down into her drink, unnerved by her boyfriend's intensity.

145

'Waitress,' Jill replied, throwing a glance across at her.

'Why d'you leave?'

'I got the sack.'

'How come?' Terri sounded concerned, but Marty wondered if the concern was actually genuine or was merely an excuse to look Jill full in the face, which is what she now did.

'Because I kept telling customers about who Fatty Arbuckle really was.'

'You mean he was a real person? I thought the name was made up.'

In revenge for the glance Terri and Marty had exchanged when she'd asked about the cigarette and coin trick, Jill affected incredulity. 'He was this fat American comic back in the 1920s,' she said coldly, her matter-of-factness her excuse to look at Terri full on. 'He had this party and got drunk and raped this actress with a bottle, and then, when the bottle broke and cut her all up inside, he wouldn't let her be taken to hospital in case there was a scandal. But the broken glass had cut into her bladder and she had all this massive internal bleeding and she died. At the inquest he got his lawyers to bring up all this stuff about how she'd had five abortions so the jury would think she was a slag and that. It was fucking sick. And he got away with it. And now there's this restaurant. The only reason I got a job there was so I could tell all the customers. I lasted a week.'

Terri looked like she'd bitten into an apple and found half a maggot. 'Ugh. How horrible.' She looked across to Marty for support. 'I didn't know that. I'll *never* eat there again, not now.' Jill shrugged like she couldn't have cared less and started playing with her pack of cigarettes.

'So why didn't your boyfriend come with you? What's his name? Paul?' Marty asked, changing the subject.

'Oh, he's not my boyfriend. He's just a good mate.'

Marty's eyebrows flicked upwards of their own accord, that being good and relevant news to some part of him. He pointed to the logo machine-embroidered on to the upper left panel of Jill's padded jacket which, though it was warm inside the bar, she still wore. It combined a vertical red P with a perspectively flat S in yellow, blue and green. 'PlayStation?'

Jill nodded. 'They ran a championship here in the summer. Part of the promotion for the new ride they're building. I won this at Tekken.'

'What's Tekken?' Terri asked, mystified.

'Fighting game.' This time the incredulity was more masked, the look less direct.

'Oh.'

Here the conversation stalled.

'Are you gonna get to the point?' Jill asked Marty finally. 'I've got a bus to catch.' This was another lie – she was going to stay at Sonya's. But what the hell.

By way of an answer Marty snapped forward in his chair, reached into his pocket and pulled out two red silk squares, which he shook out and handed to the girls.

'What d'you expect us to do with these?' Terri demanded. She'd been getting impatient too. What was Marty going to do? Show them a magic trick?

'Could you put them on?'

'Put them on?'

'Yeah. You know, Spanish-style.' He made a motion with his hands by way of illustration. 'Please. Just for a second. Humour me.' Exchanging their first real bonding glance – the solidarity of female common sense in the face of the idiocy of men – Jill and Terri folded the scarves into triangles and tied them round their heads, consulting each other to check they were in position.

'Okay. Perfect,' Marty said when they were done. 'Now. Come with me. No – you can leave your bag. We're going over this way. Just for a moment.'

He led the two women to a large decorated mirror inscribed with the name of the bar, built into one of the partitions that divided the room into its various booths and areas. Asking them both to close their eyes, he arranged them before it, side by side, positioning himself behind and between them. 'You can open your eyes now,' he told them when he was done, placing his hands on their outer shoulders as he said it and making of the revealed reflection a perfect little tableau.

Terri and Jill looked at themselves, at each other. With the hair out of the way and the difference in their complexions diminished by the muted lighting, Marty's point was immediately clear. Jill had a mole on her cheek where Terri had none, and Jill's eyes were brown while Terri's were quite green. But after that, it was just character and expression.

They could have been twins.

Looking at the two of them, Marty started to dream.

★

Once they were all back, sitting down round the table, Marty put on his most humble face and addressed the two girls haltingly, trying to sound as modest and sensitive as he could.

'I know this is sort of jumping the gun a bit,' he began, 'and I know I haven't discussed it with you, hon, but . . . well, you see, from the moment I saw Jill here in that ballroom the other day – I mean from the moment I realised it was her and not you – well from then on, right, I had this realisation.' He looked from Terri to Jill and back to Terri again, trying to guess the girls' thoughts from their eyes. It wasn't easy. 'Okay, well . . . the point is, Terri and me, right now, we're just another magic act.' Terri opened her mouth to protest but Marty held up his hand to her and simultaneously lowered his eyes in an unintentionally parodic show of self-effacement. 'No, no, come on, we might as well accept it. Maybe we've got talent, fine, but nothing marks us out from the rest. Not really. We do the same moves, the same stunts, have the same gimmicks as everyone else. We've got nothing special. We're tired, old hat. Whatever we do everyone's already seen a thousand times before. And I don't think it's us particularly,' he added. 'It's the whole scene. Harvey and Tanya, all the acts at the convention last night. Even the Power of Light. They're all the same, which is why those crappy comedy acts always win prizes – at least there's something there you haven't seen before, a fresh joke, or something. It can't be the gimmicks, cos everything that can be done with a girl and a box has already been done. So it must be the laughs.' Marty paused here and took a sip of his drink, carefully gauging the timing of his punchline. 'But the thing is, right, everything that uses *two* girls and a box *hasn't* been done. Especially if those two girls look the same. If you get my drift.'

Jill did, he could tell by the way she lowered her eyes and reached for a cigarette. Terri he couldn't read and it was her agreement he needed the most.

'Terri?'

'Of course I do, you prat,' she snapped. 'It doesn't take a flipping genius to work it out. And you're totally right. I just don't understand why you didn't tell me before.' Marty reddened. 'What did you think, that I was going to be too high and mighty to work with another girl? Ruddy hell. Anyway, it's not me you should be asking. It's Jill. What d'you reckon, Jill? How d'you fancy joining a clapped-out magic act, trying to help turn it into something halfway decent?'

Jill laughed. 'You two are really something, you know that? Christ.' She lit her fag, pulled on her drink, let the two of them sweat it out for a moment or two while she pondered. First there was Terri; Jill thought her brittle, manufactured, severe, the kind of woman you saw in the lobby of the Imperial or the Metropole attached to some corporate training course. She disliked her on instinct, didn't trust her, thought she was probably self-centred, stupid, uptight, spoilt, a prick-tease. Well, maybe not stupid, but only clever in a kind of grasping, devious way. Like when she laughed – when she laughed it wasn't humour, it was performance, laughter from the head rather than the heart. Clever but not that clever. On the other hand there was her face and it counted for a lot. Ever since they'd sat down at the same table the two of them had been sneaking looks at each other, and though at first she'd only seen all the surface stuff, the different make-up, hair and eyes, after a while Jill had begun to realise that Marty was absolutely right.

And what of Marty? If Terri was the prick-tease he was most

definitely the prick. His vanity was impossible to miss, this magician with his clean suit and his careful hair, and his spindly wrists, and his eyes blank and blue as computer monitors. He was like something inserted into the world rather than grown up in it. But he had something, too. He was definitely a twat, that much was obvious, but it was also clear that he had both brains and talent. There was something captivating about his face, maybe to do with the way that little white flick of grey hair of his counterpointed the strange intensity of his eyes. And she had to admit that he had a certain elegance on stage, that both of them had, a fluidity and economy of movement that she couldn't help but admire. God only knew what she'd be letting herself in for, getting involved with these two manikins. But it couldn't be worse than carrying on at the call centre.

She had her vain streak, too, did Jill. Though she preferred to let it peek out from beneath her hats and heavy clothes instead of parading it around as Terri did, it didn't mean it didn't exist. And that part of her was intrigued with the idea of having a twin. Some time or other, everybody's wondered what it would be like to have another version of themselves to contend with. The world would be such a different place if there were two of you. Maybe it would be worse, maybe it would be better. What it wouldn't be was so dull.

She replaced her pint, doffed her ash, put on a thoughtful face and smoked in silence for another thirty seconds. 'Yeah, all right. I'll do it. Like, what have I got to lose?'

'Wow,' said Marty, amazed despite himself – reality didn't often conform so closely to his plans. Now it was doing so, his first thought was not to trust it. 'You, er, you don't have to give us an answer right away, you know. Go back home to Morecambe for a day or two if you like; think it over.'

'Don't need to. I've already made up my mind. Assuming you're gonna pay me for my time, that is. I mean, I'm not doing this for the sake of my health.'

In the weeks that followed the earth moved a little further round the sun and the mild winter turned the corner into what promised to be an early spring. Greater London basked beneath lilac Andrex skies festooned about their horizons with toilet paper clouds in peach and mauve. Motorbikes emerged from garages and people left their overcoats at home, and groups of workers clad in distinctive orange vests laid fibre-optic cable in the roads. The odd daffodil appeared and even a plucky little crocus or two, and the carefully positioned bulbs nestling just beneath the surface of the town hall's Royal Wedding tribute bed began to nudge their way towards the sherbet light. Beckenham's trees started to bud and squirrels scampered to and fro along their branches. Schoolchildren were seen to swing their bags and whistle. People smiled and nodded to strangers in the street. Cars gave way at junctions. Playing Germany in a qualifier, England won.

Just as all this new life was at its most vulnerable and tender the weather turned, winter having decided it wasn't quite done yet after all. Unseasonally cold winds blew down from the north and lacquered the buildings, gardens, streets with a miserable taint of sleet and ice. Kids pulled spray-cans from their backpacks and set light to drunks. Following an incident in Luxembourg, football fans were banned from travelling abroad. Vicious frosts burned any green and hopeful swellings, and killed fully half of all young plants. Pundits explained that the Northern Atlantic conveyor was close to being severed and the planet's stable, temperate climate in danger of disappearing for good.

In the world of Marty, Jill and Terri all this passed almost entirely without comment. Safely installed in Marty's father's house, with the central heating on full blast, the three of them were far too occupied in putting together their new act to worry themselves with world affairs. It was, after all, an act, Marty was convinced, which would eclipse everything he'd so far done and quite possibly make him famous. Beside this, all else was of secondary importance.

Jill arrived with her precious PlayStation in tow along with a suitcase full of clothes, a backpack crammed with CDs and games, a massive lump of soap-bar hash and a penchant for playing the National Lottery. She'd wanted a way out of Morecambe and here it was, though she wished it weren't such a weird one. Magic was something she'd never given a second thought to in her entire life; it just wasn't on her map. Beyond vague memories of children's parties she'd attended as a kid, where strange child-molester types had stood behind trestle tables draped with red crêpe paper and produced dazed-looking rabbits out of moth-eaten top hats, if it crossed her mind at all it was as something that belonged to old Blackpool, sixties Blackpool, Blackpool before it had evolved into the teen haunt of nightclub, bar and Pleasure Beach that she now knew it as.

It wasn't just the magic. As she sat in her seat in the smoking carriage, dividing her time between a puzzle book and a packet of twenty Marlboro Lights, the shattered brick and concrete ruins of Stoke-on-Trent and Wolverhampton reluctantly giving way beside her to the strict pastoral of the Cotswolds, Jill realised that although she'd barely been beyond Birmingham before she never in her whole life had one good thing to say about southerners and the south. Wine bars, cappuccino outlets, Britpop, Arsenal and Chelsea supporters, anybody with a PDA, the Major government, people who worked in TV or the media, New Labour, anyone who wore a suit or carried an umbrella: all these were on her hate list. On the one hand she'd wanted out and on the other she had no love for the place where she was headed. Before she'd even got on the train she already felt uncomfortable and trapped.

But there was another reason she felt that way, one that was pictured for her right there in the window as plainly as the passing landscape, though only every time the train went into a tunnel. The fact was, Marty and Terri only wanted her for how she *looked*, not because of what she could do or the kind of person that she was, and Jill couldn't help but find this depressing. It was Gavin, again. The first thing he had asked her when he'd come up to her the night they'd met in Yates's Wine Lodge, the big one on the sea front that looks like something from *Miami Vice*, was if anyone had ever told her she looked just like Jill Dando. Up till that point no one had, and for some unknown reason she'd found it flattering – though to be fair she hadn't been aware at that point that Gavin was a total freak and pervert who wanted revenge on every unattainable woman he saw on television. But she never heard the end of it, after that. Half the reason she'd got so into the Lottery was because she'd been trying to convince people she looked less like Dando and more like Anthea Turner, though things had been really bad around that time, at their lowest ebb, he'd been beating her almost daily then and she'd been mad enough to think that something as idiotic as that might somehow save her. It was a phase that hadn't survived the move back to her parents, though the minor gambling addiction she'd developed in the process hadn't proved quite so easy to shake.

And here again her fate was being decided by her face – which wasn't really, except for these stupid resemblances, a particularly special one. The way Jill saw it she just looked . . . well, *normal*. Oh well. She'd give it a shot. If things got out of hand she had enough hash with her to spend at least a fortnight permanently stoned.

Make that a month. Half the hash she intended as a goodwill gift for her new colleagues, but when she offered it to Marty he recoiled in shock, told her it was part of his philosophy that under no circumstances did he ever do drugs – his body was his tool or temple or some such crap. He insisted that she only smoke it when his dad was out and then right down the bottom of the garden, behind the shed, so the neighbours couldn't see.

So Jill had offered it to Terri instead, but she disapproved as well. She'd tried spliff once or twice, she said, but it always made her feel sick and giddy. As for anything like E . . . they'd been clubbing once with Harv and Tan when the two of them had been on one (or, in Harv's case, on three), and the way their faces had become (white, bloodless, sheeny, eyes varnished and boiled, pupils bucket-wide), and how they'd ground their jaws (like cows chewing the cud), and the way they'd talked incessantly while making hardly any sense . . . well, Terri didn't like it much; they'd looked like aliens and it had scared her. The worst thing had been Tan spending the best part of an hour explaining to her (in between Harv's giving her repeated sweat-drenched hugs) how though she did look like Princess Diana that was really okay. Terri shuddered at the memory and Jill laughed. 'Don't worry,' she said, 'I completely sympathise.'

That sympathy was just the spark the two girls needed to help them get along. Soon, aside from work and the mammoth Tomb Raider sessions that Jill conducted stoned and solo in her room, they were spending nearly all their time together: watching TV, making shopping trips into the city, going to Guildford to visit Terri's mum. And every evening, before he went to sleep, Marty would get to hear from his girlfriend what she thought of Jill, what Jill had said that day, how cool Jill was.

What worried Marty about all this was that by far the favourite of the two girls' shared activities was making fun of him. He'd envisaged various problems that might have been entailed by bringing Jill on board, but that had not been one of them. For some unaccountable reason she seemed to see him as needing to be taken down a peg or two and Terri appeared more than eager to help her out. Once a grace period of two or three days had passed and Jill had settled in, a constant stream of what Marty regarded as jibes and asides began in response to almost everything he said and did. He couldn't ask Terri to make him a cup of coffee without Jill instructing her to tell him to fix it for himself, he couldn't sit down in front of the television without her making some comment on whatever it was he happened to be watching, he couldn't listen to his Elton John CDs without her feigning vomiting and running from the room.

Marty tried his best to ignore it. After all, although there was something of a cumulative effect, no single incident was particularly offensive in itself and he did pride himself on his ability to laugh at himself – well, within reason, anyway.

He put it down to nerves about the new situation; it couldn't be easy for Jill, he told himself, moving in with two complete strangers like this. And the problem wasn't necessarily her attitude, per se. It was that her attitude was beginning to rub off on Terri. Hearing Jill discourse on the subject, now when Marty asked her to make him a cup of coffee Terri just laughed – *laughed* – at him; told to him to make it himself and get her one too while he was at it. Or with the TV – usually he and Terri watched the same kind of thing but now she wouldn't let him watch what he wanted, insisting instead on sitting through all these crappy programmes she'd never normally be interested in, ganging up on him with Jill if he tried to complain.

Marty decided he just had to ride it out. Being the eldest and the boss, he told himself, he had to expect the two of them to tease him a little bit. If it was necessary to let them bond, then so be it. But it was extremely irritating, nonetheless.

★

Since the girls didn't seem to be managing to do it for themselves, at some point, Marty knew, he was going to have to broach the tricky subject of which one of them was going to have to alter her appearance to look more like the other. But how to do this without causing offence, that was the question. For days he turned the matter over and over in his mind, until he'd worked himself up into such a state that his inner turmoil became outwardly apparent.

'What's the matter, Marty? Something on your mind?' Terri eventually asked him.

'Don't mind him. He can't decide how many stars to sew on to his cape,' was Jill's immediate comment.

'No – it's not that. It's that new wand he wants. He doesn't know if he should get it in ebony or walnut,' Terri laughed.

'*I know* what it is. He wants us to star in Martin Mystery's Naked Mysteries and can't work out how to pop the question.'

'Yeah, yeah, very fucking funny,' Marty grumped, reddening slightly at the last suggestion, which had, in fact, crossed his mind on more than one occasion, usually last thing at night, around the time Terri undressed, climbed into bed beside him and started to relate the events of her day. But still he held back from beginning the discussion.

The problem was he didn't want there to be any *discussion* about it. He wanted Jill to change to look more like Terri. He wanted to have two Terris working for him. Why? Because the idea turned him on, simple as that. And this, of course, was the very thing he felt he could not admit.

A way round the difficulty was what he sought, a different but utterly plausible explanation. Finally, late one night, unable to sleep, he remembered something Harv had said to him in Blackpool: that he should make more of the fact that Terri looked like Princess Di and somehow work that into the act.

Pleased at finally having punctured the problem, Marty quickly fell asleep, only to awake the next morning faced with two brand-new difficulties. In the first place there was the fact that ever since Tanya had given her that E-fuelled earful on the subject a year or two earlier, Terri had been very touchy about the whole resemblance to Princess Di thing and had actually started to deny it (pointlessly, to Marty's way of thinking, but that was girls for you). Secondly, even were that hurdle to be gracefully overcome, Marty realised he would immediately knock up against that significant piece of his psyche that didn't want to create any kind of tension between himself and Jill. After all, it seemed like a foregone conclusion that a Princess Di angle wouldn't go down well with her, the Royal Family no doubt being one of those things that fell squarely into her category of southern shite.

So he nearly swallowed his tongue when, coming downstairs to get himself some breakfast, he found Jill in the lounge curled up in an armchair, completely absorbed in a battered copy of Andrew Morton's *Diana, Her True Story*. 'You? Reading that? I don't believe it,' he said, too surprised to button his lip. 'I would've thought you'd've hated the Royals.'

'Yeah, well, I do.' Jill pouted. 'But she's not royal, is she? Not born into it anyway. And plus I've always been a fan of hers. 'Specially after the way she was treated by that lot.'

'Oh, yeah?'

'You've read this, haven't you?'

'Nope.'

'Oh. Thought you would have done.'

'What makes you say that?'

'Well – you've got a bit of a thing about her, haven't you?'

'Me?'

'No, the Pope. Who else?' This was a typical Jill remark. Marty pointedly ignored it. 'No.'

'Yeah, come on. She's your type. I mean look at Terri. She looks just like her.'

Marty feigned nonchalance, but inside he was seething. Girls! Why did they always have to second-guess you instead of waiting to be told? After this there was going to be no subtle way to bring up the issue that had been troubling him. 'As would you,' he said, throwing caution to the wind, 'if you got your hair cut, put in some highlights and, you know, other stuff.'

Jill adopted an expression of mock shock. 'What sort of "other stuff"?' she asked, hands pinned against her breast. Marty flushed. He was aware, suddenly, of how much space there was around him. He wanted to do something, sit down maybe, but the spare armchair and the sofa both appeared at this instant as totally hostile, huge mouths waiting to devour him. Doing a strange kind of dance, he took three steps forward, then moved a couple of feet to the right; now he was positioned behind and to the left of Jill, and within leaning distance of the sideboard. Lean he did, though the move was such a calculated one that he didn't feel able to shift his position again, even when a strip of faux-rope trim started digging an uncomfortable groove into the tender underside of his buttocks.

'You know, we've got to sort this out,' he said, trying to sound as assertive as he could.

'What's that, then?'

'You and Terri. Getting the two of you to look more alike. If this is going to work, you've got to be absolutely identical.'

Jill swivelled round to look at him, wondered why he was standing behind her like that, not sitting down in a chair like a normal person. He was always so uptight, she thought. Why couldn't he just relax a bit? She watched, exasperated, as his eyes dropped from her face to her chest, something they were in the habit of doing.

'And right now you don't,' Marty continued. 'Not really. So either you've got to go up or she's got to come down.'

'What?'

'Either you've got to get a haircut or she's got to wear a wig or something. And one or the other of you should get some of those coloured contacts.'

'And let me guess – it's going to be me who gets the haircut and wears the contacts, right?'

'I don't know . . . maybe . . . I thought we could discuss it. Maybe if one of you does the hair and the eyes, and the other one does her skin. I mean you're a good few tones darker than Tel is.'

'Oh, come on, Marty!' Jill said softly, levering herself up on to the arm of her chair and twisting fully round to face him. 'I know which way round you'd prefer it. You'd love to have two little Princess Dis running after you, now wouldn't you? You even look a bit like her yourself. Not that I mean that in a nasty way.'

Marty couldn't think of anything past the heat in his face and the pain being inflicted on him by the rope-style trim. All his manoeuvrings, he realised too late, had only served to make it easy for Jill to pin him into this hopeless position from which there seemed no escape.

Something told him confidence was called for. Magic skills. Forcing himself to look Jill squarely in the eye, he tried a grin. 'Um. Maybe,' he said desperately, both meaning it as a confession and wanting it to be anything but.

Jill responded by looking back down at her book. 'Yeah, I thought so. And have I got to fork out for these contacts myself or do I get them paid for, seeing as how strictly speaking they're part of my costume?'

Bugger me, thought Marty, completely taken aback. *That wasn't so difficult.* And as the tension ran from his arms and shoulders, and he lifted his backside away from the stretch of relief work that had been so troubling it, he was already finding it difficult to remember what exactly it was that he'd been so afraid of. 'N-no, I'll pay,' he gushed. 'And for the haircut. Of course I will.'

Terri, of course, was delighted that a decision on the make-up had been made, especially since – on the face of it at least – it had gone in her favour. She'd been secretly worrying that Marty was going to ask her to grow her hair or wear a wig; now she knew that this wasn't going to happen she set about helping Jill transform herself with great enthusiasm, taking her into the city for a trip to the hairdresser and an extended pillaging of the cosmetics halls in the big department stores.

As for Marty, now he had his ducks lined up it was all a matter of deciding what he was going to do with them. Handy with a pencil, he'd spent most of the last two weeks working on a series of storyboard-style sketches of the illusions he was considering including in the breakthrough show, deciding – in a sudden burst of eager professionalism – to use the flip chart left over from Terri's water-filter phase as a drawing pad.

Two days after he'd spoken with Jill about changing her appearance he felt ready to summon her and Terri to the rehearsal-cum-dining room for the intial unveiling of Martin Mystery's New Mysteries.

'What's all this, then?' Jill cracked on entering. 'Gonna give us French lessons, are you?' Terri tittered and made a similar, equally unfunny comment. Marty scowled. If it hadn't been for Jill, he thought, Terri would have thought the flip chart a good idea, would have praised him for it.

Ignoring the seats he'd set out for them, the two girls sat down on the floor, Terri with her legs stuck straight out in front of her; Jill cross-legged, skinning up. 'So come on, then. What you gonna show us?'

'Er, Jill, honey – you know I'd really rather you didn't do that in here . . . ?'

'It's all right, calm down. I'm just rolling it. I'm gonna smoke it down the garden, like a good girl. Though I don't see what the problem is, seeing as how your dad's gonna be out of the house all day.'

'But the smell? It won't just disappear, you know.'

'I could always open a window.'

'Come on, Jill, please. You know it's not on.' Marty glanced across at Terri, hoping for support, but she was watching Jill with a distinctly impressed expression on her face. How was it her anti-drugs attitude no longer seemed to apply? It was true what they said, he reckoned, that women weren't logical, like men. Trying to second-guess these two was a total nightmare. You never knew what they were going to come up with next.

'Can we get on with this?' he asked finally, causing Jill to shrug and make an 'oops, aren't I the naughty girl?' face back at Terri, who laughed a second time and drummed her heels on the carpet for a moment or two before stopping suddenly, arching her feet and staring blankly at her ankles.

'What you going to show us, then, *Mar*-ty?' she said, without looking up.

'I'm going run through the ideas I've got for our new act,' he said. 'Or that's the general plan.'

'I've got some ideas if you want,' Jill informed him between licks of her well-packed cigarette paper.

'Yeah, well, if you could hold on to them for just a tick, until I've had a chance to show you the basic outline of what I've been working on? We could maybe discuss them then?'

'I think that means no,' Terri told her, and the girls pulled hoity-toity faces and rocked their heads from side to side in a blatantly sarcastic manner. Refusing to react, Marty turned and folded back the cover of the chart to reveal, on the top sheet of the flip-pad underneath it, a fairly detailed, lovingly rendered and technically quite distinguished drawing of a woman. She was wearing suspenders, high heels and a set of matching underwear complete with flounces, bows and frills – possibly in peach or powder pink, though since the picture was in black and white it was difficult to tell. More significantly, she had been securely and expertly tied up, wrists and ankles bound with ropes to a large A-frame, her feet fixed wide apart. Very wide apart, you might even say.

'You kinky sod,' Jill said.

'That is the general idea,' Marty replied somewhat sourly. He'd set by a store of sarcasm of his own in anticipation of precisely this reaction, but it didn't seem to be doing much to douse the fire currently burning up his face.

'God, Marty,' Terri chimed, which really pissed him off, since she hadn't complained the first few times he'd tied her up. Once or twice she'd actively requested it, before going off the whole idea in a typically Terri bout of contrariness.

'Terri, you've already seen this! You said you liked it.'

'No, I didn't.'

'I showed it to you last week. You liked it then.'

'Yeah, well, I wasn't looking properly.'

'Is he always this filthy?'

'Hm, yeah. He's a right old perv. You'd've thought he might've put his drawing skills to better use, wouldn't you?'

'Oh, but he's very talented.'

'Oh yes, very.'

'He's got a real eye.'

Marty tried his best to interrupt the laughter. 'Can we just stop talking about my sex life for a minute here and look at this,' he begged. 'If you must know, I copied it from a 1930s poster advertising the famous enterologist Seamus Burke. I just changed the man to a woman and updated the costume, that's all.'

Cue cackles and guffaws.

'What's enterology?' Jill asked, when eventually she'd caught her breath.

'Opposite of escapology.'

'Sounds right dodgy to me.'

'Burke used to do this act where instead of being tied up or locked in a safe or whatever and escaping, he'd do it the other way around. He'd be left behind a screen or in a bag or something with a bunch of ropes and padlocks and chains and so on, and while the audience couldn't see he'd tie himself up.'

'Um, that's a useful skill,' cheeked Terri.

Was that loaded? Or just stupid? Marty couldn't tell.

Jill was a little intrigued despite herself. 'So how'd he do it?'

'Well, nobody knows, exactly. He never told. But I know how *we'd* do it. See, we'd use a slightly different style of frame' – here he flipped the chart to reveal a diagram – 'that would, in fact, be the same both front and back, though because of the mirrors, here and here, the audience wouldn't be able to tell that. One of you, Terri say, would stand on this side, I'd do some spiel about magic ropes and stuff. Then I'd draw a curtain across the front, you'd spin the whole thing round and, hey presto, Jill would already be tied up on the back.'

'Why me?'

'But everyone would think it was Terri, seeing as how she'd now have disappeared round the back in the process of doing the spinning,' Marty explained pointlessly. His idea was bordering on genius, he felt.

'That is so fucking lame,' Jill said, pointing out the illusion's fatal flaw.

Marty looked hurt and shot a pleading glance over at his girl-friend. 'Terri?' Terri stared dumbly, pretending not to hear. She had actually thought the idea quite a good one, when Marty had described it to her the other day. But right now Jill's opinion seemed more important than her own.

'So you think it's lame, do you?' Marty demanded, realising Terri's support was not going to be forthcoming.

'Well, you know, I don't want to be rude, but it's hardly elegant, is it?' Jill said, sparking up her spliff. 'And I don't see how those mirrors are going to work.'

'Would you *please* not light that in here?'

'Shit, sorry, sorry.'

Marty glared at her, but he was secretly glad of the few seconds' respite granted him while Jill stubbed out the joint on the rim of her empty coffee mug. In the lull he decided that perhaps he shouldn't continue like this. The confident approach seemed to work when he had one or other of the girls on their own, but not when they were together.

'Well, I've – I've lots of other ideas.' He sounded somewhat more modest. 'That was just for openers.' He flipped quickly down through the chart, showing more pictures of what might be Terri, what might be Jill, in various distressed (and partly undressed) poses and positions. 'I mean, you know, I'm trying to conceive a whole major show here . . .'

'Couldn't we do something with gangsters?' Terri suggested. 'It would be really cool. We could wear suits and ties and those humbug hats.'

'Homburg.'

'Homburg. Whatever. It would look great.'

'And I suppose I could dress up in drag?' Marty queried.

'Yeah.' Jill grinned. 'That'd be good. Though I reckon if we're going to do a confrontational thing it would be cool to do it as Tekken characters or something.' She ran upstairs and came back with the sleeve insert from the PlayStation game. 'Like, Marty could be Marshall Law or Paul Phoenix or something and we could be, like, Nina Williams. She's blonde. She looks a bit like Princess Di.' She showed Marty the relevant picture.

He had a suspicion she might be taking the piss again. *I want to fuck you*, he suddenly admitted to himself.

'So you've got yourself two girls now?' Tony Quick saw fit to mention one evening around that time, when he was up late after Terri and Jill had gone to bed, watching the snooker with his son.

'Yeah,' said Marty with a grin.

'Well, you just watch it, pal. I don't want to hear from Terri that you've been messing her around.'

'What's that supposed to mean?'

'You know what I'm saying. I don't want to hear you've been getting up to any of your tricks. And I'm not talking about the magic kind.'

'Jesus, Dad. What do you take me for?'

Tony Quick didn't answer this. 'He's going to win again, this Hendry bloke,' he said after a while. 'Incredible. Ugly little sod.'

★

It was on Marty's mind for days, this brief exchange. First, how dare he, and second . . . well, of course he fancied Jill. It didn't take a genius to work it out. But it wasn't because she looked the same as Terri, as his old man no doubt thought. It wasn't that at all. It was the *differences* he found attractive – or so Marty told himself now that he was finally thinking about his designs on Jill a little more honestly. Why it should make the slightest difference whether he fancied the differences or similarities wasn't clear, but something in him shied away from admitting it might possibly be the latter, as if that touched something deeper inside him or were somehow more perverse.

Either way, once he'd admitted the attraction to himself the floodgates opened and Marty realised how well he already knew the mouldings of Jill's hair, her acrid, slightly feral smell, her cracked and smoky voice, her turn of phrase. As the days went by his fingers itched to discover the textures of her honey skin while at night before he slept his eyes locked on to hers, where they seemed to hover in the darkness just below his bedroom ceiling. She had a sense of physical self-possession, he'd noticed, that was so much more effortless than Terri's production-line disdain. She had raw, earthy qualities Marty had never thought he'd value much. Weirdly, she reminded him a bit of his sister, Rebecca, which perhaps was where the hint of perversity came in.

On top of this she was smart, contrary to his first impressions up in Blackpool. He had to be on his toes around her more than he ever did with Tel-girl. Jill appeared to see right through him effortlessly – so effortlessly that Marty had begun to worry she was actually playing games with him. Or with them both.

Well, he knew how to play, he told himself. He was an entertainer, he was good at that. It didn't seem that it would do any harm to explore a little, to see where things might go. It wasn't being unfaithful. It was more like management, getting to know the ins and outs of his new employee.

Like management.

Yeah. Just like.

That's right.

But the game proved tougher than Marty'd thought. He'd quickly found himself bending over backwards for Jill and paying her a whole range of tiny attentions, from orchestrating brushed body contacts capable of triggering bursts of adrenalin to his heart to remembering how she liked her tea. Within days, though, his lack of experience at this kind of thing had led to his becoming scared that his flirtation might be getting out of hand. What if, he'd asked himself, Terri started to become suspicious? Or what if, even worse, Jill actually began responding to his overtures and started coming on to him?

These fears had just about reached their height when he'd had that snooker conversation with his old man. Despite his indignation he'd taken the remark as a sign that the game was indeed escalating out of his control. His course of action had been to overcompensate in the opposite direction, so now, perversely, he'd become so sulky and hostile around Jill that Terri had to pull him up on it, ask him why he was being so unfriendly towards the poor girl.

This made Marty truly furious. Unable to accept that the fault lay in his failure to modulate his behaviour appropriately, he pushed the blame beyond himself. Here was his dad, thinking the worst of him, making the assumption that left to his own devices he'd get up to no good, telling him off the moment he looked like getting too friendly with the newcomer. And there, on the other hand, was Terri, giving him a hard time if he *wasn't* nice and friendly and all the rest of it, clearly blind to the games her new-found friend was obviously playing; a situation which made him now start to think of Terri as somehow not deserving of him – which in turn made him desire Jill even more.

Finally there was Jill: knowing that he fancied her, toying with him and laughing at him too, knowing damn well that the attraction was wholly animal and that he didn't even like her much. He couldn't win and, for Marty, winning was what it was always about, in one way or another.

Poor Marty.

Poor Terri.

Poor Jill.

Between the three of them they came up with a new show in the end, a thirty-minute routine featuring four illusions. Three of these were adaptations of the best on Marty's flip chart, while the fourth was the water tank escape out of *Jarrett* that he'd always wanted to do but hadn't suggested before because, in the first place, it was pretty ambitious and in the second he thought neither Jill nor Terri would be that happy about having to get wet.

'That's not a problem,' Jill assured him when he told her this.

'You positive?'

'Totally. We don't have to get wet.'

'Explain?'

'We don't have to get wet, because it's you what's going to do the escape. Me or Terri'll carry out the trick. After all, you're the magician. It makes right good sense for you to go inside the tank.'

Terri immediately agreed. 'That's a great idea,' she said, thinking it was about time Marty put himself through some of the discomfort she had to experience. 'You're forever going on about what a great magician Harry Houdini was. I reckon it would do you some good to be a bit more like him.'

Marty looked from female face to female face, two faces which – now that Jill's make-up had been pretty much perfected – looked identical. 'So that's decided then, is it?' he asked listlessly, already knowing what would happen to any objection he might raise. It would go the same way as his underwear idea, which had been voted down despite his protestations that it would haul in the crowds. (Since Marty had insisted that Jill's PlayStation characters were too esoteric, this meant they'd ended up adopting Terri's gangster theme.)

With these decisions settled there was nothing much the three of them could do as a team until Marty had either bought or built the equipment they needed and Terri had put together their new outfits, so to save money Jill disappeared back up to Morecambe until they were ready for her. When she was gone Marty disappeared inside his workshop, outside which he was rarely seen for the next few weeks. Sawing and hammering and welding and varnishing away he gradually began to assemble the new cabinets, emerging only to eat, to carry on extended negotiations with his father (whom he'd talked into stumping up funds for the project) and to scour the small ads sections in the magic press for items he couldn't manufacture himself. There turned out to be quite a few of these and during this period he made two van trips to Bristol, one to Norfolk and several into central London in order to get hold of everything he required.

Dropping Jill off at the station to go back up north, he'd experienced an incredible sense of relief. From the point of view of getting her on board the visit had been a success, but his new assistant's sweet'n'sour combo of constant challenge to his authority and subtle, superior flirting had proved too much for him to handle – Marty just wasn't used to such complex sexual politics. Still, after a couple of weeks alone with his tools and his thoughts the stress he'd been feeling began to recede and soon, he was grateful to note, his daydreams were no longer dominated by the possibilities of having sex with the new assistant but had switched back to less guilt-racked fantasies of that Las Vegas future, fantasies he'd had for so many years that they'd reduced themselves now to a kind of visual shorthand in which he saw himself as in a film, standing high above the audience on a bright silver stage, the camera swooping in from low backstage left and rising up along the line of his body before moving around to hover just in front of him; zooming in to show his blue eyes slightly wet as if from spray created by the giant breakers of rapturous applause that were breaking over the buttress of foot-lights at his feet.

Nevertheless, when the time came to contact Jill and ask her to come south again the calm and concentration Marty had redis-covered in his workshop were quickly swamped. Buzzing rivulets of dark trepidation ran down the hollows of his spine and gathered in his stomach in a bitter pool whose level rose steadily higher as the days to Jill's arrival counted down.

Yet he need not have worried. Almost as soon as she'd arrived back at the house it became clear that the scenario was no longer the same.

When Jill returned, it seemed that things had changed. As the three of them began to choreograph the show – patient days spent climbing in and out of the new boxes and devices in the dining room – Marty found that whatever it was that had sparked between them previously had gone. Part of it was that Jill had just mellowed out – she was much less acerbic than she had been during her last visit, and without her caustic comments and razor-sharp remarks super-cooling the sexual impulses Marty radiated towards her and sending them back to him in the form of tacit challenges, the conveyor of tension that had been ferrying energy between them no longer appeared to function.

So abrupt was the change that Marty found himself wondering how he'd ever imagined he preferred Jill to Terri. She didn't have the careful beauty or poise of his girlfriend; compared with Tel, her whole attitude was quite coarse. And he couldn't under-stand why he'd thought her so intelligent before. This time round her interjections and objections – those few that she made – seemed far less threatening, much less incisive. She was still Jill, she wasn't like a different person or anything, but she seemed easier to cope with, more with the programme. Maybe it was the cheques Marty was now presenting her with, regularly, once a week, making him more officially her employer. Maybe it was the make-up; perhaps transforming her into a Diana lookalike had made her more docile. Perhaps she'd got herself a man. Yeah, that was probably it. Whatever. It didn't really matter. At the end of the day she was a girl – and girls: you just couldn't fathom them.

★

In an ideal world everything would have fallen into place right then and there, before moving forward nice and smoothly. This not being an ideal world, that didn't happen. On the contrary; it was precisely at this point, Marty would decide much later, that things started to go badly wrong.

Here's why. Although the possibility of infidelity had receded to the furthest horizons of the young magician's mind, this was the moment it took centre stage in Terri's.

Since the other girl's return, Marty began to notice, Terri had become a little edgy around Jill. Her former palliness towards her fellow assistant seemed on the wane, and on the less frequent occasions that Jill made her jibes and jokes Terri didn't run with them as she had previously. Perhaps Jill's absence had given her space to reflect that it didn't do for her to let herself be led in all things by this younger woman – one, after all, with far less professional experience. Perhaps she'd simply come to the conclusion that while Jill's presence was on the one hand an opportunity, it was on the other hand a threat. Maybe she interpreted the new, more relaxed atmosphere between himself and Jill as some kind of sexual warning signal. Marty didn't know, nor did he attempt to find out. He brushed the topic under his mental carpet, attributing the change to the new seriousness that was in the air now the costumes and props had been finished and proper rehearsals had begun, and the new show had started taking on some kind of shape.

It was an interpretation that might have stood if Terri hadn't started spending odd nights away at her mother's; odd not just by their frequency but because she had never really got on that well with her mum, at least not to Marty's way of thinking. Terri was forever bitching about her mother's tendency to interfere with her life, and from the reports he got whenever she returned from one of these visits it appeared that nothing had changed.

Consequently he began to wonder if there was a different intention behind these unexpected absences. Were they designed to test him, to see if he'd give way to temptation with Jill?

The morning this possibility occurred to Marty Terri appeared without warning in his workshop, having returned unannounced from her latest sojourn in sunny Guildford.

'How's little Ms Buttons today?' she'd asked.

'Who?' Marty'd said, glancing up from an elaborate piece of stencil work, slightly annoyed by the unexpected interruption.

'You know. Buttons. Video game girl. Jill. How is she?'

'Oh. Fine. Gone into town I think. Why?'

'Oh, you know. No reason. Just wondered how she was.' Terri turned to leave but halfway out of the door she stopped, as if she'd just remembered something. 'I'm going to make an instant,' she warbled innocently. 'Want one?'

'Yeah,' Marty pouted back. *Why 'Ms Buttons'?* What on earth was that about? Was Terri trying to see how he'd react to her calling Jill a derogatory name?

Marty was intrigued. He was used to Terri's quickly changing moods and had long ago given up trying to work out the reasons for them, but what struck him about this one in particular was the powerful position it put him in. Terri's suspecting him and his being on top of that suspicion gave him a major advantage over her, he realised. It gave him a responsibility too, but somehow Marty seemed to miss that part of it, his mind fixating on the fact that her jealousy made her behaviour more predictable. Now, if Jill started flirting with him he could flirt back with far more finesse and confidence – and without his previous paralysing terror of success – simply because he understood how he could go about it and yet remain within the bounds of Terri's expectation.

He was learning.

★

What, in fact, had happened, as Marty would have discovered if he'd been paying a little more attention to his girlfriend, was that in between working on the costumes Terri had been drawing up everybody's charts. Although he was vaguely aware she'd been doing this, his failure to take her astrology seriously was also a failure to understand how important it was to her. It never crossed his mind that the charts themselves might actually have something to do with his girlfriend's changing attitude.

Ever since Jill had first arrived in Beckenham, Terri had been impressed by her. It took a special kind of person to make Terri question her picture of the world and Jill had that quality. To Terri Jill seemed solid, dependable, unshakeable, unutterably sure of herself. A typical Taurean, in other words. With her (comparably) vast music knowledge, her casual drug taking and her video game playing, she was an older version of those girls against whom Terri had had to battle when she'd moved schools. Older and wiser. Older, wiser, nicer.

Which was fine, to begin with. At the start, Jill was like a breath of fresh air blowing through her and Marty's relationship. But after Jill had gone back to Morecambe and Terri had had a chance to draw up her charts she began to get worried.

Terri was well aware that the only way a Virgo like herself and a Gemini like Marty could ever form a mutually fulfilling long-term relationship was if the Virgo could provide an anchor for the Gemini's steady, masculine side, while allowing his or her partner's flighty feminine element more or less free rein. Terri understood that this was her role and she took responsibility for it. After all, she knew as surely as if she'd had the words tattooed on to her arm that Gemini was a deeply divided sign, one that split equally between masculine and feminine; an androgynous sign; one whose divided nature made for a creative and imaginative personality but also one that too easily became capricious and superficial. But deep down, Terri felt that she was perhaps too fussy and possessive to give Marty the freedom he required. She worried that she erred too much on the side of caution, that she chastised him instead of grounding him, punished him when she should have been teaching him. Perhaps she wasn't as great a communicator as she needed to be. Both Gemini and Virgo are ruled by the planet Mercury, see, and Mercury is the messenger, which meant that Virgo's main weapon to help her Gemini male in keeping it real (according to the books that Terri consulted) was her talent for being able to communicate clearly to him the advantages inherent in her own more practical nature.

But Terri knew she lacked this talent. When she tried to communicate she always seemed to say too much or not enough, either confusing Marty or sending him into a sulk – another tendency for which Geminis were known. And she didn't seem able to help herself, to find that happy medium. She so wished she could be as self-possessed and laid back as Jill. Maybe it had something to do with her dad's leaving her, deserting her mum and her. So often when she thought about things that were wrong in her life she came back to that.

If she, Terri, was a Virgo lacking the mercurial touch, Jill was a Taurean who seemed to have it in spades. Like Virgo, Taurus was an earth sign; both signs therefore stood in the same relation to an air sign like Gemini, at least as far as romantic entanglements were concerned: they were both supposedly capable of providing definition for Gemini's free spirit, while partaking of their lover's dynamic vitality. But Jill's ruling planet was Venus and Terri sensed real danger here. Venus was all about sensuality and romance, and although very different in nature from Mercury, both planets are very close to the sun – making them natural neighbours. While it was undoubtedly the case that a Taurean like Jill would be happiest with a similarly settled and dependable partner, Terri hadn't been brought up to believe that women had much of a say in choosing – or keeping – a man. When it came to her deepest, most gut-sure beliefs on this subject it was still her parents' marriage that held sway, not her experiences with Marty and Darren. For Terri it was a man's world, and her fear was not that Jill would go prowling around Marty but that Marty would go prowling around Jill, seeing in her all those things – the groundedness, the sensuality – that Terri was (she felt) failing to provide. There was no way, she imagined, that Jill had any qualms at all about giving blow-jobs, for example. She probably even *enjoyed* giving them, hard though it was to entertain the thought.

Not only that, but the charts revealed that Venus would be in the ascendant for Marty over the forthcoming month. And Terri had just spent two weeks helping to make this girl *look* like her, all the time being pleased about it because she thought she was flattering her own vanity.

Oh, God. What had she done?

★

'Two girls, eh?' said Michael archly, when Marty finally phoned him to tell him about the new show. 'I thought you'd gone quiet on me.'

'Yeah. Twins.'

'What happened to Terri?'

'She's one of them.'

'She's got a sister?'

'No, no. The other girl, Jill, she's not related or anything. She just looks like her.'

'Oh, right. Oh, I see. Oh – good thinking! That's brilliant.'

'What?'

'Going to Terri's lookalike agency to get another Princess Di. Can't think why we didn't come up with something like that before.'

'Er, no. Not quite,' Marty corrected him (and immediately regretted doing so, feeling that he should be encouraging any impression Michael had of him as a fountain of brilliant ideas). 'No – I just ran into her totally at random. Asked her to join us and she did.'

'Well, that's excellent. Glad to see you're learning to capitalise on opportunity, dear boy.'

Michael could be such a cunt. 'Yeah, well, the new act's really going to be something. Like a total transformation. But what I really want to know is can you get me a gig?'

As it happened, Michael could; he'd just heard this morning that owing to illness the Zodiac Brothers had dropped out of three weeks supporting Bob Monkhouse at the Palace in Torquay and there was a good chance he could snag the slot if Marty so wished. Which he did. It wasn't Vegas. It wasn't TV. But it was work, good work, and it would be the perfect place to preview the show.

★

Contrary to Marty's expectations, however, the big revamp didn't wow the Torquay massive quite as much as he'd hoped. Despite good and vigorous audiences, which let it all hang out when Bob strolled on – microphone in hand, eyes a-twinkle, that million-dollar smile cut like a pastry shape into the legendary tan – the response to Martin Mystery's New Mysteries was somewhat lacklustre.

Marty couldn't understand it. The girls were good, the props were good, the choreography was spot on, the costumes looked great . . . yet something about the set-up just didn't quite bite. It was always tricky, using magic to warm up a crowd for a big-name comedian, he knew that. But this was something else.

It was Michael who put his finger on it. Marty had bullied him into taking a train down from London about halfway through the run to come and see the show, and after the performance they'd met up for a drink in the local All Bar One.

'So what d'you reckon, then?' Marty'd asked, after they'd found themselves a polished granite table, scraped up two uncomfortable cast-iron garden chairs and sat down with a bowl of olives in minced garlic, two tulip-bowl wineglasses and a bottle of Chenin Blanc between them.

'Well, Marty. You know. Congratulations. Excellent, excellent. The new girl's very good. I couldn't tell which one she was.'

'That is the general idea.' Marty nodded, smiling a slightly desperate smile. Something about Michael's tone was telling him he wasn't going to get the effusive and overwhelming reaction he needed if he was to dispel the audience-not-quite-getting-it intuitions that had been bugging him. But it was important to stay affable, not to allow himself to lapse into making any cutting remarks. 'When you, er, when you say you couldn't tell which one she was, does that mean you could tell there were two of them?'

'No, no. Not at all.'

'Oh. Good. You had me a bit worried there.'

'Not straightforwardly, in any case.'

'What? What does that mean? Not straightforwardly? What's that?'

'Calm down. Not straightforwardly, that's all.'

But Marty still didn't see what Michael was getting at and said so.

The agent took a hefty pull on his wine before responding, tipping back his head and bubbling air through the liquid before swallowing it down. 'How can I put this? I don't mean to be critical, Marty, I can see you've been working really very hard. But the problem with the show is . . . it's just *too good*.'

'What? What do you mean, too good? Are you taking the piss?' Already the 'no cutting remarks' resolution was proving difficult to stick to. 'How can it be too good? For this audience, you mean? Yeah, well of course it's too good for *them*. I mean, it's wasted, but if you could get me some decent gigs like I keep asking you –'

'No, no, Marty, listen. Calm down and listen to me for a moment. What I *mean* is it's *too good*. Literally. Your illusions. They're simply . . . impossible. There's no way they could physically be done.'

'Of course not. That's why they're illusions, for God's sake.'

'There's no need to be abusive, Martin. I'm trying to be helpful here.'

'Yeah, well, you're not making any sense.'

'Well, listen, then.'

'I am listening. You're not telling me anything worth listening to.'

Michael drained his glass, refilled it from the bottle, lit up a cigarette. 'Martin, do try to understand. I think your show's wonderful, I really do. It's the best thing you've done and I have no hesitation in saying that with a few modifications it could go really far. This is excellent material: original, entertaining, exciting. All of that. But you've got to understand that as it stands there's a fundamental problem with a majority of the set-ups. If you put a girl on one side of the stage, tie her up and put her in a sack, then make her appear tied up in a previously empty sack placed ten feet away, the audience are not going to accept that you've magically transported her if they can see two bodies struggling in the sacks *at one and the same time*.'

'But that's so's they *know*, Michael, that she's not going down through a hole in the stage and travelling along underneath it before coming up through another hole and into the other sack.'

'Yes, Martin, but isn't that what she's been tied up for, to prove precisely that? The way you've got it set up at the moment, you give away your own secret. There's only one way you could make that trick work and that's using twins. There *is* no other way and the audience, however stupid you may happen to think they are, will realise that instinctively.'

Marty blushed and went silent, stared into his drink. He hated wine, he realised. 'What about the two-boxes illusion?'

'Same deal. You see two boxes, they're both suspended from the rafters, there's no podium, no sphinx table, nothing that anyone could escape through. Your assistant gets into one of them, then she gets out of the other one. She gets back in and gets out of the first. There's only one way you can do it.'

'Two girls.'

'Two girls.'

Marty nodded. Why was the road to fame so hard and long? He suddenly felt utterly exhausted, as though he simply weren't equal to the task he'd set up before him. A childhood memory popped into his head: he was young, in his room, in the middle of a tantrum. By the time the rage was over he'd smashed his two favourite toys. 'So what do you suggest?' he asked. 'Junk it all? Start again from scratch?'

'No, no, you don't need to do that. Well, not entirely. You've got yourself a good resource and a good set of ideas. It's just a matter of deploying them right. The key thing is to construct the trick so that the audience think there's at least one vaguely possible explanation, even if it's not the right one. The *really* clever thing, always, is to put the elements of an illusion in a sequence so that everyone thinks they can follow how the whole thing's being done until the very last minute, when you pull off a climax so unexpected and amazing that it not only knocks them blind but also trashes all their previous theories. That's what the greats all have in common, that they can do that.' Marty thought of the Doug Henning 'Things that Go Bump in the Night' routine he'd once described to Harvey in the Winter Gardens Galleon Bar. That was like that; it had been precisely that quality he'd been trying – and failing – to communicate. 'Either that or the thing has to be so damn weird, so freaky, so outrageous that the audience is too busy being amazed to care how it's been done.'

Marty slumped back in his chair, letting despondency pull on his cheeks. 'Which means it *is* back to the drawing board is what you're basically saying.' He groaned. More work, more preparation, more rehearsal, more debts. He was so tired of it all.

But Michael insisted on remaining cheery. 'Yes, but like I said, not entirely. Drop the two-boxes thing – that's the one that really gives you away. Keep the sacks but make sure the girl's gone from one before she starts wriggling about in the other. The water escape where Terri – or is it Jill?'

'Terri.'

'. . . where Terri puts you in the tank, that's really good, that's classy. Keep that. And don't rely on the gangster theme for your whole routine. It's been done to death. Come up with something . . . I don't know . . . something more contemporary. Do something with computers or something like that. That's what everybody's into these days.'

Marty nodded resignedly, wondering if he shouldn't have accepted Jill's PlayStation idea after all. He leaned forward, put his elbows on the table, looked into his wine again. 'But Michael – there's another thing. Another problem, I mean.'

'Um?'

'I'm broke.'

'Oh, don't worry about that. Give me a call next week – I'm sure we can sort you out a loan.'

'So you finally think I'm worth investing in?'

'Martin!' Michael leaned over and patted him on the hand. 'Don't be like that. Of course I do! My criticisms are meant to be *constructive*, you know. I wouldn't be here if I didn't believe in you.' He drained his glass and gave Marty a sideways glance. 'Especially after you dumped me so unceremoniously before.'

'Oh. Yeah. Sorry about that. I was having a bit of a weird time.'

'Yes, well, we all have those, Martin dear, we all have those.' A group of office girls sat down noisily at the table next to theirs; Michael consulted his watch. 'Oh – is that the time? Sorry to cut things short, but I have to run. My train.'

'You're not spending the night?'

'Darling, Julie Burchill may think Torquay is chic, but I most certainly do not. Which reminds me – I meant to ask you: are the three of you staying in the same hotel while you're down here?'

'Yeah, of course. Why?'

Michael tutted loudly. 'Think think think! In the I'll admit unlikely circumstance that Anna Artspage likes your show enough to put in a good word for it in the local rag, how d'you think it's going to look when she runs into you jollying home from the Palace late one night with the same girl hanging off each of your long and lusty arms? She's going to blow your little secret, isn't she?'

Marty smiled despite himself.

'Marty! You've got to keep *everyone* guessing how you do it. I suggest separate travelling arrangements, separate hotels, secret rehearsals, the whole bit.'

'What? All three of us in separate hotels? It'll cost a fortune.'

'No, you brainless idiot. You and Terri can stay together – in fact, the more you're seen out on the town as a couple the better.

But get the other one – what's her name again, Jill? Get Jill put up somewhere on her own, get her to come to the theatre in some kind of disguise. Just so people don't suss you're using lookalikes. That's how Copperfield used to do it.'

'Copperfield? Copperfield used doubles?'

'That's how he made his name. Didn't you know that?'

'Fuck.'

'There's nothing new under the sun, Martin dear. Call me next week. Don't forget!'

'*The Fly*!' Jill said.

'What?'

'*The Fly*. You know. The movie – the one with Jeff Goldblum as that weird scientist bloke who gradually turns into a fly after his experiment goes wrong. Geena Davis as the nosy journo who falls in love with him.'

'What about it?'

'It was on TV last night. I watched it after you two went to bed.'

'So?'

'Well, have you seen it?'

'Yeah. Of course. Everybody's seen it.'

'Then you remember the teleportation sequences, with those two pods with glass doors and loads of dry ice hooked up to a computer, and whatever gets put in the first one gets zapped and then reassembled in the other?'

'Yeah?'

'Well, there's our illusion.'

'What?'

'We could do that. You, the magician, are Seth Brundle, the crazed inventor; Terri and me are Geena Davis, who he drugs and puts through his evil apparatus. It's not quite the way it is in the film, but you know. We could do it like the two-boxes illusion except better, make two really funky teleport pods, fix up some mad computer equipment and project some cool images up on a giant screen. Dry ice all over the stage . . . it would be *mad*.'

Marty looked at Terri who looked at Jill who looked at Marty who looked down at the two empty soft-boiled-egg shells lying on the breakfast plate in front of him among the crusts of dead soldiers. There was no doubting it – it was an extremely credible idea.

'Say these are the pods,' Marty said, grabbing the shells and balancing them upside-down on the holes trepanned in their crowns, suddenly enthused. 'But wait a minute. Does not compute. Like you said, it's based on the two-boxes illusion. Which Michael said just doesn't work. It's too obvious that it needs two girls to succeed.'

Jill agreed. 'Yeah. But you said he also said that wouldn't matter if the illusion is weird enough. Which it would be. Plus, with all the dry ice and computer equipment and a big fat pipe going from one pod to another, people'll think there's any amount of ways it might've been done.'

Marty pushed back his country-style kitchen dining chair and licked his fingers free of toasty crumbs. He would have wiped them on the seat of his trousers but Terri was monitoring him so he got up and went over to the sink to rinse them properly clean, staring out of the window at a clump of molehills in the garden as he did so, all the while muttering under his breath in what was a – coincidentally or deliberately? Jill and Terri couldn't tell – Seth Brundle fashion. Jill was just beginning to wonder if he wasn't going to open up the fridge and vomit some kind of predigesting saliva matter into a tub of margarine before ingesting the resulting gunk using a previously undisclosed proboscis-like tongue, when he spoke.

'The point about the film, right,' he said, tongue apparently as normal, 'is that the scientist eventually gets spliced, at some fundamental DNA-type level, with a fly. Right? And then turns into one?'

'Right.'

'So I reckon that what we need to do is somehow reflect that in the trick, using some kind of animal. Obviously a fly's not much good, on account of its being so small.' Pausing again, Marty looked at the window some more, and this time Jill and Terri followed his gaze. Beyond the miniature volcanic ridge of mole activity was a small, aged compound built of chipboard, greying wooden slats and chicken wire, in which two small and blob-like white forms alternately lolloped and shat among a scattered party pack of wood shavings, carrot tops and carved chunks of Sainsbury's 2-for-1 iceberg lettuce. 'Rabbits,' he said.

Terri laughed. 'Like, you think you're going to splice us with Siegfried and Roy?'

But the magician didn't seem to hear her. It was Michael's words, not hers, that he had carooming around his brain. He was trying to think how best to structure the illusion, how not just to plonk it down before the audience but lead them into it, give it a narrative, let them think they were on top of it and that they knew exactly what was going on until ... *kazam!* ... suddenly it wrong-footed them as an earlier and apparently insignificant detail took on key importance and the trick they thought they were being shown was transformed into something else, something completely unexpected, flabbergasting, right before their very eyes ...

Remembering a Shimada illusion he'd once seen, one in which the famous Japanese conjuror had swopped places with his assistant under the cover of a small pagoda that had been set up in the centre of the stage, Marty grabbed another eviscerated eggshell from Terri's plate and stood it upside-down in the middle of the table. Around it he cleared a rough rectangle of space, at one end of which he positioned a place mat: a laminated photograph of Buckingham Palace glued to a hard cork base, part of what was left of a set he'd bought his mum for Christmas years ago, back when he'd been around seven or eight. Taking the other two eggshells from his own plate, he stood them on it, one either side of the black-and-gold front gates.

'Here,' he said pointing at the place mat. 'That's the stage. And this' – Marty swept his hand around the cleared space, in the centre of which the third eggshell stood – 'this is the audience. We use three teleportation pods, not just two. I'm the scientist, you and Terri are the Geena Davis assistant character. I come on alone, the crazed inventor in his laboratory, and take a white rabbit from a cage, Siegfried say. I put Siegfried in pod A, and teleport him to pod B, though now of course he's actually Roy. I go over, take Roy out, check he's okay, put him back in the pod, teleport him back to A. He's Siegfried again. I go over and take Siegfried out, put him on a side table. So far, so obvious. The audience are pretty clear about there being two rabbits, with some kind of rig-up in the pods. What we actually use for both the vanishings and reappearances is a mini Pepper's Ghost illusion: we put the rabbits in boxes with false lids and use remote-controlled mirrors to project their images up on to the glass doors, meaning we can make them appear or disappear at will. With dry ice and bright lights and stuff, that can look really effective. You can even do it as a sort of gradual phasing out, like the beam-up scene in *Star Trek*.

'So. We've got rabbit in pod A becoming rabbit in pod B becoming rabbit in pod A again. Then Jill arrives, just like in the movie, dressed in a black mac like she's come in from outside. I kiss her and show her round my lab – she's my girlfriend; she hasn't been here before; I'm going to unveil my experiment for her, show her what I've been working on. This is all done in mime, there's music, everyone knows the story, everyone's seen the film.

'Okay. Next, in between making evil genius glances at the punters I suggest to Jill that she sit inside pod A. Maybe they try and shout a warning or two, pantomime-style. Or maybe not. Either way, Jill goes in pod A, she looks scared and I close the door. I go over to the computer panel' – here Marty grabbed an empty single-serving carton of Kellogg's Coco Pops and placed it between the two eggshells on the place mat stage – 'and twiddle the knobs around and pull a big lever or something. Cue lowering of a big screen down from the gods, across which now play all sorts of high-tech visuals. Then: dry ice, bright lights, and –

kazoom – Jill's not in pod A any more, she's in pod B where, in fact, she's Terri. I rush over, open the door, let her tumble out into my arms, confused and semi-conscious. I look into her eyes and check her pulse, maybe slap her cheeks a bit to bring her round. When she's compos mentis I mime to her what's happened but she shakes her head in disbelief. So to prove it to her I put her back inside pod B and run over to the control panel and do my stuff and *kabam*, she's back over in pod A. Maybe as an extra little touch when she gets back in pod B she can snag her stocking, ladder it – you can see her through the window looking at it all annoyed. And when Jill gets out of pod A that same ladder's in her tights and she points it out and complains to me about it.'

'That's great!' Terri said, enthused.

'Ah, but it's not over yet. See, next thing is, I'm so pleased with my success that I want to try something more ambitious. I see Siegfried sitting there on the table, chewing a carrot top. I pick him up. I hand him to Jill and try to usher her back inside pod A. She protests. I ignore her protestations. She runs away, holding Siegfried. We do a kind of comedy run around the stage and at one point run behind the big computer.' Marty tapped the empty boxlet of Coco Pops. 'And this is where the switch takes place.'

'Switch?'

'Switch. Because Terri, having been vanished from pod B, has meanwhile slipped out the back and got changed into the same clothes I'm wearing – black trousers and a long white lab coat. She's done whatever she needs to do to her hair so it looks like mine and put on the same pair of big protective goggles that I wear every time I fire up the machine and which in all the excitement I haven't taken off since the last time Jill came out from her pod. And with this new costume on she's gone and hidden behind the box of Coco Pops, I mean, behind the big computer. When I run behind it I stay behind it and Terri runs out, pretending to be me and still chasing Jill. She then catches Jill and persuades her back inside pod A. Once inside Terri goes over to the console and pulls the switches, levers or whatever. Bright lights, dry ice. Terri runs over to pod B. But – shit. No Jill. No girl at all. Just loads and loads of rabbits, like seven or eight, all identical to Siegfried, which come out of that fat pipe leading from the computer to pod B that Jill mentioned.

'Now our scientist's in big trouble. He's turned his girlfriend into a warren-load of bunnies. What to do? He walks around the stage, goggles still on, tearing at his hair. Suddenly he has a brainwave. Gathering up the rabbits, which by now are hopping all around the stage, he puts them all back inside pod B. He goes over to the console, types some shit in on the keyboard, sets some dials. On the big screen new graphics come up, plus a big new important word: AUTOMATIC. A countdown starts. He runs over to pod B, gets inside with all the rabbits, picks up one of them and holds it in his lap: 5 . . . 4 . . . 3 . . 2 . . . 1 . . . The counter reaches zero. Dry ice, bright lights, crazy graphics up on the screen. Brundle and rabbits disappear. The door to pod B swings open. Silence. Empty pod. And then . . . *da da daaa* . . . flash of light from hitherto unremarked pod C, which up until this point has been sitting quietly on its platform in the middle of the audience. Pod C is the same shape as pods A and B but different in design in that it doesn't have a glass front door. Instead, what happens now is that like a big black egg it cracks right open' – for illustrative effect Marty sliced a butter-streaked table knife firmly through the middle of Terri's eggshell – 'to reveal yours truly standing there, arm in arm with the beautiful Jill, holding one large white rabbit. I rip off my protective goggles and we take a bow. Applause!'

At this point Marty did, in fact, bow, folding the hand that still held the knife (now with flecks of fragged eggshell stuck to its butter coating) ceremoniously across his chest. The girls both clapped.

'What d'you reckon?'

'Superb.'

'It's a winner.'

'It'll cost a small fortune to do it right.'

'But it'll be worth it. It's really good.'

'D'you really think?'

'Oh yes, yes.'

'Well done to Jill, then, for the original idea.'

'Yes, well done to Jill.'

'Oh yes, Jill, well done. Thank you. Though just one thing.'

'What's that, then?'

'Shouldn't Jill be the one to make the switch? She's that bit closer to your height and build.'

'That'd mean, of course, that then you'd have to run round the back of the theatre and creep into pod C with me for the grand finale.'

'I suppose.'

'Is that all right?' Marty asked Jill, who gave a wordless shrug. 'Well, whichever way round you want it, I don't mind. But we're going to need more rabbits. And a hefty loan for the equipment – I reckon I can design it, but I think building it's beyond the means of the garden shed. And, fuck, we'll need someone to do us all the computer graphics for the big screen. I've got no idea at all how that stuff works.'

Everyone thought for a minute or two, during which time Marty reflected on how nimbly Terri had nabbed the glory spot of the illusion for herself, even though he'd given her what he'd actually thought was the better role.

'Oh, I know!' said Jill, her enthusiasm back. 'We could get Paul. He'd do it, I'm sure.'

'Paul?'

'Yeah, you remember. The friend I was with when you came up to me in Blackpool Tower that day. He's great with computers. He'd do it.'

'Oh, yeah.' That's right, Paul – Marty'd forgotten he was a computer geek. 'You think he'd really do it?' He wasn't altogether sure about this. That random encounter in the Tower was the one and only time he'd met Jill's friend and, as he remembered it, they hadn't exactly warmed to one another.

'Oh yeah, definitely,' Jill said. 'I'll give him a call tonight, see if he can help us out.'

'We'll need him here in person at some point, though. I mean,

I don't think I can describe to him what we'll need done over the phone.'

'That won't be a problem. He'll come down to London, if I ask him.'

Gleefully, Marty congratulated himself. So his guess had been correct. She *had* been shagging someone while she'd been back up north. Her old mate Paul. It all made perfect sense.

But then again, as things turned out, perhaps it didn't. Marty had been apprehensive about Paul's arrival from the moment Jill had suggested that he come and sort out the computer. It wasn't just the memory of Paul's belligerence in the ballroom that worried him, or the prospect that his presence might reinvigorate Jill's vituperative tongue (though the possibility of the two of them conspiring to give him a hard time wasn't one he relished). It was more to do with the fact that in the week leading up to Paul's visit Marty had begun to fancy Jill again.

The idea that someone other than himself might be sleeping with her had got under his skin; now someone else had a claim on Jill, he once again began to want her for himself. And as if the magician and his two assistants were trapped within some kind of psychological cat's cradle, a deformation in one area entailing a compensating change of relations somewhere else, this resurgence of desire was accompanied by a concomitant increase in the frequency with which Jill took the piss out of him, by a lowering in the intensity of Terri's jealous suspicions and by a widening of the recently attenuated band of cordiality that stretched from girl to girl.

With the foundations of his recently enjoyed authority thus under threat, it was a total relief to Marty when on the day before Paul was due to arrive Jill asked him if it would be okay to set up the camp bed for him to sleep on in the dining room.

'Oh,' Marty said, completely startled at the extent to which his private beliefs had deviated from reality. 'Er, of course. Sorry – I'd just sort of assumed he'd be staying upstairs. With you.'

'What on earth made you think that?'

'I don't know,' Marty stammered, shamed. 'I just . . . nothing. I'll sort out the bed.'

★

'I'm, er, sorry if I was a bit, you know, *hostile* an' that, that time up in Blackpool.'

Paul was lying on his back, his head and torso tucked inside the cabinet that Marty had built to house the computer and projector, sawdust circles on the worn knees of his jeans. Having done most of the programming, he was fitting the various electronic components into place and wiring them together.

'That's okay. It must have been a bit weird, my coming up to you like that.'

Paul seemed not to hear him. 'Jill's had a bit of a tricky time of it over the last year or two, you see.'

'So I heard.'

A small thud emanated from inside the cabinet as Paul banged his head. 'You did?'

'Yeah – she told us about getting fired from Fatty Arbuckle's.'

'Oh, that. That's not what I meant. That's normal stuff, for Jill. I'm talking about her last boyfriend, Gavin. He was a real bastard. Put her in a right mess. Those of us that know her well, we get a bit over-protective.' Paul slid out from inside the prop, stood up and dusted himself off. 'There. That's got it, I reckon.'

Marty looked at him from where he was perched up on the workbench. They were in the shed; for the last two hours it had been raining heavily. The water drummed on the roof above their heads and slid down the windows in thin, synthetic sheets. 'You've got a bit of a thing for Jill, haven't you?'

'No.' Paul looked around the floor like he'd misplaced a vital tool.

'Oh, come on, Paul. You can tell me.'

'I haven't, all right? And it's none of your bloody business, anyway. Sodding Londoners – you're all sex-obsessed.'

Marty laughed. 'What?'

'Well, it's true, ain't it?'

'Er, no.'

'Yes it is – sex, sex, sex. It's all anybody talks about down here. Look at the media.'

'That's not my fault.'

'I didn't say it was, did I? Just look at it, that's all. All right, come on. Let's switch this thing back on, see if this time it'll work.'

★

In order to pay for the major new illusion, Marty had taken out a loan of fifteen thousand pounds, more money than he'd ever had available to ruffle through his mental mitts before. Seven of the fifteen he put aside to cover the cost of the teleportation cabinets, which he was having professionally designed and built, and which were to look very similar to the cabinets used in the actual movie of *The Fly* (i.e. black, egg-shaped, and covered in heat-dissipating grilles of the kind you see on ultra high-end hi-fi amplifiers and Intel computer chips). For the construction of the big computer cabinet, the purchase of the computer to go inside it along with a projector and a screen, and the cost of paying Paul to put the whole thing together and program it ('program' being an umbrella term for Marty who, despite Paul's coaching, still had difficulty grasping the distinctions between the various types of computer coding and design) he'd allocated another three.

It took the two of them about a week to put the prop together, and it didn't take Marty long to discover that while Paul was generally an easygoing sort of bloke, the mention of Jill's name was enough to put him on the defensive. Whenever she came up in the conversation, nine times out of ten his bruised eyes would slip their focus and settle instead on that middle distance into which unrequited lovers can't help but stare, a middle distance empty of the drab slabs of reality which wall their daily worlds, containing only the image of their perfect one, smiling back at them, telling them to come on now, yes, come on.

After four days of careful observation, the magician was certain that Jill was not only aware of the feelings Paul had for her, but that she'd dragged him all the way down here to help them out just to test her power over him, the little minx. And Paul had gone for it; around his beloved he was positively doglike, super-eager, practically a leech – in total contrast to the cool, laconic persona he projected when he and Marty were alone.

For some time after Paul's return to Blackpool Marty felt suffused with a feeling of general well-being. Whether this happiness had to do with his growing sense that the new illusion was really going to be something special or whether it was directly linked to the knowledge that Jill was still technically sexually available was not especially clear.

With the props ready and the costumes done and the show rehearsed and Paul's visit to Beckenham come and gone, Marty reopened talks with Michael. The agent suggested that it would be worth doing two nights at Beckenham town hall as a kind of public dress rehearsal, partly to iron out any wrinkles in the new illusion in a proper performance setting and partly to give him a chance to see it. Marty was enthused and gratified; it was the first time Michael had requested anything like that and this new hands-on attitude of his was very encouraging.

While he and Terri booked the hall and went through their address books ringing anybody they could think of to invite, Jill designed a poster and some flyers using the new computer, which she was far more at home using than either of the other two. She and Marty spent the weekend prior to the performances standing in the High Street distributing them, an activity from which Terri managed to excuse herself by pointing out that this was a good example of an occasion on which Jill and she should definitely not be seen together. Anyway, she said, she had to stay at home to put the finishing touches to the costumes.

A strong turnout of family and friends, combined with the novelty of having a magic show on in the local town centre, meant that they had a good crowd on both nights. Just as Marty'd hoped 'The Fly' – performed as the grand finale – brought down the house, though this was partly thanks to Eric, the town hall's resident lighting nerd, taking the opportunity to live out his fantasies by putting together a smoke machine and spotlight extravanganza that wouldn't have looked out of place at a Radiohead gig. Michael said it was one of the best stage effects he'd ever seen. Marty believed him.

A week later the magician and his agent spoke on the telephone. Michael had fantastic news. Able for the first time unreservedly to praise the show, he'd been able to arrange them fully six months' work, a tour that took in some of Marty's old haunts – the Gaiety, the Inn on the Park, the City Varieties, the Camberley Lakeside – before culminating in a month at the Talk of London, the first time Marty had ever had a proper booking in the capital. They were going up in the world. By the time they got to London, Michael assured him, anything would be possible.

Chubby's grin was framed by a red bow tie, two fun 'n' fleshy cheeks, a pair of round wire old-skool NHS wire-rimmed specs and a leather flying helmet. His body was encased in a patchwork dinner jacket from one jokey sleeve of which a stubby hand was juttin' out, one finger comin' atcha. At his shoulder his name blazed forth in giant block capitals and beneath that his famous catchphrase was printed out in script. 'Come and give the helmet a big hand!' it read, lending a cosy air of interfamilial sex crime to the ad.

'If easily offended stay away,' the poster also said.

Pasted on to a blank area in the display's lower right-hand corner were two faces and an A3 banner. The two faces, colour laser prints about twice life size that had been crudely snipped to shape with a large pair of scissors (so crudely, in fact, that most of Marty's chin had been lopped off), belonged to Marty and Terri (or perhaps to Marty and Jill – these days it was extremely difficult to tell). The banner read:

WITH!
Martin Mystery's All New Mysteries
featuring...
'THE FLY'

The poster itself was pasted to a hoarding bolted to the landward end of North Pier, and was advertising Legends. Roy 'Chubby' Brown was playing Legends. Marty, Jill and Terri were playing Legends, as Roy 'Chubby' Brown's support. Legends is a drab grey building, boxy as an aircraft hangar, built far out over the grey waves at the very end of North Pier. Viewed from the viewing platform at the top of Blackpool Tower, North Pier looks something like a nightmare, a crude world of its own, a makeshift island cast adrift, the final alienated destination of the Solaris voyage of light entertainment.

Legends was the final leg of the tour before Marty, Jill and Terri returned south to take up their residency at the Talk of London.

Marty, Jill and Terri really didn't want to be there.

Marty, Jill and Terri were beginning to feel the strain.

Four months on the road had left them drained. Cafeteria meals that are too bland, hotel beds that are too soft, the constant change of venues, the eventual tedium generated by doing the same show every night . . . all these things help to emphasise and accentuate the petty rivalries and disagreements found in any touring company, and our trio was no exception. Things finally came to a head in January, soon after they'd arrived in Leeds.

By this time Jill was so bored she felt as if she had metal fatigue of the soul. It was one thing to be into video games. It was quite another to have PlayStation as her primary activity, to spend days, weeks and months plugged into the portable tellies in chintzy and claustrophobic bedrooms playing Fighting Force, Final Fantasy and Metal Gear Solid until she had arthritic fingers, RSI wrists and a neck knotted with hypertension. To cope with this tedium she stayed almost perpetually stoned, scoring whenever she could from likely-looking theatre technicians or from the lone Rasta pub in whatever town they happened to be passing through (there was always one, if you looked hard enough). In addition, she developed her Lottery-playing pastime into a total obsession, working up increasingly arcane number-spread systems and spending an increasingly large proportion of her wages on tickets.

The excitement this generated meant staying behind in her room to catch the draw results on Wednesdays and Saturdays even if this meant risking the possibility of missing her call and when, one time in Waverley, she made her entrance with literally seconds to spare she made up her mind to put a stop to what was fast becoming a compulsion (though a hundred-pound win three days later quickly convinced her otherwise).

It wasn't just the boredom. She also felt she'd got the raw end of the deal. Marty had decided to follow Michael's advice to the letter and ensure that in no town they visited were the three of them ever to be seen together. This was number one on his list of 'Tour Rules' and it was rigidly enforced. These Tour Rules had been printed up by Marty on the new computer, a machine whose possibilities for total life organisation he'd been quick to spot. About three dozen pages of meticulously laid-out timetables, instructions and budgets passed from his hands into the girls' before he realised he was just making work for himself and tired of the idea; unfortunately for Jill, the Tour Rules comprised six of these and were therefore still in full effect. Enshrined within them was the diktat that while Terri got to stay in the big hotel with her man, Jill always ended up on her own, shunted into some guest house somewhere on the outskirts of town. Terri also got to travel from place to place in the van and to go out with Marty after the show, while Jill had to take the train alone, eat alone, sleep alone, drink alone and – worse – wear a wig the entire time to minimise any chance of her being recognised.

Although the gospel of St Martin stated that she wasn't supposed to, a couple of times she slept with theatre technicians she fancied, mainly as a way of relieving the tedium. As much as she could, she kept these flings quiet from her colleagues; not because she was embarrassed or knew she was breaking any of their stupid rules – she couldn't have cared less either for their regulations or for what they thought of her morals – but because the first time it happened Terri found out and, convinced Jill was threatening the act, went into a sulk that lasted for days on end.

'If word gets out . . .' she'd wittered, until she'd filled Jill with hatred and venom, and driven even Marty half insane.

'I'm not sure the Tour Rules weren't a little over the top,' the magician had tried to say.

'Rules are rules, Marty. They're there for a reason. If you didn't mean to stick by them you shouldn't have drawn them up. They make perfect sense to me.'

It was incidents like this that transformed what had only briefly been a team back into a band of individuals. With Terri getting stroppier and cattier, revealing herself to be what Jill had previously decided she wasn't – a self-obsessed and small-minded Surrey princess – she gradually discovered the awful truth: that she'd swopped a dull life of dole and dead-end jobs for an even duller and more alienating one spent on the road, without even her friends and family around her to enliven it. With such a sheen of glamour as there had been now largely chipped away she was left turning the whole thing over in her hands and finding it inconsequential, tacky and cheap.

What percentage of the population of the towns and cities they played knew they existed? How many glowing write-ups in the local papers – or even damning crits – did they actually receive? What they did was not considered important, not at all. It wasn't as though they were pop stars. As far as Jill could see, most of the venues they performed in only survived by dint of government grant. And the audiences they did get – middle management types and their catalogue-dazzled wives if they were supporting a comedian, OAPs and school parties if they weren't – how many of them really cared how 'The Fly' was actually achieved, even if they'd enjoyed watching it? With the exception of the odd senile oldster and a handful of young children, no one was genuinely fooled. They all knew it was false-bottomed cabinets and misdirection, surely they did, and they saw much better special effects at the cinema. How many of them would really notice if they stumbled into Terri and Jill drinking together in a pub? The whole thing was absurd.

She began telling herself she should never have left Morecambe in the first place. They'd started rebuilding the old promenade, her mother had told her on the phone just recently; spending a bit of money, smartening the place up a bit. It wasn't such a bad part of the world, at the end of the day. It surprised her, but she was actually starting to pine for the things about it that she'd always derided; things like the crisp, clean air, the beautiful views, the calm half-cup of pillow-like mountains that had sheltered her ever since she was a child; for the Friday night chaos at the Battery Point boozer and the short stagger home across the hard, puckered sand; for the coughs and creaks of the gulls, and the rattle of the spindle-stiff riggings on the fishing smacks; for the reticulated cobwebs of weed that ensnared the promontories of rocks as the tide went out; for the enormous skies that rolled up out of nowhere and across which the compact little clouds her mam called dolphin clouds scudded in shoals towards sunsets so magnificent that her dad always used to say, 'That'll be Ireland on fire again; will you just look at it for the love of all beauty.'

She missed the great white Midland Grand Hotel, a ghost vessel lying broken-backed on the beach with another era stowed in its hold. She missed having Manchester, and Liverpool, and Blackpool, and Sonya and Paul all within easy reach. And she was beginning to regret having turned down Paul's offer of love, made late the final damp, awkward night before his last morning in Beckenham, an offer she'd suspected had been coming for some time and which she'd had the meanness to toy with, and mock and decline.

She'd been on the verge of walking out and leaving the others to it when something had happened to make her change her mind. One afternoon rehearsal in the run-up to Christmas, Jill had been surprised to hear Marty suggest to Terri one day while the three of them were cleaning out the cages that housed Siegfried, Roy and their nine new clones that once a week, on their night off, she stay back in the hotel for the evening while he took the other girl out for a drink or a meal or a film, to give her a break from being the secret pivot upon which their magic turned.

'Poor Jill has to spend so much time alone,' he'd said. 'It must be driving her half mad.'

Nice gesture that it was, Her Royal Highness's reaction had hardly been much of a surprise. 'On our night off? But what about me? When am I supposed to get to see you?'

'You see me all day every day, and every night after the show.'

'But Marty, it's our night off! I'm just not prepared to give it up!'

Jill had expected that would settle it but Marty had insisted, laying into Terri for being selfish with such vehemence that she'd ended up running from the room, tears flying from her eyes, saying that the two of them could do whatever the hell they liked, she didn't care.

For the first time, Jill began to wonder if Terri might be jealous. She couldn't understand it, not really. She'd have been lying if she'd said there'd never been any sexual tension between her and Marty: there'd been a bit, right at the start, when she'd first come to visit them in Beckenham. But then it would've been weird if there hadn't been – after all, she did look like his girlfriend and three's always a crowd. But she'd done what she could to defuse the situation with her comments and jokes, and it had calmed down soon enough. Since she'd come down to visit for the second time any undercurrents that had been there before had completely disappeared, as far as she was aware.

Certainly there'd never been anything anywhere near powerful enough going on to sour her and Terri's relationship. Quite the opposite. When they'd stopped getting along Jill'd just put it down to them both discovering they didn't like the other as much as they'd thought – that and a row they'd had over astrology one time, when Terri had presented her with her and Paul's charts, and tried to explain how they were perfect for each other, a piece of information to which Jill responded by telling Terri she thought astrology was a complete pile of shit, practised by idiots for idiots. She'd apologised immediately, tried to point out that her friendship with Paul was kind of a touchy subject, but she'd fired a big gun right into the heart of Terri's world and things were never quite the same again.

But now she had to wonder if that row hadn't been symptom rather than cause. What was Terri trying to do, setting her up with Paul? Was it just to make sure she wasn't a threat? Now that Jill considered it, it made perfect sense.

Her suspicions were confirmed in Leeds. Christmas had come and gone, and now it was January and they'd been nearly a full week at the City Varieties. Arriving late at the theatre one night Jill had heard raised voices coming from the other side of the closed door of the Green Room. More than raised voices, in fact: it was Marty and Terri, and they were screaming at each another.

'You want to fuck her, I know you do, why don't you just come straight out and admit it?' Jill heard Terri howl just as she was reaching out to open the door.

Jerking back her hand, she ducked into the women's toilets to wait out the storm, though not before she'd heard Marty yell a furious denial and follow it up with what sounded like a slap. Certainly it must've been something momentous, to judge by the blood-curdling female cry that it triggered.

The women's loos proved no escape: thanks to some sonic freak in the structure of the building, Jill spent the next ten minutes listening to the two-stroke pulse of Terri's sobs echo around the cubicle into which she'd retreated. When the noise had died away and it seemed safe to venture in among the animals Jill found her double sitting alone, staring at herself in the dressing-table mirror, eyes opened unnaturally wide and varnished with a layer of electricity, arm working like a camshaft as she tried to disguise with heavy dabs of blusher the bruise already purpling her cheek.

So Marty had smacked her around a little, had he? It was hateful of her, and unsisterly, but Jill couldn't help feeling a tinge of *schadenfreude* at the revelation. Friend or enemy, any girl she knew would have come to her immediately, looking for moral support; any girl, that was, but Terri, who seemed to be endeavouring to appear as tart and unfriendly as ever. And if she wasn't going to ask for help, Jill certainly wasn't going to offer it. It was hardly as if the little bitch hadn't driven the poor guy to it. She'd had it coming – Jill reckoned that in Marty's position she'd have fetched her one a long time before.

★

Marty, meanwhile, was outside in the car park pacing furiously and wishing that he smoked. He'd never hit anyone before, not anyone – he'd never even contemplated it. It had come up out of him like a reflex, or so he told himself. Terri's accusation had dislodged some vital peg wedged deep inside him, a peg which had been anchoring a dangerous distribution of forces. Like hawsers holding a ship, these forces had been suddenly released – and the effect had been to catapult his knuckles up, across and into contact with her face before he'd had a moment's chance to think.

In spite of all these mental somersaults the awkward notion still remained that his action might somehow have been premeditated, even relished. Yes, his nerve had broken, his patience had been exhausted, his resolve had frayed. But had there also been some calculation there, an understanding that by resorting to this final sanction he could prove a point, refute Terri's claims, put an end to all her questioning? Had he known deep down that by hitting Terri he could tell a more effective lie? Because it was true. He did want to sleep with Jill, and the desire to do so had been eating into him, corroding him from the inside out.

But so what? She looked like Terri, didn't she? And since they'd started on the tour she'd proved a damn sight more easygoing than his girlfriend. But had he done anything about it? No, aside from a bit of surreptitious flirting.

But Terri was behaving as if she'd caught them in bed together. It had got to the point where it seemed she couldn't bear Jill's name to pass her lips. When she did refer to her it was using that ridiculous nickname 'Ms Buttons', the one she'd invented when she'd returned to Beckenham from her mother's that day. Marty couldn't get his head round it. It was like she simply couldn't bear to share the limelight with anyone else, which seemed a possibility too absurd to contemplate, especially seeing as how if it weren't for Jill there wouldn't *be* any limelight. Unless, of course, that's what Terri actually wanted. But she couldn't want that. Could she?

Marty didn't understand. He felt miserable, powerless, guilty and frustrated. Now that after all these years he finally had the show he wanted, the show that would give him a decent shot at becoming a really serious magician, he wasn't being allowed to enjoy it. The events of the last twelve months should have made him happy, but instead he was angry, confused and depressed.

It was enough to make him want to hit someone.

Which, unfortunately, was exactly what he'd just gone and done.

He had to think this one through. He had to find some way out of this labyrinth. First things first. Don't panic; breathe. Get a handle on your breathing. One, two, three, four, out, in, out. So. Think. He knew how to get out of a maze, any maze. There was a trick to it, a trick he knew. All you did was walk along, keeping your right hand touching the wall. It might take a while, but eventually you'll end up at the exit. Don't lift your hand from the wall and keep on walking. That's all you do.

Okay.

Now.

He hadn't really *hit* Terri at all. Meaning that he hadn't made a fist and given her a thumping. She'd started going on and on about him and Jill; she'd started to frighten him; she'd seemed completely hysterical. It wasn't fair, what she'd been saying; he hadn't done anything wrong; he'd been telling her for months and months now there was nothing between Jill and him. What else could he do? He was sick of it, he'd just wanted to prove to her that he wasn't lying, he was serious, that he'd reached the end of his tether, that he didn't know how to deal with this. He'd thought that maybe if he slapped her once, hard, across the face, like male leads sometimes did to hysterical women in old films, she'd come to her senses, would understand.

But she'd moved, of course. She'd turned to protect herself and he'd caught her higher up on the face than he'd intended. He'd wanted to deliver a stinging slap to the side of her jaw, but she'd turned and he'd driven the heel of his hand up under the arch of her eye. Marty'd never hit anyone before, not even in school. He'd always used magic to squirm his way out of fights, hadn't he? He had no experience in that department, didn't understand how in order to hit someone properly you had to factor in the likely reaction of your victim seeing you raise your arm.

Keep walking.

A Shell petrol station stood across the road; Marty stared at the reflection of its illuminated tartrazine sign where it glimmered from deep in the petrol-skinned pool that stretched from his toes to the low piece of kerbing that distinguished parking from pavement. All around him white lines fretted the tarmac, recently laid but already uneven, hence the puddle. There were no cars, either parked or driving past. Damp from the recent rain shower cling-filmed all surfaces and made the car park shine like what it was – a slick of weird substance poised halfway between diamond and coal. But from where Marty was standing this glamour wasn't visible; he could see only shadows and the acid refractions of the tall yellow sign. He sat on a bollard with his head in his hands and thought of Harry. Marty hadn't seen hide nor hair of him since he'd disappeared round the corner of Lincoln Avenue in that taxi nearly fifteen years ago. There'd been no letter, no phone calls, nothing. He had searched the Magic Circle files for a Harry Carpenter, even called the Magic Castle in America, but no one had ever heard of him. Whenever he asked his dad about it Tony Quick was always vague; as far as Marty remembered he'd never liked Harry too much anyway. He was no doubt happy to forget him. Karen didn't remember him at all, the last months of their mother's illness having apparently been blotted from her memory by some childhood self-preservation mechanism, and Rebecca didn't have a lot to say about him either – not that Marty saw her that much any more, not since she'd married a Spaniard and moved to Tenerife. For all he knew, Harry might be dead. If it hadn't been for his carefully preserved copy of *Jarrett*, still the most prized of all of his possessions, he'd have had to wonder if his step-uncle had ever really existed in the first place, if he hadn't been some wild hallucination conjured by his mind to protect him from the slow death of his mother.

There! Just up ahead. The exit. Terri went on and on about her dad walking out, but he'd lost his *mother*. When he was *ten*. What was Terri's pain in comparison with his? How much more sympathy and understanding did he deserve? And how much did he get? None. That was how much. All he had was his magic, his dream. It was what life had given him in place of his mum. He had a *right* to it. It was *his*. But if he was going to have it he was going to have to learn to control his impulses, to be strong, to choreograph himself. To perform properly at all times, not just on stage. Success in all things, he'd always been certain, was just sleight of hand. He had to concentrate, not allow lapses like the one he'd let slip tonight. *Fuck* Terri. She wasn't going to get him to admit that he had feelings for Jill. What she had should be enough. He wouldn't give in. He would perfect the illusion so that from every angle it looked like the whole truth. He would remove all division between his life and his art. He wouldn't give in. Only that way would the magic come through.

Christ. Why did it have to be so hard?

The unexpected thing was that the violence seemed to have worked. Instead of opening a Pandora's box of horrors, as Marty had feared, hitting Terri seemed to have knocked whatever had been out of sync inside her head back into its slot. The show that night had been better than ever – vibrant, on the button, applauded like never before – and though Marty had had a sleepless night, kept awake by the bright light of a galaxy of possible repercussions while, next to him, his girlfriend cried herself quietly to sleep, by the next morning she seemed to have pulled herself together. Apart from the heavy foundation she was wearing, it was as if none of it had ever happened.

Still, for a couple of days Marty didn't dare to think that the crisis could have subsided that easily. It wasn't until he took Jill out two days later and Terri agreed to stay back at the hotel without so much as a whimper that he figured it was over, that the battle had been won. He'd never thought it was really possible to 'knock some sense' into somebody, but maybe there was some truth in the expression after all. Terri wasn't likely to be having sex with him for a while – and fair enough, he couldn't expect to get off without some punishment. But as he lay in bed that night after returning from his evening with Jill, his girlfriend breathing heavily at his side, her body shifted away from him, Marty felt happy. Their row had been the culmination of a time of stress for both of them, he was sure. Terri had no doubt been as frightened by how much she'd wound him up as he'd been by hitting her, but now it had happened and the tension had been released it made sense that they should take some time to address what it was within each of them that had caused the situation. For his part, Marty had it all straight in his head, pretty much. When the right moment came he'd be ready to sit down and talk it through with Terri. Together.

★

Terri was prissy and self-centred, it was true, but it might've been easier for her to examine her own role in the situation if she hadn't kept slamming up against the feeling, sitting stubborn as a stone in her gut, that on some level Marty was lying to her. It was the Jill issue, of course; her astrology and what she called her woman's intuition told her there was something going on between Marty and the other assistant, even if she had no proof of it. And if there had been any possibility at all of her realising that her jealousy and suspicions were helping to create the very situation she feared, that possibility had been well and truly trounced by Marty's moment of violence.

Terri had been brought up to believe that it was never, ever acceptable for men to hit women, whatever the circumstances. This was an absolute as far as she was concerned, as incontrovertibly true as the passage of the planets in their orbits. Provocation was a non-starter, a total irrelevance whoever the victim happened to be – and she certainly had never, ever in any circumstances thought it might be her. The second Marty struck her she'd erected a bubble around herself, built from a kind of mental Plexiglas. With this shield up, Terri knew nothing could touch her. She could be beaten, raped, abused; it would not matter. As far as she was concerned, she'd effectively removed herself from the situation until such time as the tour was over and she felt safe enough to resume control. Anything that happened to her in the interim – and anything she herself said or did – well, it wouldn't be her it was happening to, it wouldn't be her who was responsible.

She had made up her mind and, as she was so fond of saying,

once she'd made up her mind wild horses couldn't make her budge.

★

Discovering the full extent of the consequences for Marty of sticking up for her had changed Jill's opinion of him. Already she'd started to forgive him his more irritating stylings and was starting to see him in a different light. She had to admit she was impressed by his total commitment to making the show a success. She'd never seen anyone be so single-minded about anything before, except maybe Paul when he was working on his computers. Recalling how over the last few months she'd watched the magician design and build props, direct rehearsals, organise travel arrangements, deal with the continual changes of theatres and staff, and on top of all that perform faultlessly on stage every night, she began to forget that in the beginning she'd regarded him as a bit of a tosser.

While she was still refusing to acknowledge that magic might be anything apart from a cheesy and dead-end profession, Jill did understand now what high demands it made on its practitioners. Marty's stagecraft, his sleight of hand, the stuff she had to do as an assistant – it was all making her realise how difficult putting on a good performance actually was. The art of illusion? Okay, so maybe there was an art to it after all. She hadn't yet got round to liking Marty's tendency to over-organise, and she still felt that he lived in a total dream world with respect to other people's thoughts and emotions. But she was finding him altogether less of a twat than she had previously. When he'd told her, over dinner, that first evening he'd made Terri stay in the hotel, that back in the 1920s magicians that had specialised in mind-reading tricks were called mentalists, it had made her laugh. That's what he was, she'd replied, a fucking mentalist. What she didn't tell him was that she could connect with that. That she liked people who were a little bit weird, a little bit extreme. It didn't mean, though, that she wouldn't still rip the piss whenever she got the chance.

★

Terri's new unemotive, super-protective stance was completely misinterpreted by Marty. He saw her sudden calmness and self-possession as a positive, a sign that the two of them were developing a new and powerful bond. She didn't seem distant to Marty at all; it was his own self of several nights ago that now seemed far away, as if viewed through the wrong end of a telescope. They'd both been out of order, he'd done something he regretted, but Terri had understood and realised that by chilling out and forgiving him they could move on to a new stage in their relationship.

They were, he felt, both growing up.

Taking Jill out for the evening had helped to centre him. These days her company always made him feel good about himself. He felt charming and accomplished when he made her laugh, or did or said something that impressed her, precisely because she was so difficult to impress. In the fallow time between their weekly outings he found himself preoccupied with thinking up unobtrusive little close-up routines to amuse her with and one time he even did that old two-ashen-hearts number Darren had once used to pull Terri (and he told Jill its provenance, too, suspecting that the confidence would be a more effective piece of ammunition than the trick).

On this night in particular, though, seeing Jill was a relief. After he hit Terri he'd been secretly terrified that the other girl would find out and, out of solidarity and sisterhood, despise him for it. But it looked as if this fear had been unfounded, thank God. The continued success of the act depended on keeping both girls onside, after all.

Marty hadn't really noticed yet, but he was beginning to blur his two assistants into one. He was losing track of where one stopped and the other began. Jill, he'd started thinking with increasing frequency, was so much more like what he hoped Terri might be if she'd only learn to relax and take things more in her stride, and his girlfriend's restrained reaction to his hitting her was, he felt, a sign that this much wished-for transformation was under way. Terri's looks, Jill's character, Marty was starting to allow himself to think. That was his ideal.

As a general rule, most magicians favour a brand of playing cards called Bicycles. These are manufactured in Cincinnati, Ohio by the US Playing Card Company; the cards' backs are decorated with a symmetrical, heavily embellished drawing of a winged cupid riding a bicycle. This design is surrounded with a narrow white border, and it is this border – along with the cards' durable, 'air-cushioned' finish, which enables them to slide easily over each other without stickiness – that makes them so suitable for card sleight of hand: the border makes it harder to see if two or more cards are being held together or if a 'break' is being maintained in the pack in order to keep track of a particular card.

Bee brand cards – which are manufactured by the same company – don't have a border. The back design is a repeated pattern of diamonds which is printed right up to the very edge of the card in what is known as 'steamboat-style', cards of this type being first used on board nineteenth-century entertainment paddle-steamers of the kind on which the Mississippi Showboat bar in Blackpool was modelled. They are also popular with magicians, but for a different reason.

In the discipline of magic, a distinction is drawn between card sleight of hand and card manipulation. While 'sleight of hand' covers the range of moves deployed in close-up routines, card manipulation is more naturally allied with stage illusion. When magicians produce cards – singly, or in extravagant fans or water-falls – from out of nowhere, that's card manipulation. To achieve these effects, the cards often need to be held in a reverse finger palm, i.e. bent backwards and trapped by their corners between the first and second, and third and fourth fingers on the outside of the hand. In this position the card – or cards, as the best manipulators can hide up to a dozen in this grip – have a tendency to poke through the fingers and protrude slightly on the other side. As the red edges of Bee cards don't show up as clearly against the flesh as the white borders of Bicycles, experts tend to prefer them.

Marty used Bees for neither of these reasons. Though he'd once fancied himself as a card manipulator, he was actually better at sleight of hand – even if he did look down on it. So why didn't he use Bicycles? Did he just want to be different? Did he prefer the design of the Bee joker, an imp riding circus-style upon a bumblebee, over the Bicycles' fat king on a bike? Did he like the diamond pattern on the back? The truth was none of these. Marty used Bees simply because Uncle Harry had used them; like his addiction to *Jarrett*, using Bees was something enshrined in the sacredness of his past, something he correspondingly held out in front of him as an emblem for the future. It wasn't, therefore, something the implications of which he'd fully thought through. A bit like his plan for coaching Jill.

After they left Leeds, Marty decided it was about time that Jill received some tutoring in the wider principles of magic. It would help her confidence on stage, he felt, if she had a more complete picture of the discipline in which she'd become involved, prevent her from being a mere box jumper, as magicians' assistants were often called.

When Marty told Terri of his idea she registered absolutely no interest at all, and with Jill keen to give the lessons a go (anything to combat the boredom) the first of the sessions went ahead in the little lounge bar in Jill's guest house, which was generally empty of an afternoon. To encourage his student he'd dropped by the local Waterstone's and bought her a copy of the new Harry Houdini biography as a gift. It had just come out and he'd heard it was good – in his experience if you wanted to get anybody into magic, Houdini was the best place to start.

With the two of them sitting either side of small circular hammered-copper table, backsides on burgundy leatherette buttoned-cushion stools, Marty began by showing Jill something called 'the double lift', a technique fundamental to all card magic. After he'd demonstrated some of the different routines in which the technique was used he moved on to memory tricks, specifically the memorising of the order of the cards in an entire pack.

Jill protested that she didn't believe anyone could actually do this and, to prove her wrong, Marty passed her a fresh pack of Bees. After asking her to cut them he told her to lift cards off the top of the deck one by one and hold them facing away from him, while he told her what they were. He removed the top card himself to illustrate, then proceeded to correctly identify the next fifteen or twenty cards.

Jill was astonished. 'How d'you do that?'

'I told you. I memorised the order.'

'But I cut the deck.'

'Exactly. But remember how I took the top card to show you how to hold it? That's so I knew where to begin.'

'But I couldn't ever remember fifty-two cards in order.'

'Well, neither could I.'

'You just did.'

'No – see, I didn't. And that's the trick. All I remembered was two things: the word "chased", and this rhyme: "Eight kings threatened to save ninety-five ladies for one sick knave."'

'"One sick knave"? That supposed to be some kind of reference to you?'

Marty flushed. Had she found out about Terri and him?

'No, you prat.' He laughed, too loudly. '"Chased" gives you the order of the suits: C-H-S-D, Clubs, Hearts, Spades, Diamonds. And the rhyme gives you the order of the values: eight, king, three, ten, two, seven, nine, five, queen, four, ace, six and jack, otherwise known as knave.'

Jill took the pack and spread it face upwards on the table, mouthing the rhyme to herself as she worked through the cards. 'Oh, I *see*. Yeah, that's pretty clever. But wait a minute. Some of these cards have got out of order. If we'd carried on a bit further you'd've got it wrong.'

'What?' Marty was horrified.

'Yeah. The Queen of Hearts and the Queen of Spades have got all out of order. Look.'

Marty bent to check she wasn't having him on. 'I don't know how that happened,' he said, quickly scooping up the cards and blushing again. 'I'm usually a perfectionist about that kind of thing.'

'Anyone can make a mistake.'

'Yeah, but you can't afford to make errors like that, not in magic. Magic's all preparation, whether you're doing a card trick for one person or performing a huge teleportation illusion for an audience of hundreds.' Opening his satchel, Marty threw the offending deck roughly in, scattering the cards among his other belongings in a slightly theatrical demonstration of annoyance. 'Won't be using those again,' he muttered half to himself, as if the pack had been tainted by some kind of bad karma.

Then he spotted the Houdini biography he'd bought earlier. 'Here,' he said, passing it over still wrapped inside its bag. 'I brought you a present.'

'Oh,' she said, when she saw what it was. 'Thanks. I'm not much of reader. But I'll give it a go.' She flipped through the pages, stopping at the photographic plates, then gave Marty a smile and leaning over kissed him on the cheek.

'I just thought, with all this time on your hands, you might like . . .'

'It was nice of you. Thanks.'

'If you want to know about preparation, Houdini's the man. He was a total athlete, you see. Developed voluntary control over every muscle in his body, even things like his oesophagus and splincter, so he could use them to hide keys and lock picks and stuff. But he also realised that by exploiting the media he could use magic to make him a star – he was a PR genius as well as a genius of illusion. Actually, I reckon there's lots of similarities between the two things . . .'

Jill stared at him, lips pursed. 'Marty,' she said, breaking in on him, 'don't you ever get bored?'

'Bored?'

'Don't you ever get bored of doing magic?'

Now there was a question – did he ever get bored? Marty put aside the pack of cards he'd been riffling and laid his hands palm down on the table. 'Of course, sometimes.' He looked down at his thumbs, mistaking this for an opportunity to project some self-importance. 'But that's not the point. That's something you've got to get over, as a professional magician.'

'Well, if you've got any tips on how to do it, feel free to share, because between you and me, Marty boy, I'm beginning to find this tour of ours pretty rug-munchingly dull. No offence, mind.'

'None taken.' Although there was, just a little bit. 'How to get over it, huh? Well, I suppose you've just got to try and keep your mind focused on the big picture.'

'What big picture? That it's all about preparation?'

'No. You know. Money. Fame. Success. This show's definitely good enough for us to make a name for ourselves. Soon enough we'll break out of this circuit and then it won't be Blackpool and the Magic Circle any more, it'll be the Magic Castle in Hollywood and the Golden Nugget in Vegas.'

'Las Vegas?' Jill was sceptical. From what she'd seen of Las Vegas on the telly it was all tack and slot machines, just like Blackpool except a thousand times the size and stuck out in the desert without even the sea to redeem it. (Though she'd read in a magazine recently that one of the casinos had built itself a gigantic artificial beach, complete with genuine salt water and a wave machine, to compensate for this shortcoming.)

'Vegas.' Marty repeated the word with the reverence and pride a Muslim would have reserved for sounding the two syllables of Mecca, providing Jill with a sudden picture of him rolling out a craps baize and kneeling on it every morning in a private genu-flection, facing west, his forehead touched to the seven. 'Magic's dead here. It's over. It died with variety. You think I want to be the next Paul Daniels? Forget that. I want to be the next David Copperfield. The next Lance Burton.'

'Who's Lance Burton?' Jill imagined some tacky entertainer doing lame tricks in front of an audience of people dressed like bad imitations of Dean Martin and Sammy Davis Jr.

'Burton's the guy at the receiving end of the biggest entertainment contract in the history of the world,' Marty explained. 'Period,' he added, using one of the many Americanisms he'd picked up over the years in preparation for the day when he'd finally get to go there and assimilate.

'Oh,' Jill said, still unmoved. And for the first time since she'd tried to smoke that spliff in his dad's dining room, Marty nearly lost his temper with her. 'Oh? Oh? *One hundred million dollars over fourteen years*. Oh. That's right. *Oh*. Why do you think I work so hard at this, put up with all these shitty gigs, all your and Terri's bullshit day in day out?' He hadn't meant to say it. But maybe it wasn't such a bad thing if Jill knew how much he felt the two of them had been dicking him around. 'Because *I've* got my eyes on the prize. That's why. And both of you should have yours fixed on it too. I'm not pissing about here, you know. I'm not doing this for the good of my bloody health. I tell you, the three of us, if we can get this act right, we can be up there too. Maybe not a hundred-million-dollar contract, but a big Vegas booking? It's not impossible. And then we're looking at ten, twenty, even thirty thousand dollars apiece.'

'A year?' said Jill, confused again. It still didn't sound like all that much money to her.

'A week, Jill darling. A fucking *week*.'

'Oh.' That kind of money meant freedom. Real freedom. Freedom to do whatever you wanted to do, however you wanted to do it. Whenever. For ever. 'Wow.'

'Yeah. You said it. Wow.'

Jill, it seemed, was finally impressed.

'I didn't think when I took this job I'd end up right back here,' Jill quipped when the three of them convened backstage at Legends for the dress rehearsal. 'But at least I can catch up with some of my friends. I'm so narked off with sitting around in bloody hotel rooms, I can't tell you.'

'Oh, you can't do that,' Terri announced immediately, pulling a pair of plastic-looking tights up the length of her legs.

'What do you mean?'

'Once any of the locals know it'll be all round the town in seconds. It will.'

Jill didn't take kindly to this. 'So you're saying that my friends can't keep their mouths shut, are you?'

'No, I'm not saying that at all.' Terri turned to Marty, who was fiddling with a damaged hinge on one of the cabinets, trying to pretend that this confrontation wasn't happening. 'Tell her, Marty. I'm not being personal, am I? It's just that we've got to protect the show. It's our top priority. You made the rules, not me.'

Marty glanced up, looking harassed. He was beginning to curse the day he'd ever thought up those wretched rules. But he couldn't go on fighting Jill's corner for ever.' 'Fraid Terri's right,' he said quietly. 'We agreed that back in Beckenham. Sorry, Jill.'

'Oh, fuck that shit! What about my parents? And Paul? Paul already knows, remember? Or have you forgotten that he put together all those nice graphics you're so proud of?'

220

Marty nodded and upped his mental clock speed. He started thinking permutations, transpositions, combinations. A magician's skills. 'I suppose we should make an exception for family,' he said. He looked at Terri, trying to gauge her face. 'And Paul.'

Terri glowered. 'I really don't think . . .'

'What!'

'Come on, Tel, it'd be a bit fucking extreme, don't you think? Not to let them come?'

'We made a rule about secrecy and I just think we should stick to it, that's all.'

Jill stared at her. It was a weird feeling, seeing your very own face and experiencing an acute desire to punch it. She was amazed Marty didn't fetch her one more often. Fuck it, man, she would. Really she would.

'Okay. Well, that just means Marty's going to have to take me out as usual, then. And I'm not sticking a week in Blackpool without going clubbing. So Friday night, Marty, you're mine, all right? And I mean all fucking night.'

Marty reddened, shrugged, studied his hinge. 'Whatever,' he said, like this was something he'd just have to resign himself to.

'That all right with you, Terri dear?'

Terri's response was to turn, swing up her right heel, place it against the wall at around shoulder height, then slowly begin to push it higher and higher until she'd brought her body into a near-perfect vertical split. 'Of course,' she said, the words dry and constricted, almost choking her, her mouth up against her knee. 'Do what you like.'

Forget about Jill's husky voice, about her habits and her preferences, her direct sense of humour; you could tell just by the way she walked that she functioned in a wholly different manner from Terri. Terri moved with her arms and her legs; some people might have described this as 'grace', but only if they liked looking at women who were psychologically hampered by nervous timidity. Jill, on the other hand, was powered from her belly and her hips, and walking alongside her to the club Marty had to watch how he timed his own strides in order to prevent them cracking pelvises.

It took only about eight or nine minutes to get from Legends to Heaven and Hell, but when they got there they had to wait at the back of a medium-length queue. The cold sea air gnawed at their bones despite the two tequila slammers they'd done before leaving the hotel and, stamping up and down and hugging themselves (and on one slightly awkward occasion each other), they attracted the attention of the two blokes in Manchester City shirts standing in front of them, who now turned around.

'What're you like? It's not bloody cold. This is warm, this is, for February.' The boy had a waxed Caesar haircut, pale scalp showing through the combed-forward hair, a pimple-peppered forehead and cheeks. He was chewing on something.

'You're a bit dressed up, aren't'cha?' said his friend, who looked exactly the same, just three inches shorter. The two of them peered hard at Marty's suit and he had the strange feeling it had suddenly become too big for him.

'What are you two, then, brothers or something?' asked Jill.

'Nah,' said the taller of the two, 'what makes you think that?'

'Nothing, not really. Just wondering.'

'You look just like Princess Di,' said the replica, after staring in silence for a while. Inwardly, Marty groaned. Terri got this at least two or three times a week and had done for years, but she'd worked as a lookalike, after all, and so she was used to it. For Jill, though, it was still something of a novelty, mainly because it only ever happened on these evenings out with Marty – when she was on her own she had to remove her contacts and don the chestnut brown 'China Girl' wig that was the centrepiece of her daily disguise. People, Jill had discovered, had a tendency to imagine that just because you looked like a celebrity it made you public property as well, but unlike Terri she liked playing up to it – especially now she was back in Blackpool, which was after all home turf for her.

'You think so?' she said to the Manc a little flirtily, feeling liberated, irresponsible; as though she were, for the duration of the evening, someone else. She lit a cigarette and started to chat to the boys, mimicking Terri slightly with her voice, mocking her turn of phrase.

Watching her Marty felt self-conscious, awkward, excluded, a little jealous even. He told himself it was the usual paranoia about someone accidentally stumbling across the secret of the show, but really – also as usual – he wanted Jill all to himself. But one of the boys was already asking Marty questions, forcing him to join in and talk. He had a bad feeling about this one. He'd become quite adept over the years at deflecting the shit he got for being a southerner when he was touring round the north, but Jill's adoption of a stuck-up Home Counties accent – designed, no doubt, to take the piss out of Terri – would surely make things more difficult. It was looking a bit random, this one.

'You a magician, are you?' the replica said. 'You a couple, like?'

'That's right,' said Jill, giving Marty a kiss on the cheek and a simultaneous prod in the ribs.

'Up here for the convention?'

'No, not this year,' Marty said, squirming. 'We're doing a show over at Legends.'

'What, out on North Pier?'

'That's the one.'

'Show us a trick, then.'

'Yeah, go on. Show us a trick.'

Marty hedged. 'Oh, er, I don't know.'

'Oh, bloody go on.'

Now, suddenly, it was a challenge and a threat. Marty glanced across at Jill. She was smoking and waiting, expecting him to do something. Of course she was. She was winding him up, the bitch.

He hesitated. 'Well, I haven't any cards or coins or things like that on me,' he said, addressing the original, who though taller was actually the less intimidating of the two. 'But I've got one of those new self-healing banknotes. Have you seen them?'

'Don't be daft.'

'No, really. Look.' Reaching in his pocket, Marty took out his wallet, opened it and pulled out a cashpoint-fresh tenner. Handing the wallet to Jill to hold, he showed the note to his mini audience. 'A normal ten-pound note, yeah? Now. Watch carefully.' He folded the note in half, then in half again; and then – holding it so they could clearly see what he was doing – he started to tear into it about a centimetre from the double-folded corner, the routine flooding him with confidence as it had done so often in the past.

When he saw that the rip was real, the shorter of the Mancs began to protest. But Marty just nodded, brought the partly torn corner up to his mouth and bit the flap he'd created clean off, leaving a square-shaped little hole.

'Aw, no!'

He smiled and opened up one of the folds, then bringing the note to his mouth for a second time enlarged the hole with his teeth. Showing the boys the hole, he folded the note over for a third time and blew on it, opening it out as he did so and holding it taut. The hole had gone.

'Well, bugger me,' said the original. 'Let's see that.' But Marty was already putting the note back inside his wallet. 'Go on, let's see it.'

Marty just shrugged.

'That were wicked.'

'Yeah, that were wicked, that.'

'That was pretty good,' Jill admitted. 'I've not seen that one before.'

Marty glowed.

'Show us how you do it, then,' ordered the shorter one.

Marty gave the stock response. 'It's magic,' he said.

'Come on, show us,' said the friend.

Immediately the glow was gone. 'I can't show you. It'd spoil it.'

'Bollocks it will. I wanna know how to do it. Why can't you show us? What's your problem?'

'Yeah – what's your problem?'

'There's no problem,' Marty said, floundering. 'But I can't.'

'You're fockin' askin' for it, you are.' Within the time it had taken to speak a couple of sentences, the whole atmosphere had changed. Maybe they were just putting the shits up him or perhaps they were genuinely looking for a fight, but Marty had no idea which.

'He'll show you, but it'll cost you,' Jill said suddenly.

At the sound of the girl's voice, the Mancs looked confused: she'd dropped her false Terri accent and addressed them in her native Morecambe tones. 'How much?'

She smiled, took a drag on her fag. 'How much d'you think? A tenner of course.' Marty breathed out. It was the perfect response.

'A tenner? Fuckin' hell.' The two lads looked back at Marty.

'Of course,' he said, emboldened by Jill's intervention. 'You don't think *I* got it for nothing, do you?'

'Aw, well, fuck that. I ain't paying a tenner for that crap.'

'He's a pretty crap magician I reckon, if that's the best he can do.'

Just then the queue began to move. The doorman let a block

of people file past him; when his arm dropped, it separated the two boys from Marty and Jill. Jill leaned back against the wall, shook her head. Marty turned to her, raised his eyebrows. 'And I thought I was doing so well,' he said. Which made her laugh.

'Oh, they were all right. They were E-ing off their tits, that's all,' she told him.

'Really?' said Marty. 'God, I never noticed. How could you tell?'

★

Inside the club it was busy. Packed, even. The layout was straight-forward: two large rooms linked by a corridor which also connec-ted to a fire exit and the toilets. Heaven – the first of the rooms – was large and low-ceilinged, and painted a sort of toilet bowl blue. A bar ran along one side of a giant square, into which was set a large circular dance floor, bordered with benches and tables. The benches were constructed of plywood and carpeted with the same battered industrial-grade stock that lurked underfoot; in a reluctant concession to comfort a layer of thin foam cushions had been glued to their seats. The tables were also of simple construction: snot-green Formica slabs bolted on to iron pedestals, which were in their turn bolted to the floor.

Spilling off the dance floor, threading in between the tables, a group of pale, sweating eighteen-year-olds were doing the conga – to the delight of the DJ, who was not only playing the appropri-ate record but yelling encouragement over the PA.

'Go ornnn! Ye-es! You betcha. HA! Go on darlin', just do it. Laa-rvely. *Yeah . . .*'

Marty gazed around unhappily. This really wasn't his kind of scene.

'Hell's much better,' Jill shouted over the din and, pulling Marty out of the way of the derailing conga train, led him into a corridor which, if the press of bodies was anything to go by, was the most popular area of the club, no doubt because it was the only place that wasn't either of the two rooms. Unfortunately the corridor formed a natural bottleneck and in everybody's hurry to get wherever it was they were going it had been plugged solid with bodies. As they tried to force their way through, gridlock occurred and Jill and Marty found themselves stuck.

'Let's go back,' Marty yelled, unhappy that he was getting bathed in the second-hand sweat of at least three short and square-fringed local ravers, clones of the clones they'd run into outside. But Jill shook her head and told him to hold on, it would clear.

Craning his neck to try to see some kind of way through, Marty now realised that deep inside Hell a major disturbance was in progress – the real cause, perhaps, of the traffic flow problem. Before he could do anything with this information he'd been carried two feet to the right by a powerful wave of compression and, whipping his head round sharply to see what was going on, he found himself confronted by the three eager bouncers who, equipped with black bomber jackets and headset radio mikes, were shoving their way through the body jam, bursting it apart as efficiently as if the emergency exit doors further up the corridor had been thrown open and a giant plunger applied to the frame. With the bouncers powering through it the plug of bodies fractured asunder and, being just forward of the fault line, Marty, Jill and the three local ravers found themselves punched through the door and out into Hell, the security team barrelling past them and scattering them far and wide like fragments of glass.

Excited by having smashed through something, especially something made out of people, the bouncers continued on to the dance floor, piling more punters out of their way and returning seconds later with the two halves of the major disturbance locked in half nelsons, shirts and faces streaming with blood. Marty recognised one of them – it was the shorter of the two geezers they'd met in the queue. Or maybe the taller, he couldn't quite tell, what with him being all bent over backwards like that. Either way it was one less thing to have to worry about.

In contrast to Heaven, Hell was painted a visceral red; it had a small bar in one corner, and no dais. But the decor was much more fun: iron 'cages' had been constructed around the edges of the dance floor and there were various levels and booths and dance plinths, all of which were fenced round with dull wooden flames. Instead of the conga, nosebleed techno thrummed through the fetid air. Which was kind of appropriate, Marty reflected, given what he'd just seen.

'Awesome,' Jill yelled. 'Let's stay here.'

To Marty's mind it wasn't awesome at all. He hated techno. His idea of a nightclub was cocktails and cool jazz. He was even dressed in a suit – probably the only person wearing one in the entire place. He glanced nervously back over his shoulder at the way they'd come, hoping to persuade his up-for-it assistant into a retreat. But the doorway, cleared for a few glorious seconds, had already clotted up again and they were trapped, at least for the time being. 'All right,' he said and pointed in the direction of the bar.

★

Jill had broken the rules, she admitted to Marty as they sat down on a bench in the corner and sipped their drinks. She'd been to see Paul the previous afternoon, to pick up something he had for her. This was a small truth that covered a larger lie – she'd not only gone to pick something up but also to drop something off: tickets to the show for him and Sonya and her parents, all of whom she was determined would see it, whatever that bitch Terri said.

'Pick up what?' Marty asked, ignoring the confession.

'These.' She dropped her hand below the level of the table that curved round in front of them and opened it to reveal two small pale tablets, like off-colour aspirin but chunkier, with the Mitsubishi corporate logo stamped into their tops.

'What's that then? Ecstasy, I suppose.'

''Sright,' said Jill and promptly swallowed one of them.

'Only doing the one?'

'The other's for you.'

'Oh no, it's not. You know I don't touch that stuff.'

'How do you know what it's like if you've never tried it?'

'I don't have to try it. People die from taking it all the time. I mean, look at Leah Betts.'

'Marty, people die from eating peanuts all the time. People die from falling down stairs all the time. People die in wars all the time. People die from all sorts of stupid things, all the time. And Leah Betts didn't know what she was doing. I do. Come on. Just do a half. You'll enjoy it. I promise you. I won't let you drink too much water.' But Marty shook his head. Jill shrugged. 'Suit yourself. But you know what your problem is? You're scared of letting go. You're wound up like a fucking spring, Martin Quick. If you let yourself chill out a bit you might be surprised by what could happen.'

Marty stared at her. What did she mean? Over the years he'd had enough people tell him he was uptight for it no longer to affect him. But when she put it like that . . .

'Just a half?' he said tentatively.

'Just a half. See how you get on. If you like it, do the rest. If you don't, it's no big deal.' He stared at the tablet in her palm. It went right against his principles but then again, perhaps Jill had a point. He *was* too uptight. And maybe you shouldn't comment on what you haven't experienced.

'Fuck it. All right.'

'Good choice.'

'But don't we need a knife or something?'

'What for?'

'To split it in two.'

Jill looked at him as though he'd just landed from space. Placing the pill between her teeth, she bit through it and dropped two neat halves into her palm. One she gave to Marty, the other she slid down behind the foil lining of her pack of cigarettes. 'Just get it down you,' she said.

With her E inside her Jill went off to dance, something Marty didn't yet feel inspired to do. About half an hour later she came back and spent ten minutes telling him just what she thought about him and Terri and the act, half of which was embarrassingly complimentary, the other half embarrassingly blunt. Mid-way through a sentence she stopped and apologised, told him it was only the drug talking and that he shouldn't take her seriously. Then she gave him a hug and went back to dance.

Marty remained sitting where he was, sipping his vodka and Coke, feeling paranoid about everything Jill'd just told him and trying not to think about the betrayal he'd committed by taking that half-pill. He looked around the room, at the intoxicated hordes drinking and dancing and generally stumbling around; yelling, laughing, groping, not caring, having a go, having a laugh, up for it, out for what they could get. There was nothing here he wanted to emulate, that he wanted to be part of. Up on stage, looking down, that was where he felt safe. He wasn't spontaneous, it was true. But he was *good* at something. He had *talent*, and that made him different. He had routines. Ways of doing things. He had goals, dreams. He wanted something better. Was that such a crime? In America they didn't think so. In America you were *supposed* to want something better. Working hard to improve yourself, to achieve, to get ahead, that was seen as admirable over there. Not like here in this rotten little land where people hated you if you weren't satisfied with your lot. He watched Jill jigging away in the middle of the scrum, the focus for the predatory dance moves of three or four hopeful men. She had a better arse than Terri, it was true. Tighter, despite how she sat around on it all day, never doing any exercise. But the thought of her arse made Marty shiver and turn away – the last thing he wanted right now was to have to sit by and watch Jill pull.

Then suddenly, in the space of the next twenty seconds or so, the pill came on. Marty didn't know what it was at first; two minutes later he didn't care. He sat on the bench unable to move as his spine shot through the ceiling and his body seeped into the seat, and insecurities tumbled from him like the carapace of desert ice from a launching Saturn V. It was an absolutely incredible feeling, terrifying and gloriously reassuring both at once. He understood now why they called it Ecstasy.

Jill came over. 'You rushing?'

'I think so.' He could barely speak and when he did it felt strange, as if someone else were forming the words for him.

'Is it good?'

'Er . . . I think so. Will I be like this for the rest of the night?'

'No, no, it'll pass. Give it about fifteen minutes, then it'll level out. It's good E.'

'Yeah.' Marty gulped. 'Yeah, it is. Is it safe to have a drink of water?'

Jill giggled. 'Of course it is. Want me to get you one?'

'Yes, please.'

'Okay. Sit tight. Don't drink your vodka, not unless you want to kill it.'

She went off to the bar, returned with a bottle of Evian and sat with him until the rush had subsided. 'You okay now?'

'Yeah – yeah, I'm feeling a bit more normal.'

'Wanna dance?'

'Er, not right now. Think I'll sit here for a while longer.'

'Okay. I'm going to. I can't sit still. I'll be over there if you need me.'

'Okay. And . . . thanks, Jill.'

She took his hand and squeezed it. 'You're welcome.'

Left alone again, spine back below the level of his skull, Marty began to feel a little calmer. Maybe he'd go for a wander, see what was cooking. He looked towards the exit. The earlier traffic problems seemed to have subsided; he'd take a turn through Heaven, with a detour via the toilets.

Once standing upright he felt cool, loose, in control, pleased for the first time that evening that he was dressed the way he was. He felt, in fact, like he did when he was standing on stage, except now he was carrying that presence around with him. And this new-found confidence was clearly being picked up on by others: walking around he found himself acknowledging people in ways that he never did – meeting their gaze, nodding to boys, smiling at girls. Just being fully himself. And the great thing was, everyone seemed to like him for this. Boys nodded back, stepped aside to let him pass, said 'all right, mate' instead of behaving as if he weren't there. Girls gave him the eye, blew him kisses, neither ignored him nor came on too strong. It was a party, he was at it, he was there to enjoy himself, just like everyone else. This, it seemed, was the point of nightclubs – so obvious! As a teenager in Beckenham they'd been intimidating places, full of drunkenness and sudden violence, but here Marty didn't feel alienated, or wary, or frightened, or bored. He just felt amazing, a part of the scene: he was where he was, he belonged. He hadn't felt this good since he'd won *Young Magician*.

It was the drug, of course, that was making him feel this way – that was the point of taking it, after all, though Marty didn't quite understand this yet. Right now he just felt as though he'd taken a personality bath, had been sluiced free of all mental toxins. He went into the bathroom where – uncharacteristically at ease with the ocean of piss and vomit washing the floor – he splashed some water on to his cheeks. This felt amazing. He took a look in the mirror. He liked his face. It wasn't so bad. Now that he studied it, he was pretty handsome, he thought. He made to fix his hair but then thought no, fuck it, and ruffled it instead, letting out an involuntary laugh. Life was suddenly hilarious. Jesus! Jill was right. He took everything so seriously. What a joker he was. He loosened his tie. No, fuck it! He took his tie off, put it in his pocket.

Oblivious to the sniggers of a couple of teenagers standing at the urinals behind him, he left the Gents and went into Heaven, which didn't look so bad any more. The cheesy holiday camp DJ must have finished his set because a pumping house tune was playing and the dance floor was seriously heaving. The beat was infectious and Marty found himself jerking his neck to the rhythm. Of course the nightclub looks tacky and crap, he said to himself. No one cares what it looks like. They don't come here for the décor. He shook his head, astonished at himself for never having grasped this most simple of truths, and started to think about his life.

It was good, he decided straight away. The business with Terri was awful, there was no escaping that, but the thing was not to let himself be in denial about it but to face up to the situation and apologise, talk to her properly, work it all through. He'd been shying away from doing this and it now had to stop. Maybe he should even get her to split a pill with him . . . or maybe not, perhaps that was a bit hasty, he mustn't lose all perspective; the last thing she needed right now was for him to bounce out of bed in the morning gabbling like some kind of drug convert. But talking, definitely. It had to be done. And aside from that . . . well, things were going pretty swimmingly, all things considered. There was no need to be as uptight and worried as he had been over the last few months. He'd cracked it, he really had. The show was great; they'd finish here at Legends, they'd go down to the Talk, everything would be wonderful, and he'd bet that by the end of the year he'd be looking back on all this and laughing . . .

It was too much, suddenly. He was thinking too much. From thinking about the moment and his current situation, his conclusions and realisations widened and widened until they were apparently encompassing the entirety of his life – magic, Harry, mother, childhood, everything. From there they extended forward to infinity, at which point they collapsed in on themselves to form a turning kaleidoscope of insights that were grounded in nothing, that made no kind of sense. Marty shook his head, trying to clear it, then stared into space, suddenly unable to form the simplest thought. A vague sense of fear crept over him, fear that he was tumbling out of control. Vodka would kill it, Jill had said. Maybe he should get himself a drink? He felt in his jacket for his wallet but his pocket felt enormous, the size of a refuse sack, and he experienced a second or two of scrabbling panic before he realised no, it was okay, his wallet was still there.

At that moment a girl came by and grabbed his arm and asked him why he wasn't dancing. Glad of the interruption, Marty confessed he didn't know and went with her, allowing her to pull him into the crowd just as the first bars of the Chemical Brothers came on and everyone went completely *mental* . . .

★

Since she'd left Marty at the table with his bottle of mineral water, Jill had been dancing with a group of people one of whom she'd met through Paul a year or two previously. When she glanced at her watch and realised two hours had gone by, she thought she'd better go and check he was all right.

He was. She found him sitting at one of the tables in Heaven surrounded by a group of wide-eyed teenage girls – girls whom Marty had completely entranced with a series of extemporised tricks; girls with sweet cheeks and bleached hair and pupils like dinner plates and expressions of awe on their faces; girls who in normal circumstances would have responded that way only to pop stars and royalty or maybe (in olden days) to representatives or effigies of one or other of the gods. They looked embarrassed and started to peel away when Jill turned up, taking her for Marty's girlfriend.

'I came to check on you, but it looks like you're doing all right.'

Marty grinned. 'Yeah. I'm having a great time. All those babes you just frightened away were falling in love with me. I was just trying to work out which one I was going to take home.'

'Only the one?' Jill smiled.

'Yeah, well, I'm not as young as I used to be.'

'How's the E?'

'Good, actually. Nice. I'm feeling fantastic. In fact, I was just wondering about that other half . . .'

'Too late. I already took it.'

'Oh. Really? Shit. Missed out there, didn't I.'

'Well, you'll know next time.'

'What about you? You up for leaving yet?'

'In a bit. I'll maybe give it another hour. Fancy a dance?'

Marty did. The exercise brought the Ecstasy back and the drug relaxed his whole body, allowing him to move with more rhythm and freedom; at the same time it seemed to numb his sexuality and allow him to dance just for the sake of it, without any of the interfering frissons and tensions that he usually experienced in Jill's company.

★

Having moved up in the world since their last visit to Blackpool, Terri and Marty had sorted themselves a double room at the

234

Metropole, one of the grandest hotels in town and the one from within the shadow of which Marty had first spotted Jill. Jill, of course, had been put up at a guest house. Not the Eldorado but a place a little more discreet, situated at the north end of the promenade round the back of the Hotel Imperial. The Brooklyn.

To reach either of these from Heaven and Hell you had to walk north along the promenade which, once they'd finally tired of dancing, is what Jill and Marty did. Beside them the sea was flat and glassy. Eerily so, Marty thought – he couldn't remember ever having seen it so calm, not here in Blackpool in any case. There were no clouds, not a breath of wind and the stars were out, and in contrast to the chill there'd been at the beginning of the evening the weather now seemed unseasonably warm, though that was probably the drug. He felt sober, lucid, clear. He was really enjoying just walking. So much so that when they reached the Metropole, instead of saying goodnight, Marty walked straight on past without stopping.

'You not going in?' Jill asked him, surprised.

'I'll walk you back to the Brooklyn.'

'You sure? You don't have to. I can manage.'

'I know I don't have to. But it's fine. Anyway, I'm still wide awake.'

Jill laughed. 'That'll be the E, then.'

Marty nodded. 'Yeah. Though I think it's pretty much worn off. Do you think I'll be able to sleep? I can't do with being up all night and Terri finding out.'

'Don't worry. I've some Valium back in my room. I'll give you one. That'll sort you out.' They walked on for a while. 'So. What d'you reckon?'

'Um? Not what I expected. Nice. Mad. Weird. Incredible.'

'It seemed to help your magic. Those girls were two steps away from ripping your clothes off and having you right there on the dance floor.' Marty blushed. 'Hang on,' Jill said. She stopped, fumbling in her bag for something. A joint, as it turned out, which she lit with difficulty, striking dry three or four times before getting a flame. The disposable lighter she was using was all but out of gas but she didn't seem to realise this, thinking instead the problem was the (non-existent) wind and moving round to shield the ignition with her body. After she eventually managed to get lit up, she turned and slipped her arm through Marty's in such a way that when they walked on, their bodies swung, their hips not clashing but locked together in a rhythm.

Still E'd up, Marty thought, as easily as if he'd been using the expression for years. Still E'd up. But still. He sneaked a look at Jill from out of the corner of his eye. Yes, he still fancied her. But they were becoming friends and that meant he could keep a lid on it. Tonight had been really special for the two of them. Though Jill hadn't actually said anything on the subject, he'd felt for the first time that she understood the difficulties he was having. Above all he sensed that she genuinely liked him – and he her, despite all their respective faults. If only Terri would chill out a bit, everything would be fine.

'Put your arm round me,' Jill ordered, taking it and putting it there before Marty had a chance to argue. 'I need you to hold me. I'm shivering a bit. It's the pill.'

It might well have been, but with his arm snug round the girl and his hand only inches from her crotch Marty's happy, innocent thoughts were suddenly being nudged from their perch by an intense buzzing in his groin. Next thing he knew his cock had gone rigid, netting itself in the tangle of his underwear, and he wanted to fuck Jill so badly he could barely breathe.

'Hold me tighter,' she told him, fitting herself more closely into the mouldings of his body. 'I thought it was over but I've got another rush. It's the weed's brought it on.'

'Then why don't you stop smoking it?'

'Because it's nice.' That seemed as good a reason as any.

'So. You had a good time, then?' Marty croaked, his throat papery and dry.

'Um, yeah. Wicked. Let's go down by the water.'

Breaking apart, they descended the steep flight of steps that led down to the lower promenade, fitting themselves back together at the bottom and strolling for a while in silence, looking at the slumbering sea.

Then, abruptly, Jill was gone. Pulling away from Marty, she'd ducked into one of the colonnaded shelters secreted in the sea wall to their right. The magician followed her in, couldn't tell if the damp civety stench inside the small structure was due to stale urine or was just the raw, ancient smell of the sea. He looked around the walls, which were sloughing layers of paint like giant flakes of dead skin.

'What's the matter?'

'Joint's gone out. I think this lighter's fucked.'

Marty approached. 'Not a problem. Use my thumb.'

'Your thumb?'

Holding his hands out in front of her Marty repeated Harvey's trick.

Jill laughed and relit her joint. 'That's a neat trick for someone who doesn't smoke,' she said.

'Yeah, well, if I tried to light my own fags with it I'd only be kidding myself.'

'Jesus, Marty. What a terrible line. You've got to work on your comedy answers, my boy.'

Marty looked sad for a moment. 'I know,' he admitted. 'Another of my many failings.'

In the moment of silence that followed Jill examined his face and, thinking that even in the half-light drifting into the shelter from the street lamps outside it looked altogether too serious, she reached up, took the bulge of his cheek between her finger and thumb, and gave it a squeeze. But the look didn't change; the only movement came from his hand, which shot up to catch her arm as it fell. A blaze flashed in Jill's eyes and she twisted from his grip, and for a second neither of them dared take a breath. Then the moment passed and Marty was leaning in and Jill quickly thought . . . what did she think?

Stall. Stall for time.

She dropped her head. Caught Marty's hand moving again out of the corner of her eye, felt it brush past her shoulder and come round her neck. She let the spliff fall to the floor. Any moment now she was going to have to lift her head again, make a decision. She couldn't decide. She knew she shouldn't but . . . Christ, the boredom.

Fuck it. Do it. Go for it. What the fuck. Terri was such a little bitch.

Then she sensed him draw away. She looked up.

'These yours?' he said, grinning, holding her pack of cigarettes in his fingertips, like he'd conjured them from behind her ear.

Not a pass but another fucking trick. 'Oh, hilarious,' she said, snatching back the pack and reaching down to retrieve the joint from where she'd dropped it, face and thighs buzzing with thwarted expectation. She was furious and thankful, both at once. He was such a prat, really he was. Jesus Christ All-fucking-mighty.

But this time when she straightened up it was into air that held the smell of him and before she'd even got fully vertical he was on her and round her, lips on her lips, and she wasn't worrying any more about the shoulds and shouldn'ts of the thing but about whether or not she should keep hold of the spliff. Then her back was up against the damp, flaking walls and her arms had somehow decided to embrace him and his hands were up beneath her T-shirt and pulling on her breasts, she could feel the sea air on them, licking them deliciously, much better than Marty was managing with his awkward, desperate tongue, a tongue too heavy for her preference, a tongue quite likely forked. With a pang of guilt she thought of Terri, only to conclude with stoned logic that what with them being twins anyway it could hardly be construed as cheating. It served her right anyway, silly cow.

Then he was kissing her again and his hands were moving downwards from her breasts. One of them cupped her buttock while the other slid up inside her skirt, fumbling at her panties for a second before hooking them successfully. She felt his fingers probe her, then slip inside her, and they did that for a while until the hand withdrew and Marty started tugging at his fly. As he tried to lift her up on to him she grabbed hold of the tailcoats of fast-fleeing reality and told him no, not that, not without a condom, and dropping to a crouch – one knee painful on the rotten concrete, the other vibrating slightly in the air – she took him in her mouth, the blood taste of his cock realised in the countless extra intricate dimensions of the Ecstasy, and sucked him till he came.

Terri didn't do this for him, not too often, anyway. That much she could tell.

The curtains rattle back and sunlight blurts in. Marty – shocked awake – flails at the diaphanous flounces of the coverlet and tries to pull them back up over his head. This is punishment, he assumes. Discovery. He can hear Terri moving around in the room. Tall, familiar, strange. Tidying. His crime is scrawled across his face in brutal satanic inks. Pull up the coverlet. Pull it up.

But wait one minute. What can she know? There is nothing. He went out with Jill, walked her home, was back here in the hotel by four and, thanks to the Valium she'd given him, fell straight to sleep. Tel is just another punter, this is just another trick. A straight face, good patter, keep them looking where you want them looking using your hands, your voice, your eyes . . . do it right and you could have a breeze block stashed inside your trousers and they wouldn't see. He isn't used to performing in a Valium fug but there's a first time for everything.

Christ – had there been lipstick? He didn't check. He doesn't know. Though of course it would be the same as Terri's if there had. Not that she's kissed him recently or anything.

Curtains back. Marty braves the glare. She has his shirt but holds it in her hand like laundry, not like evidence. Tall, familiar, strange. Sunlight washes in. No lipstick. Jill's perfume? Aren't girls sensitive to that kind of thing? Curtains back. Terri at the window, shirt in hand, looking out.

'Oh, look,' she says. Marty pushes himself up on his elbows, too keen to oblige. She's pointing out at the water, no not at the water – he rubs his eyes. At the billboard outside their window, the one this end of North Pier, the one advertising Chubby Brown and Martin Mystery and Terri Electric (or is it Jill?). They can see it from their bed, that hoarding, it stands between them and Ireland, between them and North Pier, between them and the coffee-coloured sea. Two men in denim overalls are pasting the segments of a new poster over it, or have been; they've nearly finished, just one corner left to go, the one in which his own name was slapped. Replacing it is a PlayStation ad, one of the new 'conceptual' ones: a photograph of two pale, unearthly, androgynous-looking humans, standing limply side by side and staring blankly out. And nothing more: no cut lines, no logos, no copy, nothing at all to tell you what it was all in aid of, until you realise that the couple's nipples, just visible through the tight cloth of their T-shirts, are shaped like the four PlayStation keys. Cross, triangle, circle, square.

'It's Mr and Mrs Buttons,' Terri says.

'Eh?' says Marty.

'Mr and Mrs Buttons,' she repeats, savouring her little private joke. 'Don't you think the one on the left looks a bit like Jill?'

'Er, maybe,' Marty answers quickly. 'Maybe, yeah. I think I see.' Ho. Coverlet. Now. Up over head.

'We shouldn't be doing this.'

'Why not?'

'It's wrong.'

'Then why are we doing it?'

'I don't know.'

'It wouldn't be just because it's nice now, would it?'

'I don't know.'

'I suppose you're going to say Terri's driven you to it.'

'Maybe she has.'

'Jesus, Marty. You're so fucking crap.'

'No I'm not.'

'Yes you are.'

'I want a cigarette.'

'You don't smoke.'

'I want one anyway.'

'Well, you can't have one. It won't help you cope.'

'What am I going to do?'

'Shut up, fuck me, deal with it.'

'I don't know if I can.'

'You can't fuck me? Well, you know, thanks.'

'No, Jill – Christ, I could fuck you all day every day for the rest of my life.'

'Well, I suppose that's sort of a compliment.'

'It's dealing with Terri that I don't think I can manage.'

'You're a lightweight, you know that?'

'I know. But I've never been unfaithful before.'

'When was the last time you slept with her?'

'God, I'm not sure. Not since Leeds.'

'Well, you're not being unfaithful then, are you?'

'I don't think Terri would see it that way . . .'

'Marty! She's not going to see it any way! She's not going to find out! You're supposed to be having an affair, for fuck's sake. It's a supposed to be secret, it's supposed to be fun. Either have it or don't have it, but let's not keep on discussing it, okay? I'm here for the sex, not the moral philosophy.'

Marty was silent for a second or two. 'So I'm just a sex object, is what you're saying.'

'Basically, yeah.'

'Cool. Come over here, then. Objectify me.'

As soon as Marty and Terri got back down south Terri disappeared to her mother's. Jill had stayed behind in Morecambe for a while, to see her family and avoid any unnecessary tension. When she'd asked Marty if he wanted her to come to Beckenham he'd hummed and hedged, unable to come to a decision, and taking the initiative she'd told him to call her when he was ready to start rehearsals at the Talk. The status of their affair – and any possible future it might have – was not discussed.

Left alone for a few days, Marty had a chance to reflect on how the events of the last year had changed him. He saw them as part of a formative process, the period of his life that had properly changed him from boy into man. He'd faced the kind of adult problems that adults had to deal with and he'd dealt with them. He had a successful show, a girlfriend and a mistress. He was on his way, he felt, to becoming a star. And he was still only twenty-five.

There was one immediate consequence, he noted, of his new emotional maturity. Looking around the walls of his bedroom, the same bedroom he'd been sleeping in since he was three or four, he realised they were walls he'd now outgrown. It was time he moved on. In the past he would have agonised over such a major decision, but no longer. Not now he was a man. Tomorrow he would begin searching for a place to live in Central London. With the money that was beginning to come in he could afford it, and there was no way the three of them would want to trip between the West End and Beckenham every night. They'd go nuts. His dad was in property – it shouldn't be too hard. Maybe he could get a warehouse in East London or something, do it up. He'd heard that was considered pretty cool right now. Though he should probably just rent a regular flat to start with. Once he had a foothold in the city, things would develop naturally from there.

Freed from the company of the two girls for a while, his brief affair made an easy kind of sense. He was already getting bored with Jill. They both knew, Marty felt, that they weren't right for one another. It had been an animal attraction, a mutual fascination, a thirst for knowledge of the forbidden and unknown they'd both felt compelled to quench. But they'd done it and now it had to end. As an experience it had been okay, amazing even. He'd never had sex with anyone so in command of their sexuality before and it had been an interesting experience – she'd done stuff to him that Terri never would have, not in a million years. But though he admired that and it excited him, he wasn't sure he liked having to relinquish all that control. He enjoyed the fact that when he slept with Terri her pleasure was in his hands, her body his to command and conquer. With Jill, though, it was different. Things were much more nebulous. He couldn't tell who was pleasuring whom, where things might lead, what might happen. It was more intense but also much more effort – as well as a tiny bit frightening.

On top of that, of course, was the awful paranoia he'd been feeling that Terri would find out. He didn't want to lose her – Terri was his and she loved him, and he had to look to his responsibilities and take care of her. What would people say about him otherwise? Plus, of course, there was the show to think about. If he waited till she got back from her mum's and then gave her a sincere apology about what had happened in Leeds, and backed it up with telling her he thought it was time the two of them got a place together . . . that should do the trick.

As for Jill, well, he was pretty sure she didn't want anything more. She'd called him a sex object, for God's sake. He expected they might sleep together again once or twice in a 'goodbye' kind of a way, then that would be the end of it. Though younger than Terri, Jill was much more mature. Terri would never be able to handle the stresses and strains of an affair. She'd twisted Darren round her little finger that time, certainly, but she'd just been a teenager, then, not fully aware of what she was doing. Things were different now.

The next day there was good news, really good news: a triumphant phone message from Michael informing Marty that he'd got them the warm-up slot at *Eurovision* and had gone to Tuscany, talk next week. *Eurovision*. Marty could barely contain himself. He was so excited he had to leave the house and go for a walk, plod round the streets for a couple of hours until his heart stopped racing. At last, at last. After all these years. Television. The dream was finally beginning. Though he'd wait until Michael had given him full confirmation before he told the girls. He needed to digest it first. Plus he wanted to savour his victory in secret for a while. That was just how he was.

★

When Terri came back from her mother's, Marty apologised. The strength of her reaction stunned him. The moment the words came out of his mouth she burst into tears, threw her arms round him and sobbed into his shoulder about how she was so glad he was back to his old self again, how she'd been so scared ever since Leeds, how she'd been so frightened, how she'd been having such an awful, awful time, how she'd thought she was losing him.

'So you think it's a good idea, then, moving in together?'

'Oh yes, of course I do.'

Marty mentioned that he had in mind looking for somewhere big enough for the three of them.

But Terri shook her head. 'She can't live with us. No way. I mean – we'll be seen together.'

'I was thinking London was probably big enough for us to get away with that.'

'Marty! No *way*! What are you thinking?'

'Well, I'm not sure we'll be able to afford it, putting her up somewhere on her own.' He hadn't told her yet about *Eurovision*.

'Yes we can, can't we? We paid for it all round the country, why can't we now?'

It didn't take Marty long to capitulate. The last thing he wanted was for Jill to come to live with them, not now. But he'd wanted to make sure that it was Terri who'd insisted on it. That way when he told Jill of the decision he could blame it on her.

★

The two of them began flat hunting the following day and were shocked by how much more expensive things were than they'd imagined and, in spite of that, how absurdly quickly they got snapped up. They soon realised their initial hope of getting a place with two bedrooms – so that one could be used to store the magic props – was completely unrealistic, especially if they went through any kind of rental agency. But the small-ads route was brutal – you had to be on the telephone the moment they came out and be prepared to go and see the landlord that same morning, deposit in hand, if you wanted any chance at all of getting a place. Maybe converting a warehouse wasn't such a stupid idea after all.

Marty ended up shelling out on a Pay-as-You-Go mobile and taking Terri to crash on a friend's floor in Clapham so they could be more central while they went about their task. After a week spent chasing rainbows they found a place in Finsbury Park, not far from the Arsenal. It only had one bedroom and the kitchen was actually one end of the living room, meaning space was pretty tight, but it was affordable and on the tube and, moreover, in Zone Two. And thanks to the football stadium there were lots of B&Bs and cheap hotels nearby, in one of which they could conveniently house Jill.

Apart from some furious vacuuming to get rid of the hairs left by their predecessors' nicotine-coloured cat, to which Terri was allergic, and an accident that arched a crack across the lower left-hand corner of Marty's precious dressing mirror and left him seething about his lack of patience and co-ordination for several days, the move went ahead without a hitch. Michael came back from Italy and the *Eurovision Song Contest* booking was confirmed, and Marty told the girls the news (Jill by phone, using the new mobile, calling from outside in the street). The contest was to be held in Paris and Terri especially was very excited, immediately pointing out that they'd be able to move into a much better place really soon.

Jill seemed excited too, though she seemed more concerned about finding out how soon Marty wanted her to come back to London. She also told him she was missing him, a comment that made Marty worry that his calculations had been wrong. Might she be falling in love with him? He now realised with a gratifying tingle that this was a possibility he should not have dismissed so easily.

The kind of fee Michael was angling for from the contest organisers was by any standards extremely large – far, far larger than anything Marty had been paid previously – and, in order to do his big break justice, he intended to invest in new costumes and equipment. If he got his act together he could buy the props in time to road test them at the Talk of London, and before two weeks had passed he'd taken out a loan of twenty grand and spent most of it.

Jill returned four days before the show went up; when it did, it was an immediate hit. They got Pick of the Week in *Time Out*, then the *Guardian* did an interview (some journo looking for a British David Blaine, although what he got instead was Marty insisting he was the new David Copperfield). After that they were playing every night to real audiences of people their own age in the heart of London's famous, fabulous West End.

Magic, it seemed, was officially fashionable again.

★

There wasn't much time for their personal lives, not during that first fortnight of the run at any rate. But even Marty wasn't insensible to the feeling of unfinished business that ionised the air between himself and Jill. He'd been secretly hoping their affair would just go away, but her growing restlessness, the loaded looks she kept on giving him and the increasingly pointed remarks she was making testified against that. Now she was back here in front of him he was finding it difficult to remember he'd resolved not to sleep with her again.

This was definitely bad. It would be total exploitation to have sex with her now. Even if she wanted to, it just wouldn't be right. And it was no doubt a good thing that Marty's deeply moral instinct was there to protect Jill from herself, because as the days went by it become increasingly clear that she did not see their affair as concluded.

Her hints having proved insufficient she finally spelled it out to him over the phone, calling one afternoon as Terri and he were finishing their lunch. Since Terri was busy doing the dishes at the sink, Marty picked it up.

'Marty, is that you?'

'Oh, er, hi.' He could tell by the tone of her voice what was coming.

'We need to talk.'

'Hm – well that's great.'

'Is Terri there?'

'Yeah. Yeah she is.'

Terri looked up from her bowl of suds. 'Who's that?'

'It's Jill. She says hi.'

'What's she want?'

'What's up?' Marty asked.

'You know exactly what is up. You've been ignoring me ever since I got back to London.' This was pretty much true. When they weren't rehearsing he'd been preoccupied with fine-tuning the new props and ordering a fresh set of costumes to be made. And the one time he'd tried to take a stroll round to Jill's B&B 'to say hi', Terri had insisted on coming along. 'I need to see you. Alone.'

Well, there was no way he could deal with this now. 'Er, yeah, okay,' he said. 'Of course you can borrow it. 'Slong as you promise to give it back. I'll bring it with me tonight. See you later. Yeah, sure. Bye.' He broke the connection.

'What did she want?' Terri asked again.

'Oh – just to borrow a book. I think she's bored, cooped up in that room all day long.'

'Bored? How can she be bored?' Terri shook her head in amazement. 'This is London. It's not like we're not allowing her to go out. Oh, and by the way, Marty, I'm going to go down to see Mum Monday night, probably stay over. She's not been feeling too good again.'

'You are!' Shit, too eager. 'Er, you are? Okay, fine. No problem.'

'That's all right, isn't it? Monday's our night off?'

'Yup. That's right. Think I might get a video. I could use a quiet night in.'

★

Making sure he'd not forgotten the book he'd 'promised' to Jill, Marty left with Terri for the venue just after six. He'd hoped to catch Jill backstage, maybe slip off somewhere and have a quiet word with her while Terri got changed, but as usual she was late and by the time she turned up things were too hectic for him to get her off somewhere on her own. There was always the same atmosphere of panic and confusion the last few minutes before the curtain went up, however organised Marty tried to be and it didn't help when Jill appeared with only fifteen minutes to spare, her eyes bloodshot and tired – she was stoned, no doubt – her hair all over the place.

Terri scolded her, then helped her get ready in that patronising way she had, while Marty stole glances at the two of them in a mirror in between checking his suit for all its requisite props as he did every night. But his mind wasn't on it. All he could think about was Jill.

Announcing he was going to take a piss, he left the room and walked down a battered corridor to the toilet. His palms were wet with sweat and, too tense to relax his bladder, he made do with rinsing off his hands. By the time he returned Jill had got into her costume, the red one used throughout the first half of the show in order to get the idea of there only being one assistant firmly fixed into the mind of the audience. Terri had worked some miracle with her hair and was busy helping her with her make-up, the two girls sitting face to face like the two halves of a butterfly print.

Now he'd a chance to think it occurred to Marty that perhaps Jill had been upset when she'd arrived. Not smoking, but crying. This really worried him. What if she had some kind of freak-out? He'd really been incredibly stupid. What had he done? What kind of an idiot had he been, to create this situation? Suddenly he could feel panic rising in his gullet.

He couldn't get his thoughts to grip. What the fuck had he been thinking, up there in Blackpool? Had he lost his fucking mind? Paranoia grabbed him by the ankles and pulled him down, and suddenly everything that had happened over the last six weeks looked terrifyingly different. Most of all what looked different was Jill.

Okay, he told himself. *Keep calm. Organise, prioritise. Command, control. Focus. Focus. Concentrate. Priority number one: reassure Jill.* He sneaked another look at her. She no longer seemed the super-confident sexual predator she had during those cool afternoons they'd spent in bed together in her guest house. On the contrary, she now seemed terribly vulnerable and fragile, someone who used sex to get what she wanted because she didn't know any better; a needy person, unstable, a victim of drugs. And his responsibility. *Shit shit shit.* What the *fuck* had he been doing? *Calm, Marty, calm. You can handle this. All you need to do is talk to her. It'll be cool.*

'Fuck!' he said, too loudly.

Only Terri answered him, though without looking up from fixing Jill's face. 'What?'

'My thumb-tip! I've lost my fucking thumb-tip. It's not in my pocket. Have you seen it?'

'How on earth should I know? Can't you see we're busy here?'

'Well, did you see me put it down anywhere? I know I had it.

I definitely packed it, because I haven't got the red scarf that goes in it.'

'Did you leave it in the bathroom?'

Marty couldn't remember. Perhaps he had. He rushed out of the Green Room, up the short flight of stairs and along the grey corridor that led back to the toilets. The journey brought him closer to the stage and he could hear Ted Preece's voice booming back from the monitors. Ted Preece. Ever since that awful Pontin's gig the man had pursued them like some kind of vengeful spirit. Marty had hoped they'd seen the back of him after he'd compèred the Magical Championships in Blackpool but now here he was in fucking London – *London* – a direct result of some trendy wankers from the fashion press having decided that dour northern comedy was back in vogue. As he hurried along the corridor Marty listened to him warming up the audience. Icing over, more like. If it weren't for him and this situation with Jill, life would be perfect. But something always had to spoil it. You could guarantee that. It was sod's law.

He punched open the black door of the Gents with the heel of his hand. Yes. The thumb-tip. There it was, on the basin surround. He must have left it when he'd come in to wash his hands. He grabbed it and, checking the scarf was still packed inside, put it in the appropriate pocket, spinning back towards the exit before stopping and deciding that his bladder was now ready to let go. While he relieved himself he took the opportunity to count slowly to ten. Talk to Jill. All he needed was to get one single minute in which he could have a private word with Jill.

He emerged into the corridor just as a red-costumed body disappeared through the door of the Ladies, directly opposite. Terri. Fantastic. He checked his watch. Six minutes. He just had time. Hurrying back along the corridor, he rushed into the Green Room, where Jill was arranging their various costumes in order on the quick-change rack.

'I'm really sorry,' Marty blurted to her back. 'I know I've been crap. But things have just been so manic, with all the extra work for *Eurovision* and everything. But she's going to visit her mother on Monday and we'll get the whole night together. I promise.'

For a moment Jill didn't move and Marty found himself wondering, absurdly, if she'd somehow not heard him. Then she did move; slowly she began to turn round and by the time she was facing him something extraordinary had happened: she wasn't Jill any longer.

She was Terri.

The first thing Terri did was lift her arm and index finger in a single, stiff movement and point at him. Then she opened her mouth and let out a wail the awful sound of which would remain imprinted on Marty's brain for a very long time to come.

★

This was the point at which Jill came back in from the bathroom. 'What's going on? Terri? What's the matter?' She glanced from one face to the other, thinking Marty might have hit her again. But then the realisation of what had actually happened slowly dawned on her. 'Oh, no,' she said. 'Oh, shit.'

At the sight of her twin Terri balled her pointed finger back into a fist. 'You evil *bitch*! You evil fucking *bitch*,' she screamed before launching herself across the room. The two women tussled for a couple of minutes while Marty looked on pathetically, frozen to the spot by the sight of Jill trying to fend off her attacker. Denied blood, Terri grabbed her coat and bag, and ran out of the room, pausing only to spit in the magician's face and spike her heel into the top of his shoe with such force that it split the leather. The pain brought Marty to his senses and calling after her he limped off in pursuit, hurrying in her wake down the service stairs and out of the building. But when he finally caught up with her in the street she just screamed and screamed, her face contorted by an expression unlike anything he'd ever seen before. He'd understood she'd be upset if she ever found out, but this . . .

Putting his hands out in front of him as if she were some kind of cornered animal, he begged her to calm down, just try to calm down, but the only effect his words had was to make her take off her shoes and hurl them at him. Ducking to avoid the first, the heel of the second caught him on the cheek, though Terri didn't get to see this: she was already fleeing from her boyfriend and everything associated with him. She ran the hundred yards to Holborn without once turning to look back.

Perhaps wisely, Marty didn't attempt to follow. Instead he sat down on the kerb and tried to work out why, right at this moment, he felt so utterly detached; why everything around him had taken on a peculiar, unreal, almost two–dimensional quality. It didn't seem to be happening to him at all. It felt like something he'd seen once in a film.

He was in shock, of course, a state from which he didn't emerge until he and Jill were back in Finsbury Park and he was sitting on a chair with a vodka in his hand and his bruised foot resting in a washing-up bowl filled with ice cubes.

'She wasn't good for you, Marty,' Jill was saying. 'She wasn't right.'

'How do you know? How do you know what was right for me?'

'Well, I know you hit her.'

Marty's head jerked round in horror. 'Did she *tell* you?'

'She didn't tell me. I was there. Just outside the door.'

'So you didn't see what happened?'

'No, but I saw the bruise on her face. It was pretty hard to miss, even with all that blusher.'

'I fucking swear, Jill, I swear on my mother's grave that was the one and only time. I'm not like that, I don't hit women.'

'Actually, Marty, you do hit women, because you hit her.'

'It wasn't like that, I didn't even mean to, she moved, you see . . .'

'All right, all right, calm down. I don't think you're a wife beater. Actually, I think she deserved it. I'd have hit her too, if I'd've been you. She was driving you up the wall.'

'*Exactly*. Yes, she *was*.'

'But that's precisely what I'm saying. You weren't right for one another.'

'But we were together for years, Jill. We were a team.'

'Look, Marty, relationships end. You're both still young. Anyway, you're with me now.'

'Am I with you?'

'I don't know. Are you?'

Instead of answering, Marty took a mouthful of his drink. Jill's hand, he noticed, was starting to shake.

'What about the show?' he said eventually.

'What about the show?'

'Well, it's fucked, isn't it?'

'So we'll make another one.'

'*So we'll make another one*,' he mimicked in a whiny little voice. 'And how do you suggest we do that, Jill? I'm twenty grand in debt, the venue's probably going to sue, when he finds out about this Michael will no doubt drop me. I'll certainly lose *Eurovision*, which was going to be the turning point in my – in our – careers. I'm completely shafted and all you can say is make another show. There is no other fucking show.'

'Don't be like that, Marty. I'm only trying to help. I just don't see what else to do.' Her voice was trembling now. She felt small and far away.

'What do you suggest? Hire another Diana lookalike? Search out some twins?'

'Well, maybe. I don't know.'

'How about getting Terri to come back? How about that? Don't you think we should start there, huh? Like maybe go and see her, and apologise?' He turned and stared through the window at the building opposite, its features jaundiced by the yellow street light. Over on the sofa, Jill started to cry. 'I'm sorry,' Marty said more softly, when he heard her.

'No. You're right. I'm to blame. I really am. I'm so sorry, Marty. I'm such a stupid, selfish cow. I shouldn't have ever let you come near me. But you were so nice to me and I was so unhappy and so lonely . . .' She was sobbing too hard to talk now and, levering himself up out of his seat, Marty hobbled over to where she was sitting. Her tears gave him a strange feeling of strength – he didn't like it when she came over all superior to him, even if it was only to offer advice.

'Shh,' he hushed, holding her. 'Shh. It wasn't your fault at all. It was me that let the cat out of the bag. And I wanted you too, up in Blackpool.'

'But I shouldn't have *let* you. Christ. What kind of woman am I? I disgust myself.'

'That's ridiculous, you shouldn't think like that.'

They continued in this vein for quite some time, until in the end they went to bed. Neither of them intended to have sex, but their bodies made the decision for them. For a long time afterwards they both lay awake, separately and in silence, trying to work out what it had meant.

As Jill had predicted, Terri didn't come back. Over the week following the bust-up Marty called her countless times, hoping to say whatever magic combination of words he thought would make it better. But all his fretting and agonising were utterly without point, as neither Terri nor her mother would stoop to talking with him. Even his letters arrived back by return of post, pointedly unopened.

In the end he got in the van and drove out to Guildford, not that that did him any good; when she saw him coming up the path, Terri screamed at him from her bedroom window that she'd get a restraining order served on him if he didn't go away and leave them in peace. His father had no sympathy either – when he found out what had happened he told Marty what a prick he was, that he'd warned him about doing something like this and as far as he was concerned he could stay out of his hair until he'd sorted it; he wouldn't be welcome back home until he had.

Topping off this sack of woes was the fact that – just as Marty'd feared – Michael had abandoned him. When he heard what had happened and how it meant that the Talk of London would have to be compensated and that they couldn't do the *Eurovision* gig, he'd pulled out of their contract immediately, informing Marty of his decision in a spitefully worded note that challenged him to sue him if he dared. It didn't help that Terri had rung up the *Eurovision* organisers and cancelled on Marty's behalf, nor that she'd written to all the London lookalike agencies to warn them that Martin Mystery was a sex pest with a Princess Diana fixation and that they should think twice before sending anyone to work with him.

It was awful. His whole life had collapsed.

For the next month Marty sat around like a ghost, hardly going out, barely speaking. An especially bad day was the one on which Jill took him to sign on at the local Job Centre. For her it was all straightforward enough – she knew the routine, the system, what she had to do and say to get what she needed. But Marty was lost. He'd never drawn benefit before and got hugely upset about the whole performance, everything about it driving home more deeply the reality of his failure.

That same night they slept together again for the first time since the night of Terri's departure, despite Jill promising herself that she wasn't going to allow this to happen. But she'd pitied him; Marty had been so depressed all day that when he'd reached for her she couldn't find it in her heart not to respond. Still, she was no bleeding heart. If sex would help him feel better about himself, improve his mood to the point where the two of them could begin to move forward a little, then she was prepared to provide it. But she expected to see results.

But once the sex had started Jill couldn't bring herself to make it stop even though Marty remained as moody and withdrawn as ever. Reluctantly she watched herself sliding into a relationship and every week that passed found her sense of self a little more diminished, with the magician taking up residence in the vacated space like some kind of imp. He didn't mean to, particularly; throughout the entire period he remained so self-obsessed that it was doubtful whether he had the faintest idea about what was going on in Jill's head. But he began to inveigle his way into her soul nonetheless.

Guilt was the key that disarmed her defences and let him in, the guilt she felt for having allowed herself to sleep with him towards the end of the tour. The more guilty she got the more stoned she got; and the more stoned she got the more elaborate the mechanisms she created to chastise herself and put herself down; and the more elaborate these mechanisms the less certain she was of herself; and the less certain she was of herself the more Marty's reality, Marty's needs and desires, Marty's point of view, took command of her personality. It was a vicious circle, a feedback loop, and three weeks after they'd started sleeping together again, while Marty remainded as sullen, lethargic and despondent as ever, Jill was cooking and cleaning for him, doing the shopping, allowing him to fuck her every which way.

Not only that, but the sex they were having was becoming increasingly violent. They'd done bondage a few times together, it was one of the things she'd let him do to her in Blackpool – one of the things, he'd told her, that Terri wouldn't allow. She didn't mind; she enjoyed it herself, from time to time. But to the bondage had been added spanking and now he'd started wanting to beat her with a long thin metal cane he'd used sometimes as a magic wand. She'd agreed, only to have him hit her far, far too hard.

Furious, she'd freaked out and he'd apologised, said he wasn't interested in trying it again. But the next morning when her buttocks still really hurt she took a look in the old dressing mirror that Marty kept in the bedroom, the crappy full-length one he'd told her had once been his mother's – though what with that crack across its corner and the ugly splint that bound its broken leg Jill would have chucked it in an instant, horrible old thing that it was.

If it was looking in the mirror that made Jill realise she was in dire need of a holiday, it wasn't the welts across her backside that were the cause. The damage didn't look as bad she had thought – Marty hadn't drawn blood – and besides, it was nothing compared with the shock she got when she caught sight of herself, twisted halfway round and looking back over her shoulder, dressing gown hoiked up round her waist, and realised the most blindingly obvious thing of all.

That she looked just like Terri.

This, she now understood, was the thing that had been troubling her. She didn't mind the sex games; a bit of pain turned her on. It always had – she hadn't forgotten Gavin, after all. But she was only prepared to accept it if it was inflicted on her, on her terms, for her benefit; if, in other words, it functioned as a line of communication between her lover and herself. There was no way she was going to become a receptacle for the hurt Marty wanted to inflict on someone else. That's what she'd been to Gavin, a punchbag, and she was determined never to allow herself to be that again.

★

Paul's face looked nice in the candlelight: glowing, honest and warm. It wasn't until they'd sat down, ordered food and had a sip or two of wine that she'd realised he'd been the reason she'd come back up to Blackpool. Wanting to see her parents had just been the excuse she'd given Marty when she'd left.

It had been the right decision, too. Paul was full of hopes and dreams, and spent the meal telling her about his plans for moving out of gaming and starting up a web café. He talked and talked, telling her that the Internet was finally happening, that it was going to be as big here as in America. She'd never seen him so enthusiastic. It was the perfect antidote to the weeks she'd had of Marty's dead-end despair.

But Paul was too considerate a person to spend their entire dinner babbling about himself. He wanted to know how she was getting on. He could tell she wasn't happy. She said she was. He didn't believe her. 'If they've split up, what you still doing there in London?' he wanted to know.

'Er, well . . . I just thought I'd stick around, see how things worked out. See if he got another show together. I've got to quite enjoy the magic. And I felt a bit sorry for him really. Didn't want to leave him in the lurch.'

'You're not shagging him, are you?'

Jill missed the ashtray with her ash; small crimson sunbursts pinked her cheeks.

'Christ, Jill. And of course this wouldn't have anything to do with him and his girlfriend splitting up?'

She couldn't deny it.

'You are a twat, you know that? Jesus. You really pick 'em, don't you?'

She began to cry and, angry with himself for being so blunt, Paul moved round the table to comfort her. He suggested they leave and go back to his flat. Jill nodded. They paid the bill and left.

Back at Paul's they drank wine and Paul listened to Jill's confession.

'I don't understand it. Why don't you sleep with someone who actually likes *you* for a change? Someone who doesn't want you because you look like someone else. Someone who has some fucking respect.'

'I don't know, Paul, I really don't. And anyway, like who?'

She already knew the answer.

'Like me.'

'Don't do this to me, Paul. I can't deal with this again, not now. We're friends. I *need* you as a friend, I –'

But he was already kissing her, and it was nice, and gentle, and she kissed him back.

When, the next morning, he'd told her he loved her even though he knew she didn't reciprocate, she'd almost wanted to kill herself. The old question, insistent as ever, returned: what kind of awful person was she? Why couldn't she feel anything for the one man who might actually be good for her?

Leaving him in tears she went to Sonya's, begged her for an answer. But Sonya said she didn't know, that she was just the same. The two of them spent the day drinking tea, rolling joints and trading clichés to cheer each other up, and at the end of it Jill took the bus back over to her parents'. She spent just one night with them and then returned to London, not at all the wiser, hoping that in her absence the situation might somehow have improved.

★

It hadn't. Marty wasn't home when she walked through the door, but it was clear things were no better than when she'd left. Worse even. The sink was crammed with dishes, the fridge was empty of food, there were two finished bottles of Jack Daniels on the sideboard and beer cans sticking out of the overflowing bin; there were unanswered messages on the answering machine. Plus it appeared Marty had taken up smoking, either that or he'd taken a new lover: there were ashtrays filled with butts in the living room and in the bedroom by the bed. But she couldn't ask him about this, because he wasn't there to ask.

When he finally did appear, late in the evening, he was agitated and drunk. 'Oh. So you're back?' His eyes were dim, his face puffy and soft.

'That's nice. Welcome home, Jill.'

'Yeah. Sorry. I've been out.'

'Like I couldn't tell.'

He came over, tried to kiss her. 'Don't be like that.' She fended him off and turned her attention back to the telly.

'Talk to me. How were the folks? How was Morecambe?'

Was that a sneer in his voice? She couldn't quite tell.

'I don't want to talk. You're drunk.'

'Bollocks. I've only had a couple.'

'Yeah, right.'

'I have! Piss off.'

'Marty – I just did piss off. Now I'm back.'

'I'm sorry, I didn't know you were coming. You should have called.'

'Wouldn't have made any difference, to judge by the state of you and the flat. It looks like a bloody bomb's hit it. I thought you were supposed to be the tidy one. And since when did you take up smoking?'

'You can talk.'

'But we're not talking about me. We're talking about you. What about all the stuff you told me about your dead mother?'

'Ah. So we're talking now, are we? That's good.'

'Is it?' Still staring at the screen.

He picked up the remote, killed the set.

'I was watching that.' She took the controller from him, switched the TV back on.

'Thought we were talking?' He switched it off again.

'I'm not sure we've got anything to talk about.'

'Haven't we? I don't know. You tell me. You're the one who's been up in Blackpool, getting a length off darling Paul.'

Without answering, Jill got up and went into the bedroom. He couldn't know, could he? Had Paul called him? There was no way. He was bluffing. He was just being an arse. She hadn't even wanted to, anyway. She'd been drunk. It had never really happened. Not intentionally. She'd just needed someone and he'd been there, which meant it didn't really count. Anyway, Marty couldn't exactly take the moral high ground, not after what he'd done to Terri. The arse.

When he came in to find her she was smoking a cigarette, crying a little, rattling through her CDs for some music so that he couldn't see her fingers shake. She chose one, put it in the player, turned it on.

'I'm sorry,' he said finally, to Jill's surprise sounding like he actually meant it. 'I'm really depressed. I think maybe I need to go to the doctor.'

'I think maybe you do.' She looked up at him. 'That was a fucking horrible thing to say.'

'I know. Please . . . I'm just really, really sorry. I know it's not like that between you and Paul.'

'You're fucking gross, do you know that?'

Marty nodded, looked away.

'Do you think I haven't been worried about you? Because I have, you know. I only went so you had a chance to get your head back together.'

He sat down on the bed. 'I saw Terri,' he said.

Perfect. Now she could go on the offensive. 'Did you sleep with her? Is that what all this is about?'

Marty replied blankly in the negative.

'Am I supposed to believe that?' Careful – she mustn't push the advantage too far.

'I didn't, all right? She's had it with me. Says if I don't stop trying to get in touch with her she'll go to court, get a restraining order.' He looked glum.

'She's said that before.'

'Yeah, but this time she means it.'

'Jesus. You two. You're a right pair of jokers, you know that?'

Marty said nothing, sat there very still. Jill fumbled for an ashtray and fiddled with the CD controls, skipping forward to another song, a better one, one she was sure she liked. He was sitting there, all hunched up, cigarette burning in his hands. He was crying. She was sick of seeing him cry. She was used to men who had a bit of strength.

'I fucked everything up,' he moaned.

Oh God, Jill thought. Not again. 'You didn't do it alone, pal.' She wanted to be supportive but she couldn't be, not really. Marty hadn't moved on at all. He was still taking everything on his own shoulders as though it were all his problem, his responsibility. All three of them had had their part to play in what had happened. He had to stop acting the martyr and realise that.

'Yeah,' he said, nose bubbling with snot. 'But if I hadn't said anything that night . . .'

So he'd just proved her point. Nice. 'Christ. You're amazing, you know that?'

'What?' He looked at her, wide-eyed, not knowing what she meant.

'You're so fucking arrogant. Don't you get it?'

To her surprise, he nodded. 'Yeah,' he said. 'Yeah. You're right.'

'Come here.' She got up and went to him, lay down on the bed and held him for a while. Within minutes he'd passed out. She laid him flat on the bed, turned off the CD and went back into the living room, where she switched on the telly and smoked herself a spliff.

Money was their number one problem, it seemed. At least, it was the one Marty had begun to focus all his attention upon. From how to meet the monthly repayments on his loan to how to pay the electricity bill to the drain on their resources presented by Jill's Lottery compulsion and her marijuana habit, in one way or another the question came to dominate his every waking hour.

Perhaps this obsessing was the only way Marty could stop grieving over Terri and the show? Who was to know. Not Jill, certainly. But the situation was this: what little of the money he'd borrowed for *Eurovision* that hadn't yet been spent would get them through the next couple of months and pay the rent until his housing benefit started to come through, and after that he'd need to jump straight into a job paying about £500 a week – after tax – just to keep their heads above water. And he certainly wasn't qualified for anything that would come remotely close to that. Until he somehow found more highly paid performance work, he was stuck on benefits – and Jill was going to have to get a job.

'But I've got nack-all qualies either,' she protested, rolling her second spliff of the morning. Recently she'd started a new regime of trying not to have a smoke before lunch, but being forced to listen to Marty tear his hair out over their finances at the kitchen table from the moment they'd got up counted as an exceptional circumstance, she felt.

'Didn't you ever have any kind of work in Morecambe? I mean besides Fatty Arbuckle's?'

'No, not really.'

'Well, so you're just gonna have to go on the game, then, aren't you? Get yourself down King's Cross.'

'Marty, that's not funny.'

'Well, you must have some work experience.'

Jill pondered her three-skinner. 'I did a short stint answering phones.'

'What, like a receptionist or something?'

'Sort of. More like a call centre.'

'Computer helpline?'

'Er, yeah. That's what it was. Computer helpline.'

'Well, there you are. That's training. You could get yourself something dealing with computers.' Marty was reminded of having to hassle Terri into getting work, years earlier. Why were all the girls he met so fucking useless? He just prayed Jill could come up with something better than flogging water filters.

'Marty, it's not that easy.'

'Well, you've got to get something. Like it or not, we're in this mess together. It's your fault too, you know.'

Jill raised her eyebrows. Well, she supposed, it was progress of a sort. Taking her completed joint through to the bedroom, she put on her headphones and picked away at a word-search from a puzzle book she'd bought to while away her last train journey down from Morecambe. Marty did have a point. She was going to have to get a job sooner or later and better down here than up north. Maybe computers weren't such a bad idea after all.

Then she had a thought. It was tricky one, but . . . what the hell. He'd probably be pleased enough to hear from her. Removing the headphones, she went into the living room to get the phone and, back in the privacy of the bedroom, dialled Paul's number.

He picked up straight away. 'Hello?'

'Hey, Paul. It's, er, me.'

'Oh.' He sounded sad. 'Hi. How're things?'

'Hm. You know. Not great.'

'Still trying to save that prat from himself?'

'It's not like that.'

'Isn't it?'

'No, it's . . .'

'Martyrdom doesn't suit you, Jill.'

She couldn't find the words; the tears pricking at her eyes got in the way.

'Look, I'm sorry. That was mean.'

'Yes, it was.'

'It's just . . .'

'I know. I'm sorry too. I shouldn't have let what happened happen.'

'Well, I'm glad it did. At least you know now what you're missing.' Now she could hear the tears in *his* voice. What was it with her generation? Why was everybody she knew constantly on the verge of emotional collapse? 'I'll always be glad.' Oh, God. Was he going to start getting heavy with her?

'How's the café going?' she asked.

There was a pause. When Paul spoke again he sounded distant. More distant but more distinct. 'Good, yeah. All right. We think we've found a backer and we're looking at this dead good property.'

'Oh, yeah?'

'Yeah. On Queen Street. You know the old chapel, next to World of Leather?'

She knew the one – it had been derelict for years. All boarded up. She'd been to a party in a squat there once. 'Yeah. Near that?'

'No – not near it. The actual chapel.'

'No way! But it's amazing. Or it would be, if you got the money to do it up.'

'Yeah. We've got a long way to go, though.'

Another pause.

'Paul, I need your help,' Jill said finally.

Paul laughed quietly. 'Go on, then. What is it this time?'

Despite a sudden flush of shame for even asking, she told him how she was in desperate need of work. Did he know anyone in London, anyone on the Internet? She thought maybe she might try some of these upcoming dot.com companies, get a job as a receptionist or something.

Yeah, he knew a couple of people. Had she got a pen? He gave her some names and she scribbled them down in the margins of her word-search. He didn't have the numbers, she'd have to look them up.

She couldn't be bothered to go and get the phone book, so she called directory enquiries, even though she knew it was the kind of thing that would make Marty flip. She got the numbers, called them, spoke to some people. One of them told her to come in for a chat. The next day she went down there, met the woman in her dodgy, unfinished offices near to Old Street. Jill wasn't what she was looking for, as it turned out. But she knew somebody else who was taking on staff. Jill asked if the woman could put in a good word for her. Sure she could – she'd do it now. She picked up the phone, chatted briefly to someone on the other end, yeah, yeah they did need someone to help out in the office. Could she go round and see them right away?

Jill went round – the place was less than five minutes' walk away. They liked her and she liked them, and they gave her the job.

'I've got a job,' she told Marty when she got home, dropping down into the sofa and switching on the telly.

'You have?' He was suitably impressed. 'That was quick. Doing what?'

'Receptionist. At a web design company. I start Monday.'

'*Web design*? Jesus. That'll last about fifteen minutes. Is that the best you could do?'

'Fuck you, Marty! It's a fucking job, okay? I thought you'd be pleased, though I can see how that would get in the way of behaving like a total wanker *all* the time.'

'What does it pay?'

'Not much. But it'll be cash in hand to begin with, until they get up and running, so I don't have to sign off yet either.'

269

Marty raised his eyebrows. 'Well done,' he said.

'*Thanks.*' She didn't mention Paul's role in helping her find the work. But then Marty hadn't asked her, had he?

★

A month or two went by. Gradually the two of them fell into a new set of routines and it began to seem almost like they were in a proper relationship. With Jill out at work all week, Marty occupied his days with trying to sell off his magic props to raise some extra money. Though Tony Quick still wouldn't have him back inside the house he'd relented to the extent of allowing his son to use the shed to store some of his equipment, there being no way he could get the bigger items inside the flat in Finsbury Park. One result of this was that every time he found a buyer Marty had to go to Beckenham to pick up the relevant item before delivering it, a trip that for obvious reasons he found somewhat traumatic.

One Friday evening he returned from such a journey, which on this occasion involved the handing over of his treasured water escape apparatus to the Hackney address of one of the Zodiac Brothers, an illusionist duo he'd long regarded as being among his chief competitors. When he finally walked into the flat some time around nine, Jill was locked into a game of Crash Bandicoot.

'Hi,' she said, without looking up. 'How'd it go?'

Marty didn't answer, preferring to go straight to the cupboard over the sink, take out a chipped Duralex glass, and pour into it the last finger of the half-bottle of Smirnoff Red that was sitting on the sideboard instead of lying bedded down in the freezer where it belonged. Didn't she fucking understand it was supposed to be kept cold? And the Coke, too, the bottle he'd bought just that morning, was also out on the side, top not properly done up. Warm and already flat. Christ. He pulled open the freezer compartment, its door cracked and varnished with smears the colour of snot. Ten dead grey peas, a half-pack of Aldi sausages welded into a knuckle-duster lump, an empty yellow box of boil-in-the-bag cod which he removed and frisbeed in the general direction of the bin. And no ice.

He sat on the sofa behind Jill who was sitting on the floor. She had her back to him, as did the annoyingly orange cartoon creature she was controlling. Marty eyed it hatefully. It was running away from him, jumping over little ravines and leaping crates, and ducking and diving through an endless series of obstacles and dangers just to put distance between itself and the vortex of disaster which was engulfing him. As he watched, it glanced back over its shoulder, fixed him in the eye and smirked.

Irritated beyond belief, Marty looked away, down at the battered rug where next to Jill's red-stockinged knee a half-smoked joint poked out from between the scarred battlements of the ashtray like the barrel of a cannon. He stared at it as if it were a bloodied syringe. He was sick of her dope. The money she wasted on it, the way she spent her whole time stoned.

He hated the fact that she had that to escape into and he did not.

He hated that whenever he mentioned this she said he could help himself, that she was more than willing to share, she was tempting him to become as fucked up as she was.

He hated the fact that he'd started smoking cigarettes to compensate, despite what had happened to his mother.

He hated that he'd not been strong enough to be pure like Harry had said, that he'd pissed away his dreams for the sake of a shag.

He hated none of these things as much as having just flogged his beautiful teleportation cabinets to the fucking Zodiac Brothers.

One thing was clear. The start of everything, the single event that had triggered the chain reaction which had destroyed everything he'd worked for, was Jill's forcing that E on him in the nightclub. Heaven and Hell. It had sounded so pathetic when he'd tried to explain this to Terri, that Jill had seduced him with drugs, but the fact was it was true, it really was. He'd turned it over and over in his mind, and it was the only conclusion he could come to.

'Didn't you see? I bought some fresh cans of Coke and more vodka. They're in that bag in the fridge.'

Fucking hell. Couldn't she have taken them out of the fucking bag so that he'd see them, put the vodka in the freezer? *Christ Almighty.* The back of her head was right there in front of him, a perfect target and he allowed himself to think through the sensation of drawing back his right boot and heeling her right there in the crown. It relieved the tension a little, to imagine this, and instead of crushing her skull he hauled himself up and sloped over to the kitchenette where he emptied his unhappy drink into the sink. Sure enough, a thin blue plastic bag had been stuffed inside the refrigerator, hopeless with the shape of bottles and cans. He pulled on the bag and a can rolled out and dropped on to his foot, right on to the still tender metatarsal that Terri had damaged with her heel. Dr Pepper. *Christ a-fucking-live.*

'Couldn't you have got Coke?' he whined. 'I hate Dr Pepper. Dr Pepper's what the fucking aliens drink.'

If this was a reference to something it was one Jill didn't get. 'They'd sold out,' she told him, still not moving her gaze from her game. 'And you shouldn't swear so much, Marty. It doesn't suit you.'

'You could have gone somewhere else.'

But she didn't answer, she didn't care, the game was too involving, her thumbs were dancing on the buttons as if electricity were running through them, her body bobbing and swerving with every move the animated orange creature made. Now when it glanced over its shoulder it seemed to be checking up on *her*, to see if she was still dancing to its tune. Marty hated it as well and when it finally missed its footing and disappeared down a crevasse he experienced a quite incredible sense of relief. Music jangled but Jill tossed the handset away. Hitting the mute button on the remote, she reached out for her spliff.

'So how did it go?' she asked, sparking up. 'And thanks for making me a drink.'

'Thought you had one.' Marty dropped down into the sofa and sat there glowering, hunching, sulking, silent. For a few moments he toyed with the idea of not answering her question, but the opportunity to bitch about his lot in life was far too tempting. 'How do you think it went?' He scowled. 'It's Friday and we're in the middle of a heatwave. Half of London's trying to get out of the fucking city for the weekend. I sat in traffic all the way down to Beckenham, loaded the van up with all the stuff – on my own, naturally, nearly broke my bloody back – then sat in traffic all the way to Hackney for the privilege of selling eight grand's worth of hardly used equipment for half of what I paid for it. To the fucking Zodiac Brothers. Could hardly have been worse if I'd flogged it to the Power of Light. Except for a stop-off to spend forty quid on petrol and try to replace the two litres of water I lost in sweat, I don't think there's anything else worth mentioning.'

Jill decided not to engage him on this dangerous terrain. 'Someone at work knows this bloke who wants a magician for a big corporate event,' she said instead.

Marty pouted. 'I don't do corporate events.'

She raised her eyebrows, got up to fix a drink. 'You want another one?'

He didn't move, which she took to mean yes.

'How much are they paying?'

Jill cracked open a fresh can of cola. 'Three hundred quid, just to go round and work the crowd for a couple of hours.'

Picking up the remote, the magician changed channels without turning up the sound. The news came on. 'I was reading about some of those dot.com friends of yours in the paper today,' he said, when she brought back the drinks. 'Have you any idea how much money those wankers are making?'

'It seems to be taking off a bit, doesn't it? Paul always said it would, as soon as they worked out how to sell stuff on it.'

'Paul?'

Shit. She wasn't supposed to mention Paul. 'Yeah,' she said, proceeding cautiously. 'You remember. Paul. From Blackpool. My friend Paul.'

'I didn't know you'd been in touch with him.'

She projected a lungful of smoke up towards the ceiling. After travelling for three or four feet, it fanned out into a cloud which enveloped the stained wire and paper lampshade they'd inherited from the previous tenants. 'Yeah. I spoke to him yesterday, in fact. Turns out he's had some dealings with the people I'm working for. He's got the go-ahead to set up this cybercafé thing. He's going to put networked games on all the machines, stuff like that. In this old church. Sounds wicked.'

'Oh, right.' Marty said nothing for a second or two and Jill waited nervously to find out whether or not she'd made it out of the woods. Turned out she had. 'Well, I'm glad he's so up to the fucking minute. This whole Internet thing sounds like money for old rope to me. Makes you sick. I mean, I could be doing that. What have they got that I haven't?'

'Yeah, but that's business, innit? You didn't want to be a businessman. You wanted to be a performer.'

'I wanted to be a performer but I figured I'd be on my way to Vegas by now, not reduced to working rooms full of wankers for peanuts like some kind of fucking . . . like some kind of fucking . . . some kind of fucking *tart*.' She could hear the tears in his voice and though they failed to move her she leaned forward and rubbed him on the knee.

'Got a cigarette?' he asked.

She nodded, got one out, lit it and passed it over, then to avoid further conversation she reached for the TV remote and toggled the sound back on. Marty moaned something about how everyone in the world had more money than him. What did he think? That life was fair?

She'd put some chips and a pizza in the oven just before he'd come in and to tell by the smell coming from the kitchen end of the room they were pretty much done. Dividing what there was on to two clean-looking plates, she brought them over and sat down next to him on the sofa.

The news was on: an item about Princess Diana meeting the new Prime Minister to bend his ear on the landmines issue. Marty was apparently so transfixed by what he was seeing he was forgetting to close his mouth while he chewed.

'Close your gob, Marty,' Jill told him.

'D'you think she'd do it?'

'Who?'

'Diana.' He gestured at the shots of her on the screen with an amputated chip, tomato sauce blood liberally glubbed around its stump.

'Do what? Get him to ban them?'

'*No*. Get her to join our act.'

Jill laughed. It was the first joke he'd made for days.

'Don't fucking laugh. I'm serious. Do you think she would? I think she would.'

'Don't be a twat.'

'I'm not. Think about it. It would be great publicity. It's *Eurovision*, right, so it would be totally huge. We could get her to come and then vanish her from the royal box or something, make her appear in a Mercedes Benz suspended above the stage. It would be awesome.'

'You're off your head.'

'I'm going to ask her.' He put down his plate, got up and went over to where the phone directories were kept in a dusty pile by the side of a small chest of drawers that'd come with the flat.

Behind him Jill choked on a chip. 'You're taking the piss,' she said, clearing the blockage with a swig of Dr Pepper.

'I am not fucking joking!' Marty shouted, spinning round, a look of fury on his face.

How wrong could you be? 'Okay, Marty, okay. Jesus. So you're not joking. Fine. Call her if you like. Whatever.'

'Don't worry. That's exactly what I'm going to do. What does she have? An office? A secretary or something? What?'

'How should I know? And there's no need to shout.'

'I didn't shout.'

'I'm *sorry*? I do know what I heard.'

'I did not fucking shout, all right?'

'You're shouting now.'

'But that's because . . . *oh, fuck you*!' Marty hurled the phone directory across the room and it reared up in front of Jill like a startled bird. By the time it had crashed down on to the coffee table he'd stormed out.

'Christ.' Jill felt her temples and dumped her plate down on the floor, unable to stand the smell, suddenly, of her food. She reached for her drink and lit yet another cigarette.

She smoked, staring at the telly. Prince Charles was on now, dicking about in a kilt on the banks of some Balmoral stream with those two kids of his. Poor bastards. She couldn't think of anything worse than being born into a family like that. They were a bunch of useless cunts if ever there was one. If ever there were proof needed that money didn't bring happiness, they were it. Poor Diana. Jill might've borne a passing resemblance to the Princess but she wouldn't've swopped places with the poor cow, not for half the Royal List. Not, of course, that she was happy being broke, but still. If most of what she'd read in that Andrew Morton book was true – and it sounded like it was – as far as she was concerned it was all the argument that was needed for abolishing the Royal Family altogether. She didn't regard herself as particularly political but still she didn't see why we all had to carry on letting that inbred bunch of Nazis lord it over us. Not that we didn't deserve it. Here was half the country still looking forward to that prick becoming king after he'd tormented a girl half his age nearly to death, conspiring with that bitter old slapper he'd been poking to turn her into some kind of heir production line. The piece of shit. She felt sorry for Diana, she really did. She'd been used. She was better than the rest of that lot put together.

God she was in a foul mood, all twisted up. Maybe she was smoking too much dope after all. She should go to bed. She'd feel better in the morning.

Jill didn't sleep, at least not properly and not till late; partly the heat and partly the idiots downstairs up half the night playing indoor hockey again. This was about the third time this had happened. Two weeks previously a sixteen-year-old kid had been moved into the flat beneath them, a precocious ice-hockey talent who'd been spotted playing for a borstal team up in Scotland and was now being housed, schooled and trained, courtesy of one of the big London teams. But the boy's good fortune clearly hadn't had much of a rehabilitating effect: ever since he'd arrived the lower floor had been the site of one long summer party, complete with random people dropping in and out at all times of the day and night, speed metal continually tearing up through Jill's and Marty's floor and psychotic late-night hockey games, the main aim of which seemed to be to try to drive an ice puck through the pressboard membranes of one or other of the flat's internal doors. Why Marty wouldn't go and give them hell she didn't know – he was probably scared of them, the lightweight. Either that or they didn't bother him. Probably the latter, since he was fast asleep.

Eventually the disturbance subsided and Jill slipped into unconsciousness, only to be woken again some time around four by another noise, this time from out in the street: a joy rider or something, cars and horns, anyway. Try as she might, she couldn't get back to sleep and in despair she got up and took a couple of the Valium she kept in her secret stash. For the next three hours she lay squeezed flat between two acrylic planes of consciousness, too strung out to sleep and too tired to get out of bed, the sheets rucked up around her sweating thighs like giant versions of the felted plastic moulding used in a child's geometry set, conscious of the diazepam sluicing round her brain like engine coolant but too conscious of it to let it take effect.

At eight o'clock Marty – who'd slept as soundly as a corpse all night – unclipped himself from his side of the bed and creaked into the bathroom. With his stiff body gone the sheets seemed to swell and ease and Jill found herself lying along the edge of a crevasse in the depths of which the Valium had finally coalesced into a deep, calm pool. Gratefully she shifted sideways an inch or two and tumbled in: she knew nothing else until the pool evaporated some time after noon.

Clutching Marty's beltless dressing gown round her body, she got up and went into the living room. Marty was there, sitting at the chaotic in-tray they called a kitchen table reading the Houdini biography he'd given her in Leeds, his elbows stapling a ragged wafer of household bills and promotional flyers and magazines and forgotten dishes to the flaking wood. She didn't bother wishing him good morning, didn't see much point, shuffled instead to where the kettle stood balanced on the edge of the overflowing sink, its once white plastic smeary as if dusted for fingerprints. She shook it – it was empty, near enough. With her left hand continuously and alternately occupied with holding the dressing gown closed and pushing her hair back out of her eyes, she used her right to unplug the kettle, fill it with water and plug it back in.

Once the tea'd been made, Jill sat down across from Marty on the spare kitchen chair. 'I had an idea last night,' she said, holding her cup in both hands as though it contained some kind of precious elixir not a single drop of which she could afford to spill (which it did). Marty had opened the windows wide and there was a welcome breeze blowing through the room – the air had been unbearably hot and still these past few days. The sun streamed in and Jill moved her chair around until she was sitting out of the glare, tipping her head back a little so that her scalp could feel the benefit of the draught. She'd actually ended up liking the haircut she'd had done for the show – anything was better than that fucking wig – but since then she'd been letting her highlights grow out, partly to see what effect the change would have on Marty. So far it hadn't had any, not as far as she could tell – not unless she counted the ending of their brief foray into bondage which, come to think of it, perhaps she should. As soon as she had any cash, she resolved, she'd get her hair done properly, not that that was likely, what with money being so tight.

Across on the other side of the room the TV was on, its picture tinted sepia by sunlight, its sound turned down very low. The news, by the look of it. She didn't need sound to tell her what the story was: it was the same one that had dominated the news all week. Diana and Dodi, Dodi and Diana, Inana and Dodo, Gaga and Spanner. On this occasion they were being shown climbing out of a limo inside a street cordon in the West End somewhere. The footage had been taken at night, probably last night; it looked like a première. There were crowds and celebrities, the faces intermittently abstracted into pixelated quilts as the dozens of popping flash guns created a crazy-paving reality just beyond the reach of the camera's compression algorithms. She looked happy, Diana did, Jill thought, happy and relaxed for once. And she'd put on weight, something she hadn't noticed when she'd watched that piece on her meeting with Tony Blair. Women changed physically to become more like the men they were in love with, didn't they? Or was it that they became more like their pets? Jill shook her head, trying to rattle free a coherent thought. Her brain felt like that street scene, populated not with faces but with pixelated ideas.

'An idea for a website,' she said, reiterating her sentence, wanting out.

'Oh, yeah?' Marty grunted, still staring at his book.

Jill continued undeterred. 'Yeah. I was lying awake last night thinking: look, why is everybody shelling out so much money to play the National Lottery when they could do it all online and for free?' At the mention of the Lottery Marty glanced up at her, the tread of suspicion unfurling easily across his face. She'd promised him she'd stopped buying tickets. Was this a confession?

'And how would that work?' He was getting good at scorn, Jill had noticed.

'Well, I don't know how you'd get the ball rolling, but I reckon if you could get enough people playing it could pay for itself through advertising.' She shifted her buttocks backwards in her chair, drew up one foot and hugged it to her chest, took a sip of tea. 'It would be really simple, right. All you'd need would be this one web page with a button on it. What you'd do is, you'd go to the site and enter your e-mail address, then click on the button. And you could do that as many times a day as you wanted, up to a maximum of twenty, say. And each click would enter you in that week's prize draw.'

'And you don't have to pay?'

'No, that's free, it's free to do that.'

'So what's the prize, then? Where does the money come from?'

'That's what's so cool. 'Cos if you've got, say, a million people coming every day from all over the country – or all over the world even; I mean, maybe it could be millions and millions, that's how many visits some of these sites get – then you could sell really expensive advertising on that page. Every week a company would sponsor the button, like Microsoft or Nike or someone like that, and they'd pay a rate for that advertising depending on how many people visited the site and saw their ad. Maybe it would be a penny for every hundred people that visited or something. Then what you'd do is, at the end of every week you'd take all the names of the people who'd come and clicked, and the computer would pick one of them and whoever it picked would win a fixed proportion of the advertising money, like half or three-quarters. And the rest would be profit, after you'd paid off the costs of running the site.'

'And you think this would work?'

'Why shouldn't it work? I think it's a really good idea.'

'If it's such a good idea, why hasn't somebody done it already?'

'I don't know. Maybe they have.'

Marty put down his book and clicked the kettle back on. It was still warm from when Jill had used it and almost immediately started to boil. 'I'll tell you why not. Because it's a totally stupid idea, that's why not. Nobody'll do it.'

'Why? What's wrong with it? Loads of people do the Lottery. According to you it's a complete waste of time but people still do it.'

'If you knew anything about economics instead of getting stoned the whole time you'd know why not.'

'And like you're the economics expert.'

'Look, it's simple. You're not selling anything, you're not making anything, it's got no basis in anything real. I'm not surprised you came up with it in your sleep. If you woke up for five minutes you'd see there's no way it can work.'

'The advertising revenue, though, that would be real.'

'But who's going to pay good money to have their name up on your site? Why should they, if all you're going to do is give it away? It'll just make them look like idiots.'

'They pay for TV ads and billboards by the sides of roads, don't they? This would be a billboard on the Internet. All you need to do is to guarantee a certain number of people'll see it. That's what advertising's all about.'

'So now it's you who's the expert, right?' All this talk of billboards had reminded Marty of the PlayStation poster Terri had seen being pasted up outside their window in Blackpool, the morning after he'd first cheated on her with Jill. 'So what're you going to call it? Button.com?'

Jill looked hurt. 'What's wrong with that? That's actually a really good name. It's familiar. It's easy to remember. Easy to spell. It sums up the USP of the site.'

'What the fuck's USP?'

'Unique Selling Point.'

'You sound more like those arseholes you're working with every day.'

'There's no reason to be offensive, especially since you've not even met them. It was only an idea. Just because you've got no fucking imagination.'

'Oh yeah, that's right.'

'What the fuck's with you this morning? I was the one who didn't get any sleep.'

'Nothing's with me. Why is it my problem all of a sudden? It's you who came up with the dumb idea. You asked me what I thought, I told you. If you were going to get offended by the answer you shouldn't've asked.'

This was enough for Jill. Banging her cup down on the table – and sending her precious elixir splashing all over an unpaid electricity bill – she stormed out of the room, slamming the door shut behind her so hard that it jarred the entire flat. A minute or two later, Marty heard another door bang closed followed by the sound of running taps.

'Don't use all the hot water!' he yelled, just to piss her off even more.

Parking the cup of tea he'd just made on the coffee table, he dropped down into the giant paw of the sofa, apparently unbothered by the row that had just taken place. The sofa was old, the scabs and cigarette burns flecking its bald green corduroy the legacy of any life spent at the rough end of the furniture forest, and it's long-suffering springs moaned with pain as the magician's horny buttocks compacted them. It was a sound he'd come to find increasingly gratifying.

Spying out the remote where it lay discarded on the floor, he reached out with his leg and tried to toe the yellow button that would bring up the sound. He got it in one, which was pleasing. Some daytime discussion show was on, some housewives' magazine – the same programme Jill had thought was the news – and the talk was spurious stuff about the cultural significance of Diana's humping an Arab. A panel of twittering pundits trading thinly veiled racisms for PC irrelevancies, but of more interest to Marty was the fact that Jill Dando was hosting. Plus they'd got five-foot glossies of Dodi and Di fixed up on the studio wall and the Diana shot was one of his favourites, the one by Patrick

Demarchelier where she was sitting in whiteness dressed all in black. It was the one that most reminded him of Terri, this one. He looked at the pictures, at the presenter. It was true: Jill *was* more a Jill Dando type, really, than a Diana; coarser, less refined, not a natural blonde like the Royal. A bit tacky, when all was said and done. Still, Marty wasn't averse to a little bit of tack. It was funny. Dando and Diana, they were almost like two aspects of the same person, just like Terri and Jill. Diana the living room – no, the *drawing* room – version, all posh clothes and cocktails, and all decorative and coy; Dando what she became after a round in the bedroom, brown roots and blurred features and all a bit High Street, really, all a bit catalogue – even a shade Readers' Wives, though perhaps that was taking it a little bit far.

The fact that he'd upset Jill didn't worry him, not really. She'd get over it. She'd spent most of the last year taking the piss out of him but when he gave her a taste of her own medicine she didn't like it. Well, tough. She needed to lighten up, that was all. Anyway, he had some good news for her. He'd decided he was going to do that corporate gig she'd told him about. Quite frankly, he couldn't not: they needed the money.

It was odd, but for some unaccountable reason – and for the first time in months – Marty suddenly found himself in a genuinely good mood.

The bags were black and had the words NETWORK NETWORK machine-stitched across their flaps in white, words which were followed by three petit point circles individually embroidered in yellow, red and green. Underneath these in Blue Chip blue the familiar glyphs of the event's various sponsors were featured, sponsors whose names, names like Oracle and Exodus and Sol, sounded like they'd formerly belonged to esoteric priest-hoods.

The circles, Magda had explained to Marty when he'd arrived – early, well before the punters, so he'd have a chance to do some preparation – were part of Network Network's unique identity profile and were crucial to how it defined itself in a marketplace already maximally niched with competing cross-fertilisation salons and business opportunity groups.

'Everyone has to wear a coloured button, see,' Magda said (she was American: she meant 'badge'), 'and we've patented that.'

Marty asked what the buttons symbolised, wondering if he could somehow work some kind of routine with them, or at least a couple of good jokes.

'It's simple. Red for VCs, green for entrepreneurs. Then besides that everyone also has to wear a white sticker showing the name of their company or site. That way everybody knows who you are and what you do. Your function, I guess. It's an ice-breaker. I suppose it's kind of an American thing.'

'VCs?' puzzled Marty as Magda pinned a yellow badge on his

lapel and wrote him out a sticky white label saying 'magic'. He was thinking Victoria Crosses, red like poppies; or Vietcong, red again.

'Venture Capitalists.' Magda smiled. 'Money men.' She was tall and big-boned, and blonde and beautiful in a slightly dazed sort of way, and she had her own handwritten white sticker, which read simply 'Magda', stuck to her blouse. She looked as if she might have had Dutch ancestry, somewhere back there.

'Oh. Right. So what's yellow?' Marty asked, looking at his badge.

'Yellow means "other".'

'Other what?'

'Just "other".'

The magician frowned a little, pursed his lips. 'So you just want me to work the crowd, entertain people at random?'

'That okay? You can do it standing up, right? You don't need a table or anything like that?'

'It would make things easier, but no, I can do it standing up. I can do it lying down if you like.'

Magda either didn't pick up on that or didn't want to. 'So that's cool, then?' she asked, trying to push the conversation into some sort of endgame.

But Marty wasn't done yet. 'So,' he said a little vacantly, 'am I it?'

'Are you what?'

'Am I the sole entertainment? Or are there others? Fire-eaters or jugglers or anyone?'

'We-ll, there's you and the food icons and the wine waiters and the body ads, so you won't be all on your own.'

Marty didn't enquire about body ads; he already felt stupid enough over VCs. 'What time do I start?' he asked instead.

'Oh, whenever. Wait till the place fills up a bit. Go get a drink if you like.' The woman pointed over to where tuxedoed staff were setting up regiments of wine and beer bottles on white-tableclothed tables.

Marty nodded but didn't move. Magda was tall, he was thinking, almost as tall as he was, and actually quite sexy. 'Maybe in a while.'

'So what sort of tricks do you do, then?'

'I'm an illusionist,' Marty replied pointedly. 'I do magic. Wanna see?'

'Oh, no thanks,' she said, the logos of female defensive hostility glimmering just beneath the surface of her eyes. 'I don't like magic. No offence.'

'None taken.'

Somebody called Magda's name from the other side of the room and seizing on the opportunity she slipped away. Left on his own, Marty leaned back against a table piled high with hand-outs and hats and booklets and flyers and free CD-ROMs and foam boomerangs and fluorescent business cards and countless other items of let's-waste-the-planet's-resources-and-exploit-workers-in-faraway-export-processing-zones corporate junk, and looked again at the pile of black record bags in which all this stuff was to be stowed. Magda had told him every person who attended would get one of these and he'd been trying to think of a way to use them in some kind of routine, but he couldn't see how. He glanced up again at the design award striplights that descended on long thin poles from the raked hall's high curved ceiling to within about four feet of his head. They'd given him an idea for something but it was only a one-off and that wouldn't really do.

He checked around him. No one was looking. He'd set it up now, just in case. Then he'd go and get a beer, as Madga had suggested. Screw the punters. He'd just show them some card tricks. That would still be more than they deserved.

★

A short while later the doors opened and the room began to fill. As Marty watched the suits filing in a terrible stage fright crept over him, as bad as any he could remember experiencing. No doubt this had something to do with the two bottles of beer he'd just deposited on top of an empty stomach, but the mood seemed more than mild drunkenness, especially when the skin around the top of his arms and his shoulder blades began to tremble and prick with a chemical chill so unpleasant it almost seemed a kind of paralysis. The sensation reminded him so much of the Ecstasy he'd taken in Blackpool that he took it for an actual, physical memory, a memory stored up in his muscles rather than his brain. The strange dislocation of selfhood and space he was experiencing was certainly very much the same, the difference being that back in Heaven and Hell the feeling had been positive; it had put him in control. Here it was having the opposite effect.

He first became uneasy when, trying to get the measure of the figures in the crowd, he realised they reminded him of gulls. Not gulls in the old carnival sense of gullible punters. Gulls like the birds. Perhaps it was because, male or female, many of them wore white or pastel shirts beneath suits of dove-grey or petrol; that and the way they were standing tightly packed on the terraces of the room in little knots and bunches like a community of mews and guillemots on a terraced breakwater, jabbering at each other about the most extraordinary fact of the sun's going down. Shoulders rounded, necks extended, arms either tucked in at their sides or flapping vigorously to maintain rhetorical balance, weight shifting rhythmically from one leg to the other and back again, heads nodding, eyes looking out to both sides at once, certainly they looked like gulls, especially to someone like Marty whose great dream had only recently been shattered, whose life was in pieces and whose ambient mood was one of near suicidal depression.

To be fair, the nadir of Marty's melancholy was almost past. Having started the slow scrabble up the walls of the vicious pit of unmitigated moroseness he'd dug for himself, he was now beginning to suffer instead from violent mood swings. Which was a kind of progress, though even at the joyful end of the spectrum his moods were often accompanied by psychotic thoughts. Take the idea, for example, that had come to him during the sudden good mood that he'd experienced just the other day while watching Jill Dando on the telly. One moment he'd been enjoying a series of complex sexual fantasies involving the presenter; the next he'd been entertaining the idea of finding out where she lived and stalking her, taking surreptitious photographs of her every activity that later he could show in a fashionable London gallery and proclaim as avant-garde art, a ground-breaking concept and major comment on the narcissism destroying our society that would make his name much more successfully than magic ever could.

But he wasn't going to think about that now. He was too busy worrying about the seagulls; about how he was going to entertain them; how the very fact of being paid to work a room like this was so far from what he wanted to be doing and knew himself to be capable of doing that it was demeaning to him as an artist. What struck him above all was how the lowly status of jobbing magician contrasted with the striking confidence of the people gathered around him; how their stances and expressions, and the strangely grasping hand movements they made chorused concepts like *Succeed!* and *Acquire!* and *Believe!*; how the effect of this was demoralising to the point where he just wanted to curl up into a small ball right there on the floor in the middle of them all and berate himself while they didn't even notice and from time to time stepped on him.

The volume of conversation was already deafening, each knot of chat exciting the next in a kind of vocal convection until the room was fairly boiling with sound, roiling with terms that Marty didn't understand. Words like WAP and leverage and hit rate and churn and IPO and metatag and server and frames and MPEG and CEO and CFO and broadband and baud and banner ad and gateway and portal and OS and convergence. To have such an alien lingo to deal with when he was already having difficulty sizing up the crowd was intimidating too. It was impossible to make jokes out of what he didn't understand, or even to work out a good moment to interrupt someone and get a routine under way, interruption being a necessity because of the way in which everyone seemed to be talking all the time, everyone, there didn't seem to be a single person among the assembled company who wasn't engaged in animated verbiage, as if it were some kind of insane competition.

It *was* some kind of insane competition.

Finally – after he'd drunk another beer – Marty plucked up courage and took the plunge. Picking someone pretty much at random, he wandered up and fanned out his Bees like so many feathers. 'Would you like to pick a card?' he said, hating himself as he did so. It felt so degrading, like soliciting for sex.

'So what's this, then?' asked the mark. 'Magic.com?' He wore a red button alongside a name tag that identified him as Philip Deeg from Deutschebank. 'You need incubation?'

'Er . . .' Marty said.

The man shook his head slightly and taking a card, examined it. 'Hey!' he said, his accent a mood-inhibiting Euro-American amalgam. 'These cards aren't sponsored! You want to think about that – that's a nice marketing opportunity you're missing there.'

The two men standing with Deeg laughed simultaneously and Marty laughed with them, trying to keep them onside, to keep the routine's rhythm flowing.

'Oh, yeah,' he said. 'Definitely. Now place the card back inside the pack, if you would.'

'I'm going to put it in, right, then you're going to tell me what it is? How do I know I can trust you?'

'You can put it anywhere you like.'

'Can I keep it?'

Another titter from the group.

'That depends on whether or not you want to see what I'm going to do with it.'

'Maybe I don't.'

Marty shrugged; this was tiresome, he didn't want to have to deal with this kind of shit. He'd forgotten how hard close-up was, how combative; how you had to be right there with sharp repartee all the time.

'Ok-*ay*,' the man said, finally slotting the card back in the deck like he was supposed to. 'Jesus, you're the glummest magician I think I ever met. You should be a clown.'

This triggered another round of laughs from the cronies.

Wincing out a poor excuse for a smile, Marty cut the pack, shuffled, then reached up and produced the card from behind the man's ear.

'Hey!' Deeg said, genuinely surprised. 'That was cute! But how're you going to parlay that into click-through?'

'What the fuck's click-through?' Marty demanded.

The man stepped back. 'Hey, I was only being friendly. Is this entertainment or an interrogation?' And before Marty could protest or even apologise, Philip Deeg from Deutschebank had turned his back on him and resumed his conversation with the group.

Enervated and despondent, the young magician moved on until he found a clump of men who looked relatively unintimidating. Then he approached. 'Pick a card, any card,' he said lamely to a diminutive man with a barrel chest and sparrow legs. The man did as he was asked, but then held the card without looking at it while he continued to shunt buzzwords through the air as if the magician didn't exist. Marty waited, wondering bitterly whether he was perhaps confused and thought the card some novel type of canapé.

'What do you expect me to do with this?' the sparrow-man eventually asked.

Marty tried to keep his voice sweet, despite speaking through clenched teeth. 'Well, take a look at it, I'd like to show you some magic.'

'Er, thanks.' The man passed it back. 'Maybe some other time.'

Once again Marty moved on.

*

A short time later he was fanning his pack for a wheezing gent with blubbery lips and nose hair clipped from a welcome mat, when he suddenly got elbowed in the small of the back by a Greek. The Greek was an inch or two shorter than Marty but the reverse seemed the case; he had what they call presence, Mediterranean-style. He wore a navy-blue blazer over a white cotton shirt with an open English spread collar, three buttons undone to reveal the links of a weighty gold chain sewn into the pubis of black hairs curling at the base of his neck.

So this Greek barged Marty and jolted him forwards, and pushing out with his hands to steady himself Marty jabbed his cards into the chest of the blubber-lipped man. Being of a nervy and paranoid disposition, having long ago been bullied at school, this man now (over)reacted like he was being attacked. Jerking back, he brought his arms up and executed a kind of rabbit-like bounce; fingers flopping perpendicular to the floor like said rabbit's paws; eyebrows arched; teeth and chin moving in different directions. And as he sprang into the air he nudged with the base of one blunt shoulder blade the head of the very short woman standing just to his rear.

This very short woman now put her hand to her crown and went into a crouch, causing her complimentary black NETWORK NETWORK bag to come swinging round. The bag, being full of all that corporate bumf plus her laptop and mobile, and a light cashmere sweater she'd removed because it was just too hot in here to continue to wear it, wasn't closed, meaning that the Velcro fastener was exposed, meaning that as the bag swung it snagged the vent of a jacket of fine woollen yarn belonging to a third man standing nearby.

Assuming that someone was trying to get his attention, this man made an about-turn and, seeing the Very Short Woman somewhere below him, bent down to ask of her, 'Yes?' Which would have been fine but for his highly polished pate, which now as he went into a lean cracked hard against the skull of the guy who'd been waiting to see Marty's trick, who having come back to earth after his rabbit-like bounce had been unable to maintain his balance and right now was toppling backwards and on to the Very Short Woman. Sensing these two men in her airspace and about to collide, the Very Short Woman did what any sensible Very Short Person would do and ran forward, her black NETWORK NETWORK bag trailing behind, realising she'd better get the hell out of the way.

There followed a complex of causes and effects too tangled to describe, one of the outcomes of which was the knocking of the elbow of a waitress who had been twisting her way through the crowd in the fashion of a wind-up child's toy travelling across a highly polished and no doubt extremely expensive adult-type surface (seventy degrees clockwise and forward one foot, seventy degrees anti-clockwise and forward the other), a waitress who was trying to keep clear of the bodies, bags and beaks obstructing her way with a tray loaded with Tall But Cheap champagne flutes filled to within half an inch of their rims with sparkling wine.

And now the tray, as trays will, started to teeter.

Meanwhile the Greek who, since we last saw him, had continued to push through the press of people only dimly aware of the chain of events his earlier action had triggered, caught sight, first, of the not unattractive waitress and, second, of her toppling tray. It took only nanoseconds for his superb business brain both to register the flirtation opportunity presented and to perform fractal analysis upon the several terabytes' worth of experiential information he needed to crunch through in order to deem it worthy of a few moments of his valuable time. And so to action: unleashing the highly reflective white blocks of his feta-cheese smile, the Greek reflected down under the tray a quantum of the energy blazing forth from the design award striplights suspended in lines overhead just sufficient to neutralise the effect of the earth's gravitational pull, the result being that the tray teetered back, righting itself.

Cute move, but not cute enough; all the glasses are safe with the exception of one: the foremost and fullest, the prow of the tray. Perhaps due to a lack of adequate peripheral support, the Greek has neglected to factor in the flex of the metal, a force strong enough to overcome his stunning intervention and boost this flute upwards and outwards and off the edge of the tray. It flips in the air, passes across Marty's left shoulder, and deposits its contents all down his front, his feathers, his cards, illustrating what the sprite in Crash Bandicoot already knew to be true, which is that Marty's career has now plummeted so far and so fast as to create a sort of bad-shit black hole with the power to make real any potential disaster that happens along and which will continue to do so until such time as it can either be somehow deflected or, which is more likely, works itself up to such a furious pitch that it actually blows itself out. Which can happen. Though believe me, it is not pleasant to live through or witness. (And I know.)

Wholly unfazed by his miscalculation – not, indeed, even noticing it – the Greek executes a full body sleight and ducks under the tray, passing between waitress and magician and out of harm's way even before Marty's worked out that he's been covered in sparkling wine. By the time our rich businessman has completed his move and straightened up on the other side of the Marty–tray archway the glass has vanished completely, though the waitress, dazzled by a second flash of that wonderful smile, has not even noticed it's gone.

'Thank you,' she mouths to the Greek, all a-tremble to be in the ambit of power, which comment Marty can hardly believe. But he's too busy worrying about how to salvage his Bees from their sugary shower to do anything more and by the time he's realised that they're totally fucked and let them fall to the floor to be trampled alongside the now broken flute, the Greek has passed the waitress his card and suggested she give his office a call so they can fix a time to go somewhere flash and expensive for lunch and, the deed done, the initial public offering so neatly made, he's moved on, five or six feet in the direction he originally intended to go from which distance his voice, bassy and powerful and inflected with an Onassis-like burr, can be heard telling some poor supplicant with black curly locks and a start-up and an unmistakably rotund lower jaw, that it's absolutely no good trying to bother him any more because as he's already told him before he never in any circumstances touches anything unless it's global.

★

Out alpha-ed and with a look of fury locked on to his face, Marty pushed away from the scene and towards what he guessed were the toilets, passing by one of the many white-tableclothed tables that were serving as bars as he went. One half of its surface was occupied by green German beer bottles, drawn up in ranks, the other by half-litres of sparkling mineral water whose original labels had been replaced with bright orange ones bearing the eye-wink hieroglyph of a major Internet search engine. Of more interest to Marty, however, were the two women standing to either side of this set-up – two extremely good-looking women, Marty noted, his sexual sonar still operating unperturbed despite everything else. Both sported strappy high heels and knee-length leather coats; neither looked very much as if she wanted to be there. The one to the left vaguely resembled Nastassja Kinski; the one to the right was more Daryl Hannah. Marty flashed the latter an expression he hoped was halfway to being a grin and she flashed him back, which is to say that she opened her coat and exposed herself.

Shortly after his racing retinas had registered the undeniable reality of the girl's bust, Marty's cortex managed to process the disappointing news that although, yes, she was indeed the proud possessor of breasts, these breasts were in fact snugly encased in the top half of a flesh-coloured Lycra bikini, the cups of which were decorated with the same eye-wink logos as the bottles of mineral water. Underneath these, daubed across the girl's stomach in red body paint, was the name of the Internet search engine she'd been paid to promote.

Excite.

'Er . . . hi,' Marty managed, winching his vision like an injured climber around the dangerous overhang of the girl's torso and up to the relative safety of her face. Staring as if into a mirror, he worked it out. 'Body-ad. Right?' The girl's mouth windowed open to reveal a toolbar of teeth so perfect you wanted to click on them.

'What you 'ere for, then?' she asked, London having long ago stolen her Hs and given her two ellipses of glass in exchange for her eyes. 'You another of these dot.commies, then?'

'No – no way. I'm the magician.'

'Oh – so you're Mr Magic Man.' The girl closed her coat and

was human again. She called to her friend, 'Hey, Stella, it's the magician.' Then back to Marty: 'We've 'eard about you.'

'Only good things, I hope.'

'Just that you were coming, that's all. So. You gonna show us a trick?'

Marty shook his head.

'No?' The girl arched back, pretend-affronted, and fluttered her false eyelashes at him.

'Well, I would, only some twat just went and knocked Asti all over my cards, which has pretty much done for them.'

'Haven't you got a spare pack?'

'Yeah, of course, but my fingers are all sticky – I'll muck up the cards if I don't wash my hands first.'

'Oh.' She looked crestfallen and Marty couldn't have that – it just didn't go with the overdone make-up and the long crimps of blonde hair.

'Tell you what, princess,' he said, 'I'll make you a crown. This is real kids' stuff – I'll bet you haven't seen this done for years.'

Reaching into one of the many pockets of his suit, he retrieved three or four long thin balloons. After seasoning them with a few hefty snaps he blew them into long lemon tubes which he twisted together to form a lavish tiara. This he gravely placed on the body-ad's head.

'Cool,' Stella cooed, 'make us one too!'

'Yeah, go on, make her one,' the friend said. Marty obliged, squeaking and squeezing her out a similar design but in mauve.

Cheered by his flirtation with the two women, he strolled off to the Gents with his chutzpah restored. What had he been thinking, letting himself get intimidated like that? He'd allowed the strange language, the alcohol, the testosterone haze to confuse him. But now, as he dried off his shirt front with paper towels and washed the veneer of wine from his hands, he began to work out the game. It was just a bunch of businessmen cruising each other in a cute little financial stand-and-fuck bar, that was all and, as Magda had told him, the buttons were key. Yellows were irrelevant, journos and body-ads and liggers; he could forget about them. It was all about the reds and the greens, those were the boys, the reds in the minority but holding the cards, the greens dancing around them trying to solicit attention. It wasn't a million miles, in fact, from the Magicians' Convention in Blackpool, or at least from Marty's memory of it as an undignified mosh pit of touting and sales. Except here it was the English who seemed to be doing the selling, the freshly spanked ruddiness of their otherwise pale faces giving them a shocked, startled look that made them easy to distinguish from the smoothly tanned Europeans and Americans who made up the majority of the red button wearers.

Fine. He was remembering how to do this. He wasn't beaten yet. Unzipping the cellophane from a fresh pack of Bees and taking a waterproof marker from his pocket, Marty locked himself into one of the cubicles. A man with a plan in the can.

Twenty minutes later he was striding back into the main room, full of his scheme. Everything depended upon being able to get Magda to do what he wanted, but first he needed to locate her and manoeuvre her into position. Like a huntsman he threaded his way through the forest of nattering people, their jaws rattling like wind-driven leaves, deflecting requests for card tricks and balloon hats as he went. People were getting drunker, it seemed, drunker and more relaxed. Perhaps he'd be able to salvage something from the evening after all.

After five minutes of searching he spotted her, standing over by the entrance desk. Perfect. She was talking with a soft-spoken, bespectacled American with a neat Monkees haircut who was dressed, unlike every other male Marty could recall seeing that evening, in corduroy and suede. Figuring that not being in a suit the man probably wasn't all that important, Marty strode up to the two of them and, cleaving to his new if-you-can't-beat-'em-join-'em attitude, butted right in. 'Magda.'

'Marty.' She folded her arms and looked at him, not pleased by the intrusion but letting it ride. The blond man tilted his head and looked on with a faint expression of amusement playing across his soft features, waiting to see what would happen.

'So how's it been going?' Magda asked.

'Hm. Mixed. Difficult to get people's attention. But I thought since you're paying me for this I should at least make sure you get your money's worth.'

'How so?'

'I'd like you to let me show you something.'

'I told you already, I don't go in much for tricks.'

'Well, that's all right, then, because as I told you before, I don't do tricks. I create illusions. I do magic.'

'Is there a difference?'

'That's what I'm here to demonstrate. Here.' Reaching out, Marty took hold of her hand and led her forward. 'This is a trick,' he said. 'Watch.' He held her palm flat for a moment, then closed it up. 'What's in your hand?'

'Nothing.'

'You're sure nothing?'

'I'm sure.'

'Well, then, let's see.'

Madga uncurled her fingers and her jaw dropped. Sitting in her pale palm was a round Chinese coin. T'ang dynasty, with a square hole in its centre and dark patination. Marty took the coin and held it up and showed it around, trying to fashion the beginnings of an audience out of whoever happened to be standing nearby.

He asked Magda if she smoked but she shook her head.

'Does anybody here smoke?' Marty called out to those nearest him. Someone, a man his own age – a man who looked vaguely familiar – answered yes and offered a pack of cigarettes, one of which Marty took. He held them up, coin and fag both, so that everyone could see what was happening. 'And now,' he said with a theatrical flourish, 'for my famous cigarette through the coin illusion.'

Laughter rippled through the crowd as the magician pushed the cigarette through the hole in the Chinese coin. 'Actually, that wasn't much of a trick,' he conceded. 'Maybe if someone could time me? I could try and do it really quickly. Magda – do you wear a watch?'

'Sure,' Magda said, warming to him. She looked down at her wrist. 'But . . . wait a minute. It – it's gone.'

'What? Your watch has gone? Someone must have stolen it.

301

Or maybe just borrowed it . . .' Marty extended his left wrist, the watch strapped round it. 'It was me! But it was such a nice one that I couldn't resist. It suits me, don't you think? You want it back? You'd better take it yourself – would you mind? Sorry, but my hands are full.' He showed her the coin and the cigarette, then offered his arm. 'Wait . . . before you do, there's something trapped underneath it, can you see? Could you get that out for me?'

Carefully Magda eased out the coin that was held there. It was an English coin, a silver ten-pence piece. She passed it to Marty who took it in his left hand (the same hand which was holding the cigarette) and placed the other coin, the Chinese one, in his pocket with his right. Swopping the ten-pence into his now free right hand, he tapped it with the fag and showed it round the now sizeable audience. 'Now, unlike the Chinese,' he said, 'the English don't put holes in their coins. They don't need them, they've got holes in their pockets instead. Don't believe me? Ask my bank manager. But it's a long tradition, holes in coins, and we English, advanced as we are, haven't quite learned to do completely without them. Which is useful for magicians, because it allows us to do the following.'

Holding the coin out in front of him he tapped it with the cigarette once, twice, three times, on the third occasion pushing it right through the metal so that it was sticking out on both sides, like an axle. The audience gasped. He jiggled it back and forth to prove the cigarette was whole and then – after everyone had got a good look at the thing – pulled it all the way through. The coin dropped into his hand and he passed cigarette and coin across to Magda. 'See?' the magician said. 'I even pay you for your time.' He bowed, encouraging a loud burst of applause.

'So – you didn't like that, then?' he asked his new assistant. 'I mean, you don't like magic, or so you told me.'

Magda rocked her head from side to side, semi-sure.

'Well, I didn't like it too much either. Those were tricks, only tricks. Anyone can do those. But now I'm going to show you the real McCoy. Which is a different thing altogether. As different as the birds from the bees.'

Adopting an expression of the utmost gravity, Marty reached into his jacket pocket, pulled out a red pack of Bees and removed the cards from their box.

'Here,' he said, holding them out. 'Take these.'

'Not just one of them?'

'No – take them all. Take the pack.' A little reluctantly Magda did as he requested and immediately Marty turned and started to usher people back, creating a larger arena in which he could move. 'Make space for Magda here, make space for Magda,' he repeated loudly, calling instructions to her in between requesting that she examine the pack, make sure it was perfectly ordinary, be certain that there was nothing unusual about it.

Embarrassed to find herself suddenly the centre of attention in this way, Magda fingered the cards as if afraid they might bite. 'This is why I hate magic,' she murmured to her blond friend.

Marty returned and, sensing Magda wasn't completely at ease, took the deck from her. Almost exactly her height, maybe half an inch taller, he stood blocking the crowd from her view and talked into her eyes.

'Okay, here we are, see, a perfectly normal deck of cards.' He fanned them slowly and openly, let her see them, then handed them back. 'Here's what I'd like you to do. Check the pack again, if you would.' This she did, more readily this time. 'Okay – is there anything at all unusual about it that you can see?' A hesitant no. 'Good. Please return it to me.' He took it. 'Now, I'm going to ask you to pick out a card.' Once again he fanned the cards, with more care this time, and Magda chose one, holding it up against her chest without looking at it.

'Good,' Marty said. 'Okay, what I'd now like you to do is turn round to the table here and sign your name across the face of it using this.' Producing a black magic marker from his breast pocket he handed it to her. 'You can show the card around if you like, so that other people know what it is, but don't let me see it, and when you're done please slip it back in the pack. Anywhere you like.'

The two of them stood back to back while Magda did as the magician requested.

'Okay. All finished?'

She hadn't quite, but then she had and, recapping the marker, she blew on the card to dry off the ink and pushed it daintily back into the middle of the pack, which she then handed to Marty with a tiny, involuntary curtsey.

'That was quick,' he said, taking the cards and giving them a prolonged shuffle.

'Was it?'

'Yes. Considering you did rather more than I asked.'

Magda frowned. 'What? But I didn't.'

'I asked you to write your name across just one of the cards, that's correct?'

'Yes, and that's just what I did.'

'Oh, but you didn't,' Marty said with a smile. 'You wrote your name across all of them.' And he threw the pack of cards high into the air.

As it passed the level of the striplights it exploded apart. Cards shot away from one another on slices of air and twizzled and twirled back down to the ground like sycamore leaves, at which point it became apparent to all the spectators that every single card had the name 'Magda' scrawled across it in black.

'I told you,' Marty said, grabbing at a few of the cards and holding them up for everyone to see. 'And this is your handwriting, right?' Laughing, amazed, Magda nodded. 'But you say you're positive you only wrote your name on one of them? Which one was it?'

'Erm, the Jack of Hearts.'

'The Jack of Hearts?'

'Uh huh.'

'You're absolutely sure about that?' He looked round at the audience for confirmation and a couple of people nodded their heads.

'Okay, well, then look up there. See if you can spot anything familiar.'

Magda did, as did everyone else within earshot, and after following the line of Marty's outstretched index finger she let out an involuntary gasp. There it was, her playing card, the Jack of Hearts, with her name scrawled across it in black, lodged into a metal seam in one of the design award striplights that ran in bright lines over their heads.

Loud applause broke out all around and Marty bowed to the circle of faces. *Bet you can't do that over the Internet*, he thought to himself as his eyes scanned across them. But somehow – perhaps because the curved wall of bodies was acting as some kind of psychic reflector; perhaps because in spite of this brief bout of success he remained filled with self-doubt – the thought came right back to him: *Bet you we can.*

They were all over him, after that.

'I take it all back, what I said about magic.' Magda blushed. 'Sorry – I mean illusions. That was . . . I don't really know what to say. That was freaky.' Marty shrugged happily, glowing despite the momentary psychic pang inflicted on him by the audience. 'It was amazing, didn't you think, Dale? Marty, this is Dale Tanner, I should have introduced you two already. Dale's one of the founders of Network Network.' The magician felt a twinge of embarrassment: Dale was the suede-jacketed American he'd earlier muscled past to get Magda's attention. Still, if he'd minded he hadn't said anything about it.

'Cool,' Dale said, shaking Marty's hand. 'That was deeply cool. I'm kind of . . . speechless, I guess. How d'you do that?'

'Magic.' Marty smiled.

'Oh – yeah. But of course.'

The three of them stood nodding gently at each other while the crowd seeped back into the arena Marty had cleared, stealing glances at the magician and leaving a little circle of free space around him in a manner that suggested the existence of an atavistic awe, a cultural memory of the age-old relationship between magic and power, even these self-professed denizens of the digital future.

'About my fee . . .' Marty began, thinking this might be a good time to broach the subject of money.

But no sooner had the words come out of his mouth than a

hand broke through the charmed circle and clapped him on the shoulder. 'Marty!'

The magician turned to find himself staring the new arrival in the face. It was a round face, topped and tailed with a cardboardy fret of gingery fluff, hair and goatee both clipped to a number five grade. The features in between were freckled, ruggerish and vaguely familiar – and not just because this had been the man who'd earlier handed him a cigarette. The newcomer grabbed Marty's hand and pumped it, barking out a laugh. 'Don't you recognise me? It's me. Darren!' His small dark eyes twinkled like lacquered buttons pleated into cheeks cushioned by the beginnings of a largery bloat.

'Christ! Darren. My God – of course. I'm sorry, of course – you're just . . . well, you're just the last person I expected to see. What on earth are you doing here?'

'Not magic tricks, that's for sure. That was amazing – truly amazing. You've come on a bit, haven't you? Bloody hell.'

'Oh, thanks,' Marty answered, not sure how much of a compliment this actually was. Darren. When had he last seen Darren? It had to be, what? Four, five years ago? Not since he'd gone off to Southampton to study engineering, probably. 'God. Wow. I'm in shock.'

Darren's eyes briefly lost their glaze of alcoholic excitement, clouding over as he wondered if introducing himself to Marty like this had been a mistake. As he slid down alligator lids of forced confidence and pressed on regardless, they glinted once again. 'Yes, mate. You've really improved. That little routine was damned special. So – still a magician, huh?'

'Just about.'

'So how's it been going?' Darren asked predictably. When all he got by way of reply was a nod and a quiet okay, the three glasses of wine he'd drunk in the last forty-five minutes prompted him to ask the question that was hanging over them both. 'So how's Terri? You two still a team?'

'Er, no. Not quite. We split up.'

Darren's eyes clouded for a second time. 'Oh, right. Recently?'

'A few months back.' Marty waited for his insides to twist but they didn't; the words brought with them instead an unexpected rush of relief.

'Oh. Bad scene?'

'Yeah. You could say that.'

'Fancy a drink?' Darren asked, assuming that the blush pricking his cheeks signalled a painful regret.

'Er, well, I was kind of . . .' Marty looked around for Dale and Magda, but they'd already drifted back into the throng. Clearly he was going to have to wait to get his hands on his cash. 'Yeah. Okay.'

★

'So, what're you doing here?' Marty asked when they'd reached the nearest of the table-top bars. 'I thought you were studying engineering.'

'I was. Earned a living at it for a while, as well.'

'Oh, yeah?'

'Yeah. Did a stint as a student engineer for Tarmac for a bit. On the Channel Tunnel.'

'How was that?'

'Big eye opener.'

'What did you do for them?'

'Checked for rats.'

'Rats?'

'Yeah. Big problem with rats travelling from one end to the other with no passport. Rabies and all that. Before they laid the final track it was unbelievable down there. Made me grandma's arsehole look like the Ritz. They'd put in this temporary set-up to move equipment back and forth. Some rusted-up piece of kit scrounged up out of an old Russian uranium mine. Narrow gauge, trashed. Straight out of the Gulag. They'd just dumped the thing down on top of three feet of slime and industrial chemicals and drill lubricant. The only light came from these shitty orange emergency lamps and the slime gave off all these gases so thick you couldn't see your feet. It was like something out of *Alien*. Ridley Scott would've come. My job was to walk sections of it two or three times a week, putting down poison and bagging up dead rats by turns.'

It looked like he'd become a bit of a raconteur in his old age, had Darren. 'Lovely,' Marty said.

'That's student job schemes for you. Fucking slave labour, innit. But the whole thing was a joke. Once they had the tunnel dug and lined, the French and the British were both supposed to build these fuck-off automated track layers, which would come in from either end and meet in the middle. Spirit of competition or something like that. By the time I got there the French one was done, a fantastic machine, brought in under budget and way ahead of schedule. Naturally the British one was a total piece of shit, not finished till months after the supposed completion date. Even when it did arrive it kept breaking down. The Frogs didn't half crow over that. To really rub it in they built themselves another robot with the money they'd saved, one that would go through the tunnel in front of the track layer and clean out all the dead rats and slime and broken concrete and shit.

'Meanwhile at our end we spent so much time pissing about and arguing with the unions and all the rest of it that it didn't cross our minds to build a cleaner at all. The entire job had to be done by hand, hence the dead-rat detail, 'cause a couple of rat carcasses were enough to snag up the track-laying machinery it was such a heap of junk. The Frogs were all done and dusted and sitting around smoking fags by the time the Brits got a quarter of the way in. The whole thing was a total embarrassment.'

'So what happened?'

'Well, I'm just getting to that. This one time I was on rat detail and the time had come for the end of my shift and for some reason I was in a totally foul mood. Hung-over, probably – we did quite a lot of beering of an evening, there being fuck all else to do. Since I'd ended up as near to the French side as the British and I had passes for both, I thought, sod it, I'll walk over to Coquelles instead of heading back to Cheriton. Be the first guy to travel between the two countries on foot. Might as well get something positive out of this gig.'

'And did you?'

'Yeah. Took me fucking hours, though. And it wasn't any fun at all.'

'No?'

'No way. It was deeply fucking scary, especially seeing as how none of the pussies in my team had wanted to come with me, meaning I'd ended up going it alone. Took me about six hours to get through to the other end, by which time I was so knackered I just went and crashed out in one of the empty site offices. When I woke up next morning all hell had broken loose – the losers I'd left behind hadn't bothered to tell anybody what I'd been up to and because I didn't sign out that evening an emergency team had been dispatched to look for me. God knows what they thought, poking around in the sludge for half the night. Probably that some kind of James Herbert scenario had happened and the rats had got me. God knows. But they kicked me off the project after that.' He laughed again. 'Though I can't say I was altogether sorry to go.'

'So that's when you got involved in all this Internet stuff?'

'I still had a year at uni to finish and after that I got a job with Ove Arup.'

'Ove Arup?'

'Big engineering firm, in bed with the Norman Fosters of this world like you wouldn't believe. Offices in Fitzrovia – meaning I moved up to London.'

'How was the work?'

'Oh, it was all right. But the opposite end of the spectrum from the Channel Tunnel thing. Total desk job. Paper-pushing. Deadly dull, really. I mean, you could've done it standing on your head. But we had this totally anal IT manager working for us at the time, archetypal nerd, communication with other flesh units a total non-starter. Spent his whole time weaselling about in the computer room. But he'd installed Mosaic on all the machines and he taught me how to use it.'

'Mosaic?'

'First decent web browser. What eventually became Netscape. You've heard of Netscape, right?'

'Sure,' Marty lied.

'Well, as a teenager I'd always had a bit of an interest in computers. Cars, computers, magic cabinets – they were all basically the same thing to me. Take 'em apart, put 'em back together, make 'em do shit. Boy stuff. But I'd lost interest while I'd been at Southampton. Had other fish to fry. Then, thanks to Mosaic, I discovered the Internet and it blew my mind. Pretty soon I was spending half my day in the computer room e-mailing this old school friend of mine. Bloke called Paddy King – was doing a masters in neural nets at Sussex at the time. He was a total net junkie, brought me up to speed on how everything worked, sent me a 0.96 beta of Netscape for Mac, copies of *Wired* and *Mondo 2000*, that kind of thing. In the end I caught the fever off him. Got obsessed by it – information revolution and all the rest of it. Brave new world, blah dee blah.

'Anyway, when he graduated we started our own web development company with a couple of other mates of his. Called it SurFX – like Surf and SFX combined, yeah? We thought that was pretty fucking clever, back then. Got a small business loan, some designers on board, found cheap office space in a shitty old warehouse down in Southwark – this was before it was trendy. And the rest, as they say, is history.'

'It was a success?'

'Nah. We had cash flow problems and lots of arguments, then our three key programmers fucked off to work for BBC Online. Paddy and me, we fell out and I took a walk and Pads ended up selling what was left of the company to WebMedia.'

'So what've you been doing since then?'

'Went to work for Murdoch, didn't I, at News International, on their website. Piece of shit that was. But I'd picked up some share options when SurFX switched over to WebMedia, and now the whole Internet banana's finally taking off over here they're worth a shitload again. A year ago you'd not've thought twice about wiping your arse with them, but I'm going to give it another month or two and then cash them in. With any luck they'll pull me in about sixty grand.'

Marty's eyebrows leapt up his forehead. 'So it's been up and down, then?' he said.

'Too right it has. Been a bloody roller coaster. It's a laugh, though. I mean, it's the future, innit? It's taking everyone an age to work out what to do with it, but it's hardly going away. Whatever the media says.'

'What do they say?'

'That it's a cappuccino economy. You know, all froth and no substance. Built on delusions and tricks of the light. Gold rush stuff. Tulip mania. But if that's the case, what I want to know is how come it's the reason the US economy is outperforming every other country in the world? I mean, you don't hear Clinton complaining.'

To his surprise, Marty was feeling quite impressed by his old rival. 'Yeah,' he said, hoping to bond. 'It's certainly paying my rent. My, er, my new girlfriend's got work with some web design outfit down near Old Street just at the moment.'

'Oh, yeah? What're they called?'

Marty reddened. 'Um. Sorry. I don't quite remember. All this stuff has pretty much passed me by.'

'Yeah, you and the rest of the country. They're all desperate enough to get on board now, though.'

'Yeah?'

'Yeah – just look at this lot. See that woman over there? That's Vicky Henderson. Twenty-six, she is, Cambridge history graduate, started up her company Getaway.com with her Yank boyfriend last year to offer deals on plane tickets, package holidays, concert tickets, that kind of thing. Pads' new outfit did their site design. They're planning an IPO early next year and word is they could be looking at a valuation of around two hundred million.'

'Two hundred *million*? Christ. I knew these things were worth money, but I didn't know it was that much.'

'Yeah. For a glorified travel agent. Complete joke, isn't it? See that girl there? The short, dumpy one with the bottle-blonde hair? Twenty-three years of age, set up a company last year to sell organic beauty products over the web. She's now worth ten big ones. The bloke over there, with the nose? His outfit registers domain names and protects copyright. Right now it's worth more than Harvey Nichols and he personally is worth more than the Spice Girls.'

'How much're they worth?'

'Collectively? Around a hundred and ten. That Jewish guy there, the one with the rimless specs talking to the two banking types, just there, yeah, with the blue blazer on? His bag is virtual money, a trading credit system for use in web transactions to take the risk out of it – a way to buy stuff online without having to give out your credit card number. Doesn't work yet, no one knows if it's going to be any use to anyone. Twelve million. Rumour is he spends so much time in Yo Sushi they're thinking of giving him shares in it. The four geezers in baggies and T-shirts standing over there looking like ex-members of Dodgy? A skateboard collective from Sheffield, planning on flogging skate and skiing gear online. A million each.'

'Christ,' Marty said. 'But how come all this stuff is worth so much? I mean, these businesses, they're not actually *making* anything, are they?'

Darren threw back his head and laughed out loud. 'You sound just like one of those killjoy columnists. We live in the land of the brand, my friend. It's all about market share, first-mover advantage, potential future earnings. The received wisdom says that you can't do business this way, that all you're doing is blowing up a giant bubble that one day's got to burst. But talk to anybody here, every one of them will tell you that's all bullshit, that the world has changed.'

'And has it? I mean – what do *you* think?'

'No fucking idea. But there's that much money flying around I'm figuring it's got to be worth having a shot at getting some of it coming in my direction.'

'So you sticking with News International?'

'No way José. Quit last month with a couple of the other blokes. We're getting our own start-up under way.'

'What's that, then?'

'Can't say. It's all under wraps. In this business, the way things are, you have a good idea you'd better keep it quiet until you're ready to roll. Otherwise before you know it some fucker's nicked it and you're fucked.'

Fucked was how Marty felt. He was on his fifth beer, his head was starting to spin and the figures Darren was quoting had made him nauseous. Here he was, his existence entirely dominated by twenty grand's worth of debt, surrounded by people who were flushing that kind of money down the toilet every day and were millionaires as a result. He couldn't get his head round it. He felt suddenly old, out of date, stupid, like he'd spent five years crazily competing, only to discover at the finish line he'd been running in the wrong fucking race. He wanted to throw up.

Darren took him by the arm. 'Hey, Marty? You all right? You've literally gone green.'

'Yeah, no, I'm fine, I just feel a little light-headed, that's all. Something . . . something just came over me.'

'Hm. Want some smelling salts?'

'Er . . . dunno . . . Yeah . . . whatever.'

Putting his arm round the young magician's shoulder, Darren led him through the crowd, out of the double doors and down the empty corridor to the room that was serving as a coat check.

A skinny twenty-something was sitting at the table thumbing through a copy of *Business Week*; when she saw them approach she got up and came towards them. 'Darren? What's the matter?'

'Oh, nothing. It's fine. This is an old mate of mine. Marty. He's just feeling a bit under the weather, that's all. You know. A bit faint.' He winked and making a motion with his free hand indicated that Marty might've had too much to drink. 'Marty, Amnesty, Amnesty, Marty.'

Marty looked up wanly. Amnesty had bright eyes, hair like a handful of hay and a face that later on he'd find impossible to remember.

She peered back at him. 'You sure you're okay?'

'He'll be fine. Can I bring him back in there for a minute?

Thought I might administer some smelling salts.' Amnesty giggled and led them between the lines of coats to a hidden recess at the rear of the room. There was a grey chair here, injection-moulded, of the stacking type found in school classrooms and village halls, and while Marty sat down on it and tried to recover, Amnesty passed Darren a vanity mirror on which he proceeded to chop out three lines of lumpy cocaine.

The lines complete, Darren passed Marty a rolled-up note and held out the mirror.

'What's that?' he asked, worried that he already knew the answer.

'Charlie.'

'Oh, no.' Marty shook his head. 'I don't do drugs.'

'What? Never?'

'I did try some Ecstasy one time.'

'And how was that?'

'Fine, but . . .'

'Well, this isn't anything like as strong. It'll just put you back on your feet, make you feel okay. It's perfect if you've had too much to drink – it helps you sober up.'

Marty didn't look convinced. 'Really?'

'Really.'

'Come on, Marty,' Amnesty encouraged. 'Before somebody comes.'

'Well, if you genuinely think it'll do me some good . . .' They both nodded. 'Okay. So what do I do?'

★

The cocaine had exactly the effect Darren said it would. Ten minutes later Marty was leaning at a window looking out at the soft dark of the summer sky above the rooftops of St John's Wood, smoking a cigarette, talking. Talking talking talking, in a way he hadn't talked for as long as he could remember. For the best part of an hour he rattled on, recounting in absurd detail everything that had happened to him in the intervening five years.

Most of the time Darren wasn't really listening. When he wasn't battling with the cocaine paranoia that proximity to Marty might be somehow putting him at risk of being dragged into the same vortex of failure that had sucked down the hapless magician, the thought of Terri being single was preoccupying his brain. This was a fact far more intriguing to him than any of Marty's trials and tribulations. 'That's terrible, mate,' he said when eventually the tale of woe was concluded.

'It just looks, I don't know. It just looks completely hopeless. I mean, I know I've only got myself to blame that I messed it up. But what I've found myself asking recently is, even if I hadn't, would it have made the slightest difference?'

'What do you mean?'

'Just that maybe I was kidding myself in the first place, to think that I could be a truly successful magician. There are already so many big names out there in magic, more than the public's able to deal with. It's not such a big arena anyway and there don't seem to be any vacancies. The low-level scene is screwed. You just can't make a living. And to break through into the big time you need such an improbable talent and such improbable luck . . . I definitely don't have the second of those and I'm starting to wonder if maybe I haven't got the first.'

Darren waved his fag around in the air, satisfied that he was an authority on the subject. 'But tonight you were great,' he said. 'I mean, you've got bucketloads of talent. That's streets ahead of anything I could ever do, what you did. The most I manage now is the odd trick down the pub. You can't be thinking of packing it in.' It was important to be positive, he felt – he'd learned all about that last year in Luton on a weekend NLP workshop he'd been on.

'It's nice of you to say so. But I'm not sure I agree. I'm thinking about trying my hand at something completely different.'

'Well, I sympathise there.' Darren nodded, happy to go with the flow. 'Most of the people I know feel like that. That's why so many of them are getting into the Internet. It's all new, all up for grabs. Virgin snow.'

It was funny, he thought. You're bitter at some bloke for years because he stole your girlfriend, then one day after you'd forgotten he even existed you run into him, drink a beer, div up a line or two, and suddenly you realise he's a decent enough geezer after all. Just like you, really. Or near as makes no difference.

He reached into his pocket for his card. 'Here. Give me a bell – let's hook up for a drink or something. And you know, if you ever need a job there's lots of people I could put you in touch with.' As he made the offer, Darren worried that he might sound a little patronising. 'You'd probably be good at this e-commerce stuff, bloke like you,' he added as an afterthought. 'Ninety-nine per cent of it's all smoke and mirrors anyway.'

There. That'd do it. A little witticism. To make it better.

Soon after the Network Network event Jill lost her job. She arrived back at the flat earlier than usual one day, dumped her bag on the table and told Marty the news. Termination effective immediately. He couldn't quite get the story straight but either the start-up she'd been working for had gone belly up or they couldn't afford to pay her because of some cash flow problem or . . . or . . . or something. To tell the truth he wasn't really listening. All he heard was that the money wouldn't be coming in any more. He didn't care too much about the reason for that. He was far more interested in reminding Jill he'd told her so. 'I told you that trendy outfit wouldn't last more than five minutes,' he said.

This response naturally sparked a major row, the intensity of which was compounded by Marty's remarking that it was pretty irresponsible of Jill to go and spend money on getting her hair done right after she'd heard the news.

'I did it to cheer myself up, you wanker. And I thought you'd be pleased.' She'd not had it re-highlighted in the end, had, in fact, had most of the old colour clipped out.

'I might've been pleased if you'd had it done like it was before.'

It took Jill a minute to realise she'd heard correctly. 'It's not about the money at all, is it?' she gasped, face masked with shock. 'You just want me to carry on looking like her.'

'No, I don't,' Marty insisted, hoping that by denying it the issue would vanish. 'I thought it suited you, that's all. Can't I say anything without you leaping down my throat?'

318

'You are so full of shit.'

'And you aren't?'

'Fuck you.'

'Yeah, and fuck you too.'

Realising he was on shaky ground, Marty grabbed his bag and stormed out of the flat. He would go to the park: the sun was still high and the day still warm, and he'd spent a lot of time there recently practising his juggling and developing a new coin routine. The endless sets of dextrous callisthenics helped him think, he felt, though the truth was they helped him not to; just as they always had done they proved the perfect place for him to hide, offering the magician an alternative reality purer and more complete than any of Jill's drugs.

He didn't return home until the sun had set. When he did he found Jill passed out on the sofa, her body twisted into a pale-blue duvet like a half-eaten boiled sweet. With her head back, her mouth open, her pale throat exposed and her hair matted and slick as the sweated underarm fur of a drowsy cat, she couldn't have looked more vulnerable and forlorn. Even fast asleep she seemed to challenge him. Looking at her now, Marty realised that he was frightened of her and of the things she said.

He threw his juggling balls into the air, repeating the routine he'd been practising. It was hardly his fault she'd lost her job. He threw the balls again. He'd warned her, hadn't he? What was wrong with that? And he'd only got her word for it that she'd been laid off. Maybe she'd been fired or something, caught with her hand in the till. Perhaps she'd just been no good. She hadn't been able to buy any dope recently; maybe that had had something to do with it. Could you get marijuana withdrawal? He didn't know. But just the other day he'd found, clinging to the threads of an eviscerated towelling sock that he'd fetched out from under the bed when, finally, he'd become unable to bear any longer the moraine of underwear and clothing that had extended throughout the entirety of their bedroom (and which, like the washing up and money and dirty ashtrays and sex and what channel to watch on the bloody television had become another front in the war of attrition that their relationship had become), a blister pack of Valium, each one of its fourteen foil hymens punched through. He had no idea where she'd got those from. She hadn't said anything about going to the doctor. God only knew what else she might be on.

Having by now tried both cocaine and Ecstasy, Marty felt he knew a thing or two about drugs (lack of info on the marijuana withdrawal issue notwithstanding). And he, he duly noted, could clearly take or leave them. Jill, on the other hand, obviously had had something of a problem, one that looked like it might be becoming more acute.

Right then he made a decision. All that non-thinking he'd been doing out there in the park? It had helped him reach a few conclusions. Jill wasn't his responsibility, not any more. From now on he was going to look out for himself.

It was more an admission than anything else.

★

The next day Jill went out – she didn't say where – and as soon as she'd left the flat Marty picked up the telephone. 'Er – hi. Is that Darren?'

'Yeah, this is he. Who's this?'

'Oh, right – Darren. It's Marty here. Marty Quick?' He didn't sound all that sure.

'Marty – oh, hi. How's it going?'

'Yeah, well. You know. Not so bad.'

'Been busy?'

'Hm. Kind of. Not really.'

'Oh. Okay.'

A pause blew up, like a cloud no one had noticed skimming suddenly before the sun, and both men felt a cool wind of nervousness breeze out of their respective handsets. Running into one another randomly, having a cheery chat, swopping business cards even – that was one thing. But now that Marty had made this call the next step was meeting for a drink, which in turn meant all the hassle of building – or binning – a prospective new friendship. Either way it would entail something of an effort.

Darren's instinct was to hedge. He stabbed the Agenda button on his PalmPilot and thumbing out the writing stylus began scrolling through his immediate future, the passing of each coming day marked with a semi-audible electronic click.

'So. Shall we do beers? The next couple of weeks are looking fairly hairy and then I've got this protocol conference in Amsterdam. But I've a window right after that, last week of September.' That should give him enough time to consider whether or not he really wanted to have Marty taking up precious space in his life.

'Yeah, sure, whatever,' Marty said, his nervous breeze accelerating to a gust. He didn't even use a diary any more, having thrown his away in a tantrum following the fiasco at the Talk of London, and he was alarmed by Darren's easy command over events. Toeing the living-room door shut, he consulted the Magician's Year Planner Blu-tacked to the back. Its borders might have been busy with top hats, wands and playing cards, but its cells gaped empty, more of them occupied by spits of fat escaping from the nearby grill than by any comments or entries. Marty's eyes skipped along September, two white balls bouncing round the roulette wheel of his life. The month was blank, occupied by neither stains nor bookings. 'That week's good for me,' he said.

Darren suggested Tuesday and Marty initially agreed, but then for the sake of appearances told him no, that Wednesday would be better.

Then he did it, what he'd made the call to do. 'Darren, you know, just before you go, I wanted to run something by you. It's just an idea a friend of mine had. It's probably nothing, but . . . have you got a minute?'

'What, right now?'

'Yeah – I mean, it won't take a second.'

Darren glanced at his watch – unnecessarily, as he'd actually been playing Minesweeper when Marty rang and was intending to do so for most of the rest of the day. 'Sure,' he said, opening up his e-mail application. 'Fire away.'

Marty did; by the time the mail program's user interface was up and running and Darren had moved the small-but-perfectly-realised mouse pointer arrow over the small-but-perfectly-realised depiction of an envelope that he had to click in order to instruct his computer to dial through to the server and pick up his mail, Marty had outlined the basic idea for button.com.

Although he got his pointer into position, Darren never clicked.

'Say that again,' he said instead, lifting his right hand from the mouse and reaching for (how quaint!) a piece of paper and a ballpoint pen.

'I mean, I think it's a pretty dumb idea,' Marty gabbled, repeating what he'd said as Darren furiously scribbled a quick set of notes. 'I told my friend that when they told me. But I thought, you know, I'd just run it by you, see what you thought. Because, right, I mean, after what you said about all those people at Network Network, you know, making so much, you know, money and stuff, I thought maybe I shouldn't judge, maybe it would be worth my while to just run it by you . . .'

'Who's your friend told this idea to?' Darren interrupted. 'I mean, apart from yourself.'

'Er, no one,' Marty said. 'Not as far as I know. Why? Do you think there's something in it?'

'Maybe, maybe.' Marty could hear Darren beating out a rhythm on the edge of his desk with his pen. 'Marty – do you trust me on this?'

Marty's stomach pulsed a couple of times as his nervousness began to transmute itself into excitement. 'I suppose I have to, now, don't I? I mean, I've already told you the damn idea.'

Darren chuckled. 'Where are you?'

'Right now? I'm at home.'

'What's your number?' Marty gave him the number of the old mobile; its credit had run out a while ago but if he ran down to the corner shop he could quickly pick up a new card. 'You around all day, yeah?'

'Yeah. I'm not going anywhere.'

'Okay, well, let me do a bit of research and I'll get back to you. To tell you honestly, this is kind of an interesting idea but I don't know if it'll work. There are some legal issues. I'm going to call a lawyer friend of mine – I'll get back to you soon as I can.'

Marty put the mobile on to charge, went and bought a card, came back, emptied the ashtrays, hoovered the living room, made the bed, did the washing up, dusted the television scrubbed the bath, wiped lots of surfaces. He'd just got round to sorting out the laundry when the phone rang.

'Marty – Darren. You know that drink?'

'Yeah?'

'I'd forgotten – someone cancelled on me. You busy tomorrow night?'

For the second time that day Marty consulted his wall planner, now free of grease. Its white spaces no longer looked like absence; they looked like opportunity. 'Nope, I can do that,' he told Darren.

That evening it was Jill's turn to get a telephone call. It must have been good news – she was sitting up for once like a normal person, laughing even. 'Mags and Sonya are coming down next weekend,' she said, resting the handset against her shoulder. 'They've got tickets to that festival they're having in the park and the same night there's this big event over at Bagley's. It's all right if they crash here, yeah?'

Marty shrugged; he didn't care. 'Whatever.'

Jill went back to her conversation. 'Yeah, that's fine.' It was like watching someone in a film, he decided. She played the part of being happy and relaxed so well even he was nearly taken in.

'You deserve an Oscar,' he mumbled, supposedly to himself.

'What?' she said, squinting at him through a cloud of cigarette smoke.

He shook his head. 'Nothing.'

'Oh, just Marty being dumb,' Jill said into the phone.

Annoyed, Marty went into the bedroom and lay down on the bed, tried to think through his new coin routine. It was most of magic, this plotting, this patient mental stepping through the carefully choreographed sequences of hand and eye movements, this geometry of sight lines and gag lines and contingencies, this continual attempt to simplify, to make more elegant, to bring the necessary deception further forward in time and so divorce it as far as possible from the actual conclusion of the trick. He was an actor, his was an act, and he needed to know his part inside out and yet keep it loose enough, flexible enough, still to allow himself to improvise. After all, you couldn't expect to have one hundred per cent control over events.

It wasn't as easy doing it in here as it had been outside in the park. He seemed to have lost the trick of keeping the necessary mental focus. He tried forgetting about the coins, focused on just thinking through the principles. The key thing when performing a deception, he reminded himself, was to perform it completely smoothly while making sure the audience's focus was on something else. Perform the deception as far in advance of the plot as possible and disguise it or distract from it by using another movement to cover it. That was the heart of the thing.

Then Jill came in.

'So are they coming, then?' Marty asked her, staring at the fissures and discolorations in the ceiling, and wishing he were in a place where the ceiling was the purest white, and completely without blemish.

'Yeah. On Friday. You never met Sonya, did you?'

'No, but I remember you mentioning her. Who's Mags?'

'Oh, Maggie's excellent. We were at school together, the three of us.' Marty could see from Jill's expression that she'd travelled back there suddenly, back to school in some random northern classroom; ink-stained desks, slumped in seats, teacher droning, school blazers on. He watched her pulling on a pair of jeans, watched how her breasts hung forward as she curled to balance, how her belly rippled up. Women seemed to live so easily inside their bodies. Despite all his athleticism and dexterity he still felt uncomfortable in his.

'This festival,' he said, still looking at the ceiling and struck suddenly by the intricacy of the crack rather than the simple fact of it. 'Shall we go too? I saw a flyer. It looks quite good. Massive Attack are playing.'

Jill hesitated, instinctively suspicious. 'Can we afford it?'

'Well, I've been talking to that old friend of mine. The one I ran into at Network Network? I'm going to have a drink with him tomorrow night, see if I can't persuade him to keep an eye out for another job for you. He's got loads of contacts in the industry. And you've got some experience now, haven't you? Keep the faith. Let's not give up hope.'

They met in Joe's on Exmouth Market, a street benefiting from the dot.com boom. Joe's was a hybrid café–bar that couldn't decide whether it wanted to be American or continental. By dithering about with aluminium chairs, a zinc bar, black-and-white jazz prints, watery coffee and stale bar snacks, it had ended up becoming exactly what it didn't want to be, which was British. In this it was strangely out of sync with the other more obsessively contemporary establishments that had opened in the neighbourhood. These included an Italian table foot-ball café (in which details of leagues and tournaments were chalked up on the biscotti-coloured walls alongside enthusiastic write-ups clipped from lad mags); a reservations-only tapas rest-aurant with an open kitchen and smoke-grey marble floor; and a basement DJ bar styled according to the red and black aesthetic of a 1970s digital watch. Alongside these Joe's Athena air of eighties yuppie kitsch seemed almost like old London auth-enticity.

Darren was at the counter when Marty arrived, sipping a Hoe-gaarten, leaning into it, in fact. His right foot, snug inside its khaki Caterpillar workboot, was notched on to the brass rail that ran around the bottom of the bar; his left was planted firmly on the floor, toe pointing slightly out. A vinyl bomber jacket with a gathered waist puffed around his upper body. The jeans he wore were the washed-out blue of a Barclays cheque.

Glancing reflexively around the room like any person carrying out a deception, Marty traipsed up to him and tapped him on the shoulder.

Darren turned round. 'Oh, Marty, hi. Let me get you something. Beer?'

Marty took a Becks and they sidled through the close-packed chairs and tables to a vacant spot over by a plate-glass window overlooking the small area of paving stones and trees and benches opposite the post office at Mount Pleasant, more of a triangle than a square. The view was of the traffic roaring by up Rosebery Avenue and the action paintings of accreted pigeon shit, abstracts in Chinese White and Recycled City, spattered over every surface.

Forget the small talk; cut to the chase.

'Well, I'm very glad you called me,' Darren said, furrowing his mousy brows in order to advance an impression of being focused and intent.

'So you think there's something in it, then?' Marty asked. He was feeling detached from the situation, sceptical, and was thinking that Darren's earnest expression sat awkwardly on his puffy face, his artist's prejudice making it impossible for him to imagine anyone taking business genuinely seriously.

Darren sipped his beer. 'That's difficult to say.'

'It's pretty stupid, it seems to me. There's nothing to it, right? It's got no substance. I thought so. I mean, once I'd put the phone down I wished I hadn't told you, the world's not that straightforward, people aren't that dumb. I shouldn't have wasted your time. I don't know the first thing about business, I mean, I just promised my friend . . .' Already he was preparing to give up on it, out of embarrassment as much as anything.

But to Darren Marty's behaviour betrayed not embarrassment but modesty. 'No, not at all. You gave me the perfect elevator pitch, the best I've heard. Right now, anything too complex isn't cutting it. You want to get a start-up off the ground, you want to get investment? The people with the money are so overwhelmed with projects that if you can't light their fire in three minutes flat you might as well forget it. It's like Hollywood or something. The simpler, the more straightforward the idea, the more chance you've got of getting it to fly. No – the idea's not the problem. I mean, it needs back-up, research, a business plan, all that stuff for sure. But that's not what worried me.'

'Oh.' Marty blinked, surprised.

'No, what worried me was whether or not the thing counted as a lottery.'

'. . . ?'

'Yeah, see, to run a lottery you have to have a government licence, the law's really strict on that, and obviously there is only one licence available and Camelot's already got it.'

'Um. Yeah. Of course. Hadn't thought of that.'

'There might be ways of routing round this – you could set up offshore or something, that's what the Americans have been doing with their gambling sites, setting them up in the Caribbean or Tuvalu or wherever, getting past national restrictions that way. But it's complicated and expensive, and basically it's hassle you don't need if you can help it. So that's why I wanted to call my lawyer friend to check it out.'

'And did he?'

'Yeah.'

'And?' At Darren's feet was a bulging black cycle courier's bag which he now picked up. Setting it before him on the table, he fetched out a small sheaf of slightly dog-eared papers, then dumped it back down on the floor. At the sight of documents, Marty prepared himself for another bout of despondency.

'There's no statutory definition of a lottery,' Darren said, flicking through the top few sheets. 'But according to the legal precedents there are three elements that you need to have before you officially count as one. You have to be distributing prizes, that's first. Obvious enough. So your friend's idea does that. Second, you have to be distributing them according to chance rather than skill, making you a lottery instead of a competition. The idea does that too. Which means it's the third requirement that's crucial to us.'

'And what's that?'

'That you need to be distributing prizes to participants who have provided what is termed "valuable consideration".'

'What's "valuable consideration"?'

'That's the sixty thousand share options question. What it is is this. With a lottery, people have to give something to the organisers in order to be eligible to enter. Most lotteries it's money; basically, you buy a ticket. That's valuable consideration. But it might not be money, it might be information. That can count as valuable consideration too.'

He passed Marty a piece of paper; it was entitled 'Insolvency' and subtitled 'Current Law Cases, Reference: 95/2849, Jurisdiction: UKEW'.

'Two years ago this company MegaBase got screwed under the 1986 Insolvency Act for offering people the chance of winning something in a prize draw in return for providing information about themselves. The idea was to set up a market research database, which could then be sold on for profit. It turned out that this counted as valuable consideration and that by the terms of the act they were running a lottery. They didn't have a licence for that. So they got closed down.'

'So that means button.com won't work?'

If Darren weren't so impressed by Marty's magic skills he might have had to wonder just how bright he was; the boy clearly didn't have much of a head for business.

'You're convinced it's not going to happen, aren't you? No, it doesn't mean it's not going to work. I'm telling you all this MegaBase stuff to illustrate just why it is your idea's so bloody beautiful. The thing about the button is, it sidesteps this issue perfectly. It *doesn't* require valuable consideration, because no one needs to provide any information in order to enter.'

'But you need to put in your e-mail address.'

'Yeah, but that doesn't count. It's acceptable for people to identify themselves, that's clear enough. According to my lawyer friend we're safe on that.' Darren was beginning to use the 'we' word rather a lot, Marty noticed. 'Reader's Digest and Which and companies like that have been doing what's basically the same kind of operation for years, but by post. They do a mailshot containing two envelopes, one labelled "Yes" and the other labelled "No". Then they ask you if you're interested in buying some piece of junk or other and to incentivise you to return one of the envelopes they promise to enter you in a prize draw. It doesn't matter which envelope you send because by returning an envelope at all you identify yourself and that's useful to them. *But that doesn't count as valuable consideration as far as the law is concerned.* If button.com sold on its database of addresses at any point it's possible that could turn them into valuable consideration. But as long as it doesn't do that it should be safe. Plus I reckon if we get a decent geek on board we could get a site set up that just takes the details of whoever's come and clicked on the button without them having to enter any info at all. Porn sites do it all the time.' The faint beginnings of a blush. 'Apparently.'

'So it can work? It's not completely stupid?'

'Marty mate, it's incredible. Awesome. It's, like, total fucking genius. Do you know what you've got here? What you've got is the first example of a whole new Internet genre. It's so simple, it's so beautiful, it's so obvious – but no one's thought of it yet. It's exactly the kind of thing everybody's on the lookout for.'

'Really?'

'Sure. Look. The only way people are making money on the web right now is by selling advertising. The retail sites, the Amazons and so on, they're not making hardly anything on sales. Like I told you at Network Network, everybody's losing money hand over fist. What money the big sites are making they make from selling ads. But to sell ad space you need a lot of eyeballs. The search engines charge the most right now because they get the most visitors – everyone uses them all the time, they're first ports of call. Sites like Netscape and cnn.com and BBC Online and Amazon come in a fairly close second. But what your friend's hit upon is a way to channel traffic for traffic's sake. It's like, let's cut out the middleman. Button's not offering a service and piggybacking ads on the back of it, which is what everybody else is doing. It's appealing directly to people's greed – and there's no better principle. Any economist will tell you that. I mean, it's obvious, right?' Darren leaned forward a little, brought his hands up as though they were cupped around a crystal ball and lowered his voice. 'Marty, I'm telling you, I think this thing could be fucking huge. I'm not exaggerating. I think this is the new Hotmail. And I'm willing to put my money where my mouth is.'

'What do you mean?'

'I think your friend should do this and I'd like offer to be his business partner.'

'You?'

'Absolutely. Whoever he is he's going to need someone to help him put this thing together, someone with experience. And I'd love that someone to be me.'

Marty went bright red. He hadn't expected this, not really. He'd allowed himself an occasional what-if, but other than that . . . He'd honestly expected to be asking Darren to put out job feelers for Jill by this point in the conversation.

'Well, you know, I'm not really sure. My friend . . .' The magician hesitated, realising the sudden need to be extremely careful about how he chose his words. 'They're, uh, quite shy. Not business orientated, not really. I think the idea was more a joke than anything else. I don't know how they'll feel about me going off and getting it all set up like this . . .'

Darren leaned back, showed Marty two empty palms. 'Whatever. Don't pressure him. Let him think it over. All I'm saying is I'm here if he needs me. But promise me one thing. For Christ's sake be careful who you talk to about this. Once it gets out of the bag it'll spread like wildfire and someone'll steal it. They will.'

Marty could feel segments of sweat wedging up inside his shoulders. He needed time to think. He changed the subject, turning the spotlight back on to Darren. 'But what about your other project? The start-up idea you were telling me was all so hush-hush? What about that?'

'Yeah, well, we had a bit of a disaster on that front last week. The idea was to be the UK's first online wine distributors. People would come to our site and order wine, and it would be shipped to them anywhere in the world, direct from the manufacturer.

We'd set up agreements with vineyards in France, South Africa, California or wherever and cut out the middleman, see. Same basic principle. It was gonna be called biggrape.com and we had the name registered, the funding lined up, the first agreements organised, everything. But then just last week this other company launched, worldofcorks.co.uk. Exact same set-up as ours, but they beat us to it. Got the media attention, got prime-mover advantage. Pulled the rug right out from beneath our feet. Our investors have run a mile. Can't even get them on the phone.'

'Shit. That's bad luck.'

'It might have been more than that,' Darren muttered darkly, his eyes condensing into bitter little pills. 'We think they might have hacked into our server, stolen our business plan.'

'No way! Does that kind of stuff really happen?'

'All the time, mate, all the time. Wine distribution's a cut-throat business. You'd be surprised by the amount of ex-government types who get involved. Wine's a big deal at MI6. Some of the stories I could tell . . . But it's impossible to prove anything, unless you actually catch them in the act. If you never remember anything else, remember this: information wants to be free. The lesson's simple – keep schtum. If we'd kept our mouths shut instead of getting all excited and blabbing about it endlessly to all our mates . . . well, we only had ourselves to blame. It comes back to what I said before – don't say a word about the button unless you're sure whoever you're talking to is a hundred and ten per cent trustworthy. Which counts out pretty much anyone in any way connected with the Internet.' He pulled back his lips, set his teeth, and gave Marty his best and biggest grin. 'With one exception, naturally.'

★

If by this Darren was telling Marty he was one hundred per cent trustworthy, he was lying. If the magician wasn't being completely honest with him, neither was he being completely honest with the magician.

It had to do with somebody called Terri.

Ever since that night at Network Network, Darren had been unable to push the knowledge that his ex-girlfriend was single from his mind. Over the past few years he hadn't had too much luck with women. He'd had several relationships, but none of them had lasted beyond the crucial two or three months. A pattern had developed: as soon as any of the girls he'd met began to make too many demands upon his time, he lost all patience with them. Attraction quickly turned into contention, arguments flared up and, rather than try and work them through, Darren tended to piss off down the pub, where he soon discovered he was happier in the company of his mates. Again and again he found himself asking himself why it was that girls seemed so eager to give him a hard time; again and again he failed to come up with an answer. Most of the girls involved didn't know the answer either, though they sensed it; one way or another, within a few weeks of knowing him they'd picked up on the fact that he was unconsciously comparing them with somebody else, somebody better than them, somebody against whom they didn't measure up.

Guess who.

No surprise, then, that after Marty's phone call Darren couldn't help himself from thinking well, why not? Why not ring her up? You know, just to see. Couldn't do any harm. He didn't need to tell Marty; he'd understand. They'd split up, after all. And anyway, the way Darren saw it Marty still owed him one from five years ago; with the advice he was giving him on this button.com thing, he owed him two. He couldn't very well complain.

The only number Darren still had for Terri was her mother's. He'd always got on pretty well with Avril Liddell; unlike her and Marty, the two of them had seen pretty much eye to eye. So he called her up. 'Hi, there, Mrs Liddell, how are you?'

'Who's that, then?'

'Bit of a blast from the past, I'm afraid. Don't know if you'll remember me. It's Darren Watt.'

'Darren! Of course I remember you. How nice! I was thinking about you just the other day, wondering how you're getting on.'

Darren told her, adding a little parent-friendly embellishment.

'So,' he said, when news had been exchanged, 'I was wondering . . . is Terri there?'

'Of course she is, dear, of course she is. She's been living here since she split up with that awful boy. Good riddance to bad rubbish, I say. I'll just get her for you. *Terri*! Come down here, darling, I've got a surprise for you. It's that nice boy Darren on the phone.'

Five years previously that kind of comment from her mother would have put Terri off a boy for ever. Indeed, part of the attraction of Marty had always been that Avril Liddell didn't really approve. But things had changed and, ten minutes later, Darren had a date.

Keeping schtum was one piece of Darren's advice Marty decided to take. All he said to Jill about the conversation he'd had in Joe's was that Darren was keeping an eye out for jobs for her and that he'd thought there was a good chance of him coming across something suitable. To steer the conversation away from anything more probing he'd then given her the festival tickets, which he'd picked up from Ticketmaster while he'd been in town.

They had a pleasant week together, the best they'd had for some time. At the end of it, on the Friday afternoon, Mags and Sonya arrived from Blackpool and that was good as well. The four of them went into Islington for the evening and came home with a takeaway. They ate it in the living room, then sat around until three or four in the morning gradually transforming the scraped foil punnets of purple korma and orange tikka into a smokers' graveyard of weathered butts and roaches. Jill was animated, laughing – shrieking even, though Marty wondered if there was a note of mild desperation in the way she sucked the marrow out of Mags's and Sonya's jokes. But his secret put him on the periphery and, sick from smoking too many cigarettes and unable to relax, he finally left them to it and went off to bed.

Next day around midday the four of them trickled out of the flat and up the road, where they negotiated the snaking maze of steel crowd control barriers and funnelled into the park. It was a lovely day, hardly a cloud to mar the clear blue sky, but at the same time there was something overcooked about it, some turmoil in the air that suggested this was summer's end. Marty didn't like the heat and he didn't like the T-shirt he was wearing, and he'd made a mistake in wearing shorts, he now decided, because they were making him feel self-conscious about his legs. Once inside the perimeter, though, it was too late to go back and change.

It was a festival. Clumped at the southern end were several large music marquees interspersed with smaller tents containing food outlets and bars; the major outdoor stage was situated a little further to the north, divided from the temporary village by a wide gravel path. Beyond that, in a kind of natural bowl or dip up near to where the railway line sliced past, was a second stage and sound system, somewhat smaller in scale. And there were lots of people, lots and lots of people, all milling about. It was fun, in theory anyway.

Marty and the girls trailed around for half an hour or so, checking out what was on offer. It seemed that buying a ticket wasn't sufficient to entitle you to know who was playing when; if you wanted to plan your afternoon you had to fork out five quid for a programme. None of them wanted to do that because it seemed like such a rip-off, but then Mags spotted one that someone had discarded on the grass. She grabbed it and the four of them clustered round.

'Let's go and see Spiritualised!'

'But they're on at the same time as the Propellerheads.'

'Ohmigod, Roni Size is on now!'

'Ohmigod, ohmigod!'

They ran off in search of Roni Size.

After they'd located the correct marquee they danced limply for a while, until a tall man with a Space Invaders T-shirt and a square afro the colour of furniture wandered up and began to talk to Jill. Marty watched him out of the corner of his eye, not quite sure exactly what was happening, though he thought he could probably guess. Turning away from the man, Jill cupped her hand to Sonya's ear; Sonya nodded and passed the message on to Mags. Yeah, yeah. Where? Sonya pointed out the guy and Mags went with him through the crowd.

She came back with eight pills which she palmed out to the others – with pretty good sleight of hand, Marty noted.

But when it came to his turn he shook his head. 'I don't really do drugs,' he said apologetically. Guilt made him glance across at Jill – would she see this for what his gut told him it was: a fumbling attempt to find some kind of moral thread he'd be able to follow through the mess he'd already begun to orchestrate?

'Oh.' Sonya smiled, giving him a slightly curious look. She placed a pill on her tongue and washed it down with a couple of glugs of Club UK mineral water.

'You don't mind, Mart, if I do?' Jill touched him on the arm and he shook his head but noticing the other two girls looking on – Sonya glancing sideways, dark eyes receding, Mags with her fingers frozen a half-inch from her lips – he realised that the line was for their benefit. He felt a distance suddenly open up between the two of them, as if Jill were no longer standing there beside him but was already where he wished her to be: seated on a train speeding north.

'You go ahead.'

'You're sure you don't want anything?'

Mags reiterated the offer. 'You're sure you don't just want a half? My treat.'

'No, really, it's okay. Thanks.'

The girls turned away and began to dance, three pairs of see-sawing hips plus an occasional fist in the air. Marty watched as their E came on, able thanks to his experience in Heaven and Hell to detect the point at which the beats ceased being barrages of sound particles that merely bombarded them and became rocking waves of sound under the transformative influence of the drug. But once the change had taken place he became bored and, drifting out of the tent, went hunting for a bar.

Hours later – after that marquee and then another and then Massive Attack outside on the big main stage – they sat with the crowds on the paperchase grass, passing joints between them. Marty declined as ever, apparently content to work his way through the best part of a pack of cigarettes. In front of them was the sun, bleary, descending, a water chestnut dressed with an egg drop of cloud; to their rear fingers of rhythm from the reggae tent felt the pulse of its techno neighbour and bounced back as blunt knuckles of sound.

'Okay. Back to the flat?' Marty said hopefully.

Jill half nodded, not really sure.

'How far is Bagley's from here?' Sonya asked.

'Bagley's? Jesus, you still want to go there?'

''Course. We've still got more pills.'

Marty looked at the three of them, scared by the dampness of their satin skin, the bored blanks of their eyes. 'I don't know where you get the energy.'

'I do.' Jill lay back on the grass, crushing flat a paper cup that got caught beneath her shoulder blade. 'X . . . T . . . C . . .' she murmured slowly, tasting each letter as she let it out. 'You should do a half, Marty, really. It's the same as we did up in Blackpool that time. It's top gear.' All week she'd been hoping he'd do a pill with the rest of them and that they'd recapture something of what they'd found together on the promenade that night. But he clearly wasn't going to and so that, she supposed, was that; though any real feeling of disappointment she might have had was being swamped for the time being by the MDMA flooding her own brain.

The ground felt like a pillow, like a cloud. It hardly felt like anything. She was cushioned, floating, her feet and hands were made of rags and twisted silk. She was a Cabbage Patch doll, she was Bagpuss. She squinted up at Marty; the sun was busy just above him, burning a hole into the photograph that was the sky, and his features were cast into pure profile. He reminded her of Professor Yaffle. This made her laugh. London, Morecambe, Vegas, Paris – what difference did it make when taking one little pill made you feel this good? Marty, Paul – what difference? She had no idea what love was any more. Or even if she ever had.

Two strangers had already come up to her that afternoon and told her she looked like Princess Di. That was normal, now. She was getting used to the weird looks people gave her, the second glances. When it had been Jill Dando, back at home, it had only really got to her because it had been Gavin who had started it. But now she was discovering the strange alienation that results from having people look at you not because of you, but because of someone else.

Coming on top of her strong suspicion that Marty's only attachment to her was as another Terri, the experience had made her start to wonder who she was. She didn't seem to have a fixed point any more; when she looked back through her life all she saw was a series of reflections. And it was leeching all the life from her, this notion; daily, now, she had the feeling that she had no solid core at all, that she was just a collection of planes of light, like a character in a video game. Like Lara Croft.

The feeling always started in her stomach and radiated outwards in a gently fizzing ball; it was frightening, and it could come at any time: eating, washing, watching television, walking down the street. It had got so bad that being high seemed the only way to bear it. Valium, dope, E . . . in the past they'd made her feel she had some kind of substance, that she existed. Now they made her feel that her new lack of substance didn't matter, that it was okay to let herself drift apart in this slow explosion of elegantly spinning mirrors.

'Yeah. These are sorted pills, man, really sorted,' Mags agreed. 'I've still got a bit of that speed. You could have some of that, Marty, if you don't want a pill.'

'I think maybe I just need to eat.'

They hauled themselves to their feet and joined the mass of people flowing out of the gates, Marty already cold in his shorts, a dull headache building in his ventricles from the four pints of beer he'd drunk. Then it was back to the flat via the Acropolis kebabery – lots of customers; much waiting; the girls unable to decide what they felt like eating (probably nothing, in fact); Marty all the while aware of exasperation from the queue behind them shining like a sun lamp on his neck. And the waxy chips and vaginal kebabs and pellucid chicken burgers they finally got round to ordering were only half consumed after all that, their remains piled high on the already overflowing coffee table in loose-wrapped paper shrouds turned transparent by osmosed gouts of cooking oil, stinking up the room.

Stomachs lined, the girls got changed and took more E, then set out for Bagley's. Marty didn't go, wasn't in the mood, he said. Perhaps he was half hoping they'd fuss around him, flatter him, try to convince him to come along – maybe even pressure him into trying some drugs so he could break his rule and not have to take responsibility for it. But they didn't and though Jill was a little torn, Mags and Sonya were glad he wasn't coming; he'd been quiet and internalised all afternoon and neither of them was finding him easy company.

The minute the door clicked closed behind them Marty began to shake. All day long he'd been able to think of nothing but button.com and the turmoil in his mind was killing him. The nicotine in his system wasn't helping either; he'd thought that cigarettes were supposed to be relaxing, but he was wound up tighter than a clockwork robot. No wonder they'd done for his mother. He paced around the flat, rubbing his face and pushing his fingers through his hair. Making decisions, he realised now, was not his strong point. As ever, his strategy hadn't got much beyond setting events in motion, then sitting back and waiting in the hope they'd overtake him. It seemed easier that way: that way he wouldn't have to take the blame.

He took a bath but it didn't calm him so pulling on some jeans and sticking his feet into his favourite shoes – a pair of broken-backed Italian loafers – he slouched down to the pub on the corner where he pumped twenty quid he didn't have into the trivia machine and drank Smirnoff and Coke until his blood ran cold.

Returning home he passed out pissed, only to be woken – stomach full of acid foam and room still swimming – when the girls rocked in some time after four.

Jill came into the bedroom and began to hunt for something in the dark. In the process she knocked a glass of water that was standing on the bedside table all over Marty's arm. 'Shit,' she said. 'Sorry, Marty, sorry – I didn't mean to wake you up. I was just on the lookout for some skins. Sorry – we'll be really quiet, I promise. I won't disturb you again.'

But she did: fifteen minutes later she was back, casting around in the mess on the floor for something else. When she left she forgot to close the door, enabling the noise from the mini party in the living room to come drifting in. In the end Marty had to get up and kick it shut, but he misjudged slightly and badly stubbed his toe. More annoying than the pain was the suppressed giggling that followed hard on the heels of the slam – which couldn't have been that suppressed considering how he could still fucking hear it. They were laughing at him, he knew it; bunch of bitches, who did they think they were? This was his flat, for fuck's sake. He was paying for it. Sinuses blocked with mucus and the vodka he'd drunk sapping moisture from his brain, he coiled himself beneath the duvet, folding a flaccid and coverless pillow round his head in a vain attempt to keep the world from shuddering in.

Then music. Or thuds, at any rate. Music and voices; someone singing; a door banging below. Then the unmistakeable sounds of indoor hockey. Jill must have said something to the other girls because now he heard the living room door open again and her voice hiss, '*No – Sonya, don't*! and Maggie laughing and Sonya saying (shouting), 'Fuck 'em, the little fucks, I'll sort 'em out.' And she did, too: while Marty cringed she stomped down the stairs, five foot two of wire and weather-beaten northern vitriol, one of those girls who'll sail out for an evening braving freezing fog wearing nothing but a miniskirt and a halter top, then walk five miles home from some grotty club in a pair of three-inch Shelly's spaghetti straps dragging her drunken boyfriend and his best mate behind her by the hair and thinking nothing of it.

He could hear her quite clearly as she piled down the stairs and started beating on the front door of the flat below with what was quite possibly a brick, saying nothing yet. She was saving that for when the kids inside made the mistake of opening up, which they now did, only to receive a barrage of abuse the like of which Marty for one had never heard.

'You fucking cock-sucking piece of rank fucked-up scab of pissing cunt snot,' was how it started. 'That's my best friend upstairs you're keepin' up with your stupid fucked-up games, you gobshite little runt.' The kid made an attempt to answer back but it proved futile: Marty could only guess at exactly what happened next but it involved a lot more banging and a lot more swearing, and concluded with the electric sound of breaking glass.

If the magician had been worrying that he was going to be called upon to perform some kind of rescue he needn't have; a moment later he heard Sonya pounding her way back up the stairs.

'I'll call the police on you, I will, you bitch,' the hockey prodigy shouted at her receding form, his voice a little cracked with tears.

'Like fuck you will, bog slime,' Sonya klaxoned back, for which comment she was applauded by the couple on the next floor up who'd appeared in their matching dressing gowns to find out exactly what was going on. Rather than being angry at being woken up (Marty's fear), they were apparently delighted that someone had finally had the bottle to do something about these little bastards who'd been plaguing the entire building for so long.

The music from downstairs boomed louder for about ten seconds and then cut out, and soon there was quiet again, or near enough. As he dived back underneath his pillow Marty dimly heard Mags say it was nearly time for *Teletubbies*, whatever that was. 'Perfect come-down TV' supposedly. All it meant as far as he was concerned was that he might finally get some fucking rest. He found the other pillow, made a sandwich for his head and, pulling the duvet up around him, returned to the foetal position. More and more it seemed to be the only one in which he was able to fall asleep.

Then there came a wail, a wail that penetrated the sleeping magician like a bright and speeding wire. Not because of its volume, which was relatively low, but because its frequency and tonal quality were almost identical to the wail Terri had produced the night she'd discovered he'd been cheating on her with Jill. For a fraction of a second before it woke him the wail enjoyed a brief life in Marty's dreams, where it took the form of a small child in pain, his little sister, maybe, but years ago, his sister Karen screaming from within a house without any walls, a house he couldn't reach. No walls and no stairs either, and it was difficult to see because of the oscillating light and he couldn't feel his feet. Then he was awake and wrapped up in sheets – the duvet having long ago been cast on to the floor – and the wail was here and it was real, and it was coming from the living room.

The clock. The clock said 6 a.m. and this was the final straw. Using his fury to catapult him out of bed, Marty retrieved the duvet and, pulling it round his waist like an enormous skirt, barrelled out of the bedroom and through the tiny hall. 'For fuck's sake, please,' he yelled, throwing back the door. 'I'm trying to get some fucking sleep here. Just what the fuck is going on?'

The girls were lined up on the sofa, huddled together inside the vapour of a major joint, tears running down their faces, TV on.

'Oh, Marty, don't,' said Jill. 'It's terrible. It really is.'

'Awful.' Sonya nodded.

'Terrible.' Mags sobbed. She pointed to the screen. On it there was a man, an anchorman, standing in a grey dawn somewhere else, wind messing with the remnants of his hair. He too was crying.

'What the hell is this?'

'It's Diana,' Sonya said.

'Diana? Diana who?'

'Princess Di. There's been a car crash. She might be dead.'

Marty stood there, considering this. 'You stupid cainers,' he finally said. 'You woke me up for that? Jesus Christ. I'm going back to bed.'

He didn't, though. He went and took a piss and drank some water from the tap, and then, standing vacantly in the bathroom staring blankly out of the window at the watery dawn, duvet round his ankles, wondering whether he felt terrible or just numb, he slowly realised that the thought of Princess Diana in a car crash really turned him on.

The moments that followed seemed trapped, caught like the violet pane of sky the planet had pinned against the metal window frame. Images percolated through the acid in his bowels, shot up his spinal cord and spouted in a lateral band across his brain. He felt sick, felt better. Felt wide awake.

A car crash.

Princess Di.

Fucking hell.

Scrabbling into his dressing gown, Marty hurried back to join the girls.

★

It wasn't clear yet whether she was dead or not.

'Thought you didn't give a shit?' Jill said accusingly, the static of distress interfering with her voice. She was shockingly pale and despite the bob of auburn hair Marty thought she looked more like Di than ever, as if the icon's imminent departure from this world had at last freed up that space.

'Um. Sorry about that. I'm not feeling too good. Got a bit

pissed after you lot went out last night and then . . . well, I didn't get too much sleep.'

Sonya squeezed out a hard little blush. 'My fault, yeah?'

'Don't worry about it. It was about time someone told those little wankers downstairs where to go.' It was an act but a good one and Sonya fell for it. For the first time bonded as a group, the four sat and watched the news bleed out, the coverage consisting largely of a live feed of the newsman with the flasher mac and the receding hair, standing weeping in the rain and going on and on about what an incredible woman Diana was and how he'd met her once and how much he personally had loved her, and how if she died it would truly be the death of all beauty, love and hope.

The details were somewhat cloudy and it seemed for a long time that, although injured and in hospital, the Princess might survive. Then the rumours that she'd been in the company of Dodi Fayed began to filter in, followed by snippets of information about the car, the underpass, the pursuing press, the scenes at the Paris Ritz. Very gradually a picture was coming into focus. Then she was dead and then she was alive again, and then she was dead, definitely dead, and the newsman with the tears and the hair could not bring himself to speak, and the camera stayed with him anyway and this was very strange for television, it was like the earth had stopped turning almost, anyone would think the universe had come to an end.

The three girls wept and smoked and uttered short mantras of mutual support until, bored with sitting still, Marty offered breakfast. About the idea of eating, though, there seemed something faintly blasphemous, so when he and Sonya made a trip outside it was just to stock up on fags and juice and newspapers. (There was nothing in them, they'd gone to press hours too early to catch the story.) Outside, the streets were silent, like it was Christmas Day or Cup Final Saturday or something – or rather, like the memory of them, there no longer being any festival or occasion all-encompassing enough to bring London to a halt.

Early afternoon Mags and Sonya had to leave for Blackpool

and after tearful embraces and a telephone call to the station to check the trains hadn't stopped running out of respect (Marty unable to help raising his eyebrows at that, although he had to acknowledge that with the trains any excuse would do) the magician and his girlfriend once again found themselves alone.

It was to become the UK's equivalent of the Kennedy assassination. An entire generation would be unified by knowing the answer to the question: where were you when Princess Diana died? Terri knew and so did Darren. They were in bed together, asleep, having spent most of the previous night re-consummating their relationship.

It was only the second time they'd seen each other. They'd had lunch on the Wednesday, as they'd arranged over the phone, Terri coming into town to be treated by Darren at Quaglino's. Neither had been sure what was going to happen, if the reunion would be anything but awkward. But as it turned out they'd got on like a house on fire. Terri was as beautiful as Darren remembered – more so, in fact. Gone was the blonde, fey teenager of old; in her place was a serious, spike-haired brunette, dressed in a power suit and oozing attitude.

'Wow,' he said, when he first set eyes on her. 'I nearly didn't recognise you. What happened?'

Terri affected to look mystified, then ducked her head and touched her fingers to her hair. 'Oh,' she said, smiling slightly, 'I got bored with being blonde. It's pretty recent. Do you like it?'

'I love it,' Darren said.

She looked him up and down. 'And you! You've put on weight.'

Darren dropped his gaze. 'I know.'

'But it suits you. And I *like* the *beard*.'

She reached up as if to touch it then stopped herself, making Darren's belly flush with warmth. 'I think the table's ready,' he said. 'Come on. We can talk over a glass of wine. I can't believe it! It's so good to see you.'

Talk they did, for the remainder of the afternoon. One bottle turned into two. Confessions were made, apologies offered and gracefully accepted. Inevitably, Marty's name came up.

'I ran into him, you know, just recently,' Darren said, after Terri had given him her version of the final months of their relationship.

'Oh, yeah?' the young woman prompted cautiously.

'He told me about it. The two of you splitting up. That's what made me think of getting in touch.'

'What, cos you knew I was single?'

Darren grinned. There was no need to deny it; they were too deep into a flirtatious groove now to have to worry about things like that. 'Maybe.'

'I'll bet his version was a bit different from mine.'

'Well, you know, he certainly spared me some of the more, er, extravagant details. But to give the guy his due, he was pretty open about what a prat he'd been.'

'Total arsehole more like.'

'Well, yeah. Absolutely.' Being fair was one thing, but there was no point in giving Marty too much credit. Darren wasn't here to talk Terri into getting back together with the magician, after all.

It was past five when they eventually left the restaurant and parting at the tube they eyed each other longingly, both of them intensely drunk. A date for dinner a few days hence had already been arranged.

★

Darren still had his red Triumph with the leather trim and early evening Saturday he drove down to Guildford in it to pick up Terri as agreed.

'You've still got it!' she thrilled when she saw the little car.

Darren blushed. The Triumph had, he felt, long since passed into the realm of naff; the only reason he still had it at all was that at no stage over the last five years had he had the money to buy himself another set of wheels. 'Yeah, well, it's like an old friend in many ways . . .'

Terri slid into the passenger seat and let the fluted hem of her light summer skirt ride up in order that the leather might rub against her thighs. 'God, it feels good to be back in this after Marty's gross old transit.'

'Well, you know . . . there's always something to be said for sticking to a classic . . .' Darren mused, while he tried to calculate the chances of the clutch holding up if he risked a little wheelspin as they pulled away.

It was interesting for Terri, seeing Darren again after all this time. She'd already discovered that his company provided her with a yardstick against which she could measure herself. One of Avril Liddell's most oft-repeated commonplaces was that 'people *never* change', and in the old days Terri had been fond of repeating it herself. But after what she'd been through in the past few months she knew that it was only the people in the endless soaps her mother watched whose characters were like stuck records. Real people – young people, anyway – changed all the time. Look at her. Five years before, when she'd been going out with Darren, she'd been sassy, confident and sure of herself, capable of taking what she wanted from life. Then she'd met Marty and she'd become weak, insecure and subservient – probably because, as she now understood it, he'd been a stand-in for her dad. Now, seeing Darren, she felt confident again, and in charge. Terri liked that feeling. She wanted to keep on having it.

It was experience that had caused the change, of course, not Darren's presence; experience and all the personal growth stuff she'd been investing in since Marty and she had split. But being around Darren brought it out, made her feel that she had achieved something for herself that was tangible and real.

Darren knew nothing of this. Since their lunch date on the Wednesday he'd been working up an insecurity over that remark

Terri had made about him putting on weight. There and then he'd made a resolution to cut down on the beer and get himself in shape, and first thing the next morning he'd got on the phone and made an appointment for an induction session down at his local gym. But the earliest slot they had available wasn't for another week and in the meantime he had plenty of time to worry that over the past five years he'd let himself slip out of Terri's league.

To compensate for this perceived shortcoming he decided to try to impress her with his business acumen. He gave her the same spiel he'd given Marty at Network Network, more or less; though this time round it was a bit lighter on the boyish mat-eyness. But it retained the emphasis on money.

Even so, Darren didn't really feel he was engaging Terri's interest. In the end, out of desperation, he hinted at a new venture he was involved in. 'Between you and me,' he said in a low voice, leaning towards her across the table, eyes glinting fortuitously in the light coming from the single candle placed between them, 'I think this could be as big as anything yet seen on the Internet.'

Terri's interest, it seemed, was piqued. 'Are you serious? How much do you think it might be worth?'

Darren glanced from side to side, as if to check that the nearest diners weren't wine-swilling corporate spies formerly of MI6.

'*Hundreds* of millions.'

'You're kidding!'

'Shh!' He shook his head. 'I don't kid. Not about that kind of money, anyway.'

'So what is it, then?'

Darren sat back in his chair, not yet aware of the trap he'd constructed for himself. 'I can't say.'

'You mean you're not going to tell me? After building me up like that? Darren!'

'I – I'm sorry. But I can't. It – it's not mine to tell, not really.'

'What?' Terri looked horrified. 'Don't you trust me or something?'

Shit shit shit. And just when he was doing so well. 'It's nothing personal, honestly, I promise you. I'd tell you if I could . . .' The lie descended upon him like an angel through parting clouds of Chardonnay. 'But I've signed an NDA.'

'What's an NDA?'

'A Non-Disclosure Agreement.' With the patience born from relief Darren explained what this was.

Terri tutted and made a little pout. 'I wanted to hear,' she said.

'Well, I promise you'll be the first person I tell once the contracts are signed.' Darren smiled, congratulating himself on the successful saving of what had nearly been a disastrous own goal. He'd made a nice clearance too — now the two of them had a reason to keep in touch. 'So come on,' he said, thinking it was high time the conversation's tack was changed. 'Tell me a bit more about what you've been up to.'

Terri brought a finger up and rubbed at the corner of her eye. 'Nothing half so glamorous as all that.'

'Well, you must have been doing something,' he insisted with clumsy enthusiasm.

She looked at him and cocked her head. 'I'm not sure you really want to hear about it.'

'Try me.'

'Well, you know, basically, Darren . . .' She let out a painful sigh. '. . . I've been in counselling.'

If the corporate spies had been tuning in, they would have heard Darren audibly deflate. 'Counselling?'

'Like I said to you the other day, after splitting up with Marty I was really depressed. I talked to Mum about it and she took me to see the counsellor who'd helped her after Daddy left and . . .'

'Your mum saw a *counsellor*?' Darren shared the common English prejudice against therapy.

'It's no big deal, Darren. Lots of people do it. It's just, like, *talking* to someone, basically.'

Darren nodded, lit a cigarette, put on his serious face. 'And, er, did it help?'

'Not really. Not in the beginning. But then I went on Prozac . . .'

'You went on *Prozac*?'

'Jesus. Calm down. You make it sound like heroin or something. I mean, do you know the first thing about it?'

Darren had to admit he didn't.

'Well, then. Anyway, I was only on it for three months.'

'Did it work?'

'Can I have one of those,' she asked, pointing to his cigarettes. Masking his surprise, he took one out and passed it to her.

Terri took it. 'There's lots of things about me that are different,' she continued blithely. 'In lots of ways I'm really a completely different person.'

'And that was the effect of the counselling? And the, er . . .'

'The Prozac. Yeah.' She puffed on the cigarette and blew the smoke out quickly, without inhaling properly. 'I learned so much about myself, about what it is to be . . . to be a woman. There's so much about me that's not the same. So I suppose you could say that's what I've been doing recently. You know. Changing.'

'It sounds pretty heavy.'

'It was. But it got easier.' She said it with the pained resignation of someone who's just survived a war.

'Do you want to talk about it . . . I mean, what else is involved in this, er, transformation.' Darren ventured a grin. 'Apart from dyeing your hair.' But Terri's eyes blazed up at this.

'Shit, sorry, I didn't mean – I didn't mean to imply any of this was superficial.'

She darted him a hard emerald look and took another shallow drag. 'I don't know,' she said lightly, returning to his first question. 'Boring things. Being nice to people. Giving them the benefit of the doubt. Talking to Mum about something other than clothes. Getting in touch with my dad again. I suppose it should mean being able to forgive Marty for what he did to me as well, but I just . . . I just don't know if I'll ever really be able to do that. He caused me so much pain . . .'

She bit her lip and, bringing her left hand to her mouth, turned away as if to cry.

Instantly, Darren moved his hand to cover the one she'd left lying conveniently on the table. 'And what else?' he asked softly, keen to move things along.

Terri brightened. 'Giving up astrology.'

'Giving up astrology? But you were so into it!'

'I know. But Martha – my counsellor – made me realise that it was one of the things that was trapping me. She said it was basically "a toolbox of character archetypes", which is great to help you understand all different types of people when you're young, but which eventually you need to grow out of. She gave me all these wonderful books and stuff, which are much more up to date.'

'Like what kind of stuff?' It had been a while since Darren had read a book. It wasn't that he didn't like to read – he used to read a lot. But he'd got out of the habit and what with so much being on offer these days he didn't know which ones to choose.

'Oh, I don't know. Lots of things. I just finished a great one though. It's called *Saurian versus Simian: Men & Women under the New World Order*. It's all about how, because of the way we've evolved, there's these two sides in each one of us that are always competing. Sort of a cold-blooded, individualistic side, left over from when we were fishes and lizards, and a more sociable, warm-blooded half that came from when we were apes.'

'Sounds amazing.'

'It is. I'll lend it to you.'

'Yeah. I'd definitely like to read it. Maybe it'll help me understand, you know, what you've been through.'

In reply Terri flashed him a shy and dazzling little smile of a kind that Darren could not remember seeing on her face before, which was yet strikingly familiar. It was only when he saw the television news the following day that he realised where he'd seen it last. Not on Terri, but on Princess Diana. Obviously a smile couldn't outlive its host, couldn't transubstantiate. But the next morning that's how it would seem.

★

After the serious atmosphere that had descended on their meal, Darren had fully expected to be driving home alone. But when the Triumph pulled up outside Terri's house once again she took him by surprise. 'So,' she said, after a moment's silence. 'You coming in for coffee?'

Even more than the words it was her tone that caught him out. She sounded more cheerful than she had all evening and when he looked across at her he saw the sparkle had come back into her eyes. 'What about your mum?'

'I told you, things have changed. And anyway, she's staying over at her boyfriend's tonight.'

'Avril's got a *boyfriend*?'

Terri giggled. 'Yeah! He's called Jason and he's seven years younger than she is. Can you believe it? He's quite studly too.'

'No way?'

'Yeah. I tell you, even I wouldn't mind a bit of that.'

'What if you had the choice of him or me?'

Terri's serious voice returned. 'Darren – don't take the piss. It's not fair.'

'I'm not.' And leaning across the gearstick he kissed her. When she didn't resist he kissed her again.

Some time now passed before they left the car, and one cup of coffee, one bottle of Moët and half a gram of charlie later – Terri's puritan views on drugs being one of the things that the Prozac and the counselling had helped her jettison – the old flame had been rekindled. Which didn't mean that when Terri's mobile rang early the next morning they weren't both out like lights.

It was Avril. 'Terri, I'm sorry, darling, were you asleep?'

'Uh . . . yes, I was.' Terri was, to say the least, annoyed at being woken. 'What time is it?'

'It's past nine o'clock, dear. I didn't want to wake you, but I thought you should know. Something awful's happened.'

The key phrase jostled the plates of Terri's consciousness. 'W-what? What's wrong?'

'Is Darren there?' Obviously whatever was occurring was not sufficiently bad for her mother to miss the opportunity to extract this important piece of information.

'Yes. Why? What's happened?'

'There's been an accident. A terrible thing. It's Diana. She's dead.'

'Diana who?'

'Diana Spencer, darling. Princess Di.'

Terri sat bolt upright, stunned awake. The news couldn't have been more shocking if her own death had been announced. It wasn't just that Diana had formed part of her mental make-up for so many years now that the woman had become practically an integral part of her own psyche. It was that she was an icon, an immortal. She *couldn't* die. It was like with the Queen Mother or something. It just wasn't even conceivable.

Fumbling for the remote, Terri switched on the television.

★

'Morning, gorgeous,' Darren said sleepily, when eventually the blither of the news reports coaxed him awake. 'What?' he demanded, feeling Terri's body shake the bed. 'Have I said something funny?'

But it wasn't laughter, it was sobbing.

'Terri, honey, why are you crying?'

Terri explained.

'Oh my God.' Darren didn't know what to say.

'It's true. It's fucking true. Isn't it terrible?' The sobs came even harder than before. Darren moved to try to comfort her but she struggled from his embrace, begging him to go and make some coffee and leave her on her own for fifteen minutes.

'I don't want you to see me like this. Not after we had such a lovely night last night. Go on – go and make some coffee. Everything's in the jars next to the toaster. Milk's in the fridge. I'll be fine by the time you get back. It's because of . . . you know . . . how I look. It's touched me really deep.'

'I understand,' Darren said softly, and falling quite naturally back into the pattern of duty and deferment that he'd followed when they'd first gone out as teenagers, he pulled on his jeans and trudged down through the strangely familiar house (redecorated since his last visit – Avril must have found some cash from somewhere) to do as he was told.

In the kitchen he switched on the portable to keep up with events. He hadn't realised that Diana and Dodi Fayed were a couple. From the fuss they were making on the television he realised he'd probably been virtually alone in this, but then he didn't watch the TV news that often and tended to turn directly to the financial section whenever he picked up a newspaper. Celebrity gossip, unless it was about the Barings or the Guinnesses, held no interest for him.

Like so many young men, Darren's emotional register was less well represented by a nice smooth curve than by a series of jagged steps. He tended to be either a cold fish or a sentimentalist, jumping sharply and often unexpectedly between one state and the other. Now he was about to experience just such a change. As the kettle boiled and the story unfurled, and a shaft of sunlight came through the kitchen window and illuminated a pinboard stuck with gonks, pages cut out from the *Little Book of Calm*, and Polaroids of Terri and her mother and their friends, a tremor of unfocused emotion shook Darren's frame, allowing a new perspective to open up before him. How anti-people he'd become, he realised. How impoverished he was.

Whether because the intoxicants he'd ingested the previous night were still active in his system or because the spark he'd held for Terri was now blazing merrily inside his chest, love and coupledom suddenly appeared of much more importance to him than they had at any point in the previous few years. Adding water to the coffee granules now became an activity of the most profound significance and, his dopamine receptors rippling with blunt shivers of activity, Darren's wrists went weak as he was overcome with a sensation of the purest truth and light and love.

Carrying the tray laden with cups, sugar and milk carton up

to Terri's bedroom was almost beyond him, so enervated did he feel.

When he got there Terri took one look at him and knew something was wrong. 'What's the matter, Darren? You look awful. Are you okay?' She'd stopped crying now and her eyes were dry, if still a little red. 'You look worse than me.'

Darren set down the tray on the corner of the divan. 'No, no, it's nothing. I'm okay.'

'Oh, baby, come here. Let me hold you. I know, it's so upsetting.'

'Yeah, it is, it is. It's awful. Awful and . . . *it's just so sad*.' And letting Terri hold him in her arms, Darren began to weep.

After a minute or two of this he recovered himself and climbing back beneath the covers the two lovers lay arm in arm, drinking their coffees as they watched the news come through. Half an hour later, as it became apparent that the reporters had no news and were chasing their own tails, he picked up the remote and muted the sound.

'What d'you do that for?'

'Terri, there's something I've got to tell you.'

Terri sat up, expecting the worst. 'Yeah? What's that?' She'd not done a lot of cocaine before and while making love last night she'd had to battle one or two paranoias of her own, paranoias that she'd not felt since she'd started on the Prozac.

'It's about Marty.'

'Oh, yeah?' So at least it wasn't another girl. God, he wasn't about to confess to being bi, was he?

'I should have told you already, I suppose, but I didn't know that we were going to sleep together last night. And then when things moved in that direction I just thought that was more important, to go with the flow, like, you know . . .'

'Oh, Darren. I know you wanted to have sex with me. Come on. Spit it out.'

Darren looked ruefully into his nearly empty mug. 'Well, it's like this. You know that idea I told you about over dinner? I mean the one I told you I *couldn't* tell you about . . .'

'The one that's going to make you rich?'

'Er, yeah. That one. You see . . . Well. The fact is, it's Marty's.'

'*What*?'

'It is. It's his. That's why I didn't want to tell you.'

Terri was incredulous. 'You mean you're going into business with Marty? You mean Marty's going to give up magic?'

'Yeah, maybe.'

'I don't believe it.'

'It's true.' As Darren had feared, Terri looked horrified. He waited while she lit a cigarette.

'Well, then you'd better tell me what this earth-shattering idea is. I've a right now, don't you think?'

Darren nodded. Squeezing the voice of his conscience to the back of his mind and concentrating on the bigger vision of love and truth and light he'd had down in the kitchen, he outlined the idea for button.com.

If she'd thought the idea ludicrous, or thought it excellent but vented fury at his not telling her, he'd have been prepared. If she'd been so thrilled that dollar signs had clanged up and displaced her eyes, he'd have been ready. But when she turned down her lips, stubbed out her cigarette and sat with her knees pulled up to her chest in silence, he had no idea what to do.

'What d'you think?' he asked eventually.

'He is such a total bastard.'

'What? What do you mean?'

'I'm sorry, Darren. It's not your fault. You've done nothing wrong. It's that snake Marty. There's no *way* he could have thought up that idea and there's only one person he knows who *could* have thought it up. And that's Jill.'

'Jill? Are you sure?'

'Yes, I'm sure. This mysterious "friend" of his. He didn't say whether or not she was female, by any chance?'

Darren thought back to the various conversations the two of them had had. 'No . . . no, he didn't. I mean, I definitely got the impression that he was male. That the friend was male.'

'He is *such* a bastard. I don't *believe* it. He was planning to fuck her over too.'

'How can you be sure? Maybe she asked him to ask me.'

'Then why didn't he tell you that? What would be the point?'

Darren shrugged, his earlier sentimentalism fast on the wane. 'I just don't see what you're getting so concerned about. It's her battle, isn't it? Shouldn't she fight it? And anyway, I thought you hated her, after what she did to you.'

'Yeah, well, I got over that,' Terri said, in a voice that made it sound rather like she hadn't. 'It wasn't up to her to have self-control. It was up to him. Either way she doesn't deserve to get ripped off by that . . . by that *arsehole*.' She got up from the bed and pulled on her dressing gown, her nakedness making her feel suddenly insecure.

Darren still felt somewhat confused. 'How come you're so sure the idea was hers?'

'Because I'm sure! She was the only one out of the three of us who knew anything about computers. And then there's the Lottery thing.'

'The Lottery thing?'

'She was totally obsessed by the Lottery. She spent a bloody fortune on it, most of what she earned, from what I could tell. She claimed she regularly won most of it back, but I didn't see much evidence.'

As what remained of his sentiment soured into embarrassment, Darren began to wonder if once again he'd said too much. 'So, er, so what do you think I should do?' There was no way he wanted to lose control of the idea, but with Terri coming over all moral like this he needed to be careful. The last thing he wanted was to be put in a position where he'd have to choose between her and it.

'Well, he hasn't actually told you he's going to go ahead yet, has he?'

'Not in so many words.'

'Then I suppose it's his move. We'd better just wait and see.'

Terri's use of the first person plural did not escape Darren's notice; after all, he'd deployed it this way himself to build rapport with Marty. But it made him wonder what her agenda was, especially now that they'd slept together.

'There's none of that charlie left, is there?' she asked casually.

The next morning Jill was up at seven, having gone to bed the previous night at eight and slept for eleven hours straight. On waking she rushed out of the house and reappeared twenty minutes later laden down with seven or eight different papers. Marty made some comment about this being a tad extravagant but she pretended not to hear him and sparking up the first cigarette of the day (she'd run out of weed) she started going through her haul. Stomach rumbling, no food in the house, the magician stomped off to get a half-dozen bagels from the Jewish bakery on the Seven Sisters Road; by the time he returned Jill had dismembered her haul of media and distributed the various fragments over coffee table and floor and sofa in what looked like an attempt to reconstruct the wreckage of the doomed Mercedes from papier mâché.

Marty toasted his bagels and made some tea, before joining her in looking through the coverage. The lead story – occupying the whole front page of both *The Times* and the *Guardian*, and honoured with a full-colour cover wrap-around by the *Sun* – was the body's arrival back on damp English turf. Prince Charles had been cropped from most of the photographs in order that attention would fall solely on the coffin, though despite being borne aloft on the earnest shoulders of the eight scarlet-clad pall-bearers this could not, in fact, be seen, hidden as it was by a royal standard infested with a pride of lolling cartoon lions.

The *Guardian* boasted an eleven-page tribute pull-out, *The*

Times a fourteen-page photo album tribute souvenir. The *Sun* told how the heroic French docs had massaged Diana's heart with their bare hands (the last lucky mortals to be touched by it, they implied). They also detailed the contents of the dead woman's stomach by describing the dishes chosen during her 'Tender Last Meal' (the meat or the emotion? It wasn't clear). On the facing page Earl Spencer – same celeriac skin as the pall-bearers, same army face – stood outside the gates of his pad in South Africa and painted a portrait of a press up to its elbows in his sister's blood.

And the press seemed to agree. Self-flagellation was the dominant mode. Mother Teresa peered out from the grey scale like a mole rat, calling for prayers and mortification. The *Mirror* and the *News of the World* both carried pictures of Federico Fellini and praised him as the seer who'd fingered the evil of the paparazzi before anyone else. If only we'd listened, the op-eds wailed, if only we'd sat through to the end of all those boring subtitled films. The writers were positively pleased that the speeding cameraman at the head of the pursuing motorcycle pack had been called Romuald Rat; it lent the power of paranoiac coincidence to their pain, endowed their sixteen-point lashes with real bite.

The images of the icon, strewn everywhere, had turned the living room into something that resembled a stalker's shrine. Diana Diana Diana, her face psychopathically collaged with all those porn shots of the extravagantly obliterated car, its surface tessellated into triangles of light, its crushed carapace and stag beetle angles made significant by being juxtaposed with the dozens of powdery, eternal images. Reaching over, Marty picked up a copy of the *Sport*. Jill hadn't got to it yet and it was lying off to one side, unopened, one of his favourite Diana shots on the cover: Diana on holiday, leaping for joy in the sea, arms out as though she were levitating, head back, sunglasses on; dressed in an orange bikini nearly the same colour as her tanned Kodacolor skin; chin, teeth, nose curved into a laugh, wave spurting at her groin like Neptune's cum. 'FREE AT LAST!' lied the headline, alongside the information: 'Seven paparazzi held in manslaughter probe; Diana death pics on sale for £1 million . . .' Below this in an inset box Earl Spencer hoped that 'death would be a merciful relief for his sister', as if her shattered corpse could still somehow feel. Tailing off the page were four purple stanzas dragged from Auden, the *Sport* trying to recuperate its coverage for posterity, for art.

> *Born a lady, died a saint . . . Pages, 2, 3, 4, 5, 7,*
> *13, 14, 15, 16, 17, 18, 19, 20*

Marty stared at the montage for a while, thinking of Terri, then turned to the first spread. *Doomed Di's last minutes alive*; CCTV snaps of Dodi and the Royal; another porno close-up of the bonnet of the car looking enfolded and mysterious and labially complex. On pages four and five, *Oh my God, the Boys*, sandwiched between thick borders plump with sex ads; girls with their legs spread like the split bonnet of the Merc: *Girls Online; Real Satisfaction; Pauline's Pure Pleasure; Come Be My Tampon; Live One-on-One.*

Tits, sex, girls; the most famous woman on earth; another tribute to cut-out-'n'-keep, on this occasion opening with Arthur Edwards's legendary snapshot, the one (you'll remember) where the sun shines through Diana's skirt to reveal her 'shapely legs'. *Adults Only*, even here: *Hard Discipline, Hot Party Babes, You and Me Go at It!* Details of the Di affairs, secret sex chats, weird stalker calls from Kensington Palace to the home of 'millionaire London art dealer' Oliver Hoare. *Teen Whore; Bored Housewives Desperate to Talk*; Di at the gym – *OUTRAGE: The Picture they Never Should have PRINTED* (showing the picture, naturally); Di in tears, upset. On the back page, voiced with real righteous anger: *VULTURES! A Flashbulb was the Last Thing Di Saw.*

It was unbelievable, terrifying, the world had gone insane. Marty began to get another hard-on.

'There's no way she's going to join the act now,' he said despondently.

'Don't start that nonsense again.' Jill was sitting perched on the edge of the sofa like a kingfisher on a river bank, chin resting on her knees, an oversize turquoise fleece hanging limply from her shoulders. He had the feeling she was holding something back, some resentment for something he'd done over the weekend perhaps, something he'd said, some way in which he'd behaved. Again he hated her and had the sudden urge to hit her, as if by driving his fists into her face he could punch whatever secret she was keeping out into the light.

Before anything could happen the letter box clacked and an envelope, a flyer for a new pizza outlet (USA Pizza! & BBQ!), and a copy of the the *Finsbury Park Fun and Free Advertiser* slid into the hall. Marty retrieved the letter; it looked vaguely ominous. Perversely hoping for bad news, for something that would ramp up the tension between the two of them, he tore it open eagerly. It was the final instalment of the bill for the *Eurovision* costumes. He carried it through into the living room and dropped it on to the spread of papers. 'That's another three grand we owe.'

'Oh.'

'Is that all you can say?' He wanted it to come to a head, he wanted to scream at her for the money he'd spent over the weekend. He wanted to smash up anything that might remain between them.

'Well, we knew we were going to have to cough up for them at some point. It's no big surprise.'

'And where exactly is the money going to come from?'

But she wouldn't rise to him, wouldn't even look up to acknowledge the expression of despair he'd so carefully assembled, wouldn't do any more than shrug. It wasn't till later that he was able to have a real go, when he found her in the bedroom writing out a cheque. She'd tried to turn away and hide it from him as he'd entered but he saw it and snatched it from her hands. In her hooped schoolgirl writing she'd written 'Diana Memorial Fund' where it said 'payee'. There was no amount yet specified.

'How much were you going to send them? Or were you just going to be really generous and leave it blank?' He threw the cheque-book back at her and stormed into the living room, slamming both doors as he went. A few minutes later he heard footsteps, a sob, a click. When he went to look for her she'd left the house.

She came back late, didn't speak a word, played Tekken and Mickey's Wild Adventure, passed out on the sofa. Marty went to bed alone; the next morning when he woke Jill wasn't to be found. Around ten the doorbell rang: it was the costumes, pink and shrink-wrapped like cuts of supermarket meat, the last thing he wanted to see.

Around twelve there was a phone call. It was Jill. She was crying.

Marty felt cold. Disaffected. Glad. 'Where are you?'

'I'm at the Mall.' So she wasn't crying for him, then.

'What're you doing there?'

'You've got to come. It's . . . I just can't describe it. It's . . . there's something amazing happening here.' He sighed. 'Marty – you've got to come. It's important. And can you bring the packet of incense? The one that's in the bedroom?'

'What the hell do you want that for?'

'Marty!' Through tears. 'Please just bring it, will you? For God's sake.'

★

He arranged to meet her at the foot of the steps leading down from St James's but then took an age getting dressed, slowed by the serious consideration he was giving to the idea of not showing up at all. Finally he was ready – white trainers, Gap khakis, a navy-blue Ralph Lauren polo shirt with a small hole in the armpit where the seam had worked loose, a couple of fingertips of wet gel for his hair.

He set out for the Underground feeling edgy, off-kilter, tense. The newspapers were in their stands out in the street, the shots of Di, Dodi, Charles, Camilla, William and Harry temporarily displaced by images of Trevor Rees-Jones and Henri Paul. For the most part these were accompanied by conspiracy theory head-lines that were the press's first attempts – sensing danger, the possibility of a genuine backlash – to protect itself. As ever, the *Sport* grabbed Marty's attention: *KINKY SEX SECRETS OF DI'S DEATH DRIVER; DIANA BODYGUARD HAS*

TONGUE TORN OUT *(turn to page two)*; *PAGE 3: KAREN BARE!*

The headline only pushed him further into his toxic trough of cynicism. Was this the national conscience? Was this the self-styled Fourth Estate? However bad he felt about his plan to steal Jill's idea, he could be sure at least that he'd never be as bad as the hypocrites and lechers running the tabloids. Look at how they tore at the memory of Diana, shredding her between them like pigs at a feast the very moment they were pretending to revere her as a goddess or a saint. It was hot again, hotter – Marty was pleased to note – than it had been the previous week, despite the newspapers' insistence that Diana's death had happened on the final day of summer, despite all those supposed liberals acting like gin palace prostitutes in their eagerness to show how easily their corsets of rationality could be worked loose. He couldn't understand this need to make the woman into some kind of Proserpina, a people's princess, a golden chain that would link the grimy galaxies of the prosaic streets and suburbs to the mystical courses traced across the night's screen by the stars. He couldn't grasp the ancient longing this expressed, nor perceive the individuals here at all, just a collective single force of folly and blind will. Precisely as he always had done he could see only an audience, a mob.

Fired by this burst of righteous anger, Marty clenched and unclenched his fists as he strode. He lived in a nation full of liars and creeps who bayed like bloodthirsty hounds at the prospect of disaster and disappointment, who fêted the image of morality even while they sucked the blood from its veins. He'd been so stupid, such a fool, tried to do things the long way, the hard way, the way he'd been told.

But no more.

Reaching the station entrance he disappeared underground and twenty minutes later he emerged at Piccadilly, blinking in the sunlight, the sky stretched bright above him like a sheet of cellophane. Down the incline he went, dodging the crowds dappling the pavements, the slope of Lower Regent Street giving him the impression of being strangely tall. But this sudden gigantism diminished with every step and little by little he shrank in size until, feet hatching the black and white lines of the Pall Mall zebra crossing, London once again swallowed and digested him, just one more lowly pedestrian among all the others hurrying along its speckled streets, of indeterminate age, pressured and peered at, outsiders until they were safely back inside.

Bundled at the foot of the steps leading down to the Mall, felled by the shadow of the grand old Duke of York, Jill was waiting. She was sitting half in and half out of the sun, her feet drawn up beneath her, a pair of the yellow-lensed sunglasses that had been fashionable the previous year shielding her eyes against the glare. And smoking a joint, which since she'd run out of dope on Sunday evening meant that yesterday she must have been out buying more.

'You can't smoke that here,' Marty told her when he reached her, vaguely clocking the fact that the Mall had been closed to traffic and was simmering with meandering groups of people.

'No one cares, not today,' she replied, taking a last drag before putting the tip of the joint to the flagstone she was sitting on. Marty watched as she carefully rolled a ball of burning marijuana and tobacco from its paper cradle out on to the step. It lay there smouldering for a moment, a bloodied furnace of light, until with one sweep of the leather sole of her sandal she transformed its orange chemical life into a long black charcoal smear. Tucking the remainder of the bone-like spliff into a crevice of her bag, she revealed the existence of the suspected packet of weed.

'Did you bring the incense?'

Marty winced: he knew he'd forgotten something. 'Shit! No – I'm sorry.' He didn't sound it. 'What do you need incense for anyway?'

Jill said nothing, bending to pick up a bouquet of flowers instead, an enormous pale meringue of lilies clasped in a wrapper similar to those in which the costumes had been delivered earlier that day. At the sight of these Marty's righteous fury blazed up again. How much fucking money was she spending? But he bit his lip, not sure if he was letting the matter ride or biding his time.

They walked out under the trees and along the edge of the orange macadam, heading in the direction of the Palace, Jill wishing now that she hadn't asked him to come. It had been a mistake, a vain hope engendered by the atmosphere here and perhaps some vestigial traces of the E . . . she had to stop doing that stuff, it was softening her brain. She'd had this notion that getting him to come down here would somehow move him, trigger something meaningful within him. But now he was here in front of her – jaw forward, nose sharp, tiny wedges of cast lip and spittle inset at each side of his mouth, irises like slow moats of creeping cellular desire – she could see that it had been a ludicrous idea, that she hadn't thought it through at all. She realised she was never going to be able to get him to open up to her, that he had closed himself off to her for good.

But still the atmosphere – the atmosphere here. It was quite incredible. Jill had never been to India or anything like that, she'd never even set foot off British shores except for a pointless school trip she'd once been on to Calais, which was more about seeing the insides of a child-mutilated coach and spending a couple of hours coursing around in the heady, dizzy, sugar-rush atmosphere of a vomit-stained ferry than having any real experience of the alien land. But she'd heard about Indian festivals and had seen them on TV, and the impression she had was that they were something like this, something like what was going on right now, here in her own country, under the leaden English sun.

It was the incredible sense of quiet, of calm, that did it. It was like being, she felt, in some kind of open-air temple or cathedral, the trees lining either side of the road like pews as yet unturned; the Palace like an altar, low and distant and rectangular and gold. But what made it better than any church she'd ever visited was the absence of ritual, of dogma, of patronising sermons, of tiresome hymns. Just people and flowers, that's all, people and flowers, flowers flowers flowers, flowers piled up in great heaps under the trees, strewn like palm fronds underfoot, flowers in people's clothing, in their hair or in their eyes.

Canvas shoulder bag banging on her hip, glasses slipping on the sweat that filmed her nose, Jill threaded through the crowd intent as a knight, her bouquet held before her like her sword, the magician trailing in her wake. Round they went, round to the enormous tongue of flowers that lolled before the Palace gates, a tongue not far off being long enough to lick the lions standing at the western corners of the Victoria Memorial as if they were kittens, to cleanse them of the afterbirth of petals and coloured water that ran, nandi-style, across their smooth bronze backs.

As they walked Marty's pupils turned to pinpricks in the sunlight and his irises began to loosen into pools. He flicked his head from left to right, disorientated by the dozens of little shrines on either side of them, shrines complete with wreaths and photographs and incense sticks and messages so saccharine with sentiment that in any other circumstances they'd have made him want to laugh. But the hundreds of images of the Princess, repeated to infinity in every direction he looked, were beginning to unsettle him. The impression he was getting was of being led into the epicentre of some unbelievably elaborate practical joke and he was half starting to expect that at any moment it was going to be revealed that the replicated faces belonged not to Diana but to Jill and Terri, that the crowds weren't here to mourn the tragic Royal but to mock him for the manner in which he'd so foolishly fouled up his life.

At their destination a police cordon had been erected in order to control the manner in which new bunches of flowers, like small dabs of coloured sherbet, could coax the tongue ever further out beyond the black teeth of the gates. Reaching the front, Jill signalled that she wanted to add her offering to the pile, then waited until a yellowjacket beckoned her through. She tripped forward like a lamb, skittish and stoned, her very modesty an acknowledgement of all the eyes she knew were watching. Two of them were Marty's; looking at Jill now he wondered if the crowd would spot her resemblance to the dead princess and, caught up in a wave of misplaced hysteria, kneel down and start to genuflect. Perhaps they'd even leap on her and tear her limb from limb?

But no, there was nothing, not a tremor, she was just another woman laying flowers and for the first time Marty asked himself if, in fact, there had ever been any real similarity between Jill and Terri and Diana after all; whether perhaps the whole thing hadn't been a figment of his imagination, something projected out on to the world from the dark velvet folds at the centre of his own fickle, ambitious head.

When she came back she was crying and confused, relying on the policewoman to return her to her entrance point. As she ducked beneath the TensaBarrier, Marty took her hand and, his grip powerful and brutal, pulled her through the press of bodies and across into a patch of shade thrown by the Memorial.

It was cool there, out of the sun.

'How much did you spend then, on those flowers?' he said suddenly, the words as vicious as any slap.

'What?' Jill was still cascading tears, her brain still having trouble registering what it was she'd just done.

'How much?'

She heard him now and pulled back her hand, but Marty grabbed her by the wrist and gripped her tightly, more tightly than he'd ever held her before.

'I don't know! Does it matter?'

The magician brought his pale face close to hers, eyes hard and round as marbles. 'Has it not struck you, you stupid junky, that we are totally fucking broke? Huh? Has it not crossed your burned-out little mind that we can't go blowing a week's worth of food on fucking flowers for this kind of fucking crap?' He was still holding her wrist and now he pulled it towards him while he used his free hand to rifle through her bag, searching out her weed. 'And how much was this?' he demanded once he'd found it. 'You bought this yesterday, didn't you? It wasn't enough that you should spend all weekend partying, E-d out of your face with your stupid fuckwit friends – you had to go and buy even more of this shit. Can't you stop smoking it for five fucking minutes? Can't you give it a break, just for one single pissing day? What the hell are we supposed to live off for the next fortnight, you stupid bitch? How are we supposed to pay the rent, or the electricity? Did you think about that, you dumb cow? Did that thought make it into the dope-shrivelled sultana you've got for a brain? Huh? Well? Huh?'

He had no alliterative options on Hs, it seemed, and in order to maintain momentum he let drop her wrist and, taking the baggie in both hands, tore it open, ripping it along its two side seams in order that the mossy green skunk, pungent as the mounds of rotting flowers, could fall in a clump upon the ground. Urgently, angrily, like some kind of petulant and posturing bullock, he dragged it into the pavement with his foot.

A gradual downwards creep across Jill's face flattened her initial expression of sorrow and distress into a taut blank mask, as if her skin were slowly turning to beeswax. Why was he doing this to her? What had she done? What kind of weird, fucked-up world had he been living in? Is this what had been going on behind those eyes of his for the past few months, eyes that might just as easily have been mirrors for all they revealed about what he thought or felt? She listened to him flip open the top of his head and scoop out these fistfuls of anger, she watched as he pulled on her wrist and pulled out her grass and trampled it with his ugly, so ugly, running shoe. She watched him say 'Huh?' again and again, watched his mouth form the sound, and though she didn't actually seem to hear it she knew how insistent he'd meant it to be.

Her brain was ice floes, blood clots, gridlocks; she had to let a few tense seconds pass before whatever it was that had been obstructing it flushed clear. Then: a thought. An idea for an appropriate response. Balling her hand in a fist, she pulled back her arm and punched Marty right in one of his precious blue eyes.

It hurt so much that she thought she might have cracked a knuckle, but the pain felt so good that she wanted to do it again. Shame; after grabbing his face and doubling up the magician managed to scuttle out of range. Jill slid her throbbing hand into the holster of her armpit and flipped the safety off her tongue.

'You BASTARD!' she screamed, the cry turning a hundred – two hundred – heads. 'You total piece of SHIT. How DARE you!' They could hear her down under Admiralty Arch the shout was so loud; the length and breadth of Green Park, people were jolted from their meditations. She moved in and went for him again, attacking him with the heel of her undamaged fist as if she were stabbing with a knife. 'You piece of shit, you've fucking ruined my life, I'm sick of your shit, I fucking hate you, I hate the moment I ever fucking met you, you fucking loser, you fucking loser piece of *SHIT* . . .'

On hearing himself called a loser Marty rallied – he wasn't going to take *that*, at least, and with a rush of blood round his skull he lunged back, catching Jill full on the side of the head with the open panel of his hand. She froze for a moment, checked by a temporary disabling of her inner ear, then launched herself fully at him as Terri had once done at her, talons out, hoping perhaps to scratch off his face. Half blinded, he tried to fend her off and they mauled until, with a sudden cry, Marty twisted away and began clutching at his crown, reeling from some kind of crippling blow.

Unable to maintain his balance he dropped to his knees, every-thing around him swirling as if he were riding on a waltzer: people, lions and flowers with their colours combed out. When things eventually began to sift and settle he found himself in a different reality, a reality in which Jill, bag on the floor, sunglasses broken, bruise already swelling on her cheek, was being comforted by two womble-like women dressed in heavy woollen skirts and opaque old stockings, and those weird, rubberised shoes that lace through four pairs of eyelets and have only the thinnest kind of a sole.

Now that his vision was almost back to normal, Marty could see that one of the two crazy shoe wearers was hefting a heavy walnut walking stick, generously endowed along its length with the awkward oval amputations of subsidiary branches. It was with this, presumably, that the old bag had brained him – and now she pointed it at him, crooking its splayed handle into the bite of her arm like it was some weird antique gun. 'Just you keep away from her, you horrible little man!' she cried, her jaw a wobble of folds and flour sacks, her eyes hard little fruit plucked from the same tree as her stick and dried to woody kernels over several generations.

'I would have thought on a day like today you'd have more respect,' her friend added, holding sobbing Jill against her breast in a matriarchal tableau sufficient in symbolic power to inspire almost any human male with the deepest and most arcane of gendered fears. Desperately Marty cast around him for support but there was none; everywhere he looked he saw faces filled only with hatred, as if his worst pre-performance nightmares were being visited on him all at once. He still didn't see it, though, he still didn't see what it was he'd done. 'Bu . . .' he began in feeble protestation.

The woman with the stick was having none of it. 'Why don't you just go home? Go on. Go away!' She gestured with her weapon a couple of times as though he were some kind of filthy and unwanted stray and then, planting the stave down on the tarmac and placing one foot either side of it, she stood warrior-like, immutable, her mouth set into an utterly implacable arc.

'Yeah, piss off, you *bastard*!' Jill yelled, lifting her head from the pillow of the second woman's bosom. 'I don't ever want to set eyes on you again.'

Knowing he was beaten, Marty twisted off his knees and clambered slowly to his feet, wiping off his gritty hands on his sweat-drenched polo shirt. 'The feeling's mutual, bitch,' he wanted to say but couldn't, on account of his throat having choked itself almost entirely closed. Without looking back at Jill, he strode off in the direction they'd come, head held high but eyes bursting with tears of shame, trying to remind himself that this what he'd wanted while all around him people backed away as surely as they would if he'd been revealed as one of the photographers who'd hounded Princess Di, as if he were some kind of demon conjured from the emotions of the day, something pre-verbal and pagan – a hooded man, perhaps, a goat's head or an imp, some thing that had crawled up from a crack beneath the city to remind them of the old ways of the land, of a time when we still needed the grace of golden chains, of a time when that which was feared was hated and revered, when that which was hated was obeyed.

For the next few hours Marty wandered the streets, or tried to; most of the time he was, in fact, inside, performing traditional rituals deep in the brothel embrace of several pubs, crossing himself with shot glasses sloppy with piss-coloured fluids, feeling sorry for himself. By seven he was in Soho, adrift in the yellow and beige plastic tack of the McDonald's on Shaftesbury Avenue, pressing greasy slabs of coagulated cow into the vacuole of his jaw. He'd fallen in the street somewhere, not in the Mall, somewhere else, and he'd torn his chinos at the knee. A ketchup-splattered Happy Meal lay raped and eviscerated on the plastic tray in front of him, broken fries and crescents of bitten burger discarded amidst shreds of torn packaging that would outlast him by three hundred and twenty-seven years. He wanted a cigarette and, turning his face from the miniature crime scene, he leaned across to the couple at the next table and scrounged a Marlboro Light, carefully taking the white tube between two stained, straightened fingers and bringing it to his lips like a man who has just confronted the terrible realisation that his one true talent is as a torturer.

An hour earlier he'd had the dislocating experience of walking up Haymarket as the rest of London came out from work, so drunk he'd had to stop several times and hug various items of street furniture in order to stop himself from being overwhelmed by the interleaving channels of tired, stressy people thundering homewards in their summer suits. Their tunnel vision had made him feel homeless, parasitical, and he'd come in here and eaten in an attempt to sober up.

He sucked on the cigarette and it grounded him, the nicotine bringing the disparate, spinning shards of his mind to bear on a single level plane that, though still rotating, did it slowly and coherently, like the opening logo from one of Jill's video games. It didn't have a similar effect on his body; when he tried to stand he had to grab the table's edge to steady himself, feeling for a moment like the assistant in one of his own illusions, the one where feet, thighs, head and torso are divided up into four boxed sections and shunted from side to side. He stood for a moment breathing carefully, persuading the various components back into their rightful places before moving slowly out into the street. He didn't want to go home. He didn't know if he could *get* home, not in this state. What could he do? Where could he go?

Looking up, he saw that he was standing by the back entrance to the Trocadero complex. He could go there, to the new IMAX cinema; he'd wanted to do that for a while. Swaying forward, he circumnavigated the building and took a series of escalators to the appropriate floor, where he paid what seemed like an excessive amount of money for a ticket and entered the theatre just as the film – a documentary about a group of climbers attempting to scale Everest – began to play across the vast screen. Clumsily, causing a mild disturbance, he stumbled into an aisle seat a few rows from the top.

The images were powerful enough – and Marty's drunkenness extreme enough – for him to half believe that he was actually there, being carried across the slopes of the goddess-mother Chomolungma in some kind of sedan chair. At one point the camera yawed so realistically over the edge of a crevasse that he actually managed to fall out of his seat. But as the storyline developed and the documentary makers became aware that some people in the party up ahead of them had been killed in a sudden mountain storm, the alcohol began to boil off a little and Marty's body and mind were able to realign.

Back outside in the street he craved more nicotine, and crossing Shaftesbury Avenue swayed into Soho, searching for a shop. He'd stopped thinking, finally. The barrage of guilt and anger that had been bombarding him ever since the Mall had ceased and he felt gloriously empty and silent.

Then, in Rupert Street, a woman approached. 'You look like you could use a bit of company,' she said.

Instead of walking on as he normally would have, Marty stopped and turned, and studied the play of the lights from a nearby video arcade across the pearly skin of her face. 'How much?' he asked. She didn't look much like Jill or Terri or Diana; she was short, a little plump and mousy-haired. But she was a woman and that was close enough.

'Don't worry about that,' she said, plucking at his sleeve. 'Come on, my place is just round the corner.'

He was still drunk and she knew it but he didn't know that she knew it – he was still too drunk for that. He stood his ground, determined he wasn't going to be taken for a ride. 'How much?' he insisted, his voice pitching itself higher than he would ideally have liked.

She looked him straight in the eye, showed him nothing. 'Sixty,' she said.

He weighed it up. He was broke. 'How much for . . . you know. A blow-job?' His throat cracked as he said the word; you might even say his voice broke.

She looked away, tucking her tongue into the hole left by a broken tooth. 'Thirty. That more in your range, love? Come on, then.' Taking his elbow, she tried to pull him away.

Marty hesitated. 'Er – w-wait a minute. I haven't got that on me. I've got to go to the cash point.' It was true enough. 'What's your address?'

She answered him with a question. 'What bank do you need?'

He couldn't think fast enough, ended up by telling her, 'HSBC.'

'Come on, then. I'll go with you. There's one just around there.'

Now he had no choice but to let her lead him to it. He stole glances at her body as they walked, finding her attractive enough for the drink to start stealing back into his brain and make him think this wasn't such a bad idea after all. He wondered if she had decent tits. Would she let him feel them while she sucked him off? Maybe he should get an extra tenner out, in case he needed to convince her of it. He looked at her mouth. How strange to think that was where his prick was going to be just a few minutes from now. How weird that some girls could do that with strangers, for money, while others – Terri, for example, to pluck a name out of the air – couldn't manage it even with a man they claimed to love. How different people were from one another.

He thought about Jill, allowing himself an uneasy glimmer of pride at the thoroughness of the argument he'd manufactured at the Mall. She'd never stay with him now. With any luck she'd piss off back to Blackpool and leave him in peace; leave him with button.com too, of course. Well, he wouldn't feel guilty. Whatever was coming to him, he deserved it. Hadn't it been he who'd bothered to find out what it was worth – or whether it would even work? Hadn't he had to slog for years with his show? Hadn't he had his whole life destroyed because of her tempting him and feeding him drugs? Hadn't he himself been forced into becoming a whore himself, reduced to tarting his art around business conventions? This woman beside him; he understood her. He identified with her. They were both desperate people, fighting for survival in London's bleak urban desert, and now the city had brought them together for one moment only, offering them mutual consolation in the only way it knew how: by taking the violence they harboured towards one another and through some strange alchemy transmuting it into a gift. They'd make the exchange and when it was over he'd leave, move off into the night, and maybe her heart would go out to him and his to her too, but at the end of it they wouldn't even know each other's names. The situation had, Marty thought, an extraordinary *poetry* about it . . .

He looked at the woman again, at her hair pulled back in its ponytail, at her shiny Plasticine face. He couldn't do this. He was drunk. What on earth did he want to do this for?

'So what's your name?' the girl asked him.

'Er . . .'

'Well? Have you got one or haven't you?'

Marty hesitated. Then he stopped. 'I don't know,' he said. 'I've absolutely no idea.' And then, finally, Marty made an actual decision. Turning on his heel, he ran.

★

He ended up walking all the way back to Finsbury Park, perhaps to punish himself, possibly because he wanted to be truly alone and in the city walking was the simplest way of achieving that. As he travelled the sky clouded and turned to rain; autumn began. The drops were rounded, deliberate, regularly spaced; but for perhaps the first time in his life Marty really didn't mind them falling on him, even welcoming the way they blotted his shoulders and leached the gel out of his hair.

He arrived home around midnight to find that both doors had been left open: the main door to the building and the front door of flat B. His first thought was that he'd been burgled, but he knew immediately this wasn't the case. Sure enough, when he looked at what had gone missing it was only one variety of thing. So Jill had come back, then. Come back and gone.

Well, fuck her. As anger, self-hatred and frustration completely overtook him he flailed through the flat, hitting things, kicking things, screaming *fuck her fuck her fuck her* until his throat was raw and the neighbours' lights started to click on. Kicking over the coffee table, he sprayed half a cup of cold and mouldy tea across the sofa. He cleared the surface of the dresser with a sweep of his arm, pushed over the television, drop-kicked his satchel, tore his magic books from their shelves, stuffed the unpaid bills stacked up on the kitchen table into the bin. He threw his box of fekes across the room, scattering coins and scarves and decks of cards and thumb-tips into every corner. *Fuck it fuck it fuck it.* With nothing left to damage in the living room he ran into the bedroom, where he put his foot through his old fibreglass sword cabinet, long since co-opted for storing his dirty laundry in.

Then he saw the mirror: his mother's mirror, the mirror he'd inherited when he was just ten years old, in whose reflection he'd first seen himself as a great magician. He stared at the crack he'd clumsily put into the corner and at the long broken leg, still held together by his father's makeshift old splint. For years he'd thought of having another leg made but it had never seemed quite right, somehow, to get it replaced. He'd wanted it kept the same, always the same. It was the only thing he really felt he had left of his mother.

Time dries wood glue, even the best; dries it out, makes it brittle, turns it to dust. Whether the heat of that year's long summer had finally been too much for the ageing adhesive; whether the bond had been weakened in the move; whether the rumpus Marty had been creating in the flat had fatally unsettled it was impossible to say. But whatever the cause the forces that had held the mirror's leg together through eighteen long years of service now finally gave out. They'd had enough. With a silent exhalation, a quiet parting of desiccated molecules, the elements of the splint ruptured asunder and with one short preliminary jerk the mirror collapsed, catching on the radiator as it fell and shattering into half a dozen shark-fin pieces which tumbled easily from the husk of the frame.

In silent horror the magician stared down at the fragments and the pale set of faces – complexions slightly mottled, hair flattened by rain – they contained. The first face he recognised. It was the face of Terri. The second one ... it looked like Jill – though whether Jill Dando or Jill Kingcraig he couldn't tell. The third showed him the tired and pained visage of Princess Diana, something close perhaps to the icon's real face. From the fourth his mother's ghost rose up to greet him, her eyes directly meeting his. But in not a single shard, however much he looked, did Marty see an image of himself.

Grabbing the van keys from the drawer in which he kept them Marty fled the flat, not even bothering to shut the door behind him as he went.

'Terri, darling. Terri! Wake up!'

'What? Why? What is it? Can't you see I'm asleep?'

'I know. I'm sorry. But I think you'd better wake up.'

'But Darren's here.'

At the mention of his name, Darren shifted heavily in the bed.

'I know. But . . .' Avril Liddell switched into a stagey whisper. '. . . it's *Marty*.'

'What?'

'He's here as well. Outside.'

'What!'

'Outside in his van. Asleep.'

It was true. He was.

Five minutes later the three of them were dressed and in the kitchen, attending a hastily assembled summit. A quick reconnaissance from the vantage point of Avril's bedroom window had confirmed that Marty's van was indeed parked directly outside the house, two wheels up on the pavement, its driver passed out inside.

'What shall we do?'

'We can't just leave him there.'

'Do you want me to go and deal with him?' Darren offered heroically.

'I think we should just send him packing,' Avril counselled.

Terri rubbed her face. Even through the fug of tiredness she could sense the approach of a crucial opportunity, clear as the headlights of an oncoming lorry on an otherwise deserted road. Her hurt and anger, she realised, had all passed. It was Marty, now, who was stumbling along the tarmac. She was in the driving seat. 'I think *I* should talk to him. I'll do it in the lounge. You two wait here in the kitchen.'

'Darling, do you think that's wise? He might be violent.'

'It's all right, Mummy. Anyway, it's . . . complicated. And I'm sure Darren will protect me. Won't you, Darren?'

Darren grinned.

Darren's features were the last ones Marty had expected to see before him when he woke. The idea had been to throw himself on Terri's mercy in the hope that she would expunge his guilt, but after a drunken drive all the way to Guildford in the middle of the night he'd realised that waking her in the small hours of the morning might after all not be the best way to elicit sympathy. The effort required in coming to this intelligent conclusion had so exhausted him that on reaching it he'd fallen immediately asleep.

'Darren? What the . . . ?'

'Mornin', soldier,' Darren said, opening the door of the van.

'What are you doing here?'

'What do you think?'

'You and Terri . . . ?'

Darren tipped his head. 'Sorry.'

Marty was so disturbed by this turn of events that he couldn't even speak. Instead, he just gasped a bit and looked confused.

'You'd better come in. She wants to talk to you.'

It was a few seconds before the magician worked out that a fastened seat belt was the reason for the difficulty he was having in climbing from the van.

'Might as well leave the keys in the ignition.'

'What? Why?'

Darren looked down at the offending wheels.

'So that I can park this properly for you. Go on. She's in the sitting room.'

Flashing him a dark look, Marty started up the path.
'And behave yourself!'

★

They sat facing one another, Terri in an armchair, Marty vulnerable on the expanse of the settee, Avril making her presence felt by delivering two milky cups of tea. When she'd gone Terri lit up one of Darren's cigarettes.

'You're smoking!' Marty observed perceptively.

'Yes, well, I think I've got you to blame for that.'

He looked down into his tea. 'I've done a bad thing, Terri.'

'You surprise me.'

'You know, don't you?'

'Yes. Darren told me.'

'Shit.'

'You're an idiot, Martin.'

'I know.'

'An arsehole and a fool.'

The lashes felt good across his back. 'I know.'

'What I don't understand is why? I mean, what did she ever do to you?'

Marty started to cry. 'Nothing.' His voice sounded very small.

'If anyone had the right to do that it was me. It should have been me who got to punish her, not you.'

'I know.'

There was a pause while they both sipped their tea.

'I'm sorry, Terri, I really am. For . . . for everything.'

'Save it, Marty. Right now I'm really not the slightest bit interested.'

'Can I have a cigarette?'

Terri raised her eyebrows and tossed him the pack. 'What would your mother think,' she jibed as she watched him light one up.

'I don't care what she'd think. She's dead.'

'I know she's dead, Martin. But what I'm beginning to wonder is if you've only just worked that out yourself.'

'What!' He looked up, amazed that she should dare to speak the truth.

'Come on. Get over it. You've got to learn to take responsibility for things, you know. We all have to, in the end.'

Which might have been the moral of our story if Terri hadn't been merely parroting words uttered, under different circumstances, by her counsellor.

Marty dropped his head again. 'What am I going to do, Terri?'

'I don't know. What are you going to do?'

'Jill left.'

'You don't say.'

'I want to kill myself.'

'Don't be pathetic.'

'I don't see what else . . .'

'Well, why don't you try calling her?' This had the merit, Terri realised, of being the most obvious solution.

'How? Where?'

'Duh. At her parents', possibly?'

'I don't know if she's there.'

'Well, when exactly did she leave?'

'I don't know. Some time yesterday afternoon.'

'My guess is, then, that she's probably back in Morecambe already. I can't see her wanting to stick around in London for long.'

'I haven't got the number.'

But Terri had. It was still in her address book, scribbled out yet faintly legible, its legibility ascertained two days previously when, having become acquainted with the network of secrets that was button.com, she'd begun considering the best means for ensuring that she and Darren both remained involved. She'd already made up her mind that should Marty prove reluctant to allow her to be a part of it – share options included – her first recourse would be the threat of shopping him to Jill.

'Mum! Darren!' Terri called. 'Why don't you come in here? I

think that you should hear this. Marty's about to make a telephone call. To Jill.'

★

For Terri it was a moment of total triumph. That instant when, after several minutes spent listening to the incoherent series of grunts and explanations and apologies that comprised Marty's half of the conversation, she got to watch the boy who had treated her so cruelly put down the phone and say the following words: 'She doesn't want it.'

'What!?'

'She doesn't want it. She doesn't want to have anything to do with it. She doesn't want to have anything to do with it – or us – ever again. She says we can have it if we want. She's going to move in with Paul and help him run his web café.'

What Jill had in fact said was that she thought the idea unbelievably selfish and evil, the result of his and Terri's and, yes, London's bad influence on her. A typical southerner idea, in short. If they wanted it, they could have it. She didn't care. There was more to life than money and that kind of nasty, grasping success. One day perhaps – though she didn't hold out too much hope – this was something that maybe even Martin Quick would learn.

Avril Liddell knew nothing about any web café and all she knew about button.com was what Darren had told her of the project while the two of them had been waiting nervously in the kitchen (though he hadn't omitted a small speculation about the kind of money that might be involved). This did not prevent her from casting judgement on Jill's decision. 'I think she's a very sensible young woman,' she announced, her blinking eyes expressing all the satisfaction of a mother hen who has just reassembled a brood scattered by a passing tractor.

No one else said anything, not for a while, although Terri did permit herself a smile – a smile which only Darren saw. It was a smile very similar to the one he'd seen her make for the first time the other night, the one that – in retrospect – he thought might have been some weird portent of the death of Princess Diana. Except that this time round there was something about it that wasn't quite the same. Its ambit, its arc . . . to someone who hadn't known Terri as long as Darren had, these might have looked identical. But there was something else, now, something perhaps in the distribution of crease lines around the eyes, or in the degree of dilation of the pupils . . . Something, anyway, that betrayed a not quite perfect modesty, a hint not of relief but of self-congratulation, something that transformed the smile into something a little bit . . . reptilian.

Darren liked this all-new Terri. She was definitely his kind of girl.

Plus these days she gave absolutely fantastic head.

Look at Martin. Look at his hands. Long hands, slender fingers, unobtrusive knuckles with joints so efficient they might be components of some elegant machine. Look at his hands; don't look at his face, a tapering face with a nose sharp, triangular, a little equine. Don't look at his hair, shaved to an even number five grade in the very month when that old mullet of his became genuinely trendy. Don't look at the Vans sneakers cushioning his feet, or his stone-coloured combats, or the IBM Solutions for a Small Planet T-shirt that was handed to him at a server convention. Don't look at his eyes of Microsoft blue, a colour he's now well acquainted with. Don't look at any of that. Try to concentrate on his hands.

His hands. Just what is it they're doing?

They're holding a mouse. Or rather, one of them is. The other is hovering over the keys of an expensive laptop put together in an Irish assembly plant leased from the government by a company called Dell.

He's about to deliver his first presentation. The script is all ready; Darren, Terri and he have spent days writing it; with one click of his finger it will start scrolling slowly upwards across his screen. They've all agreed that it should be Marty who should read it today, on account of his experience of performance.

They're in a boardroom, high up on the twenty-somethingth floor of a smoked-glass building positioned on the eastern edge of London's Square Mile, trying to raise money for button.com.

A building which looks and feels to Marty like it might itself be a computer chip, an extravagant and gigantic processor fixed on the motherboard of the City.

Glancing to his left through the boardroom's floor-to-ceiling window, Marty can see clear over the roof of the more modest tower opposite and past the twin blue peaks of the world-famous Tower Bridge to a waterfront of refurbished warehouses. Beyond that he can see the tallest spire in Europe, a cyclops trapped amid treacherous drained basins and the tangled razor wires of elevated railway lines, the single red light on the pyramid at its summit blinking away in distressed amazement at having been lured so far from the Pacific Rim, its spiritual home.

In the boardroom is a single table, a vast lozenge of mahogany, and Marty, Terri and Darren are sitting on one side of this. Opposite them, precisely distributed in a curve whose very gentleness is designed to intimidate, are five employees of the London office of Technology Pacific, the large American investment bank.

Five grey Herman Miller Aeron chairs with Pellicle™ suspension and Kinemat™ tilt support their buttocks, elbows and shoulders, but the sense of inviolate confidence each of them quietly exudes comes not from these but from the hundreds of millions of dollars they together have the power to put to work. Marty knows from the names written on their business cards that three of them are men and two women, but purely by looking at their faces – unpassionate and androgynous as those of clean-shaven Roman sentries – he can't tell which gender is which.

Marty hasn't ever imagined that his life would come to this pass. Since he was a boy he'd understood that it would involve the climbing of a very high and very sheer wall, and he'd chosen one and gone at it with all of his will, and in the end he'd scaled it, just about. But all along the idea had been that once he'd managed to swing his thin legs over the top, on the other side he'd find a ladder, a ladder leading down to a beach. This beach would be quite idyllic, caressed for ever with a warm, gentle breeze and populated – not too densely – with beautiful and interesting people who would welcome him as one of their own.

They would lead him to a waiting lounger in the cool shade of a lofty palm and, laying him down, would bring him things like cocktails and fine foods and other, more curious pleasures. And in return, he would entertain them with his magic.

But the view from the top of the wall had not been like that. The view from the top had revealed another wall, and then another and, beyond these, yet further walls, which crossed and crossed again until they formed a vast net of stone that weighed down and trapped even the vast range of angry and hostile mountains that underpinned it, mountains whose jagged ridges were alive with dark turrets and bright citadels, whose slopes had been made unpredictable by the scarring histories of thousands of blind, marauding tribes, whose members would almost certainly prove impervious to the power of all Marty's carefully studied tricks.

The magician's mind flips back to the boardroom. The ten blank eyes in front of him are windows on to this world; the light from his laptop illuminates an entrance. The land over the threshold is America.

His right forefinger clicks and the words start to scroll. Opening his mouth to speak the first of them, young Martin Mystery finally steps through.

AUTHOR'S NOTE

The word Bee, the Bee logo, the Bee Ace of Spades, the Bee Honeycomb, the Bee Diamondback design, the Bee Tuckcase design and the Bee Joker are trademarks owned by the United States Playing Card Company, and are used here with kind permission. Katrina Palmer, Joseph Robinette and all at the USPC Co., I thank you; thank you too to Amazon.co.uk for awarding me their Year 2000 Bursary Award, which went a long way towards helping in the writing of this book.

In orbit around every book is a small system of friends and acquaintances foolish enough to allow themselves to be caught in the project's gravitational field. On this occasion those deserving of gratitude include: CJBF for research into the legal viability of button.com; Sean Geer and Anne Prendergast for being sane enough to convince me not to do it for real; John Browning and all at First Tuesday for letting me come and spy on them; Chrissie and John at the Brooklyn Hotel, Blackpool for letting me have that extra room; Azeem Azhar and Emily Spencer for dot.com insider stuff; Plug and Nauca for providing refuge in Japan; Tom Loosemore for Channel Tunnel tales; Aladin for insight into the light side of the Force; and Scott Penrose for the loan of his copy of *Steinmeyer's Jarrett* (you can have it back now Scott, honest). Above all I'd like to acknowledge the input of Paul Kieve, a real, live master of illusion, whose guidance and knowledge I simply couldn't have done without. The information you gave me was correct, Paul – the mistakes are all my own work.

On a more personal note, thanks are due to: Jess Cleverly, for helping me out of two major holes (editorial and financial); Katie Owen, for timely advice; my agent, Jonny Geller, for sticking by me through some tough times; my parents, for their patience and support; and too many friends for me to list. Thank you, all of you. War is hell.

Finally, a note about the text. All the opinions expressed in this book are the characters' own, and should not be understood as belonging to the author. *52 Ways to Magic America* is a work of fiction, and no information contained within it has any truth status beyond the book's own – artificial – world. Having said that, if you'd like to know more about the mysterious NB, you should visit the excellent (and vicious) www.tvgohome.com; while Jill's account of the Fatty Arbuckle–Virginia Rappe tragedy was largely drawn from Kenneth Anger's *Hollywood Babylon*, a copy of which she picked up a couple of years before we get to meet her in the second-hand bookshop just past the clock tower on Morecambe's promenade. Unbeknown to Jill, however, at least one other version of these events exists. In his book *Frame-Up: The Untold Story of Roscoe 'Fatty' Arbuckle*, Andy Edmonds claims that the comic had the blame for Rappe's death pinned on him by Paramount movie mogul Adolph Zukor, and was denied the opportunity to tell his side of the story by campaigning journalists looking for something to symbolise the threat then thought to be posed by Hollywood to the moral fabric of the nation. Whatever the truth of the matter, Rappe's past as a call girl and her multiple abortions were dredged up at the trial and largely on the basis of his victim's 'questionable character' Arbuckle was acquitted.

Innocent or guilty, Arbuckle certainly didn't go unpunished. As a result of the scandal his movies were subsequently banned from the screen by the notorious Hays Office, and his career was destroyed.

Don't let this happen to you.

James Flint

Habitus

'Set against our culture's precarious leap from the space age to the digital age, *Habitus* is a sweeping epic comedy in which cosmos, characters and molecules are wrought with equal grace and verve.'
Douglas Rushkoff

This magnificent novel entwines the history of science into the bizarrely linked stories of three people and the first dog in space. Joel, Hasidic maths genius; Judd, Hollywood misfit and obsessive gambler; and Jennifer, precocious Stratford schoolgirl, are all struggling to make sense of their terrestrial existence. Meanwhile, Laika orbits the earth, monitoring the unpredictable and extraordinary ways in which their lives intersect.

'A witty, often erudite, stylish commentary on our pre-millennium condition. Not a science fiction novel but a science novel.'
New Scientist

'Flint updates the Huxleyan novel of ideas into a science-fictional epic with an impressive degree of complexity.'
i-D

'A captivatingly entertaining experience of a distinctly unusual kind.'
Time Out

Scarlett Thomas

Going Out

'Fans of Coupland and Murakami:
Here is your new favourite author.'
Matt Thorne

Luke wants to go out but a rare allergy to sunlight has kept
him housebound for 25 years. His only experiences of the
world arrive in his blacked-out bedroom on the TV, over the
internet and through the nightly visits of his best friend Julie.
But now he has vowed to find a cure. So, with a home-made
space suit, a camper van and a bunch of unreliable friends,
Luke and Julie embark on a journey along the B-roads of
Britain that might just change their lives forever.

'Surreal and inventive, A warm and comical study of life outside the
London orbital, *Going Out* does for provincial Britain what Frank
Capra did for small-town America.'
Independent on Sunday

'An absorbing, sympathetic story.'
Esquire

'Fresh . . . original and well written.'
Jockey Slut

'Insightful and entertaining.'
Big Issue

Ed. Nicholas Blincoe & Matt Thorne
All Hail the New Puritans

Alex Garland; Toby Litt; Scarlett Thomas; Rebbecca Ray;
Nicholas Blincoe; Daren King; Matt Thorne; Ben Richards; Bo
Fowler; Candida Clarke; Geoff Dyer; Simon Lewis; Matthew Branton;
Tony White; Anna Davis

All Hail The New Puritans is the controversial anthology of
new British writing.

'This is an important collection. Whether you agree with the New
Puritan Manifesto or not, if you care about writing you must read
this book. Discuss it with your friends, revile it, love it – you
can't afford to ignore it. The New Puritans have mounted a
formidable revolution.'
The Times

'It is exciting to find so many good stories in one collection . . .
Thorne and Blincoe have challenged the writer to do something
original and that is exactly what the New Puritans have done.'
Daily Telegraph

'The stories achieve a vital, vivid immediacy . . . the best thing about
these stories is that they're so palpably happening now.'
Salon.com

'An impressive showcase of hard–edged contemporary fiction.'
Boyd Tonkin, *Independent*

All Fourth Estate books are available from your local bookshop.

For a monthly update on Fourth Estate's latest releases, with interviews, extracts, competitions and special offers visit
www.4thestate.com

Or visit
www.4thestate.com/readingroom
for the very latest reading guides on our bestselling authors, including Michael Chabon, Annie Proulx, Lorna Sage, Carol Shields.

London · New York